THE URBEX TRIP

E.M. Lund

This is a work of fiction. Names, characters, places, and incidents either are the product of the author's imagination or are used fictitiously, and any resemblance to actual persons living or dead, business establishments, events, or locales, is entirely coincidental.

© COPYRIGHT 2026 by E.M. Lund

All rights reserved. No part of this book may be used or reproduced in any manner whatsoever without written permission of the publisher except in the case of brief quotations embodied in critical articles or reviews.

AI was not used to write this book, to create the cover art, or in formatting.

NO AI TRAINING: Without in any way limiting the author's and publisher's exclusive rights under copyright, any use of this publication to "train" generative artificial intelligence (AI) technologies to generate text is expressly prohibited. The author reserves all rights to license uses of this work for genAI training and development of machine learning language models.

Warning: Not intended for persons under the age of 18. May contain coarse language and mature content that may disturb some readers. Reader discretion advised.

Cover Art Design by: Kelly Moran/Rowan Prose Publishing
Photo Credit: Adobe Images/Deposit Photos
First Edition
ISBN: 978-1-961967-79-3
Rowan Prose Publishing, LLC
www.RowanProsePublishing.com
Published in the United States of America

For Suzu.

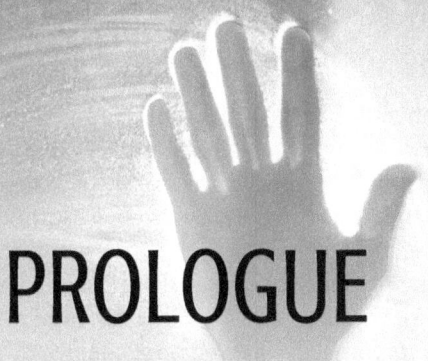

PROLOGUE

The Royal Oceanview Resort, Okinawa, Japan

Sunday July 20, 1975

It was only ten to midnight, but in a moment, the party would be over. Dead. Killed by the young woman in red.

She moved through the crowd, hair hanging in her face, feet dragging and catching with each step. The guests murmured, whispered, and parted around her. The gala opening of the Oceanview Resort was in full swing, and the speeches were just about to start.

Pupils over-dilated, eyes glittering too brightly, the young woman brushed past the startled wife in the pearls and the geeky teenaged son in the too-large suit.

None of these people really mattered. Not to her. To her, there remained only *him*—him and the resort.

Onstage, the manager of the Oceanview hesitated, microphone in hand, sweat beading his brow. It was high summer in Okinawa, and the glass-walled lodge had absorbed the humid, tropical heat, making the air inside thick and muggy. Making it difficult to breathe.

Behind his thick spectacles, the manager blinked rapidly, a nervous tic.

"Tell them what we did." The young woman spoke. Her voice was without power, a bird's shrill warble, her chest hitching for breath. Reaching for the stone pendant she wore around her neck, she turned to the crowd. They murmured their alarm, a fluttering of fear.

"Tell them about the caves," she demanded, veins pulsing in her neck as, with a jerk, she yanked the pendant free. She held it high by its cord. "Tell them about the *Utaki*."

The manager's throat worked, his own neck flushing. "Security," he pleaded, voice straining with effort. "Can someone please—"

"Darling, who is she?" the wife interrupted, and the young woman fought a sudden, terrible urge to laugh.

The wife *knew* who she was. It was clear from her face. The anger and embarrassment etched into her features.

"She's no one. A crasher. One of those insane protestors," the manager said, placating his wife, wiping his brow with the sleeve of his tuxedo. *Blink. Blink.*

"When you see the red smoke, you'll know what this place is." Finding strength beneath the fear, strength in her own anger, in her own betrayal, the young woman stepped forward. The guests closest to her stumbled backward, now openly afraid. "You'll know what you've been part of. *All of you.*"

A tall man, reeking of hair cream, authoritative in a dark suit, took hold of her. He opened his mouth to speak and cried out instead. A curl of red smoke rose from the back of his hand, and he released her, reeling backward, hot, hungry flames licking up his arm. The crowd surged away, a ripple of panic catching and spreading. The air filled with the sweet smell of barbecuing flesh, the chemical stink of melting polyester.

The red smoke. She reeled backward, her vision blurring. It was *inside of her* now.

As the man rolled shrieking on the ground and several of the guests rushed to smother him with the confetti-strewn tablecloths, the young woman turned, stumbling as if blind, making for the doors at the back of the lodge.

The dried-out husks of dead cicada shells crunched beneath her feet as she followed the meandering forest path through the dappled moonlight to the foot of the Ocean-Viewing Platform.

She tipped her head back, hot tears spilling into her ears. The platform rose high above the thick forest canopy, offering stunning panoramic views of Okinawa Island. The crown jewel of the Oceanview Resort.

At least, that was what the brochure said.

But the platform was still unfinished, webbed with scaffolding. Breath catching and crackling in her lungs, she started up the concrete steps, her knees locking as she climbed. She had to see it one last time. The island of her birth. The ocean. *Everything he stole from me.*

But the stiletto heel of her shoe slipped on the wet slab of the final flight, and she went down hard on her hands and knees. Head spinning, nauseous from vertigo and cloying heat, and exhausted by the vast fear that had long since taken root inside her, she clambered to her feet. The midnight Okinawan sky was above her, scattered with stars.

She risked looking down at the forest. The burning light of the lodge was bright. The remaining guests milled around inside, ants in a formicarium. Little confused specks vibrating anxiously within its glass walls.

Indistinct, but shaky with alarm, a voice called out somewhere down below.

Doubt tugged at her through the haze of her pain and confusion.

Was it him? Was he coming after her, even after everything?

But she couldn't stop. Not now.

It was too late.

She ascended the final few steps, emerging onto the top level. Up here, boat lights sparkled like jewels out on the oceans—two vast black seas on either side of the island, both visible in one panorama.

The view. It was as breathtaking as he'd said it would be.

She gazed out, the resort spread beneath her, like a village in miniature, a child's toyland. The ocean air tasted of salt, and a hot breeze blew, rippling the distant fields of sugarcane and drying the tears on her cheeks.

Reaching the edge, she peered, trembling, over its blunt lip. Below, in the gloom, clustered the frightened faces of the guests who'd followed her.

So there wouldn't be any doubt, she stepped out of her shoes and nudged them side by side on the ledge. The cold concrete bit into the soles of her feet as she curled her toes over the side, the hot night wind whipping her red skirt around her legs.

She raised her fist and held the stone pendant tight against her chest.

The red smoke. She could sense it, the malevolent presence of it, billowing on the wind behind her. It was very close now and thicker, more distinct than it had ever been. In recent weeks, it had begun to infest the home she shared with her mother, to curl in the edges of the closets and seep through the gaps in the sliding paper screens.

And now it had claimed her.

The caves. The *Utaki*. Together, the two of them had unleashed something ancient, something terrible.

She owned her part in it. This place could have her soul. But he refused to believe. The deaths were accidents, he insisted. She was losing her mind, he said. He had never seen the red smoke.

But if she were gone, the smoke would surely come for him.

It would come for them all.

Her terror built to a crescendo and then evaporated.

With a soft sigh, she tipped over the ledge. The watching guests whooped their shock as she plummeted. Her dark hair streamed behind her, her clothing a carmine blur against the inky blackness of the Okinawan night. In flight, she knew no more terror, no more guilt, no more fear.

She was still clutching the stone pendant in her fist the next day as she lay supine on the stainless-steel table. The coroner had to break her frozen fingers with a ball-peen hammer to pry it loose.

So that it could be returned, in a sealed plastic bag along with the rest of her effects, to her next of kin.

PART ONE

THE OLD OCEANVIEW

"How could anyone who was not a god predict the future, shaped as it was by human psychology, human behavior, and pure chance?"
—Yukito Ayatsuji, *The Decagon House Murders*
(Translation: Ho-Ling Wong)

1

Yamaoku City, Shiga Prefecture, Japan

The evening of Saturday, July 6, 2019

This place makes me feel like I'm inside somebody's womb, Eloise thought, ducking under the half-curtain and entering the bar. *A womb that's been pumped full of smoke.*

It was cramped, dark, and humid inside. The tiny structure seemed to have started as some sort of shack. With zero insulation to speak of, even the best efforts of the wall-mounted air conditioner, its yellowed plastic casing furred with dust, weren't enough to keep the place from becoming a hotbox every summer. This was Eloise's third year working in Japan as a teacher on the English For All Program, but she still hadn't gotten used to the immense, soupy heat of the Kansai summer. It never let up, even at night.

Especially at night.

She stood in the doorway, blinking for a moment, tears pricking her smarting eyes. Inhaling deeply, she let the sweaty-armpit stench of stale beer fumes seep in through her nostrils.

Kemuri was the rural town's only real bar, and as the name in Japanese suggested, it was always filled, as it was tonight, with smoke. Smoke from the teppan grill, smoke from the patrons' endless cigarettes. It floated about the high rafters and swirled around Eloise's legs like dry ice.

Jaw grimly set, she threaded her way through the crowded space, squeezing past the bar. She was making for the outside. Eloise and her fellow English-teacher friends always opted to sit outside, even at the height of summer, when the hot night air was practically suffocating. They'd even brave the maddening itch brought on by the mosquitos, which seemed to have a particular taste for their foreign blood.

As she drew closer, the mellow crimson glow of the outside area filtered through the opaque plastic curtain. Over many years of business, a thick layer of brown oil appeared to have formed on most of the bar's surfaces. The curtain, too, was foul and filmy with grease. She suppressed a shudder of revulsion, peeling the flap of plastic aside and squeezing through. Her pulse was pounding in her ears already, her hands numb and tingling at the same time.

I'll be fine. I always am. Just as soon as I get some alcohol in me.

Outside, a string of naked red lightbulbs dangled from the canvas canopy overhead, illuminating drunken faces. In the center of each table sat a glowing mosquito coil, releasing an acrid, burning stink reminiscent of ceremonial incense. Tate was there, holding court at their usual bench with Linh, Steph, Satoko, and—

Kenji.

Swallowing, lips sticking to her teeth, Eloise tried to smile and managed not to fall down the trick step. Time appeared to stretch out, to become elastic, and it felt like an eternity had elapsed before she finally arrived at the table. Linh spotted her first and waved, knocking her disposable wooden chopsticks—the kind that always gave you a wicked splinter—off her plate and onto the dirt floor.

Eloise took the bench seat opposite with a quick smile. There were calls for more beer, more grilled chicken skewers and salted cucumbers on sticks, another set of chopsticks for Linh.

The first frosty glass mug of beer tasted phenomenal. The cold burn hit the back of Eloise's throat, and she gulped greedily, even as the freezer-chilled handle seared the flesh of her palm. Licking the foam off her upper lip, she tasted salt. Almost immediately came the familiar rush of relief that alcohol always brought to her in social situations, the tension slowly seeping out of her muscles.

It's okay. You're okay. Now focus.

"We shouldn't have any real trouble getting access," Tate was saying. "But just to be on the safe side, we can't tell *anyone* what we're up to. We gotta keep it on the Q-T. Urbex isn't strictly legal. I mean, okay, *technically*, it's trespassing. On paper, the old Oceanview is private property, but in reality, it's completely abandoned."

"How abandoned?" Steph gazed at Tate with glazed-over eyes, chin propped in her hand.

"Like nobody-even-gives-a-shit abandoned. The resort isn't even guarded, no razor wire, no security cameras. There's only the one road up the cliff, but we can hike it. My plan is, we stay at a cheap backpacker hostel near Naha and get the bus to the Takagusuku region of the island, hit up the resort early the next day. I need as much daylight as possible to get all the shots I need."

"What's Urbex again?" Linh asked, not looking up from her phone, her thumbs flexing across its surface.

"Linh, I've explained this. It's short for urban exploration. It's a niche hobby where you explore disused buildings and structures, like hospitals and power plants, and just soak up the atmosphere. I document all my excursions on my blog. It's a good way to present my photography, you know, pursuing a consistent theme."

"Your *blog*?" Steph's lips peeled back from her teeth in a grin. "Jesus, Tate, it's almost 2020."

Tate ignored her.

"And Japan is pretty much the best place in the world to do Urbex due to how safe it is here—no drug addicts lurking in dark corners with needles poking out of their arms—and because of all the abandoned structures that've just been left lying around after the economic bubble burst in the eighties. Mostly extravagant venture capital stuff like hotels and amusement parks."

"Can someone fill me in?" Eloise took another sip, the fat lip of the glass mug chinking painfully against her front teeth. Tate held up a finger, shoveled the last of the grilled chicken into his mouth, then chased it with a gulp of beer.

"The Oceanview." He licked sauce off his lips. "It's this old luxury resort I've been dying to explore. Correction: it *was* a resort. Now, it's just a junked-out heap of concrete, but it's in this amazing location, high on top of these cliffs overlooking the sea in Okinawa. The story of it is insane. It was built when they expected all this tourism to come in for this ocean exposition they were holding in Okinawa in the mid-seventies."

"Expo '75? The World's Fair?" Kenji looked interested, but Tate continued as if he hadn't spoken.

"It was only open for one season. The whole project was doomed from its inception. There were all these bizarre deaths—suicides. The locals said the resort was built too close to a sacred burial ground, that the developers had angered the spirits of the people buried there. So, they shut down operations in 1975, the same year it opened. Crazy shit, right?"

Okinawa. Eloise had heard it described as a kind of mini-Hawaii, a string of beautiful subtropical islands located halfway between Japan and Taiwan. It had its own distinct history, culture, cuisine, language...

Catching the interest in her eyes, Tate grinned, exposing perfectly straight teeth. She'd first met Tate at a welcome party during the EFA Program's Tokyo orientation. The immediate culture shock had hit everyone pretty hard, and some of the new recruits were grappling with the revelation that their home country wasn't the origin of the world, as they'd been led to believe. During an alcohol-infused conversation on cultural stereotypes, Tate had bragged that, despite his All-American smile, he'd never even had braces. *Just naturally straight*, he'd said, pausing for effect, eyebrows dancing. *Ugh*, Eloise remembered thinking to herself. Physically, Tate was her type. Built, strong jawline, confident. But Tate's appeal had quickly faded once she'd noticed how he insisted on making everything, no matter how innocuous, sound like a reference to sex. Eloise suspected he was compensating in some way, that this was just a front for some deep-seated insecurities. And what was it Steph always said? *Tate'll sleep with anything that can't run away fast enough.* Despite Tate's best efforts—he'd waged a serious charm campaign against her during his first few months here—gorgeous Steph had never been remotely interested in him.

"Mmm. Thanks anyway." Steph shook her head. "I'm not looking to get grudge-cursed in some crusty old ruin. Especially not with you."

Linh was nodding along. "Besides, we've got plans for next weekend, right, El? We're going to Nara. We're going to feed crackers to the deer and go inside the big Buddha."

"You can visit Nara and go up inside a deer's rear end any time," Tate sniffed. "You do realize this is our last three-day weekend before our contracts are up for this year. In other words, before they're up *for good*. Don't you want to go to Okinawa for Marine Day? It's so apropos! Come on! Oh! Kee! Nah! Wah!" He started pounding on the table, trying to get a chant going, but no one seemed willing to join in.

Eloise rolled her eyes along with Steph and Linh, but she already knew she was going to say yes. She knew it the second her phone pinged with Tate's group chat alert.

Property of Kenji Ohkawa. That was the legend printed in spiky block letters inside every book in the immense pile left outside of her apartment. There were so many that when she'd opened her door to leave for work early that one morning, a few weeks into her fresh start in Japan, she'd almost caused a landslide.

By that point, Eloise had been getting desperate. With suitcase space at a premium, she hadn't been able to bring more than a few thin paperbacks over with her on the plane. Import books were murderously expensive, and the town's small library had nothing in its tiny English section—technically, it was a shelf—save about twenty volumes of a manga about a robot cat, translated into English, and a variety of out-of-date travel guides. eBooks were a thing, yes. But staring at screens too long gave her migraines. And if you asked Eloise's opinion, there was nothing that could replace the feeling of a book in her hands, the whisper of the pages, the buttery smell of old paper.

She'd mentioned her love of reading to Kenji only in passing. Staffroom small talk at the junior high school where he taught Phys Ed and Eloise was the assistant language teacher. And the casual kindness of his gesture had taken her completely by surprise.

That first year on the Program, still raw from everything that had happened back in England, she'd isolated herself. Kenji's books were her only real form of companionship, and through reading them, she'd gotten to know Kenji himself. His taste. His mind. He was sharp, with a dry sense of humor, writing little notes to himself in the margins that he'd apparently forgotten about.

When Steph arrived at the start of Eloise's second year, she'd dragged Eloise out of her shell, brute-forcing a friendship. Steph would show up at her door with toaster oven-baked cookies, mind set on showing Eloise endless funny cat videos on her tablet. Thanks to Steph, Eloise gained a social life and started to see more of Kenji. Not just at stiff town events but more informally. Like when the foreign English teachers all got together at Kemuri. But Kenji never mentioned the books, and Eloise was never sure if she should bring them up.

But even now, Eloise found herself spending an inordinate amount of time imagining being alone with Kenji. Just the two of them, in some intimate, dark setting. She spent hours mentally planning out every detail of how the evening would go, what she'd wear, and what they'd discuss. She would thank him for the books. Something stupid like that. When she saw his name in Tate's group chat, the one proposing this excursion, she'd found herself hyper-focusing on the possibilities, obsessing over various what-ifs.

"Have you two been to Okinawa?" Steph's question was for Kenji and Satoko.

"Like five times," Satoko said. "A couple weddings. You know, it's cheaper than Hawaii."

Kenji nodded. "I go every year. It's the pre-graduation class trip at school. We usually take the kids around the main sights. Shuri Castle, the Kaigungo..."

"The what?" Tate's brow wrinkled.

"Uh. It was the Japanese Navy's underground HQ during the Battle of Okinawa. There are still shrapnel marks on the cave walls from where they committed suicide with hand grenades." Kenji interlaced his fingers atop the table. "There's a war museum there now. And we also take the kids to the Himeyuri Peace Museum. You know, the Lily Corps? They were the schoolgirls mobilized as nurses during the conflict. When things got really bad, they were told to go home, turned out of the makeshift cave hospitals into an island in the grip of total war."

"Jesus," Steph said.

Eloise swallowed, trying to imagine it, to see herself as one of those girls. How abandoned they must have felt. How betrayed. The enormity was hard to grasp, like trying to pick up sand with chopsticks.

"Yeah. Okinawa's a beautiful place with a very somber history." Kenji looked down at his hands, his floppy black hair falling over his eyes.

"That's awful." Tate exhaled, steepling his fingers below his lips, pausing. He seemed, to Eloise, to be counting the beats, not dwelling on the topic at hand like the others. Just waiting it out until he could safely continue talking without being thought an asshole.

"There was another thing I wanted to bring up regarding the trip," Tate said finally before slurping the dregs of his beer. "Safety. Urbex is a dangerous sport, so if you're coming, you've got to come prepared. The old Oceanview is falling in on itself. I read that the construction was all messed up, to begin with, like the architect was a total nut job. There's supposed to be all these staircases that lead to nowhere and doors that just open out onto dead drops. Oh, and, uh, we should make sure we're prepared for possible dangerous animal encounters. I'm talking wild boar, snakes, bears. After all, this is *extreme* tourism."

Extreme tourism. Those words would have been pure catnip to Chris.

No. Please. Don't think about Chris now.

Eloise took another sip of beer. Her hand was shaking.

"I don't think there are bears on Okinawa. You're thinking of Hokkaido." Satoko had been gazing at Tate as he was making his pitch, the string of bright bulbs reflecting in her dark eyes like a constellation of stars. Eloise wouldn't have minded being friends with Satoko. She had long, fawn-like eyelashes and always dressed elegantly, hiding her prominent, childlike eye teeth behind her hand whenever she laughed. Satoko worked for the Board of Education at the city hall, so her face was a familiar one to all the local EFA Program teachers. But she was always so formal, so businesslike, that the opportunity for any kind of personal conversation had never presented itself.

Tate sniffed. "Right, well, what I'm saying is, we should make sure to go prepared. We're not going to be assholes about this. Urbex is all in the preparation. Flashlights, hiking boots, long pants, maybe gloves, though it'll be hot as balls."

"It's hot as balls here, too." Linh groaned. "Can't we just go hang out at the beach?"

Tate closed his eyes briefly. "All right, listen. I'll level with you. This trip isn't just fun and games for me. I'm applying to film school in LA next year, right? And I need to submit a ten-minute short. I was thinking documentary-style, and this place would be freaking *perfect*. Otherwise, my life's going to end up like a Norman fucking Rockwell painting. Law school, like my dad wants, then before you know it, I'm trapped. The third Caldwell boy to join the family firm. I don't want to be remembered in history as a fucking nepo baby. I may as well kill myself right now. Is that what you want, Linh?"

Linh stared at Tate, chopsticks in her mouth. Slowly, she lowered them to the table.

"Look," Tate said, swiping his tablet to life. "I found scans of the resort's old seventies brochures online." He flipped the screen, and Eloise caught a glimpse of geometric-print wallpaper, models in colorful tights posing on banana-yellow leather chairs. A chandelier sparkled above their heads, and they held their champagne glasses high, faces frozen in eternal laughter.

"Just look at this place. It must have been a *seriously* ambitious venture, with tons of money poured into it. The height of opulence, a great place for a getaway—until it all went downhill, and the guests started *checking out* of existence, one by one..."

Tate's enthusiasm wasn't catching. The group was again displaying subtle signs of disinterest: shifting in their seats and checking their social media accounts under the table.

"Come on, guys," Tate said, a hint of desperation in his voice. "You still haven't heard the best part. The resort's haunted by a *presence*. The locals call it the Red Maiden. Legend has it that her soul is attached to the ancient gravesite somehow. There's been all kinds of sightings of her over the years."

"Ah, here we go," Steph said, locking her phone with a *snap*. She looked up at Tate. "I *knew* it was gonna be haunted."

Tate grinned. "Yeah, so the local legends claim the Red Maiden appears every year *on Marine Day*. Mostly, she appears in the form of a beautiful young woman in a red dress. Sometimes, she crawls on the ground, dragging her long, black hair through the dirt. If you encounter her, she'll ask you what time the party starts. Tell her you don't know, or panic and give her a random time, she'll slit your throat. The only way to escape her is to tell her: "It starts before it ends." Then she disappears in a cloud of red smoke." Tate sat back on the bench, triumphant.

Kenji smiled, shaking his head. "*Yurei?* Every middle-school kid in Japan has heard ghost stories like that. And that one's not even original. It's a total rip-off of *Kuchisaké onna* and *Teké-Teké onna*."

"A total rip-off," Satoko repeated, her eyes suddenly glittering with what looked to Eloise like excitement. "I love ghost shit."

"What's *Kuchisaké onna?*" Linh asked Satoko.

"*Kuchisaké onna* is the legend of the split-mouth woman. You encounter her on a dark street at night. She carries a pair of scissors and wears a surgical mask. She asks, "Am I pretty?" Say yes, she kills you with her scissors. Say no, and she reveals her mouth, slit from ear to ear. Then she asks again. If you say yes this time, she cuts your mouth to match hers."

Linh grimaced, hands hovering over her ears as if she could hardly stand to hear anymore. "And the other one?"

Satoko's grin widened. "*Teké-Teké onna* is my favorite. She's the ghost of a girl who died in an accident. Her legs were cut off by a train. All she can do is drag herself around by her arms, making a scraping sound. We call it *teké-teké*. If she catches you, she cuts off your legs, too."

"Jesus." Steph lowered her chopsticks, mouth hanging open.

"They're both types of *onryo*. That means vengeful ghost. They're trapped between this world and the next. They can't move on. And that makes them...angry."

2

"*Hey, hey, hey, American boys and girls!*"

Linh shrieked, and Eloise's heart clamored with sudden terror, adrenaline spurting through her in hot bursts.

The middle-aged man who'd just slammed his beer mug down on their table grinned, leering at them. The naked bulbs bathed his face in a bloody glow. He was quickly joined by an entourage of salarymen from the next table over. This sort of interruption wasn't uncommon, especially at Kemuri. The foreign contingency of Yamaoku City often drew the attention of locals.

Tables were pushed together. There were calls for more beer, grilled chicken skewers, and salted soybeans in furry green pods. Soon, a drinking game got underway, one with intricate rules that the salarymen struggled to communicate. Not that it seemed to matter.

Later, the salarymen began interrogating them. What exactly did they think of Yamaoku, and what exactly was it that had brought them to the remote valley town in the first place? Their shared answer: "Teaching English," seemed to dissatisfy, but what other answer could they be expected to give?

No one comes to Japan to teach English. They come to see Japan. Or to escape from something.

El grew silent, withdrawing into herself as she tuned out the shouting and laughter and focused instead on Kenji, who was leaning in to talk to Steph, his mouth close to the curved shell of her ear. He was deeply tanned, skin a rich brown under the lights.

The first time Kenji came out drinking with their group, Steph pulled Eloise aside, her breath hot and beery, and hissed, "He's gorgeous, isn't he? You could hang your jacket on those cheekbones." Eloise had shrugged Steph off, mumbling something about sweaty gym guys not being her type, but she'd caught the glint in Steph's eyes.

"What say we decamp?" Steph suggested as Tate, roaring, hooked an arm around Kenji's neck. Eloise felt a rush of relief.

The salarymen barely even looked up as the girls picked up their drinks and plates. Eloise assumed the main draw for them had been Tate's floppy blond hair and muscles, anyway. It was like how the moths flittering around the naked bulbs overhead were attracted to the light.

Settling down at their new table with their heavy beer mugs, they watched as Tate received back slaps and fist-bumps and posed for a round of selfies. His white face was luminescent in the gloom, smushed between those of the grinning salarymen, who all seemed to have gone alarmingly red. A bout of arm-wrestling ensued soon after. Rolling her eyes, Steph was the first to look away.

"It's like a frat boy kegger out here. Jesus wept." She crossed her arms on the table in front of her. They were very tanned and covered in soft blonde hair that glinted gold in the light. Eloise looked down at her own arms. White. Skinny. Spattered with freckles.

Only the one scar, though. Maybe she hadn't been as serious about it as she'd thought. It was hidden, anyway, by the thick band of her watch, the sweatband she wore underneath it. *Who freaking wears a watch these days?* Steph had said once, laughter in her voice.

"I'm glad we moved out of splash range before the barfing begins," Linh said, grinning. "Also, I think I'm done. Does anyone want my beer? Any more, and my Asian Glow's going to be bright enough to power the whole town."

Eloise blinked and nodded, pushing away the darkness that threatened to wash over her. She reached for Linh's glass and drained it. How many was that? She'd lost count. Not enough. Not yet.

"...So, we're going on this Okinawa trip, then?" She heard the impatience in her voice. She was tired and getting a headache. Who cared about the drunken salarymen who'd hijacked their evening? She came here tonight for two reasons—to bask in Kenji's presence and to find out who else was going on the trip.

"I might," said Steph. "Linh?"

"Eh, maybe. Why not? I guess the Nara deer aren't going anywhere." Linh smiled, showing the deep creases in her cheeks that weren't quite dimples.

Eloise's heart leaped a little. She'd been hoping Linh would go. Unlike Steph, Linh could be relied upon not to ditch her and go off with some random guy. Linh didn't seem to be into guys. Eloise actually wasn't sure what Linh was into. It had never come up.

"Satoko?" Steph prompted.

Satoko opened her mouth to respond, but she was interrupted by the arrival of Tate.

"You've gotta come with, Satoko. I need Japanese speakers to do the talking for us in case we get into any trouble for trespassing." Tate wedged his bulky body onto the bench beside Linh, who hastily scooched over to avoid having to get too snuggly. "*Native* Japanese speakers," he added, this remark directed at Eloise.

What happened to his fan club, she wondered idly, and she could *feel* herself spacing out. Disassociating? Is that what they called it?

I want to go home. Not *home*-home, of course. That was six thousand miles away. But back to her tiny one-room apartment. The cocoon of her futon. The blissful escape of a book.

"Do your own bullshitting," Steph said. "Use those patented *gaijin* charms of yours, and you'll have the local police eating out of your hand and kissing your ass at the same time."

"That doesn't sound physically possible," Linh mumbled. Knowing Linh, she was probably picturing it.

"Kenji's coming, though...aren't you?" Steph looked up at Kenji, who nodded vaguely. He stood behind her, waiting for her to scooch over and make room for him. He rested his hand briefly on her shoulder before taking a seat. Eloise looked at the two of them side by side, chewing on the inside of her bottom lip. Kenji, tall and muscular, with those soft, understanding eyes, and Steph, with her lovely, bright face, her bubbling confidence. She always had at least two guys seriously pursuing her at any one time, and she seemed to have exciting plans every weekend. She was messy and scatterbrained, forever running late but never apologizing for it. And Eloise had seen the little red bubble on her phone indicating her unread message app notifications. Inexplicably, the number ran to triple digits.

Why is someone like Steph friends with someone like me?

It wasn't the first time she'd pondered that question. Her hunch was that they had a symbiotic relationship. On some level, Eloise used Steph for social interaction, something she was still afraid of after what had happened back home. At the same time, though, she knew it had to be good for her. As for Steph? Well, maybe she was using Eloise, too. Using her to make herself look better, to boost her own ego. Not that it required any further boosting. Every guy wanted to date Steph. And Steph was very male-oriented. All she ever seemed to want to talk about was men and her favorite variation on the theme, *Eloise* and men.

"Why don't you ever go for any of the guys? Tons of them show interest in you, but you're so quick to reject them," Steph said to her once after one of the get-togethers she'd engineered.

Eloise had declined to swap numbers with a guy, and for some reason, Steph seemed annoyed about it. "It's like, they do or say *one thing* that doesn't fit your lofty ideals, and you cut them dead. What's with the sky-high standards, Els? You take everything so *seriously*. You should have some fun. You don't need to keep them around after they've provided their services, of course. Just do what I do—use and recycle."

Steph consumed men like a praying mantis. She was always hungry for male attention. She *fed* on it. Steph might have had confidence to spare, but her attempts to draw Eloise out of her shell often had the opposite effect, leaving Eloise feeling hounded, frigid, defective.

Sometimes, I hate her.

Eloise tightened her grip on her mug of half-drunk beer, the glass handle slippery with condensation. She saw herself lifting the heavy mug high, bringing it crashing down against Steph's temple, the dull *thud*, the shocked yelps of the others, the bench scudding backward as Steph toppled onto the table face-first.

Eloise gasped, suddenly breathless.

What the hell is wrong with you? Normal people don't have thoughts like that. They just don't. If you can think something like that, then you really must be evil. As evil as everyone back home said.

She closed her eyes, trying to regulate her breathing. In for three, hold for three, out for three.

The mind is its own place, she told herself shakily, lifting the beer mug very gently to prove that she could. As she tried to take a sip, her teeth clinked against the fat glass lip again. *Thoughts are just visitors, let them come and go.* She fought the intrusive image down into the murky depths of her mind swamp, letting it sink beneath the silt layer.

Calmer, Eloise opened her eyes, blinking against the harsh red glow of the bulbs. Her eye fell on their original table, where the salarymen had been carousing. The table was empty.

"So, everyone else is in, right?" Tate looked around at them all. There were some noncommittal murmurs.

"You said it's technically trespassing? You said it's...what was it, again? Oh, *illegal*?" Steph smiled, not really serious, just yanking Tate's chain. Realizing this, he grinned with delight.

"Come on. Nobody's going to care about a bunch of *gaijin* poking around some old unattended ruin. So. All in favor of getting out of this tinpot town and having some actual fun this three-day weekend?" He raised his own hand high.

"*Tate*," Eloise gasped. Not only was he being rude, he was hanging her out to dry. Ordinarily, Tate would say something American like *podunk town*. "Tinpot town" was an Eloise-ism he'd obviously co-opted.

"No worries. It *is* a...what did you say? *Tinpot* town?" Kenji smiled, his soft eyes on Eloise. "I like it. I never heard that one before."

"Okay, so *provisionally*, let's say everyone's in." Tate slapped his palms down on the table, sucking air through his teeth.

"Shall we call it, then?" Kenji was the one who got up from the table first, even though he'd been the last one to sit down. "I have to be at school early tomorrow. Got to coach baseball practice."

"Right, right. How are we splitting this? Per person? Eloise, can you spot me? I promise this is the last time. I'll get it back to you next week. After payday. Cool?" Tate raised his brows in her direction.

Not cool, Eloise thought, irritated. *You're the one who organized this night, and you don't even have enough on you to cover your share? Really?*

God, Tate really reminded her of that guy in The Secret History.

The one who gets murdered by all of his friends.

"Great! Okay, I need a final headcount by, let's say, Wednesday. El, can you book the flights and find us a hostel?"

"Just tap the big icon that says *English*, Tate." Eloise wanted to smack him. It wasn't in her job description—at least not officially, on her contract where it was supposed to matter—but as a third-year EFA who by that point spoke halfway decent

Japanese, she found herself performing extra duties as a de facto babysitter for every clueless *gaijin* that came to this town. The EFA Program liked to pluck fresh graduates, and some of them arrived in Japan barely functional. Tate was the worst of them all. There'd been the debacle with the heated toilet seat in Tate's first month here. A low-temperature burn, and he'd needed a medical interpreter to accompany him to the town's small clinic. It had been left to Eloise to explain to the elderly doctor just how the clueless American had managed to create the ruddy stripes that banded the backs of his upper thighs. Then there was the incident at the dry cleaners...

"Come on. Be a good egg, Eloise," Tate said, treating her to one of his most winning, most infectious smiles, and she smiled back, traitorous mouth twisting in reciprocation despite herself.

"Maybe you guys should get some travel insurance, too." Steph grinned, slinging her backpack over her shoulder. "I mean, it's not like this excursion doesn't come with risks. Structural collapse. Wild boar attacks. Death by *yurei*."

Kenji signaled for the bill, but the bar's owner waved away their money and leaned in to say something in his ear. Kenji translated: "It's been covered already. By those salarymen guys."

Humming through his nose, the owner set about collecting their glasses.

"I love Japan." Tate grinned as he got to his feet. "How could anything bad happen here?"

3

Steph ran through the bamboo forest, leaves whipping her face. The ground was mulchy underfoot after the pre-summer rains. Tangled roots threatened to snag her, trip her. Lungs on fire, sweat stinging her eyes, face flushed from the heat, she stumbled to a stop in a moonlit glade. Bent over, hands on knees, she coughed hard until she caught her breath.

At the mid-point of her run, she always played this little mind game. She conjured a dark figure from the shadows, a faceless man pursuing her with a sharp, glinting knife. If she couldn't outrun him, he would drag her to the ground, stab her, and keep on stabbing until the last breath seeped from her lungs. It was a simple scenario, effective enough. There was no need to embellish. Perhaps it was a sick thing to imagine, but it was certainly effective. Just one of the mental tricks she'd developed over the years, tricks she used to push beyond her limits.

Running was a habit she'd taken up in high school after Mom remarried and had the twins. Anything to get out of their cramped trailer and away from the surround sound screaming and endless shitty diapers. Anything to get away from the ever-watchful eye of her new stepfather, Don. Running was a ritual, Steph's time to decompress and work through things, and as long as she carried bear mace, there was never any real need for concern.

No need for bear mace at all in Yamaoku, though. If you asked Steph, one of the best things about Japan was the near-absolute safety she could take for granted here. She could stay out all night and fall asleep on the first train in the early morning light, unmolested. She could head to the convenience store at four a.m. when insomnia hit. Buy herself a hot can of coffee, sit in the park, and slowly sip it as the gray light of day seeped into the world. She could go running through the bamboo forest at midnight and encounter no one.

Eloise always said she was insane, that she was taking unnecessary risks. But Eloise was the type of person who kept the door on the latch whenever she was home. Her personal safety paranoia always amused Steph. People like El tended to see murders and rapes as random criminal acts, things that happen to the unfortunate few. The ones who just happen to cross paths with an unhinged individual. But Steph knew the statistics and that the majority of homicides and rapes are carried out by people known to the victim. The real creeps are always far closer to home than you'd ever expect.

Speaking of creeps—

This trip that Tate was proposing. She couldn't imagine actually *going*. Not now, not knowing what she knew about him. Could she? Gooseflesh crept along her flushed arms. She'd underestimated Tate. She'd thought he was just another rich, prep school pig, but she'd been wrong.

Dead wrong.

Was she going to do something about it, then? Talk to the school? The police? She'd be risking retaliation from Tate. Was he dangerous? Or just disgusting? Should she just stay quiet, let the semester end, and let Tate fly back home scot-free?

She could send an email to the Program. Anonymously. They were meant to be responsible for them, weren't they?

She would have to do *something*. She was involved now. But she needed more time to think. And if Eloise was going on this trip with Tate, then Steph couldn't let her go alone. Ever since they'd met, Steph had felt an odd sense of responsibility for Eloise, the same kind of responsibility she felt for her students. Eloise needed someone. Steph had to look out for her. And Steph had never had a real best friend who was a girl before. Other girls never seemed to like Steph all that much.

All right. That simplified things. If El went, Steph went. And if she got the chance to talk to Tate alone—

Suddenly, she stiffened. She wasn't alone in the clearing. There was some kind of creature crouched a few feet in front of her. It reminded her of a raccoon, only with brownish-grey fur and no rings on its tail. A tanuki, then. But why hadn't she scared it off?

The tanuki watched her, its dumb, dog-like eyes glowing red in the beam of her phone's flashlight. The bamboo forest had grown preternaturally silent, as if cut off somehow from the rest of the town. Even the cicadas had paused their singing. There was just silence. And the tanuki. And Steph.

Animism, she thought wildly. Japanese spiritual beliefs. Gods, or *kami*, that exist within all aspects of nature. Rocks, trees, rivers, animals.

A second later, the tanuki turned and scurried off into the darkness. There was nothing spiritual about the undignified sight of its furry rear undulating from side to side, its little hind paws propelling it away.

Steph blew out the breath of air she'd been holding, the loose hairs lifting off her forehead. Her phone needed charging, and she needed a shower. Badly.

But as she dropped her hands to her sides, preparing to set off, something stopped her.

A flash of moonlight, reflecting off something smooth, off to the side.

She waited, breath held, eyes narrowing, trying to focus. Somewhere beneath the swelling din of the cicadas' encore, there was something odd. Something artificial.

Dink.

She listened, confused. She tried to place the sound. It was something familiar. She knew that much. The kind of noise you never think much about. Like a microwave ping or a doorbell chime.

There was no fear. Fear would come a moment later when the night air broke around her with an explosive crack, and hot adrenaline flooded her veins.

Run, Steph, you need to run…you need to go…Now!

Then she was running. The ground squelching beneath her feet, branches clawing at her eyes, her breath coming in short hard bursts. The crack had been a branch snapping under someone's foot. Now there was breathing, panting, excited. Just feet behind her.

Dink.

The road opened up ahead of her, the indistinct blur of a passing car whipping by up ahead. The road was public. The road was safety.

Something snagged in her hair, tugging her head back hard. A tree branch? Or a hand, grabbing?

Grunting in terror, Steph went down to her knees, clawing at the back of her head. She grabbed a hank of her hair and ripped it loose from the branch it was tangled in. Then she struggled to her feet, emerging under the bright streetlights onto the supposed safety of the road.

Please, please, just let me get home!

Chest bursting with white-hot pain, she ran up the gentle slope, finding the open culvert where the stormwater rushed away, spotting the house with the white siding and the third-floor window that always housed the same sleeping cat. Oriented now, she broke left at the bank of humming vending machines and cut across the parking lot of the walk-up apartment building where she, Eloise, and Tate all had studio units.

She thought, for a second, about banging on El's door, but her lights were off, and all Steph could focus on was getting inside. Drawing the lock against the night, making herself safe. She fumbled with her keys, dropped them, and risked a glance over her shoulder before bending to scrape them up off the floor with clawed, shaking fingers.

The parking lot was empty.

Stabbing the lock with her key, she let herself in and slammed the door. Jamming a hand against her mouth, she tried to slow her breathing, which sounded much too loud in the inky silence of her hot, dark apartment. With numb fingers, she threaded the metal chain clumsily across.

Just breathe, Steph, you're okay, you're all right, just stay very quiet and breathe.

She was still slumped against the blissfully cold metal some minutes later, her breathing steadier, heart rate almost normal again, when she thought she heard footsteps crunching across the gravel outside.

The door to the apartment two down from hers clacked open and then quietly closed.

She knew whose apartment it was.

Jesus fucking Christ.

Still too afraid to turn on the lights, she used her phone's screen to investigate a throbbing on her shin. A shallow half-circle had been cut into the soft flesh, its shape a perfect replica of the hacked-off bamboo stem she must have fallen on.

As she hissed and prodded at the black, glistening cut, her brain finally placed the strange noise she'd heard in the forest just before the attack.

Dink.

It was the sound of a phone camera recording.

The creep had been filming her.

ROYAL OCEANVIEW HOTEL AND LEISURE RESORT SET TO OPEN THIS SUMMER
The Daily Okinawan, June 17, 1975
By Miyoko Fujiwara

A new luxury hotel and leisure resort is due to open in the former Takagusuku Park nature preserve next month. The ambitious resort project is one of a number of new ventures launched to capitalize on the upcoming Okinawa Ocean Exposition and World's Fair. The exposition, which will run from July 20th through January of next year, will commemorate the return of the Okinawan islands from America to Japan. With a central theme of "Oceans" and a catchy slogan: "The Sea We Would Like to See," the exposition is certain to bring fresh tourism to the main island of Okinawa.

The new resort complex is the brainchild of businessman Satoshi Imamura. Imamura, a hotel magnate from Osaka, dreamed up the concept of the luxury resort during a family snorkeling vacation to Okinawa. An avid surfer and lover of the ocean, Imamura selected the resort's location, a plateau high atop the bluffs of the Takagusuku Park nature preserve, for its stunning views.

A press release quotes Imamura: *"What better place for ocean lovers to relax than Okinawa, with its emerald seas and sugar-sand beaches? I envisioned a hotel and leisure resort where families can vacation together, enjoying the island's lush nature and sea breezes. The name Oceanview is apt, as both the East China Sea and the Pacific Ocean are viewable at the same time from the vantage point of the resort's Ocean-Viewing Platform. I hope that all guests will leave refreshed and imbued with a feeling of deep peace after a stay at our resort, which sparkles brighter than the seas themselves."*

Despite Imamura's words of confidence, the resort's development has been marred by a series of setbacks. A construction worker was crushed to death in a structural collapse, and rumor has it that many of the resort's facilities are still unfinished, including the aforementioned "Ocean-Viewing Platform," and as such, are unlikely to be operational in time for the grand opening.

Furthermore, Imamura has faced harsh criticism from local residents and Buddhist monks from a nearby temple. They allege that the Takagusuku Park nature site is host to a cluster of ancient tombs, which the new resort infringes upon.

Imamura, however, appears impervious to naysayers and went on record to dismiss concerns over the so-called sacred site, saying: *"I hired a monk from a respected temple myself and had him flown over at great personal expense to bless the site and the construction process before we broke ground, so I have zero concerns about facing the wrath of any angry spirits. It is true that there is a gravesite complete with an ancient tomb of the traditional Okinawan "Turtle-Back" variety located close to the site. However, the insinuation that my beautiful resort is in any way culturally or spiritually disrespectful is nothing but slander, steeped in prejudice against mainlanders, and one that has no basis in theological or geographical fact."*

The resort's soft open will commence on July 14th, with the pool and waterpark facilities opening to the general public free of charge for one week only. A gala opening event will be held on Sunday, July 20th, with select VIP guests set to enjoy a banquet and musical performances.

FAILED RESORT TO CLOSE FOLLOWING STRING OF BIZARRE DEATHS, HOTEL DEVELOPER STILL MISSING
The Okinawa Sun, October 18, 1975
By Jim K. Masunaga

The Royal Oceanview Hotel and Leisure Resort is to close its doors this winter after only a single season in business. The ambitious resort project, built at huge expense on the former Takagusuku Park nature preserve, was spearheaded by Osaka businessman Satoshi Imamura. At the time of this publication, Imamura has been missing for the past twenty-three days.

The resort has been the site of a series of bizarre and unsettling incidents, beginning with a string of construction worker deaths and the shocking and very public suicide of a local young woman, rumored to be Imamura's mistress. The tragic incident happened during the resort's gala opening party when nineteen-year-old Nanoha Shimabukuro jumped to her death from an unfinished concrete structure.

Another tragedy occurred when a child drowned in the resort's waterpark. Facing a wrongful death lawsuit initiated by the child's parents, the billionaire hotel magnate Imamura paid condolence money to the family. Additionally, he vowed to introduce more stringent safety procedures. However, his image suffered further irreparable damage when a string of apparent guest suicides occurred one after another during the first summer season.

"Lots of people check into hotels to kill themselves," Imamura was quoted as saying, a prime example of the callous, self-serving nature that earned him the nickname 'Ghoul.' He went on to state: *"These incidents, while regrettable, are not the responsibility of either The Royal Oceanview or its parent company, Imamura Lifestyle Developments."*

With so much tragedy tarnishing the resort's reputation, locals staged a protest on August 29th, blocking the only access road to the resort for several hours in an attempt to dissuade paying guests. They attribute the tragedies at the resort to a curse, which they claim has been triggered by Imamura's selfish decision to build on grounds that infringe upon an ancient *Utaki* or holy site.

Imamura was reported missing by his wife on September 26th, when he failed to appear at a family function in his home city of Osaka. According to friends and relatives, there had been great concern of late about his mental state. Described as being 'paranoid' and 'distressed,' there were fears that he may have taken his own life. A police search of the resort, however, revealed no sign of Imamura, who is now believed to have fled Japan in a desperate attempt to evade creditors.

PART TWO

OKINAWA

"In order to induce the process of decay, water is necessary. I think that, in the case of women, men are the water."
—Natsuo Kirino, *Grotesque*
(Translation: Rebecca Copeland)

4

Naha, Okinawa, Okinawa Prefecture,
The evening of Saturday July 13, 2019

"*Snake!*" Linh gasped, eyes wide, horrified. "Oh, my God, is that *real*?"

The waiter grinned, brandishing an enormous glass bottle that contained amber liquid and the coiled, intact corpse of a viper, fangs bared as if to strike.

"You've got to be shitting me. People drink that?" Tate's lip curled in disgust.

"The guidebook says it's called *Habushu*," Eloise said, flipping through the pages of the pocket-sized book she'd picked up at Naha airport. "It's made of *Awamori*, an Okinawan distilled liquor, bottled with the body of a *habu* snake indigenous to the Ryukyu islands and aged until consumed."

"I don't think so. No. Thanks." Tate shook his head at the waiter, and Eloise felt a momentary rush of relief until Steph opened her mouth.

"Are you kidding? We have to try it! Five glasses, please!" She flashed Tate a challenging look, and he backed down.

"*Habu* snakes mate for up to twenty-four hours," the waiter said conspiratorially in English, a twinkle in his eye. "*Habushu* will make you good in bed with the ladies." Steph and Linh both cracked up over this, but Tate simply stared at the coiled corpse of the preserved snake, his mouth slightly open. The waiter poured five glasses and left, re-instating the bottle of snake wine on a high shelf behind the bar.

"It's not poisonous, is it?" Linh asked, pushing her glasses up with her knuckle.

"Venomous," Steph corrected her. "If you bite it and you die, it's poisonous. If it bites *you* and you die, it's venomous."

Linh narrowed her eyes at Steph. "Thanks for the biology lesson."

"It *is* venomous," Eloise said, turning the open guidebook around to show them a photograph of a yellow-brown snake resembling the one in the bottle. "The venom contains cytotoxin and hemorrhage...hemorrha*gic* components. Bites cause nausea, vomiting, hypotension, and potentially even death if you don't get prompt medical treatment. As well as extreme pain in the afflicted area." A bead of sweat slid down her spine, and the hairs on her arms prickled despite the heat of the night.

She couldn't *stand* snakes.

Tate grimaced, lifting his small glass of amber liquid to the light as if expecting to see venomous swirls floating there.

"Hey! Save some for me, man."

Eloise's stomach did a little leap, a sensation reminiscent of the slight chop turbulence they'd encountered on landing earlier that day.

Kenji made it.

"Drink this," Satoko said quickly, pushing her glass of *habushu* in front of Kenji as he took a seat. Kenji picked up the glass and knocked it back without hesitation, to the impressed gasps of the others. His eyes found Eloise's, and he smiled, putting the glass down on the table with a muted *thock*.

They'd arrived on Okinawa Island around one in the afternoon and headed straight from Naha airport to the beach. It was beautiful here. The sand was the color of raw cane sugar, and the ocean was so crystal-clear that Eloise spotted shoals of tiny fishes darting between her toes.

The sun went down early, around five. Used to endless summer days back home in England, where it stayed light as late as nine p.m, Eloise still found the early sunsets in this part of the world strange. The setting sun had formed a burning red ball low on the horizon, spilling sun glitter on the ocean below. The evening sky had been beautiful, too, a gentle gradient of colors shifting from pastel orange, to pink, to lilac, to deep indigo.

Limbs heavy with delicious exhaustion, they'd crunched up the white gravel path to their hostel, little stone lanterns and puff-ball bonsai trees lining the way. An immense, gnarled banyan tree hung over the building and offered welcome shade in the heat of the afternoon. Satoko checked them in, and the hostel owner, a stocky guy with a tanned face and short, spiky hair, had recommended a good bar down the street for dinner. They'd already been drinking for an hour by the time Kenji arrived.

The bar had communal-style seating, and when a group of other visibly foreign travelers entered, Tate and Steph waved them over. One was a beaming English guy with some meat on his bones and an air of dishevelment that was immediately disarming. He was accompanied closely by a dark-haired girl with huge, beautiful eyes, who seemed to be his girlfriend. Also in their group was a tall American guy with broad shoulders and piercing blue eyes, who sat down beside Eloise and flashed her a quick smile, and a lanky blond guy with glasses who kept blinking nervously.

They ordered more *habushu*—which actually tasted quite nice—so they could share the shock of discovering it with the new additions to their table. The guys all took a glass, but the girl with the lovely brown eyes, whose name was Mishka, opted out. Eloise took a second to appreciate how her boyfriend—called Ollie—didn't react to this. He didn't tease her or try to pressure her into drinking it by putting her on the spot. Eloise couldn't help liking him immediately. She thought he was cute, too, although he wasn't conventionally good-looking. He had a cheeky, winning smile and bright eyes, with facial hair that was past the stubble stage but hadn't yet committed enough to be called a beard. You could hear the smile in his voice when he spoke, along with an almost imperceptible lisp, only really noticeable when he said things like *pass the soy sauce* and *fantastic*. He spoke with a South London accent, which seemed to be an affectation, but it came across as charming anyway.

They ordered most of the items on the menu for the whole table to share, in the Japanese social eating style. Ollie and Mishka had been there for a few days already and knew what to order. Satoko and Eloise dished up everyone's plates from the communal ones. The main dish was a kind of stir-fry containing crumbly tofu, chunky bacon, and *goya*— a vivid green bitter gourd with a knobbly rind. There were thick slabs of fatty pork in some sort of sauce, as well as a dish of what looked like little black eggs clinging to stalks.

"Those are sea grapes," Mishka explained. "Very salty, and they burst in your mouth."

Eloise dished up a plate of some sort of rubbery meat. "What's this?" she asked Mishka, who waved it away, her mouth twisting.

"Pig ears," she said, making Eloise smile.

"Bullshit." Eloise looked closer. She suddenly remembered reading somewhere that Okinawans ate a lot of pork—every part of the pig but its squeal.

"Ugh," Steph groaned, leaning away from the offending dish.

"Poor piggies," Linh said, grabbing a piece with her chopsticks anyway.

"You think pig ears are gross, you should try eating *Balut*. I had some in Manila. Mishka nearly puked just watching me eat it." Ollie grinned, clearly cherishing the memory.

"No, I didn't," Mishka said. "*You* chose to eat an unhatched duck fetus. If anyone should have been puking, it's you. It still boggles me how you kept that down."

"You refused to kiss me for a week after that, didn't you, babe? Oh, speaking of disgusting eggs, have any of you ever had a Century Egg? They bury it in clay and leave it to ferment for months, and when you finally eat it, the yolk part's navy blue, and it tastes like toilet cleaner."

"Can you stop, hun? People are trying to eat."

While Ollie and Mishka continued talking about the culinary misadventures they'd had traveling around Asia, Eloise finished dishing up her own plate. "*Kwatchii sabira*," she mumbled, taking a bite of the fatty pork. It melted into almost nothingness on her tongue, so salty it sent jets of saliva arcing inside her mouth. It took her a moment to realize that the others were staring at her.

"Oh, it means 'Let's Eat' in Uchinaaguchi." She swallowed her mouthful, wiping sauce off her chin with the complimentary damp towel the bar provided.

"What is that? Like, Okinawan?" Steph frowned. "It sounds so different from Japanese."

"What made you decide to move all the way to Japan to teach English, Eloise?" Ollie spoke around a thick mouthful of chewy Okinawa soba noodles. "I mean, is that what you want to do as a career? Teaching?"

"No, it was..." Eloise swallowed.

Go on, Eloise. Tell them. Tell them what you did. What you ran away from.

"It was just...something to do after uni."

"Teaching sucks." Tate sniffed.

"It's not the greatest. We're more like human tape recorders than anything else. But the kids are cute." Linh shrugged.

Ollie introduced himself and Mishka as a pair. "I'm Ollie. This is Mishka, she's from Brisbane. We met traveling in Thailand." His eyes were fixed on hers. "I was backpacking with a group of mates from back home after uni, but I completely ditched them to go off with Mishka, didn't I, babe? We've been to six—bugger me, is it seven? Seven countries together, and I think—is it Taiwan next? Yeah. Then, after that, we're planning to make a pitstop in Dubai and then fly from there back to the UK. Mishka's agreed to come with me and meet my family because, well…" Ollie trailed off then, an embarrassed smile on his face. He took Mishka's left hand and held it up so they could all see. Satoko quickly covered her mouth to conceal a shocked smile while Steph grabbed Mishka's hand and pulled it over to her side of the bench.

"It's just a cheap pearl ring, but it was all I could find to propose with. I'm saving buying the real bling until we get back," Ollie explained, and Mishka tugged her hand away, sitting back in her seat, a shy smile on her lips.

"He proposed on the beach last night," she confessed coyly. "I have no idea how we're going to make it work—which *country* we're going to live in—but all I know is that love…love exists. And I've found my person. My soulmate."

Soulmate. The word jabbed at Eloise's brain. Soulmates didn't exist. Neither did love. Not really. It was all just chemicals when you thought about it rationally. Dopamine. Oxytocin. Human beings were just flesh bags swirling with chemicals. Love, like free will, was an illusion.

"How's your journey been, mate?" Ollie said, turning his gaze to the tall American sitting beside Eloise. He'd been mostly silent until this point, and Eloise had been too self-conscious to look at him, but she'd noticed his forearms. She always noticed when a man had nice forearms, and this guy had a particularly good pair. Well-muscled, with tanned skin and a modest amount of soft golden hair, and those ropey veins you saw on guys that worked out. They ran along the insides of his arms from just under the wrist, and Eloise had to fight against a mad impulse to press her thumb against one. He had nice hands, too. Strong-looking, but not too rough.

She put down her wooden chopsticks and angled her body to one side to get a better look at his face. They were all sitting crammed together. It was a tight fit. He looked back at her, down at her, without lowering his head, and she wondered if she'd ever seen such a young man with a mustache that thick and full before.

Why, though? she mused, distracted.

"Eye-opening, I guess," he said, smiling at Ollie, his voice warm and slow. "Been mostly backpacking solo around Asia. Avoiding the real world and the folks back home."

"What's your name?" Eloise murmured, fixated by the pale blue of his eyes, how the light color contrasted with the deep navy rings around the outside of the irises.

"Miles," he said after a protracted pause, during which he let her dangle. Eloise fought back a wave of embarrassment. *It's not like it was a tough question.*

"Hey, Miles, *Movember* ended eight months ago," Tate wise-cracked, and they all laughed, Miles included, before his face suddenly darkened.

"Don't make fun of me, man. I was born with a cleft palate. I had to have all these surgeries as a baby. The mustache hides the scar. Not cool, bro. Not cool at all."

There was a horrified silence that lasted for several seconds. Tate made a clicking sound in his throat. Nobody seemed to want to be the first one to speak.

"Ah, I was just joking with you. I lost a bet with a couple of buddies, actually, and hence, had to grow the 'stache. You need to lighten up, man, talk about stiff. What about you?" Miles elbowed the quiet blond guy sitting on his other side, and he jerked in his seat as if he'd been goosed.

"I'm...Jan. I am a marine biology student in the Netherlands. I'm here on a solo trip. I arrived last night and will go to Ishigaki Island by boat tomorrow." Jan removed his glasses and began cleaning them. Eloise noted that he hadn't touched his snake wine.

"Oh, that sounds cool," Linh said. Tate nodded, looking bored. "Just passing through, huh?"

They ordered another round of drinks.

5

When they arrived back at the hostel an hour later, they were all nicely drunk, voices a few decibels louder, laughing at things that weren't particularly funny, and generally enjoying each other's company. They'd lost the Dutch guy at some point, but his absence barely registered.

The only one still stone-cold sober was Mishka, who hadn't ordered any drinks at all, contenting herself with the complimentary iced water. She opted out of taking a bath with the rest of the girls, too, saying she'd used the beach showers that afternoon.

Eloise almost tripped over her own flip-flopped feet as she and the other girls dashed, giggling, down the covered stone walkway to the communal baths. The guys had gone ahead, and they could hear them talking, burbling water flowing somewhere beyond the half-curtain emblazoned with the kanji character for *Man*. Ducking under the curtain on the other side that read *Woman*, they entered a dressing room equipped with amenities. There was a row of sinks and mirrors, hairdryers hung up on brackets beside them and wicker baskets to store their clothes.

Eloise poked her head around the sliding door to the outside. The moonlight shone down on the surface of the glittering water. It was all one big, stone, open-air outdoor bath, but a bamboo divider ran down the center of it, segregating the men from the women.

"Oh, my God, you could totally see through that screen," Steph said, her head popping over Eloise's shoulder.

"What?" Linh squawked, looking panicked. "I'm down for skinny dipping with you girls any time, but are we seriously going to trust those *men* not to peek?"

Steph turned, grinning at Linh. "What if we even the score and peek right back?"

"I'm going in with a towel wrapped around me," Linh announced, marching naked back into the changing room and whipping one of the hostel-provided towels off the shelf. "If you ladies value your modesty, I suggest you do the same."

"Oh, there's no towels allowed in the…" Satoko started to say but quickly trailed off. She, too, grabbed a towel off the shelf.

The hot water was scalding, almost too hot to bear at first, but they soon acclimated. Eloise kept her towel wrapped firmly around her, with the loose end tucked tight under her armpit.

"Who all's in there?" Steph called out, swimming through the steaming chest-high water to the far end of the bamboo fence.

"It's me," Tate called back. "And Ollie and Kenji."

"Where's Miles?"

"Right here, sweetheart," Miles said, leaning his head around the far end of the divider and grinning into their side of the bath.

They shrieked, even though they were suitably covered up. Miles hooked his elbows behind him, resting them on the stone ledge of the bath, leaning his head back and closing his eyes.

"Nice tattoo," Steph said. "What is that, a rooster? I can't make it out."

Miles opened one eye. "Yeah."

"No tattoos in the bath, Mister. Manager said so."

"If they don't like it, they're gonna hafta come in here and remove me."

Eloise couldn't see the tattoo from where she was, but she didn't want to go any closer.

Linh blinked behind her steamed-up glasses. "Are you guys all, uh, naked over there?"

"As the day we were born," Miles said, opening both eyes and craning his head back even further to look in on them again.

Eloise clamped her arms tight against her sides to make sure the towel wasn't in any danger of unpeeling itself and sank up to her chin in the steaming water.

"Maybe give the ladies some privacy, huh?" Ollie suggested. There was a sloshing sound, water displacing, and Miles disappeared from view.

"They're wearing towels. That's disrespectful to the sacred practice of communal nude bathing. What would the ancient Romans have to say about this, hmm?"

"Oh, my God, I can see his butt," Steph said, eye pressed to the bamboo divider. "Peachy. I give it a nine. Would be a ten without the tan line."

"*Stop it*!" Linh hissed, scandalized, splashing water at Steph.

"Come take a peek, Els," Steph said, gesturing for Eloise to join her.

"No way," Eloise muttered. "How wasted are you?"

"Oh, come on. You know you want to peek at the boys. Well, one boy. *We* know you want to. *He* knows you want to. *Everyone* knows you want to!" Steph's voice was getting louder and louder.

"I think I'm done bathing for tonight," Eloise said, and she knew she sounded prim and prissy. She was spoiling the fun and making things uncomfortable for everyone else. At the same time, she was too embarrassed to care.

Wading through the hot water as fast as she could without losing her dignity and face-planting, she hauled herself out onto the wet slab. Then, without even rinsing off, she trotted into the changing room, slamming the sliding screen door behind her.

Inside, she scrambled to dry off and change back into her clothes. As much as she liked Steph sometimes, admired her, even, she could be such a demonic bitch when she wanted to be. Eloise had lost count of the number of times Steph had put her on the spot and put her down in public to make herself look better by comparison. What Eloise didn't know was why she bothered. Steph was beautiful, really beautiful, with the kind of face you usually only saw in the movies or on TV. She was vivacious, confident, sharp. What did she have to gain from crushing Eloise's ego except her own sick satisfaction?

"El?" Steph opened the sliding door and stepped in. "I'm sorry. I was only teasing. I didn't mean for..."

"Save it," Eloise said. "Really, Steph, whatever. It's fine. I'm going back to the room. I overheated, that's all. I need some cold water."

"Do you want me to come with you?" She could hear the regret, the wounded tone in Steph's voice, and she hated her for it.

Great, make me out to be the bad guy.

"I'm fine," she said, ducking under the curtain and making her escape.

Eloise was lying out on the tatami mats in their room, a cold washcloth on her forehead, the air conditioning unit blowing directly on her, when Steph's face appeared above hers.

"I'm sorry," she said, and at this angle, she looked like a basset hound, hair limp from the steam, hanging down on either side of her face like floppy ears. The effect was definitely comical.

Eloise tried to hold on to the feeling of being annoyed with Steph, but it was slipping away from her.

"Fwends?" Steph asked, using baby talk for the irony, to make her laugh. Eloise knew that if she stayed mad at Steph, she'd be the bitch by default. That was the way it always went between them.

Sighing, she sat up.

"Friends. So? Did you see anything interesting?"

"It was no fun spying without you. By the way, Kenji was worried when you disappeared."

"No, he wasn't," Eloise said. "And I don't care, anyway."

But she did care. That was the problem.

She'd asked him out once. An impulse three a.m. text, fueled by one too many cups of hot sake heated up in a pan of water on her one-ring burner stove. He said yes immediately, and Eloise had burned her fingers on the sake bottle, blinking at the glowing rectangle of her phone's screen in drunken disbelief. She kept it simple—after-work drinks at Kemuri, where else? But the day before their proposed date, he sent her a follow-up text: "Who's coming tomorrow?" and it was like she'd just swallowed a boulder. Heart thumping with embarrassment, she sent out a mass text and managed to get together enough people to make a decent-sized group on almost zero notice. But the night was a wash, she barely managed to speak two words to Kenji. After that, she tried to find comfort in the thought that at least Kenji was none the wiser about her intentions. But sometimes, late at night, lying awake on her futon in the darkest hour before the dawn crept in, her mind tortured her with agonizing thoughts. *He realized you were asking him out*, her mind said. *Realized too late and panicked at the idea of being on a date with you.*

Did Kenji *know* about her? Did *any* of them? No one had ever said anything. But one Google was all it'd take, surely?

The thought was not a new one. It surfaced often, whenever she was skipped over for a social invite, whenever she caught the eye of one of her friends, and they didn't smile.

No. Couldn't be. If they knew, none of them would ever talk to her again. She was sure of it.

"Uh-huh," Steph said maddeningly. "Listen, everyone's going to gather in the communal room and drink more. Miles and Tate already went to the 7-11 to buy more booze and snacks."

"Okay," Eloise heard herself saying.

Great, maybe if everyone got drunk enough, they'd forget about what a pissy little baby she'd been back there.

"Where's everyone else?"

"Already hanging out. Come on!"

Sighing, Eloise allowed Steph to grab her hands and pull her to her feet.

6

The communal area was a Japanese-style room with tatami mats and a low, lacquered table. The manager, Nakamura—*Just call me Nack*—was there, sitting cross-legged and strumming some sort of string instrument. The smiling, silent woman next to him turned out to be his wife, Masami. She wore her hair in thick curtain bangs that concealed the majority of her face. There'd been no sign of Masami earlier when they'd checked in. Just Nack, red-faced and spiky-haired, grinning behind the check-in desk. Rubbery black wetsuits had hung on the walls behind him like limp, drowned bodies.

"Is that a *shamisen*?" Steph asked Nack, indicating towards the odd, long-necked instrument.

"It is a *sanshin*," he answered proudly. "*Sanshin* means three strings. Our traditional instrument. It is genuine snakeskin."

"Are you okay?" Kenji asked Eloise, making her jump. She'd been spacing out and hadn't noticed him sitting down beside her.

"...What?"

"You're scratching."

"Oh...yeah. Mosquito bites. I'm just tasty, I guess. I'm always the first one to get bitten."

Kenji grinned, meeting her eyes for a second. "Your blood must be a delicacy to them. It's not every day they get to feast on a cute British girl."

Steph choked, water coming out of her nose. "Wow, Kenji, smooth!"

"Shut up." Kenji grinned at Steph, tossing her the box of tissues that was on the table.

"We need hot spoons." Steph screwed the cap back on her bottle of water and leaned in close, appraising the throbbing welts on Eloise's flushed legs. "Heat cooks the protein the mosquitos inject into you. That'll eliminate the itch."

"Or, I mean, we could just use bug bite gel." Kenji pulled a plastic cylinder out of his pocket, popped the cap off, and rubbed one end of it against Eloise's leg, his tanned hand holding her skin taut. The applicator had stiff plastic bristles, which scratched the itch deliciously as the cold gel soothed the throbbing. She closed her eyes in bliss, and when she opened them, she realized Steph was watching her with an unreadable expression on her face.

"Better?" Kenji paused, looking up at her, too. He had very thick eyebrows, and his eyes were a light shade of brown that actually looked amber under the fluorescent strip lights.

"All better. Thanks."

"Konbanwa. Konbanwa."

Voices floated from an old cabinet-style television set, playing away to no one in the corner of the room. Eloise was surprised to see it. She hadn't realized TVs that old still worked. Maybe it had been retrofitted.

The two anchors, a grey-haired, jowly man and a pretty young woman, had just lifted their heads from a deep, synchronized bow. Their expressions were solemn. Apparently, they were about to deliver the evening news.

Tate and Miles walked in, laden down with plastic bags from the 7-11. Tate had a tense expression on his face, and he put his bags down on the low table with a little more force than was necessary. Condensation immediately began to slalom down the sides of the bags and puddle onto the table beneath. Miles followed suit and dropped his plastic bag of drinking snacks onto the low table as well, accidentally knocking the remote onto the tatami mat. The TV screen went dark and silent.

Linh began rootling around inside the bags. "Did you get me an electrolyte drink?"

"I got whiskey—just cheap stuff—carbonated water so we can make highballs, box wine, uh, beer...beef jerky, stuff like that. And some of those pre-hangover prophylactics. You know, the supplement drinks in the little bottles. I want to set off early tomorrow, like *sunrise* early, so we get the whole day to explore the ruins and take pictures."

"What ruins?" Ollie asked, reaching for one of the cans of Orion beer.

Tate blinked, hesitating. Eloise and Steph waited, watching Tate's face to see how he was going to handle that little slip. After a few seconds, though, Tate shrugged.

"We're heading to these remote cliffs tomorrow, to this old, abandoned resort. Just to explore, take some pictures. It's kinda why we came here, actually."

"Ew, why?" Mishka wrinkled up her nose. "That sounds horrible."

"Mate! I *love* abandoned places," Ollie said, his voice suddenly thick with excitement. "It's the atmosphere, like they exist in some kind of nowhere space outside the bounds of real-time. *Liminal* space."

"What does *liminal* mean?" Mishka's beautiful dark eyes flashed with irritation. "Anyway, *we're* not going with them."

Ollie frowned at her. He opened his mouth to speak, thought better of it, paused, took a big breath, then tried again. "If you don't want to go, babe, that's fine. Maybe I do, though. We've been together every day since we met, practically. It's been months. Am I not allowed to do my own thing anymore?"

"Uh-oh, trouble in paradise," Steph whispered, leaning in close to Eloise, her hot breath tickling her ear.

"The more the merrier, man," Tate said, shrugging. "Right, girls? Kenji?"

"You can't be serious," Mishka said. "This is your idea of fun?" She turned to Tate. "You said it's abandoned? How long ago? Is it dangerous?"

"In the seventies. But it's not—*that* dangerous," Tate muttered, clearly not wanting to be caught in the middle of what was apparently their first-ever lover's spat.

"So where is this abandoned resort?" Miles hadn't taken a seat with the others. He was standing by one of the thick wooden support beams that held up the roof, leaning his back against it, his hands hooked casually onto his belt. "You said it's remote? How remote are we talking?"

"It's...up on the cliffs. It's, like, a forty-minute bus ride from here. The east coast of the island."

Nack stopped plucking random notes on his *sanshin*. He lifted his face, his mouth slightly open. "The old Oceanview ruin? Don't want to go up there. There's some *bad* history in that place. Terrible things happened there."

An ancient oscillating fan, spinning away in the corner, turned its cold breath on the back of Eloise's neck, making her shiver.

"Yeah, yeah, we've all heard about the curse. The red maiden. The red smoke. The way she—" Tate made a comedic gurgling sound, drawing his finger across his throat. "We know about the construction accidents, the suicides, and *duh-duh-duh-duh-duh*. I've read all the rumors online, but do you want to know what I think? I think it's all bullshit. There's no creepy red maiden. No curse. No spooky shit. It's just another failed monument to the extreme excesses of the era, an abortion of a project dreamed up by a rich, terminally bored guy with more money than sense."

The hostel owner's smile slipped, and his expression darkened unpleasantly for a moment. "If you think so, why are you going?"

Tate licked his teeth.

Nack waited a moment for an answer, but when none was supplied, he shrugged and packed his instrument carefully into its case. As he got to his feet, he frowned. "You check in?" he demanded of Miles, eyes narrowing.

"Yeah."

"You the one with the surfboard?"

"No."

Nack hesitated for a moment, then gave his head a little shake. "Sorry. My short-term memory is, you know, not great. Good night."

The group murmured politely as Nack disappeared into the hallway along with his silent wife. Eloise sensed that their group had disappointed him in some profoundly significant way. Maybe it had something to do with the fact that they weren't surfers. She hoped they hadn't done or said anything culturally offensive.

"There's a *curse*?" Mishka hissed. "Oh, hell no. Count me out. My plans for tomorrow involve laying out all day on the beach with a book over my face. Not getting my extremities twisted off in a junked-out pile of rubble by some long-haired, creepy Japanese ghost girl with a grudge."

"I think I'll join you guys," Ollie said recklessly. "You don't really mind, do you, babe?"

"Whatever. Knock yourself out," Mishka said, her voice going cold and hard. "I'm going to bed."

The others mumbled awkwardly as Mishka left, closing the sliding door a little too hard behind her so that it jumped and skidded in its grooves. Ollie looked slightly deflated for a moment but soon perked up and started animatedly discussing the history of the old resort with Tate.

"So technically, it's not restricted, but the Marine Corps banned US servicemen and their families from going there. Some sort of accident. It was a structural collapse, I think?" Tate cracked another beer. Was that his sixth? Seventh? Tate had an impressive tolerance. Eloise didn't think she'd ever seen him drunk. "Anyway, a group of them were messing around up there, having a party. The guy was probably wasted and wasn't looking where he was stepping. We should be fine as long as we follow some basic safety procedures. Hiking boots, flashlights, stuff like that."

"The Marines?" Miles still hadn't sat down. He was watching Tate, a curious look in his unusual blue eyes.

"Yeah, you know, there's a huge US military presence here. I think something like 25 percent of Okinawa Island is taken up by US military bases. Sometimes, they act out and commit crimes and stuff. The locals protest a lot."

Miles narrowed his eyes. "Those *bases* maintain deterrence against possible threats to Japan. You do realize that, don't you?"

Tate opened his mouth to respond, two angry blotches of color high on his cheeks.

"Uh, uh, uh. Excuse me? Boys?" Steph raised a hand. "No politics. Can we not? Thanks."

"Are you...are you joining us, Miles?" Eloise ignored the sharp, angry look of betrayal Tate shot her. It wasn't an invite. If Eloise was going to force herself through a social situation, she generally wanted to know who else would be there. It helped, somehow. Although, it pissed Steph off every time. "Do you want a freaking guest list?" she'd snapped at Eloise once in frustration.

"Hmm. You're leaving at sunrise? I'm not really what you might call a morning person." His blue eyes held Eloise transfixed.

"You and me both," Linh said, chugging bottled water.

Tate clapped his hands. "You know what we should do? We should play *Never Have I Ever*."

This suggestion was met with a chorus of groans.

"Please, Tate. We're not in college anymore." Steph wrinkled her nose.

"I can't handle any more booze," Linh moaned.

Tate grinned. "No worries. You've never done anything spicy in your life, Linny."

"What would *you* know about what I've done in my life, *Tater*?"

But they were interrupted. The sliding door shot open, and an old woman appeared in the doorway. She had snowy white hair pulled into a tight lacquered bun and wore a pale salmon-hued kimono and white tabi socks. Head bowed low, she shuffled across the tatami mats and slid aside a section of the wall, revealing deep shelves piled high with towels. A white-gloved hand reached up, groping blindly for them. Eloise remembered seeing the old lady earlier, sweeping the exoskeletal shells of dead cicadas off the stone path near the bathhouse with a crude straw broom. She'd noticed the white cotton gloves and wondered why the old lady wore them in the heat, but it wasn't all that strange. It seemed that taxi drivers and police officers wore them year-round in Japan.

The others barely glanced at the old woman.

"So, we'll leave at sunrise or soon after, yeah?" Tate looked around, checking for assent. "We'll get the bus going to the Takagusuku Park area and then hike up the hill to the old resort. The views of the ocean should be amazing."

The old woman froze, still bent over, clutching a stack of towels. Her head twisted to one side, and she stared at them with her yellowed, rheumy eyes. The others were still talking, and only Eloise noticed the stricken expression on the old woman's deeply lined face.

"*Yana*," she muttered, her voice barely audible above the conversational din.

Still laughing at something one of the others said, Tate's smile slowly faded as he took in Eloise's look of shock. He craned his neck to look at the old lady behind him. Then he raised a hand in the air, calling for silence.

"What did she say?" he asked Eloise.

"Takagusuku cliff. Oceanview..." The old woman's eyes glistened. "*The red smoke.*" She dumped the towels in a heap on the floor, abandoning them, shuffling with an almost preternatural speed back to the sliding door she'd entered by. Her tabi socks whispered to a stop against the tatami as she paused in the open doorway, her bent back facing them.

"*Stay away.*"

The creaking fan breathed another icy gasp onto the back of Eloise's flushed neck.

Then, the old woman pulled the door shut behind her.

After a moment's stunned hesitation, Tate released a peal of laughter. "Wow, talk about local color!" He pulled his jaw to one side in grotesque mockery. "What crypt did she come crawling out of?"

But nobody else was laughing.

7

Hot vomit splattered across Eloise's sandal and bare shin. Satoko's body jack-knifed again, ejecting the half-digested remains of her dinner over the gravel. When she finished, Eloise and Linh hauled her, feet dragging, to the bench out in front of their stand-alone guest house.

Eloise went to get a bottle of water from the humming vending machine, and Linh gingerly plucked the vomit-soaked loops of Satoko's hair out of her mouth and wiped her face with a clean towel handkerchief.

"I'm sorry," Satoko burped, hand clawing the air for the bottle of water as Eloise returned. "I don't usually drink this much."

"Don't worry about it." Eloise was no stranger to public displays of vomiting. Heaven knows she'd been the hot mess herself enough times. Fresher's Week at uni had been a complete pukeathon. But these days, Eloise never seemed to get that drunk, no matter how much booze she sank.

Does that worry me? Maybe it should.

"I thought that if we got wasted together, it would just...happen. I mean, that's how it happened last time." Satoko looked up at Eloise and Linh, her eyes bleary, her chin shiny with puke. Then she let her head hang, her hair covering her face.

"What's she talking about?" Linh mouthed at Eloise, her wide eyes confused behind her thick glasses.

"But all he cares about is Steph," Satoko moaned. "He's been completely *ignoring* me. I'm such a *stupid*."

Linh leaned forward, parting Satoko's hair like curtains. "You're not stupid. What's going on, hmm?"

"Tate," Satoko said, lower lip pooching out.

"*Tate*?" Eloise heard the note of disgust in her own voice. And surprise, yes, but only for a moment. Tate had worked his way through half the female population of Yamaoku. Why not Satoko, too? She'd actually be more surprised if he hadn't.

"We hooked up. Once. Last month. He was *perfect*. He's hot, he knows what he's doing in bed, and most importantly, he's leaving soon, so Shun would probably never find out..."

Linh frowned, eyes flicking to Eloise for help. "Shun is...?"

"We're getting married. I *hate* him." Satoko's cheeks billowed out, and Eloise took a hasty step backward, but Satoko merely burped again.

"Oh, hey. Why are you marrying a guy you hate? Why cheat on him when you could just, you know, break up?" Linh looked like she was trying really hard to understand. Eloise, meanwhile, was fighting a sudden intense flare of dislike for Satoko. Her prim, demure act was disingenuous. She was a complete fake. And because of her, Eloise was missing the party. She grabbed the bottle from Satoko's limp hand and splashed what was left of the water over her shin and ankle, washing away the other woman's vomit.

"I don't have any choice. Our families planned it all out. My dad and my older brother are both dead, so it's up to me to support everyone else. Mom. Bah-chan. My little sister, Emiko. Gan-chan, our Shiba Inu. He's got kidney disease. And Bah-chan's got an insulin pump. Anyway, Shun's not *that* bad, as far as guys go. He's *dependable*. It's just that I don't want to have to get married *yet*! There is so much I still want to do!" Satoko knuckled tears out of her eyes, dislodging her feather-light artificial lashes and smearing them across her pale cheek.

They reminded Eloise of disembodied insect wings. "I want to travel more! I want to live abroad!"

Linh chewed her lip. "You can't get married and still do that?"

Satoko snorted indelicately. "No. Shun doesn't like—*foreign* stuff. And once we're married, I'll have to quit my job. Lucky me. I get to spend the rest of my life doing housework and cooking dinner for him. Meanwhile, he goes out after work and gets blowjobs from girls in pink salons, just like the other guys in his department."

Linh winced. "That's disgusting. You don't have to marry a guy like *that.*"

"You don't know what you're talking about," Satoko sniffed. "That's what marriage *is*—a business contract. The husband works and pays the bills. And the wife does the housework and takes care of the kids. And if the guy wants to fool around and have some fun after work, there are ways he can do that without anyone getting hurt. It's not *cheating* if he pays for it."

"But that's *horrible.*"

Eloise studied Linh. Her cheeks flushed with emotion. One hand hovering in the air just above Satoko's knee. Her lips moved silently as if voicing words of internal disbelief.

Eloise had heard about these kinds of relationships, marriage as a business contract. The pragmatism with which a lot of people here viewed it. The old Eloise would have found it all too devastating to even think about. But the old Eloise was a romantic. And anyway. The old Eloise was dead.

Maybe it's really better that way, she mused, gazing absently at the mascara dribbles sliding slowly down Satoko's cheeks. *If everyone's clear on the rules from the start, then nobody has to get hurt. Nobody has to have their heart ripped out of their body while it's still pumping, and then stamped on.*

And nobody had to end up at the police station at two in the morning, arms tacky with dried blood, phasing in and out, wondering what the hell happened to their life.

No. Stop. We're not thinking about that.

"It's normal." Satoko sniffed, her tone suddenly defensive. "It's normal here. You don't get it. At least I don't have to work at a desk all day anymore. I don't have to do hours of stupid overtime. I get to stay home all day, take the kids to the park, and go to lunch with my friends. And I won't have to *suck some guy's gross dick* anymore. That part can get outsourced." Satoko's eyes blazed.

"How can you not care?" Linh asked, her voice almost cracking. "What about love?"

Satoko snorted once more, dragging the back of her hand across her chin.

There it was again, that hot flicker of dislike.

"You don't know anything," Satoko said bitterly. "Once I'm married, that's it for me. You're supposed to leave behind your...your *sexuality* and become a dedicated wife and mother who never has a single impure thought. Well, I came on this trip to *get laid*, and I'm not leaving until I get what I want. If Tate's no good, I'll try that other guy."

Linh laughed then, softly, as if she thought Satoko was joking.

Eloise wondered if Satoko's drunken brain was actually processing this conversation, or if she'd wake up tomorrow with a complete blackout. Eloise had experienced a few blackouts during her uni days. She'd found them terrifying at first. Gaping voids of empty time during which she'd done things and said things that were lost to her forever, those memories not just inaccessible but never even formed in the first place.

Like the night Chris died, you mean?

Eloise bit down on her lip so hard she tasted blood.

"What guy?" Linh asked after a few moments of awkward silence, during which her laughter had hung on the humid air. "Miles?"

"Yesssh," Satoko slurred. "I like his eyes. God, I love blue eyes." She made a sound low down in her throat, like a strangled sob.

Then, her forehead connected with the top of the bench, causing a loud and painful-sounding *thud*.

"Eloise? *El*?"

Eloise blinked, realizing that Linh was trying to speak to her. She'd been miles away. 6,000 miles away. Over two years ago. A crowded pub, sweaty bodies crammed together. The stench of stale beer. The metallic taste of fear on her tongue.

Linh sighed. "Help me with her, El. I think we'd better put her to bed."

8

"So much for our sleepover," Steph said to Eloise beside her, chin resting in her hands. She was sprawled on her front atop her crisp white futon. It was still early, comparatively speaking, but Satoko was sparked out, and Linh was halfway there, glasses, water bottle, bug spray, and phone strategically placed by her pillow. She had her earplugs in and her eye mask on already.

"Stop talking," Linh groaned.

"I think it's time for a game of *Would You*?" Steph said, rolling over and propping herself up on one elbow, her eyes glittering in the dim light as she looked shrewdly at Eloise.

"Please, no more games." Eloise sighed. She wasn't in the mood for any more Steph that night. She was tired, irritated from having to mop up Satoko, and all she wanted was to drift off to sleep thinking about, well, never mind.

"Come on. You used to love to play." Steph pouted. "It's like you're so distant lately. We never have fun anymore, not like we used to. You always *used* to tell me when you had a crush on a guy. Why is it different this time?"

"I've told you. I don't have a *crush* on anyone. Why can't you drop it?"

"But we're *best* friends. It's not cool of you to start shutting me out all of a sudden. At least not without letting me know why."

There was an anguished pause.

"Would you," Steph said, lifting her hand and making a fist, bumping it sideways against her cheek. Her tongue probed, stretching the opposite side out in a grotesque parody of a sex act.

"Bloody hell. That's vile, Steph."

Linh sat up, uncorking her earplugs and tugging her eye mask down to her chin.

"Wait, I missed it. What did she do?"

Steph rolled over obligingly and repeated the performance for Linh.

"Eww." Linh giggled with scandalized delight. Okay, you did the verb, so do I get to choose the object?"

"If you're playing, too."

Linh flung back the covers, grinning.

"Erm, then...Miles."

Steph whipped her head around to look at Eloise, a tight grin of amusement on her face.

Eloise's heart sank. "I'm not playing," she said, a finality in her tone that made Steph groan.

"Come *on*, Elly-Wheeze," Steph said. "You're being a major bummer."

"*Fine*. The answer's no. That's no to the verb, regardless of object, FYI."

Linh grinned. "Would you kiss him, though?"

"Linh, rules! You forgot to act it out. You're ruining the game. Would you, though?" Steph put her head to one side as if imagining it. "I would if he shaved off the mustache. I do love a bad boy."

"He seems kind of mean, though," Linh said.

"He seems like a complete jerk. But that's the *entire* appeal," Steph grinned. "When he's a total asshole to everyone...except you. Ugh, fucking dreamy."

"Oh, puke." Linh wrinkled her nose.

"What would *you* know, Linny? Some of us actually want to live a little while we're young. I'm surrounded by prudes."

"I'm not a prude," Linh mumbled. "I just think that playing around with random guys is a zero-sum game. Not to mention dangerous."

"I'm not stupid, Linh, thanks. But listen. Why do the guys get to have all the fun? We have a right to enjoy sex, too, you know. To enjoy *variety*. Am I supposed to live like a nun until marriage just because man's the most dangerous animal? If you're a straight woman, you've got no choice but to date your only natural predator. It's messed up, but that's just how it is. And to be completely honest, I think that's part of the thrill."

"You're a lunatic," Linh said, smiling with mild exasperation.

"Wait, wait, I'm getting a text." Steph snatched up her vibrating phone. "It's Tate. Ugh. They're at the beach for a midnight swim, and they want us to join. Jesus, look at this. He said, *bathing suits optional*." Steph's lip curled with disgust.

"Goodnight!" Linh quickly plugged her ears and tugged her eye mask back up before burrowing under the covers.

"Linh…" Steph started, but Linh cut her off, her voice muffled.

"Nope. I'm just a cozy, toasty blanket burrito. I can't even hear you."

"I bet Kenji's with them." Steph turned to Eloise. "Wanna go swimming?"

She didn't, particularly, but she knew Steph would go whether she went along or not, and the thought of that made her anxious.

"Absolutely no skinny dipping. And no embarrassing games involving exposing intimate body parts or divulging personal secrets." Eloise leaned forward, brows rising, wanting Steph to know she was serious.

"You can trust me," said Steph. "Grab your swimsuit."

9

On the beach, everything was in darkness. The sky was a glittering dome above. The stars were sugar crystals spilled over black velvet. Eloise inhaled deeply, smelling salt, the rotten tang of seaweed. It was so dark she couldn't see where she was putting her feet. She could barely even make out Steph in front of her. The scant starlight seemed to have gotten caught in the strands of her friend's hair, giving it a faint shine. Lazy waves lapped the beach not far from where a small campfire was glowing down to the final embers. There were tall, dark shapes gathered around it.

"Looks like all the boys came down," Steph said, slowing her pace. It wouldn't do to answer a summons as sexist as Tate's with any measurable degree of eagerness. "Look, there's Kenji. So, do you want to make your move now, under the stars, or wait until tomorrow? Hooking up in the ruins of an old, haunted resort, that would make a killer story to tell the grandkids."

Eloise reached out and grabbed Steph's warm, soft arm, spinning her around.

"Cut the shit, Steph," she hissed. "Just drop it. This is literally your last warning."

"And you are literally the queen of denial," Steph said evenly. "But fine. Don't say I didn't give you first refusal."

"What's that supposed to mean?" Eloise dug her fingers into Steph's bare flesh, making her wince and hiss air between her teeth. "Sorry."

"Hey!" The yell came from Tate, who'd spotted them first. "What, it's just the two of you?" The disappointment in his voice was palpable. Kenji stood beside him, but the licking firelight barely reached his face. The other two figures, judging by their height and bulk, were probably Miles and Ollie.

I can't make out any landmarks, Eloise realized with a stir of fear. The nearby beach cafe, the boathouse out in front of it, even the markers she'd watched bobbing on the waves that afternoon. Everything seemed to have been swallowed by the darkness. It was like there was nothing left here anymore except this dim, glowing patch of beach and the vast, empty ocean quietly roaring beyond the shore.

When they entered the smooth, silty water, it was still pleasantly warm, even without the heat of the sun.

"Here comes the shark," Tate grinned, kicking off against the sandy bottom, making straight for Steph.

"Punch it on the nose. That's the only way to deal with a shark. Assert dominance!" Kenji said.

"I smell blood in the water!" Tate circled Steph, sniffing. "Which of you ladies is running a code red?"

Steph gasped with furious indignation, and that was when Tate, bobbing up behind her in the water, yanked down one of the triangles of her bikini top.

"Wardrobe malfunction!" he yelled, and Steph shrieked, whirling around, thumping Tate's shoulder hard, a loud, wet *smack*.

"Fucking asshole!" she yelled, then she disappeared, ducking under the waves. She stayed under just long enough to make Eloise's breath quicken with panic before resurfacing with a colossal splash. Then, a furious struggle ensued as Steph made a failed grab for Tate's shorts.

While the others were playing, Eloise bobbed away. She was a fairly strong swimmer, but she was still afraid of Tate or Steph grabbing hold of her and ducking her underwater. In the dark, out here with no lifeguard and no one to call for help—it was better to be on the safe side. Pitching back, she started floating, hands trailing by her sides, gazing up at the stars above.

"Do you see the plankton? It's glowing," Miles said all of a sudden. Eloise hadn't even sensed him growing close. She let her legs drop, falling upright. "What?"

"See? The blue glow."

Eloise looked around, breath catching in her throat. The ocean was awash with an electric blue light, a billion sparkling dots all moving and flowing together. She moved her hand through the water, marveling.

"It's beautiful."

"Bioluminescence," he said. "It's the same thing that makes fireflies glow."

She looked over at the others, who were still horsing around, yelling and splashing.

"Say goodbye to your shorts, shark boy!" Steph screeched, waving something dark and floppy high above her head, smacking Tate with it. "You like it, huh? You fucking *like* it?"

"Those are your friends?" Miles asked, irony in his voice, his eyes challenging her.

"They're all right," she said, immediately on the defensive.

"I'm drowning!" Tate squealed. "Quick, Steph, lend me one of your front-mounted flotation devices!"

"They're just kids," Miles said. "What are they, fresh out of college? First time out in the big wide world without mommy and daddy to hold their hand?"

"Maybe," she said. "At least they're out here. Most people back where I come from, they never even move out of the county."

"You could do better," he said, reaching out, fingers lightly brushing her bare shoulder. She looked down, realizing he'd just replaced the strap of her bikini top after it had fallen. The gesture was overly familiar and presumptive. She took a step back, the sand cold silk beneath her feet, and crossed her arms over herself.

"Hey, you guys. It's no fair if only Steph and I are naked. Everyone's gotta get in on the action." Tate swam up to them, brandishing a bikini top in one triumphant fist, like a trophy.

"It's too dark to see anything, anyway," Steph rationalized. "And it feels amazing like this!"

What the hell, Eloise thought. *Next year, you'll be back home, where everyone hates you, and the only job you're likely to get is stacking shelves at Tesco's. At least make some crazy memories to look back on while you still can.*

She'd never swum naked before. It wasn't actually all that different in terms of sensation. But the thrill of it was undeniable. And it was too dark for her to feel self-conscious. She could barely make anything out beyond the vague globes of Steph's bobbing breasts and the flash of Tate's pale buttocks when he duck-dived.

Kicking and gliding through the neon clouds of plankton, she was actually starting to feel sort of okay when she suddenly realized what the blue glow reminded her of.

Tell-tale blood splatters, illuminated by luminol.

Long-hidden secrets, ones that lurked there all along, exposed only by chemical trickery.

But they never found the knife, Eloise, did they? How different do you suppose things would be if they had?

Eloise reached an unexpected dip in the sea floor, the sandy bottom falling out beneath her feet. Gasping, she swallowed a mouthful of warm, gritty ocean. Kicking against open water, she glided forward, blinking the salt droplets out of her stinging eyes, trying not to lose sight of the shore.

10

"What happened to the others?" Steph asked Kenji, bare feet sinking into the cool sand as they walked towards one another on the beach by the outcrop. Steph had gotten the jump on Tate, streaking up the beach with her bikini top and bottoms clutched safely in each fist. Once she'd gotten a decent distance away, she'd quickly hopped and wriggled back into them.

That was when Kenji had emerged from the ocean, from the gloom, calling out to her. The others were lost somewhere in the darkness.

"Beats me," Kenji said lightly, his California accent reminding Steph of family summers spent on Pismo Beach long before the divorce. Zinc on her nose, riding back to the motel, limbs heavy with a delicious feeling of sun-drenched exhaustion. Mom bitching about the sand in the floor wells of the Mustang.

"You've got seaweed on you," Steph said, brushing the slimy green tangle off his muscled arm.

"What, you don't like seaweed?" he quipped, his teeth shining in the dark. They were very straight, except for one eye tooth, which sat at a slight angle.

"We didn't all grow up on the beach."

"Burbank."

"Big difference. It's, what, a thirty-minute drive to Santa Monica?"

"Well, that depends on the traffic."

"Do you miss it?"

Kenji didn't answer for a few seconds.

"Not really. My mom and sister are both here. But I don't know. Japan seems different since I came back. I missed the high school experience that everyone here shares this collective nostalgia for, you know?"

"Mmm. I heard it can be hard for Japanese people who grew up abroad to re-integrate."

"It makes people treat me differently when they find out. They're always like, oh, so you must speak English like a native. You're so lucky. But it's like there's this—divide. This is a weird analogy, I know, but to me, it's like when a baby bird falls out of its nest, and someone comes along and picks it up, and after that, the mother doesn't want it anymore because now it smells like a human. It feels like that."

"Kenji..." Steph said, mildly perturbed by the sudden turn their light-hearted conversation had taken. She was still drunk and didn't want to get into anything heavy. All she wanted was to have a good time. That way, she wouldn't have to think about tomorrow. About her nebulous plan to hash things out with Tate. Potentially *dangerous* Tate. Was he, though? She still wasn't sure if she really thought it'd been *him* stalking her in the woods. If not him, though, then who? Some random creeper?

She shook her head and tried to focus, one hand inching down to finger the scab on her shin.

"I don't know what that's like, but you know...that thing about not touching baby birds? It isn't true. Mother birds don't reject their babies just 'cause someone touched them. Birds actually have a really shitty sense of smell."

Kenji laughed—a mirthful rumble that seemed to emanate from deep within his chest.

"Thanks, that makes me feel a lot better."

"You could always go back, you know?"

"Maybe someday. I don't know. I'm not sure I fit in anywhere anymore. That's the thing. After spending most of my life being dragged around the globe like carry-on baggage, I feel like I'm always stuck in this...this nowhere space. Everyone else has somewhere they belong. But I don't feel like I fit in anywhere."

Steph reached out and touched his wrist. His skin was hot beneath her fingers. "Hey, come on. You'll be okay. For what it's worth, I do know how you feel. I got dragged around as a kid, too. My mom moved us all the way to *Wyoming* when she met my asshole stepdad."

Kenji was silent for a second. He cleared his throat and stepped back. Then he sat heavily down on the sand, patting the spot next to him.

Smiling wryly, Steph sat down beside him. There was a peaceable silence for a moment as they both gazed out at the black ocean, watching the bluish frills that edged the gentle waves.

"What was that like?" Kenji asked her, still gazing out at the sea. "Having a stepdad, I mean. I've never met my stepmother. If you can call her that."

"Horrible. He was actual human trash. He—"

No, I'm not going there.

"You know what, never mind."

"What?" Kenji bumped her shoulder with his. "You can tell me."

"No," she said, hearing the hardness in her voice. "I don't want to."

He looked at her then. She could sense it, his eyes on her. It wasn't a new sensation.

"That's okay," he said. "Whatever you want."

She sighed. When she'd spotted him out here, she'd thought about Eloise. About how she should probably try to sound him out for her. See if she could do a little matchmaking. Be a good friend. But right now, she just didn't want to. She was tired of always thinking about Eloise.

"Steph?" Kenji asked, and she looked up to find him gazing right at her. The stars glittered in the intense blackness of his eyes, and as Steph inhaled, her breath caught in her throat.

He didn't say anything for a moment. Then he shook his head and turned away.

"Never mind. Good talk. I mean, thanks."

"Anytime," she shot back, huffing a little air through her nose. *He's sweet. Maybe not as much of a meathead as I thought. But whatever.*

She brushed the sand off her shins and started preparing to clamber to her feet. That was when Kenji reached out, placing his hand on her knees, gently pushing her back down.

"Stay a while longer," he said, and she frowned at him, confused.

His warm hand was still on her knee.

"Why?"

"Because..." He swallowed. "Because I like you. I've always liked you. Okay?"

Steph waited to feel surprised. It didn't happen.

I guess I knew that. Maybe El knows, too. Maybe that's why she's been so weird with me lately.

Anger flared inside her, sudden and unwelcome. How was that fair? She'd never done anything to lead Kenji on, so why did she have to suffer Eloise's disapproval?

She's supposed to be my friend. My best *friend.*

She'd only come on this stupid trip to help her. To keep watch over her with Tate. To be a wing-woman for her with Kenji. *What is our friendship even based on, anyway?* Steph had shared her deepest desires and fears with Eloise. She opened up to her like she'd never opened up to anyone. And it had taken her too long to realize that Eloise was holding out on her, that what she'd thought were intense heart-to-heart talks was really just her speaking into a void. Because Eloise never gave anything back.

Steph *didn't* know her. Not really. Because Eloise didn't want her to know her, she had been keeping her at arms' length this whole time. The realization was crushing.

Was she just using me this whole time? Did our friendship ever mean anything to her at all?

Kenji was still gazing at her, his eyes hungry, fixed on her mouth.

Fuck you, El, she thought, focusing on her anger, trying to ignore the corkscrew of pain and hurt twisting inside her.

She reached for Kenji's neck and pulled his face down towards hers.

He responded instantly, grabbing her by the upper arms and knocking her hand away. He pulled her hard against him, taking the lead.

He smelled like sunscreen and the citrus shampoo they'd all used back in the hostel's bathhouse. Their bodies were cool from the ocean, but the heat between them was enough to burn her skin. All of her nerve endings were singing, a dragging, excited feeling in the pit of her belly.

His lips were smooth and tasted slightly of salt as they kissed. Despite his clear enthusiasm, he was hesitant, far too gentle with her.

No. Not like that.

She put her arms around Kenji's broad, smooth shoulders, opening her mouth, feasting on him. His hands kneaded her bare flesh, his weight pressing her down against the sand.

Then, finally, she stopped thinking about Eloise.

She stopped thinking about anything at all.

11

Eloise was lost somewhere in the blackness. Somewhere beneath the vast bowl of the sky above, studded with stars.

Below her, the hard crust of the dried sand scraped her bare feet. She knew which way was left because that was where the ocean was, still pounding against the shore. The hostel was somewhere to the right. She was trying to find the road, but she couldn't *see* the road.

It can't be that far, she told herself. *Just keep walking away from the sea, and you'll find it at some point. Surely?*

Sand crunched behind her.

She sucked in a terrified breath, heart thundering in her chest, adrenaline spurting through her veins, whirling around to face her attacker.

Go for the eyes, the groin, whatever you do, don't freeze up—

"Hey! It's just me. Did I scare you? My bad. Man. You really need to learn to watch your—you need to be more aware of your surroundings."

Miles. He had her by the upper arms. His face bent down towards hers so she could see him in the gloom. He had scars on his face. She'd never noticed them before. They were all down his right cheek, shallow furrow marks, long healed and barely even perceptible if not for the way the shadows filled them. And there was a deeper, wider scar midway down his neck.

"You did. You scared me," Eloise gasped, her heart still hammering as he released her. "I was trying to find the road."

"Well, you almost fell off the overhang there. About ten feet ahead of you."

Eloise turned back. She couldn't see anything.

"Oh, man." There was a smile in Miles's voice now as he looked past her. Descending a few steps into the darkness, he leaned forward, hands resting on his knees. "Wow, they are really going at it."

"Who is?" She walked up behind him and tried to focus her eyes. She could see them now—two figures intertwined on the sand some distance below.

"I don't know, I can't make them out. Steph, probably. Who's the lucky guy, you think?"

Steph? Eloise took another step forward, her throat tight, eyes stinging from the salt. But Miles put his arm out, blocking her from going any further.

"Don't go falling on top of them."

While she was still trying to force her eyes to adjust to the dark, someone yelled indistinctly from somewhere in the distance, somewhere parallel to the ocean. She placed the voice. Tate.

"If you lot can hear us, come towards our voices!" a second voice yelled, this one more intelligible. It had to be Ollie.

Then that had to mean...

Eloise's eyes finally focused in the dark. She could see Steph's face now, blue under the moonlight. Her beautiful features were contorted in pleasure. Her eyes were closed, Kenji pressing her into the sand. The muscles in his back were flexing and tightening.

No. She can't. She can't be doing this. Not to me.

But she was. And from the looks of things, she was enjoying it, too.

Eloise stumbled backward.

"Hey..." Miles said, but she turned her back on the overhang and shoved past him, running blind in the opposite direction.

There was a sharp pain in her chest. A cold knife stuck between her ribs. It hurt so much she could hardly breathe around it. The stars and the lights of the town flashed and grew distorted through the blur of her tears. All she could think about was getting back to the hostel, curling up in the dark, being alone.

But where was the hostel? If she kept the ocean behind her, she'd be able to find the road. Find the road, and she'd be able to make it back.

The balls of her feet sank into the sand, and she kicked up wet clods of it as she struggled, gasping, through the darkness.

I'm not shocked, she realized, her lungs and thighs burning from the effort. It was no big surprise that Kenji was into Steph, most men were. No, this feeling was...anger. Hot, burning, anger. Steph had done this on purpose. It couldn't be more obvious. It was so...so *calculated*. That was the part that Eloise couldn't take. She'd done it just to hurt her.

Why? Why would she do that? What did I ever do to her?

She found the road and followed it. Crunched along the white gravel path that led through the complex of wooden guest houses. Under the moonlight, she recognized the hulking figure of the banyan tree that hung over the reception building. The jagged gravel stones bit cruelly into her insteps and made her gasp with pain, so she ran on the dry, coarse grass instead, its rough blades scratching her feet. Eventually, she made it to their guest lodge and threw herself down on the splintered picnic bench outside.

She needed to calm down before she went in there. She didn't want to wake Linh or Satoko. She needed to get a grip on herself. She was gasping for breath, her chest shuddering.

A bird twittered in the trees above her. Its call was soft and melodic. Maybe a nightingale or a reed warbler. She wasn't sure if either of those birds lived on Okinawa. She was lost, wretched, so impossibly far from home.

A home that doesn't want you, anyway.

God. She *hated* Steph. She should have *known* that she was a snake. And all this time, Eloise had rolled over, quietly taken it whenever Steph treated her low-key like actual *shit*. Whenever she claimed she was "just telling it like it is" or "just being real." She'd been *grateful* to Steph for adopting her, for being her friend. Steph had come to her at a time in her life when she'd just about given up on the thought of anyone wanting to be around her ever again. And so, she'd forgiven Steph every single time she trampled on Eloise's feelings or put her on the spot in public.

For a while now, she'd been planning to make a clean break with Steph after their tenure on the EFA Program ended. After EFA, there'd be no more shared experiences, nothing new to discuss. No need for dramatics, no need for a tearful bust-up. She'd just gradually stop commenting on Steph's socials, start leaving her on read for longer and longer periods of time.

But not now. Now, she was furious. Now, she wanted to make Steph regret betraying her.

Her mind ran free with thoughts of hurting Steph. Of separating her from the others the following day in the resort, bashing her brains in with a chunk of concrete, shoving her off the blind-drop edge of the cliff. Steph's body crashing against the ocean rocks far below.

Eloise was hyperventilating, the world tilting wildly around her.

It's happening again. It's all happening again.

Choking back panic, she forced herself to hold her breath and count to three. She forced the air out, counted to three again, and breathed in. She had to slow her breathing. Then, her heart rate would follow. It had always worked before.

While she was busy trying to breathe, Miles appeared out of the darkness of the night. His expression was mild, not exactly empathetic, but not completely detached either. He took a seat on the bench opposite Eloise but said nothing for a minute or two. He just sat there, arms stretched out in front of him on the table, fingers interlaced.

She wiped the snot and tears off her upper lip with the back of her arm, glad that she didn't particularly like him, that his opinion of her didn't matter. At the same time, though, it was sort of nice of him to have come after her. Maybe he wasn't a *complete* tosser.

Eventually, he broke the silence.

"I think your foot's bleeding."

Eloise looked down. It was hard to see in the dark, but the electric amber glow from a nearby stone lantern picked out something wet and shiny streaked across the top of her foot.

Beyond caring, she hiked the foot up and rested it on the bench top, like some kind of yogi contortionist.

Miles made a small sound of amusement in his throat.

"It's nothing," Eloise said with relief. "I knocked off a toenail. The little one. Used to happen all the time when I did ballet."

"That's a lot of blood, though. I thought maybe you stepped on some glass."

"I didn't even feel it."

"There's plenty of guys out there," Miles informed her.

"It's not about the *guy*," she croaked. "I don't care about the *guy*. I thought I did, but it was more like, like, the idea of the guy. It's *Steph*." She knuckled away an unwelcome tear, sniffing hard, suddenly infuriated, not with Steph but with herself.

"So, she's a bitch. Just cut her off."

"I've been trying," Eloise hiccupped.

"Yeah, it looks like it," Miles said, giving her a wry, lopsided smile. The bird in the trees above their heads twittered once more.

"You know, funny story." He paused to scrub the back of his hand against his chin. "My Nana's one big wish in life was to go to the Vatican City and see the Pope. She was a *staunch* Catholic. And I mean, like, the *staunchest*. They had these tours at her church, you know, they'd take a whole group of them over the pond to Italy, anyone who wanted to go. But Pop-Pop wouldn't let her. He was always in her ear, you know? Telling Nana she wouldn't be able to handle going that far from home without him. I always said to her, Nana, why don't you ignore him and go anyway? But she'd make excuses, like it was really *her* that was the one standing in her own way, and not Pop-Pop. Fear of flying was the big one she used. I told her, Nana, think of the odds. Do you really think you're important enough in the grand scheme of things that it's going to be your plane? She got all mad. She was all, "Peanut..."—she called me Peanut—"Peanut, are you saying I'm not important?"

Miles huffed air through his nose, his voice warm with amusement and affection. "Then, one day, she up and divorced Pop-Pop. Not very Catholic of her, but anyway, she finally made it to Rome and had the trip of her life. She was sick. I guess she knew it. She died the next year."

There was a pause while Eloise digested this.

"I'm...I'm so sorry about your grandmother. Really. But what's that story got to do with my situation?"

"Huh?" Miles looked confused. "What? Nothing. Not everything is about *you*, is it, Eloise?"

She stared at him incredulously, his features hazy and indistinct in the dark.

"You're weird," she said finally, out of a distinct lack of other, more astute things to say.

"So what? Everybody's weird." He grinned at her, showing perfect teeth that glittered. "Listen. Give it a year, you won't give a shit about that guy *or* Steph. I personally guarantee it."

She made a sound in her throat, a noncommittal gurgle.

"I mean it. Time pulls you along. Things lose significance. It's so gradual you don't even notice it. You wake up one day, and you realize you stopped caring months ago. You've got your head full of other things now. New people, new places. New emotions. It's all transitive. At least, that's what I'm banking on. That's really why I'm out here, I guess. Remember..." He scrubbed his chin again.

"Remember how I said I was out here traveling alone? I was being purposefully vague, I guess, but—fuck. I guess I'm just embarrassed. I don't mind telling you, though. If you'd be willing to listen?"

Eloise nodded.

"I was traveling with my girlfriend. I mean, my fiancée. Katie. She's a nurse. Things started to break down between us before we even left the States. I don't even know how it happened. It was like we forgot we were meant to be on the same team. We were supposed to be in love, but it didn't even *feel* like it anymore. I can't even pinpoint when it started to change. I didn't know what she *wanted* from me. Maybe there's someone else back home. Fuck if I know. I woke up one day, and she was gone. That was it. She left a Dear John on my pillow. Our dads are best buddies, our moms golf in a league together. The wedding date was set. I know I have to go back at some point and deal with it somehow. She'll spin it so that it's my fault. I guess I'm just delaying the inevitable."

"That...that really sucks. I'm sorry," Eloise said, hoping he wouldn't think she was pitying him.

Miles sniffed. "Yeah. Well. Fuck her, right? And fuck your friend Steph. We've got to move on, don't we? Do you think you're going to even remember Steph's *name* when you're thirty? When you're in a great relationship with someone who actually sees you, and you're super successful in your chosen field? Meanwhile, Steph's back in bumfuck Nebraska. She's slinging suds at some seedy highway bar, slapping sweaty truckers' hands out of her back pockets."

"*Stop.*" Eloise surprised herself by giggling a little. What he was saying was ridiculous, petty, *bitchy*, even, and she knew he meant it to sound that way. Just to hammer home how stupid and petty and bitchy *she* was being. This whole thing with Steph was juvenile. On some level, she knew that and was embarrassed by it. She was supposed to have left the drunken histrionics and the immature girl-on-girl spats back in her university days, if not before that.

"I'm sorry," she said. "I know it's not really comparable to what you've been through, is it? It's just that things with Steph are always so *intense*. I'm an only child, but she's always been like a sister—a sister I seriously can't stand a lot of the time. But I think I'd kill anyone who tried to hurt her. I hate her, but I sort of love her at the same time. It's completely dysfunctional. I just want..."

"What?" Miles's eyes were soft and understanding in the dark. "What do you want?"

She wondered what it really would be like to kiss him with that mustache. The thought made her squirm inside.

What the hell is wrong with me?

"You don't know what you want. That's the whole issue, isn't it?" He inclined his head to one side, studying her. The subtle tells of her features. She looked down.

I do know what I want. The things other people take for granted. Connection. To be loved. For someone to believe in me. Believe I'm a good person inside.

But those things were gone to her, gone forever.

Miles reached across the table, taking hold of her wrist. His hand was so warm. The gesture was friendly and comforting, but she picked up on a flicker of interest. The coaxing inflection in his voice, the way his eyes were fixed on her.

Ohh. Okay.

She mulled the idea over, rolling it around in her brain, seeing how it might fit.

They sat there in the dark for a while, bugs bumping mindlessly against the glass casing of the stone lantern, the hot night air alive and singing all around them.

"Are you coming with us tomorrow?" she asked finally, looking up into Miles's eyes, which in the darkness had lost their beautiful blue hue and simply looked black.

"If you want me," he said softly, and the bird, whatever it was, stopped singing.

PART THREE

LEISURELAND

"I've no doubt in my own mind that we have been invited here by a madman—probably a dangerous homicidal lunatic."
—Agatha Christie, *And Then There Were None*

AWOL MARINE WANTED FOR QUESTIONING IN CONNECTION WITH SUSPECTED DEATH OF IOWA GIRL IN 2012

Marine Corps says man is dangerous and should not be approached.
Life on Okinawa.com Sunday, July 14th, 2019
By Jim Fraser

A manhunt is underway today for a US Marine stationed out of Air Station Futenma. 25-year-old Adam Preston Davis absconded from the base and was declared officially UA late Saturday evening. He is currently wanted under suspicion of being connected to a 2012 case involving a missing young woman in the continental United States.

IMAGE ERROR 404 NOT FOUND

Presumed deceased: Cadence Marie Walker pictured here in her junior year of high school, in 2011.

Although the Marine was officially off-duty at the time, the alarm was raised when Davis failed to report to a summons at his post late Saturday evening. Davis is officially wanted for questioning in the United States in connection with the disappearance of the girl from his hometown of Cedar Rapids, Iowa, in May 2012. Senior Cadence Marie Walker went missing following her high school prom, which Davis also attended as the date of the victim's close friend.

IMAGE ERROR 404 NOT FOUND

25-year-old Adam Preston Davis and Cadence Marie Walker, aged 18 at the time of her disappearance, are pictured together in this undated photo released by Cedar Rapids police.

From a distinguished military family, Davis joined the Marines in 2013 after obtaining his high school diploma and has been stationed in Okinawa since 2017.

At the time of Miss Walker's disappearance, Davis was cleared of all suspicion, owing in large part to an "iron-clad" alibi provided by his father, a Marine Corps colonel. But new suspicion fell on the young marine following a recent development in the case. Last week, a partial female skeleton was discovered by a dog walker in a lakeside woodland area. The location is close to a cabin that Davis's family owned at the time of Miss Walker's disappearance. An arrest warrant was subsequently posted by the Cedar Rapids police on Saturday at noon Japan time.

IMAGE ERROR 404 NOT FOUND

PFC Adam Preston Davis, pictured here in uniform in 2017.

"We are conducting searches, but while it's a small island, there's no shortage of places to hide," a representative for the Marine Corps said on Saturday. *"There's a strong possibility that he has already taken his own life, but if he is still alive, then he could be holed up in any one of the many caves across the island, or he could have hitched a ride on a fishing boat and be halfway to mainland China by now."*

If Davis is indeed still present on the island, locals are warned that he should not be approached under any circumstances. *"We consider him to be dangerous,"* the representative told this reporter. *"He is certainly trained. He has United States Marine Corps training, so we don't want to pressure him to the point where he may become a threat to the local populace. Our hope is that he will come to his senses and turn himself in quietly so that this matter can be handled without anyone getting hurt."*

When asked whether it was possible that Davis could be armed with a firearm, the representative declined to comment.

If you have any information or think you may have seen Davis or any individual who might resemble his description, please contact local police or your commanding officer immediately.

12

*O*kinawa, Okinawa Prefecture

*The morning of Sunday July 14, 2019
(The Day Before Marine Day)*

Eloise found Tate out by the road, taking pretentious lungfuls of the morning ocean air. His navy polo shirt was fresh on, his khaki hiking pants were unwrinkled, and his boyish face was neatly shaved. He had his butt parked against the low stone wall in front of the hostel and was waiting for the others to assemble. Outwardly, he seemed calm, but there was a nerve jumping in his cheek right next to the fleck of shaving cream he'd missed. He was clearly anxious to get going, but that wasn't going to be happening anytime soon.

Eloise felt like shit. Her ripped-off toenail stung like a bitch, and she'd probably had no more than two or three hours of sleep total. The night had passed in fits and starts, and she'd been phasing in and out of dreams of Steph. In her dreams, Steph was dead, her body buried in a shallow grave in the bamboo forest. The knife was hidden in the toilet tank of Eloise's tiny Yamaoku apartment. Dream-Eloise knew she needed to move the murder weapon and dispose of it someplace, but there was a party going on at her apartment. Tate was making highballs in her cramped kitchenette. Linh, Satoko, and Kenji, in their underwear, were playing strip Uno. A thump at the door made her heart constrict with fear. Not the police, but Miles, a big smile on his face, holding a huge jar of snake wine as a party offering. But it wasn't a snake inside the jar.

It was Steph's head.

Giving up on sleep well before dawn, Eloise had gone to the outdoor bath and submerged herself under the painfully hot water, trying to block out her thoughts. It helped—a little. Taking a moment to be alone in the stillness, to watch the daylight seep in and slowly stain the world around her with color, she'd begun feeling a little steadier.

When she left their room, Linh was in a panic over some misplaced instant film, and Steph was still fiddling around with her straighteners, filling the room with the acrid stench of burning hair. Satoko was in the bathroom. She had been in there for a while, and Eloise felt bad for her. Hungover puking and an old-style Asian squat toilet must be a really hellish combination. They called them Squatty Potties, and even the most regularly cleaned ones seemed to stink of fetid urine.

"It amuses me that you thought ten minutes was enough muster time for four women," Eloise said, wondering if she could banter Tate out of his state of barely contained tension.

"Well, you made it."

"I was up hours ago."

"Yeah, well, so was I. I went down to the beach to watch it get light out. It was actually really incredible. It was full daylight before I even knew the sun had come up, and the sea was full of really old people swimming. I didn't even see them in the dark. They probably do that every morning. Maybe that's their secret. You know, why Okinawans live longer than anyone else."

They weren't alone, out by the road. Ollie was looking more disheveled than ever, bending over and messing around inside his backpack. He wore a hangdog expression on his flushed face. Eloise had no doubt he and Mishka had exchanged a few more choice words last night over his decision to ditch his new fiancée and go off with a bunch of strangers they'd only just met.

Miles was nowhere to be seen. Last night, he'd agreed to come, but Eloise wasn't sure he'd make good on that promise. He and Tate seemed to clash, and it was clear he didn't think much of the rest of them. Okay, he seemed like he might be interested in her. But she couldn't imagine what, if any, appeal she might hold for a guy like Miles. Still, the resort itself was a compelling location. She thought about the photos she'd seen of the place online and the articles Tate had posted to their group chat. The sad stories about the guests that had died there. The woman who'd thrown herself off the high platform. Eloise imagined herself as the woman, looking down across the island, her last earthly sight the two glittering oceans on either side. A thrill of fear went through her, making her shiver despite the fact that the morning was already oppressively hot.

Kenji emerged from between the low wooden buildings. Eloise forced herself to look at him, wanting to know if last night's encounter with Steph was visible on his face somehow. He looked the same as ever but didn't smile at her as he joined them. He seemed hungover, in fact, his face puffy, holding a bottle of some kind of chalky, salty-but-sweet electrolyte drink against his chest with one curled wrist.

She wondered what would happen between him and Steph going forward. *Probably a whole lot of nothing.* Steph wasn't exactly the relationship kind of girl, and besides, she was leaving Japan for good in a few short months. *Why even bother in the first place?*

Eloise didn't do casual sex. It wasn't a morals thing. It was just that she couldn't get attracted to anyone without some sort of emotional connection. She'd assumed it was the same for everyone. Fundamentally. So what did Steph get out of it?

"You're such a *dead doe*," Eloise had spat after a night out in Tokyo. On Steph's insistence, they'd taken the bullet train to the tangled concrete jungle of Japan's capital. All so they could go to some club Steph had heard about online. Eloise hated clubbing.

Even in university, the only part of nights out she'd actually really enjoyed was when they all went back to someone's flat afterward and got cozy. They'd make a ritual of it. Taking off their makeup, changing into pajamas, and ordering pizzas. They always watched some cheesy nineties film on VHS, a predictable slasher, something so groan-worthy that it begged for audience participation.

So she was already in a bad mood, tired and uncomfortable in her tight dress and the heels that pinched her toes when Steph ditched her in Tokyo at two a.m. Abandoned, just so that Steph could go to a tawdry pay-by-the-hour love hotel with a guy she'd felt 'electricity' with on the heaving dance floor. Eloise had waited out the rest of the night in a twenty-four-hour McDonald's. By the time Steph finished her hungover walk of shame the next morning, shuffling along the bullet train platform towards Eloise, the bad mood had crystallized into a hard chunk of fury in her chest that seemed to have replaced her heart.

"A dead doe? What's that supposed to mean?" Steph had groaned. A baseball cap was pulled low over her smudged mascara eyes as they stepped inside the train, which, with the smooth curves of its futuristic interior, resembled an airplane cabin. Wincing, Steph yanked down the window shade, falling heavily into her seat, blocking out the insipid morning sunlight.

"It means that men are the hunters, and we're the prey. Like it or not, that's just the law of nature. It's like how guys get all fired up to go and hunt down deer with their buddies, and then they haul the carcasses back and nail the heads to the walls of their living room as trophies. But if they were just out driving in the truck and they hit a deer that leaped out in front of them, do you think they'd whoop and holler and get on the blower to the local taxidermist? No. They'd be sickened and probably feel sorry for it. They'd dump it on the grass verge and drive on. That's *you*. You're a dead doe. You're roadkill."

"You need feminism," Steph had gasped. "That is literally the most misogynistic piece of crap I've ever heard come out of another woman's mouth." But later, as the G-force of the bullet train pressed them back into their seats, Eloise thought that Steph might have been crying quietly under the angled brim of her cap. Eloise had never said anything like that to Steph again. The memory of it now made her stomach lurch with guilt and wretched self-hatred, and her anger towards her friend faded, but only a little.

Steph came stumbling out onto the roadside barefoot, hiking boots hanging around her neck by their laces. She looked pale, washed-out, and younger somehow. Without the usual sweep of black eyeliner on her upper lids, her face had a bare, unfinished look about it.

"I need coffee," she croaked. Her eyes were bloodshot, reptilian.

Eloise watched as Steph plopped down on the dusty roadside. She shoved her bare feet into thick hiking socks and laced her boots over them.

"Satoko's still puking," she said. "Linh's going to be a while, too. She lost her nose ring in the bath."

"Fine," Tate said, smiling tightly in a way that indicated it was not, in fact, fine.

There was a crunch of dry sand behind them, and they all turned to see Miles step out onto the road from the beach side, his brown leather boots scuffing against the asphalt. He scanned the road in both directions for traffic before acknowledging them.

"Mornin'."

He strolled over, already lightly sweating in the early heat. Eloise could see it glistening on his tanned cheekbones.

"Are those the clothes you were wearing yesterday?" Steph's nose wrinkled in distaste.

"Yeah. What? I've been backpacking through Asia. You think I'm carrying multiple wardrobe changes with me?"

He was wearing the same gray T-shirt from the night before, but now it was mottled with white, frostlike patterns—dendrite crystals of salt distilled from his own sweat.

Satoko was the next to join them, looking put-together in full hiking gear. She wore a long-sleeved top and a pair of baggy shorts made of some sort of khaki-colored, nylon-looking material, with black, shiny leggings underneath the shorts. Her hair was tied back in a ponytail that poked through the gap in the back of her outdoorsy-brand baseball cap. She wasn't wearing heavy hiking boots like Steph and Eloise. Instead, she wore a kind of light neoprene shoe with thick rubber treads. Everything she was wearing looked brand-new. Eloise's raw toenail stung inside her old leather boots. She looked down, noticing the cracks across the toes. She'd forgotten to oil them.

Despite the snazzy hiking gear, Satoko didn't look so hot. Her lower lids were puffy, and there were broken capillaries ringing her eyes like crimson crow's feet.

"Ugh, I drank way too much," Satoko said, her voice gravelly and faint as if it was an effort just to speak.

"Any update on Linh's ETA?" Eloise asked her.

"Her what? I didn't see her." Satoko readjusted the straps of her hiking backpack.

"She's got one more minute, and then I'm going in to get her." Tate's air of breezy, unbothered nonchalance was growing noticeably threadbare and starting to unravel around the edges.

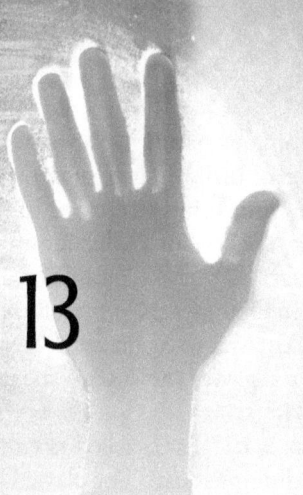

13

Linh stepped out of the bathhouse's dressing room, dragging the sliding door back along its track behind her. Out of time, she'd had to give up her nose ring for a loss, which annoyed her. The piercing would probably close up by the time they got back.

Great. Just great.

Stepping out from under the covered walkway and crunching across gravel, she heaved her backpack onto one shoulder with a ragged sigh. But feeling her skin prickle and tighten, Linh came to a sudden stop, white stones spurting beneath her boots.

Someone was watching her.

A faint whispering sound—cloth brushing against cloth.

Linh whirled around to see the old woman right behind her. But that was impossible. The gravel—why didn't she hear her approach? The old woman was bent so far over that Linh couldn't even see her face, just the back of her head. Her yellowish-white hair was very sparse, the pink scalp visible underneath, like the exposed belly of a half-plucked chicken. The old woman's gnarled hand came rising from her side, her kimono sleeve flapping. Her arm was almost mahogany brown. Her wrist was knobbed all over with varicose veins. It reminded Linh of petrified wood. There were black markings all over the back of the woman's hand, and at first, Linh thought they might be liver spots or bruises, signs of poor circulation, old age, but that wasn't it. Some kind of tattoo? Linh had heard that the indigenous Ainu people of Hokkaido in the far north tattooed their lips and arms. But she hadn't heard anything about a similar practice in Okinawa. Not that she really knew much of anything about Okinawa, to begin with.

Were the gloves she'd worn the previous night meant to *hide* the markings?

"What is it?" Linh asked politely in Japanese, but the old woman did not speak. The clawed hand groped for Linh's, but a sudden reflex made her snatch it away in disgust.

"Charm," the old woman whispered finally in English. "Keep you safe."

Linh realized the old woman meant to give her something. Fighting back the hot, bilious lump of fear that was rising in the back of her throat, Linh reluctantly held her hand out to accept it. The old woman dropped something cold and heavy, something made of hard material like stone or metal, onto Linh's trembling palm. The old woman's cronelike fingers curled above it like a dead spider.

"Here," the old woman rasped. "She sleeps...The maiden. *The red smoke...*"

"What?" Linh's voice was very loud all of a sudden in the fresh, clean air of the morning. The old woman's head jerked, and she looked around as if afraid that someone might be watching. Then, she folded her hands one over the other in front of her. It looked like she was trying to approximate a bow, but she was so bent that she could neither go down any lower nor straighten up. Linh's heart fluttered against her ribcage like a caged, panicking bird as the old woman turned and shuffled jerkily away. Kimono flapping, gravel spurting out from underneath her lacquered thong sandals. Then she disappeared into a narrow, shadowy space between two of the old wooden buildings.

"Linh!" Tate's voice was abrupt and disapproving behind her, and Linh whirled around, letting out a small shriek of surprise.

"What?" he frowned, jaw clenched.

"The old lady...that old woman from last night," Linh managed at last. "She just gave me this."

She uncurled her fingers, taking her first close look at the object. Tate craned his neck to see as well.

"What is it?"

Linh chewed her lower lip. "I don't know. It looks kinda like—like half of a yin-yang symbol. It's sort of familiar, but I'm not sure why."

"It looks like a tadpole to me. Or a fetus," Tate said. "With a hole in it. What's it made of?"

"I don't know. It looks ancient. Some kind of metal?" Linh poked it with a forefinger. Little flakes of dirt, or maybe rust, had rubbed off and adhered themselves to the skin grooves in her sweating palm. "She said it was a protective charm."

"Well, whatever. Maybe Kenji or Satoko knows what it is. You're ready, aren't you? Because we're burning daylight here, and I want us back down off the cliff well before nightfall."

"I'm ready. I was just coming out to join everyone," Linh said, closing her fist around the little object. She didn't really want to keep it, but the old woman seemed so insistent. What did she need a protective charm for? A shiver ran through her, her stomach tightening.

Following Tate, Linh removed one of the stretchy black hair ties she wore around her wrist and looped it through the hole in the object and back through itself, forming a tight knot. With the little stone secure, she slid the hair tie back onto her wrist.

"Yeah, that's a magatama," Kenji said without too much interest. He took the small stone from Linh and held it up to get a better look at it. "They're a kind of bead used in ancient jewelry, dating back from prehistoric Japan. They used to be made of stone, clay, stuff like that. By the end of the Kofun period, they started making them out of jade. These days, you can find them in gift shops all over the place."

"So, it's just like costume jewelry," Linh said. That was a relief. She was worried the old woman had handed her some kind of expensive family heirloom. She'd have felt terrible about accepting it if that had been the case.

"That one looks old, though," Kenji said. "Originally, magatama seem to have been used as religious objects—for ceremonial purposes. Whenever historians dig up old tombs and burial sites, they almost always find a necklace strung with magatama beads buried with the corpse. Some kind of funeral rite, maybe."

"So, they're found on Okinawa, too?" Steph asked, blinking against the hot sun, clutching a can of coffee like it was some magical hangover elixir. Right. Okinawa had its own ancient history, quite distinct from that of mainland Japan. Geographically speaking, it was actually much closer to Taiwan than Tokyo. Linh remembered reading that somewhere.

"Yeah," Kenji said. "The Noro priestesses of the Ryukyu islands were wearing magatama necklaces as early as the twelfth century."

"Noro?" Linh took the magatama back from Kenji and slipped her wrist through the hair tie again. "Do you know a lot about Okinawan history and religion, Kenji?"

"Not too much. I majored in Japanese history in college."

Steph wrinkled her nose. "What is it, exactly, though? It looks like a yin-yang symbol. Is it?"

"What's that?" Kenji looked confused.

"You know, like dark and light, good and evil."

"I don't..." Kenji trailed off as Linh started scratching one into the sparse gravelly dirt of the roadside with the toe of her boot.

"Oh, like the *inyo* symbol," Kenji said. "They're not related as far as I know. The magatama's shape could represent any number of things. Animal fangs, an unborn fetus, the moon, even the soul. No one knows for sure."

"That crazy old bat from last night gave you this?" Steph frowned at Linh. "Did she say why?"

"She said something about it being a protective charm. She said it'd keep me safe."

"That old lady wasn't all there, Linh-Linh," Eloise spoke for the first time, touching Linh's arm softly.

Linh shook her head. "One more thing, Kenji. The old woman had these...I want to say tattoos? On the backs of her hands. She was wearing white gloves last night, so I didn't notice them before, and they seemed pretty faded. But I thought only the Ainu people, up in Hokkaido, had a tradition of tattooing?"

"*Hajichi*." Kenji nodded. "Indigo tattoos. They were indicators of social status meant to mark the transition of Ryukyuan women from girlhood to womanhood. They're symbols of female spiritual power, but they were banned when Japan annexed these islands. After that, the practice dwindled. You almost never see them these days. They became stigmatized, a source of shame."

"Fascinating as all this is, if we don't get going now, we might as well not bother going at all." Tate was almost vibrating with impatience.

Steph scowled and opened her mouth to speak, and a dark shadow fell on their faces. They looked up in unison to see the belly of a helicopter flying very low in the sky above them. The chop of the rotor blades and the thrum of the engine filled the air, and as it passed over the beach and out over the ocean, it whipped up a whirlwind of sand and ocean spray.

"Jesus!" Tate yelled. All of them had been temporarily deafened by the sudden noise. "I thought that was going to land right on top of us!"

"That'll be the US military, then," Ollie said dryly.

"US *Marines*." Tate whooped. "You gotta admit, that was pretty fucking impressive."

"Hey, look who I found."

Miles was back. When he'd wandered off a few minutes before, Linh hadn't cared. Things were already tense enough with Steph and Eloise at each other's throats over Kenji. The last thing they all needed was a stranger like Miles stirring the pot. And his eyes unnerved her. The weird, empty blueness of them. The way he kept them fixed on Eloise. Steph didn't seem to have picked up on that yet. But when she did, Linh had a feeling she'd implode. And Linh would be the one dealing with the fallout, as usual.

Although, maybe that would be for the best. Something needed to happen to get Steph to wake up. Linh was beyond frustrated with the whole Eloise thing.

"Did you see the bird just then?" Tate asked, a challenge in his voice as he narrowed his eyes at Miles. "What do we reckon? Osprey? Venom?"

"Hell if I know." Miles barely even glanced at Tate, facing the girls instead. It took a second for Linh to realize why.

"Is that a *kitty*?!" She sucked in a gasp of delight, reaching out to stroke the soft, fuzzy black head that poked out of Miles's chest pocket.

"Must have been born only a few days ago. Look, its eyes are still barely open. I didn't see any sign of the mom. There was a crow lurking, so I couldn't just leave the little guy."

The girls were all gathered around Miles now, crooning in soft voices, shoulders jostling for space as they reached to pet the little kitten. Tate closed his eyes briefly. He looked like he was in pain.

Oh, suck it up.

"Just put it back where you found it, and let's get a move on," Tate whined, his very existence irritating Linh. If it weren't for Steph and Eloise, she wouldn't give a guy like Tate the time of day.

The girls all turned as one to look at him, and Linh noted that the other two looked as scandalized as she felt that Tate would even suggest such a thing.

"Callous *man*," Steph sniffed.

"A *crow* was hunting it!" Eloise massaged the tiny pink paws.

"The poor *baby*!" Linh crooned, pleased.

"It's probably riddled with worms and fleas," Tate scowled. "Come on, just put it back."

"I'll take it into the office and see if Nack will take care of it," Kenji offered, holding his hand out. Reluctantly, Miles removed the kitten from his pocket and handed it over. Linh's heart wrenched as the tiny creature squeaked, its fluffy legs splayed like a frog. Its impossibly tiny, pearlescent claws poked out of the ends of its fuzzy little toes. So cute. So utterly helpless.

14

The sun was high in the sky above when they finally reached the foothills at the base of the cliff. The hills were thickly wooded, and the only available road didn't seem to get too much traffic these days—it was overgrown and completely blocked to vehicular access in numerous places. The largest blockage came in the form of an enormous, blackened tree that seemed to have been struck by lightning years ago. The foliage met overhead in a thick canopy that cut off most of the sunlight, allowing only a few scattered beams to filter through. It was surprisingly loud under the muffled canopy, the woods alive with the sound of chirping insects and the rustle of burrowing creatures.

They'd lost a good chunk of the day already, with all the distractions delaying Tate's proposed sunrise departure. Then, his complete misreading of the bus schedule had them waiting for almost an hour under the blazing sun for the next bus. He was still sulking about that, but the others were in high spirits, laughing and joking together as they followed the shady road up the steep incline.

Eloise hung back in the rear of the group, trying to practice mindfulness, to be present in the moment with the trees and the nature around her. She was glad Steph was walking up at the front of the group with Tate and Kenji. Maybe they could just stay out of each other's way for the rest of the trip. Linh, Ollie, and Satoko followed at a short distance, chatting about the differences between British and American English and where Canada fell on the scale between them.

Which left her paired up with Miles.

She'd been sneaking glances at him as they strap-hung on the crowded bus to the nature preserve. Well, she strap-hanged. He was well over six feet and didn't need to. He wasn't really what you could rationally call handsome. It was clear that his nose had been broken more than once, for example. His hair was brown but cut so short it seemed colorless. It was probably easier to deal with that way, backpacking to a different country every other week. Eloise felt a pang of regret that she hadn't been more adventurous herself, hadn't used her paid time off to visit other places in Asia, hadn't left her comfortable, well-situated base in Japan.

Moving halfway across the world to live and work in a place where almost everything is different from how it is back home—that's not adventurous enough for you anymore? Not enough of a distraction?

The scornful voice in her head belonged to the Eloise she'd been over two years ago. A young woman paralyzed by fear of her own formless, colorless future, of the world in general, of the prospect of being stuck for good in the prison of her hometown, or even worse, the narrow confines of her own mind.

Miles didn't speak to her as they walked. He was sweating—they all were—but it looked a lot better on him than it felt on Eloise. She was sticky and grubby, but the moisture sparkling on Miles's tanned cheek gave him a look of freshness, of robust health.

He must work out a lot, Eloise thought. *Either that or he's one of those annoying guys who naturally has that kind of body despite stuffing down hotdogs and cheeseburgers.* The thought made her stomach growl. They left too early for breakfast, and the seaweed-stuffed rice ball she'd snagged at the convenience store near the bus stop had barely even touched the sides.

He caught her looking just then, his smile revealing white, even teeth. American teeth. Even his moustache was glittering with sweat. *I could never*, she thought, a horrified thrill running through her body like an electric shock as she tried not to imagine kissing him. Her dad had worn a moustache at some point. That was before he left, obviously. She didn't remember it. She didn't remember much of him as a person, but it was there in the old photos. The ones where she was a chubby toddler with errant pigtails, her face smeared with chocolate, one strap of her dungarees always unfastened and hanging loose. Miles's mustache horrified her on some deep, Freudian level. But the mouth below it was pretty, the lips smooth and pillowy, so incongruous with the roughness of the rest of his face.

"Hot enough for ya?" Miles grinned.

She smiled at the cliché. "It's not the heat. It's the humidity," she said, wiping the sweat off her own naked upper lip. "What made you decide to travel here? Have you been to mainland Japan yet? Or did you come from there?"

But Miles didn't answer her. He'd stopped dead.

Eloise turned back to look at him, clutching the straps of her backpack and rocking back on the heels of her hiking boots. He was standing absolutely still, those striking blue eyes fixed unblinkingly on a section of the dense forest that hemmed the road.

"Miles?"

He moved ever so slightly then, reaching up to rub his jaw with his knuckles, frowning like he was deep in thought.

"Don't move," he growled to Eloise.

"Why?"

She took a few steps towards him, and he suddenly grabbed her, his firm, sweat-slick arm clamping down over her collarbones, the other arm snaking around her to press and hold her forearms down. She didn't cry out. She knew that he was just messing around, trying to scare her. Should she play along or call his bluff? She wasn't sure which one he'd prefer. She wanted to play the cool girl, but there was a thin line between cool girl and doormat, and Eloise was never sure where that line was.

She stayed quiet, thinking.

What was he staring at? Something in the trees? Eloise scanned the tangle of dense, green foliage, but she couldn't see anything. The silence persisted. Miles's heart was pounding hard against her back.

"Miles?" she whispered finally, abandoning all pretense towards coolness. "What is it? You're scaring me."

"It's nothing. I thought I saw someone. In the trees."

So, he *was* trying to scare her.

"What? What *kind* of someone?"

"Nothing. You know what? Never mind."

"Hey!" Tate yelled back at them from up the hill. "Stragglers will be cut loose, you know!"

"Come on," Miles said, finally releasing her from his hot, hard grip, not looking at her as he brushed past. She caught a glimpse of his face, though. Those blue eyes. They were colored with something like fear.

Miles moved ahead, climbing the road ahead of them with measured, economical strides. Eloise hung back a moment longer, staring into the trees.

She breathed in a lungful of hot, cloying forest air.

Nothing. There was no one there.

15

After around an hour's hike, a chunk of whitewashed concrete came into view, poking out of the tree canopy ahead at an angle perpendicular to the road.

The white building had a red-tiled roof, a little curved flourish on each corner in a style that seemed to draw inspiration from one of Okinawa's most famous landmarks, the Chinese-influenced Shuri Castle. Tate got all excited, thinking they'd reached the resort's main guest building, but when they drew closer, it turned out to be a stand-alone structure too small to be part of anything but itself. A gatehouse of sorts, perhaps, but the gate itself was long gone.

"At least it's a sure sign we're nearly there," Tate gasped, as much from the exertion of the climb as from excitement. The group had now bunched up together, and they were all united in their exhaustion, desperate to finally take a real rest.

"Eloise." Steph was at her elbow, voice low. "Is everything cool? It's just you've barely looked at me all morning."

"Super cool," Eloise responded breezily, aping Steph's American accent, something her friend was always slow to pick up on. It was cruel of her, though, she supposed. Why did Steph always end up making Eloise feel so *guilty*? Anger swelled within her, beating back the guilt. She wanted to hold on to that anger. To let it strengthen her.

"I noticed you've been buddying up with Miles a bit." Steph seemed to be choosing her words carefully. "I'm not sure we like him, Els."

"Really? We don't? Wow, thanks for letting me know. But for your information, I actually don't fancy Miles. Although, he is interesting."

"*Fancy*," Steph said, rolling the word around on her tongue, relishing it. Her eyes crinkled as if Eloise had just said something fantastically funny. "You haven't let one of your Britishisms slip out in quite a while, you know. I've missed them."

"Mmm," Eloise said, looking past Steph, through her. It was small things like that, little jabs and digs. *Britishisms*.

"All right, gang, let's press ahead." Tate turned, walking backward, thumbs looped through the straps of his backpack. "Watch out for *habu,* okay? Apparently, they like to hide out in cool, dark places like inside rock walls and old buildings."

"I thought snakes liked the heat. My cousins used to keep garter snakes as pets, and they needed this special heat lamp." Linh smiled wryly. "Auntie Anh was freaking terrified of those snakes. I still think the only reason the boys got them was to scare her off snooping through their room. It didn't stop me from raiding their computer for their collection of fansubbed anime episodes, though. Nothing was getting between me and my Sailor Moon fix."

"Wow, I had no idea you were an actual *anime nerd*." Tate's voice was filled with mild disgust, even as he grinned. "I'm going to have some fun with that info."

"Excuse me. The term is otaku. That means *aficionado*. I appreciate the art form."

"Right, some of us came to Japan for the culture." Steph wrinkled her nose at Tate. "We didn't all come here just to mack on Japanese chicks."

"Shut up," Tate smiled, his lips drawn tight across his teeth, glancing over his shoulder at Satoko up ahead.

After walking for a few more minutes, they had to stop for Linh to shake pebbles out of her boots. Then they had to wait for her to relace them.

"This hike is taking forever. Talk about an inconvenient location," Linh groused as Eloise helped her tug her laces tight.

"Well, I read that they wanted to put in a funicular, but they couldn't get the planning permission. I'm guessing they had a courtesy bus, at least." Tate flipped the cap off his canteen and took a greedy swallow.

Eloise didn't have a canteen or a fancy hiking flask like Satoko, just a flimsy plastic bottle of mineral water, its original contents already long drunk. She swallowed, her tongue darting out to swipe her dry lips.

It was like Steph read her mind. "Hey, can someone give me some water? I'm thirsty." She looked entreatingly at Tate.

"Where's your canteen, Steph?"

"Didn't bring one."

Tate's grin faded, then returned, wider than before. "Well, that was smart, Steph. I thought I told you. Come prepared. It's like you deliberately put in the effort *not* to listen to me. And why are you wearing shorts? My instructions were clear. Long sleeves, long pants, hiking boots, and enough water for *each person*. What part of that was too difficult for you?"

"It's just a little hike up a cliff. You're really getting off on all this, aren't you, Tate?"

"We passed a spring a few minutes back. Remember? It should be clean enough. Go ahead, we'll wait."

Steph stared at Tate, her thumbs looped through the straps of her backpack. Her face was shiny with sweat. Her curls stuck to her forehead in limp whorls.

"You know, I was reading up on Urbex stuff online, and one of the rules you're supposed to follow is that the whole group sticks together. No one goes off alone."

Tate blinked, clearly affronted that Steph would use his pet interest against him. Despite herself, Eloise couldn't deny that this little stand-off was entertaining.

Then Tate sighed. "Fine. But this is the last detour. Anyone else need water?"

Eloise and Linh held up their empty plastic bottles. Tate sighed again.

Fifteen minutes later, once they'd all refilled their bottles and canteens at the spring—as Tate said, it seemed clean enough, and it tasted amazing, cold and almost sweet—the group was back on track, drawing close to the gatehouse once more. But as the red-tiled roof came into view again, their attention was arrested by something else.

At first, Eloise couldn't make out what she was looking at. A dark red puddle stretched across the road, right on the very spot where they'd stood minutes earlier, arguing about water. And strewn throughout the puddle were chunks of what looked like meat.

Furry meat.

Linh released a muffled squeal of disgust into the heel of her hand, whirling away from the *thing* on the road. Undaunted, Miles headed over to it and crouched down, sifting through the lumps with a stick.

"It's a deer," he said. "Look, here's the head." He rolled one of the larger lumps over, revealing a glassy black eye and a small open mouth full of blunt yellow teeth.

A deer. No antlers were visible in the mess.

A dead doe.

"Looks like it was pregnant, but I think..." Miles poked the largest lump of flesh. "I think something ripped the fawn out."

Eloise wondered if she was going to throw up. The sweat was cooling rapidly on her arms as if the sight of the mangled creature had chilled her right through to the bone. Though she wanted to, she couldn't tear her gaze away from the puddle of deer parts.

"Jesus." Tate leaned over the mess, his lips parted in disgust.

"It wasn't here ten minutes ago." Steph's voice was high, shaky. "How did...*that*...get there?"

Nobody had an answer to that question.

"I don't *like* this. I want to leave. Okay? Whatever that is, it's not good. This is the part where the smart people leave. Don't you think?" Steph looked around at the others, seeking their agreement. "I mean, this is like every horror movie cliché rolled into one."

"It's just a fucking deer, Steph." Tate straightened up, turning his look of disgust on her now. "We're not *leaving*. We've come all this way. The resort's just ahead."

"It's not just a fucking *deer*. It's fucking deer *tartare*. What kind of animal does that to a deer? What even preys on deer? On Okinawa? Huh, Tate?"

Eloise watched the two of them argue back and forth, taking dim note of how Miles was walking away from the group, disappearing from sight as the sloping dirt path snaked around the next corner.

Suddenly, Steph stopped arguing back, her beautiful eyes growing wide and wild.

"Oh, my God." Her voice climbed to a reedy, paranoid register. "Oh, you've set this *up* somehow. *Fuck*. You're trying to scare us. You've got a buddy—an accomplice—someone you sent ahead. This deer's just the start of it. You've probably rigged the whole resort with creepy shit like this!" Taking a step back, she threw her hands up, laughing with furious disbelief.

Tate smiled with delight. "Steph, *dear*. Have you got heat stroke? Or are you just batshit insane?"

"Yeah, come on, Steph. I think that's a stretch." Linh started walking again, giving the puddle of deer parts a wide berth.

"What...you're still *going*?" Steph's mouth fell open as Linh shrugged. "*Eloise*?"

Eloise opened her mouth to speak, but someone else spoke first.

"Guys." It was Miles, reappearing where the trail curved. "I just saw it. The resort. It's right ahead of us."

If she wanted to make a point, to show Steph she wasn't just going to follow her lead anymore, like some domesticated, brainless sheep—

It's just a deer. Just a dead animal. Not some omen. Not some presage of death. It's just...roadkill.

Eloise moved past Steph, averting her eyes from the puddle, heading after Miles.

She heard Steph huff angrily and could almost feel the hot puff of air on her cheek.

When she reached the bend in the road, she glanced back. Steph was still hesitating, scraping her hiking boots against the road, shuffling agitatedly on the spot. The trail disappeared back into the trees. It would take a long time to hike back down. A couple of hours, at least. Alone. Under the dark, rustling canopy of leaves.

Steph was looking back down the hill, too, chewing on her thumbnail.

"Shit," Eloise heard her whisper.

They pressed on. The bugs were still singing in the overgrown vegetation that fringed the road, a cacophonous, hissing din that reminded Eloise of air slowly leaking out of a cracked-open bottle of soda. The air itself seemed to fizz with the racket they were making, a blanket of sound so thick and so overwhelming that it even drowned out the crashing of the ocean waves a long, long way below.

16

When they rounded the final bend, the resort's main hotel building was suddenly *right there*, nestled in a saddle dip just below the crest of the cliff. A long, meandering concrete structure led to several stacked stories at the far end, which rose above the trees like a bloated wedding cake.

The hotel's façade, right in front of them, was smooth and white and bland and didn't appear to have any right angles anywhere. Everything was curved, even the windows, which resembled nothing so much as oversized ship portholes. The building was peppered with them—empty black holes. It was like the resort itself was a grotesquely overgrown spider possessed of hundreds of blind, staring eyes.

The low roofs were so flat you could walk on them, and the whole thing looked somewhat bare and unfinished. The hotel had an odd look about it, almost retro-futuristic. The architecture style was something Eloise had seen before, dotted about here and there in Japan, leftover relics of the 1970s and '80s. It was called Streamline Moderne, according to Tate. However, there was nothing modern about those rounded walls, the almost nautical design, and the thick, bubbly, opaque panels of dingy glass that were designed to let in natural light.

The group stopped at a sparse gravel area in front of the building. It had probably once been a parking area. The front of the hotel was blackened as though it had been burned out at some point. Smudged shadows depicting the hotel's name were still legible above the gaping hole that would once have been the hotel's grand entryway. The letter plaques had long since fallen off the dingy plastic movie theater sign-style paneling and gotten lost or been taken as souvenirs, but years of sun exposure had bleached out everything around them, leaving darker imprints, the ghost of the old hotel's signage.

THE ROYAL OCEANVIEW LEISURELAND RESORT

"That's a mouthful. And why did they call it 'The Royal'," mused Linh out loud as they all gazed up at the decrepit building.

"Just to sound fancy," Tate explained with a knowing tone. "No real reason. The developer who built this place was a rich nutjob, after all. The whole thing was this one guy's crazy fever dream. It's proof of what happens when you've got too much money and nobody around with enough balls to tell you when to rein it in. I want to try to find the petting zoo that used to be here. I read they used to have pangolins there—freaking *pangolins*. You can't keep pangolins in captivity. The guy was completely bat-crap crazy. That's what makes this site so tantalizing. See? It's the sheer weirdness of it all."

Tate was already moving forward, bulky DSLR clicking away, grinning through the viewfinder. Excitement radiated from him like body heat.

Eloise hung back, squinting into the far distance. There was some sort of tall, spindly structure way back in the hills beyond the main building, rising out of the canopy of overgrowth. There were no walls, just wide, plain slabs of bare concrete connected by open stairwells on alternating sides. It reminded Eloise of an old M.C. Escher painting, and she was seized with a wave of vertigo so powerful and nausea-inducing that she had to look away.

That must be the "Ocean-Viewing Platform" those old articles mentioned, she thought. *Guess they never did get around to finishing it.*

"Let's take a group pic for posterity." Linh rummaged through her threadbare backpack and brought out a bulky plastic camera with smooth, rounded edges. It looked like a child's toy—more an approximation of the concept of a camera than anything else. Eloise watched with mild interest as Linh flipped the back open and slotted some kind of cartridge into its works.

"Okay, everyone, get in close, under the sign. I'm going to set the self-timer. There is to be *no* goofing around, okay? There's only ten shots to a pack, and this is the only pack I brought."

"Jesus, what even *is* that faux-analog piece of hipster junk? Just use your phone and slap on some dumb filter." Tate's voice dripped with sarcasm. "It's 2019, Linny. That thing is an over-priced piece of cheesy plastic novelty crap marketed to hipsters who want to look cool and retro without learning the first thing about photography."

Linh sighed. "Just let me take the photo, eh?"

"Knock yourself out," Tate responded, mouth twisting.

Rolling her eyes, Linh propped the camera up on the partial remains of a nearby chest-height stone wall. It probably once had parking instructions nailed to it. Now, it was half-crumbled away, covered with creeping vines. The front of the hotel building was covered with them, too. Thin, spidery, mossy veins snaking every which way, their tiny grasping tendril-like filaments clinging tenaciously to the sun-bleached concrete.

"Go!" Linh yelped, bolting out from behind the wall and taking her place in the front of the group. She bent forward from the waist and threw up a peace sign, eyes crinkling behind her glasses. The others obliged, posing properly in deference to Linh's financial concerns, smiles plastered to their faces while the red eye of the camera blinked and faded.

"What the heck, I'll take one, too," Tate said, sauntering over to the stone wall and fiddling about with his DSLR. Meanwhile,

Linh plucked up the instant photograph her camera had just ejected from its slot and began flapping it impatiently in midair.

"Don't shake it," Tate said, closing his eyes for a moment, as if pained.

"It's a Polaroid," Linh responded archly, shaking it even harder.

"It literally *isn't*." Tate closed one eye and scrutinized his camera screen.

Linh continued shaking the picture.

"Okay, everyone back in position," Tate ordered, shouldering past Linh and covering the distance back to the others in a few quick, leaping strides. Linh, however, hadn't moved.

"Come on, Linny, it's a ten-second timer. Get your butt in gear."

Linh stared at the plastic rectangle of instant film in her hand.

"What?" Eloise was the first to stop smiling. There was something in Linh's expression that shouldn't have been there. "What's wrong?"

Linh looked up, eyes blank as she looked through the others, focusing on the hotel façade behind them.

"You guys," she said finally, in a faint sort of voice. "Come see this."

"Ten-second timer!" Tate whined impotently as Eloise and Steph went over to Linh.

"That's...huh." Steph snatched the photo from Linh's stiff fingers.

The photo showed the eight of them huddled together in the center of the frame, the hotel's negative-impression letters hanging just above their heads.

"Must be some kind of dud film," Miles suggested, looking over Steph's shoulder. "Maybe a defect, concentrated in that part. Take another one."

"It's not a dud film." Linh looked up at Tate, her eyes narrowing. "Is it, Tate?"

Tate snatched the photo from Steph, who'd been holding it at arms' length as if she didn't want to get too close to it.

"That's freaky." Tate brought the photo close to his nose. "Your eyes haven't come out, Linh."

It took Tate pointing it out for Eloise to finally realize what was wrong with the photo. Where Linh's eyes should have been, there were only two blank, black holes.

Eloise swallowed, tasting metal on her tongue.

Pushing the photo into Eloise's numb hand, Tate went over to his DSLR. It had taken its ten-second timer photo as the girls broke from the group and walked over to check out Linh's picture.

He blanched, silent as he scrolled back through the DSLR's photo reel for them all to see.

The photo was in clean focus, every detail of the hotel's crumbling, graffiti-strewn exterior rendered to perfection in the top-of-the-range camera's fifty-megapixel glory. But the black holes in place of Linh's eyes were there in this shot, too. She was closer to the camera, her face upturned, her mouth open. Her eyes didn't resemble holes in this one. They were shining black orbs, all massive pupils, no brown irises, no whites. Tiny pinpricks of light glittered inside them like two dark galaxies spinning with stars.

A bead of cold sweat slid down Eloise's spine. Somewhere, a seagull cawed.

"What the hell," Steph muttered.

"Haters gonna say it's photoshopped," Tate quipped, grinning at each of them in turn. He was the only one smiling.

"It's not *funny*." Steph's tone was caustic. "Prank photos? *Seriously*, Tate? First those stupid ghost stories about the red woman or whatever the hell you were on about, then that disgusting dead deer carcass, now this?"

Linh looked at Tate, her face ashen, her skin waxy. She gave herself a little shake, then grinned, her lips stretching over her front bunny teeth. "How'd you do it?" She laughed and flipped her Polaroid over, inspecting the shiny black backing. "I don't mean on your DSLR. I wouldn't put it past you to rig up something devious, some weird lens or filter or something, but when did you touch my instant film?"

"I didn't touch your dumb hipster film, Linh. I swear, I had nothing to do with this. Man, this is so freaking cool, though. It's going to make amazing content for my blog." Tate shook his head and chuckled. "A cursed photo. That's some gnarly shit. All right, no one's gonna believe it's unedited, obviously, but it'll still make for killer clickbait."

Could it have been Tate? What *else* could it have been? Eloise studied his face, the all-American smile, the eyes impossibly blue against his tanned skin. For just a moment, as he turned his head towards her, there were ragged, oozing black holes superimposed where his eyes should have been.

Don't. Stop it.

"Keep trying to scare us, Tate." Steph snatched the instant photo out of Linh's grasp, looking around as if she was expecting to spot a trash can. She was trembling slightly, two angry, hectic spots of color burning high on her cheekbones. "Just know that I'd sooner die than give you the satisfaction. I'm going to burn this. Who's got a light?"

Miles rummaged in his pocket and held up a gold click-wheel lighter.

"Don't *burn* it. Jesus. I want to get footage of that. And please stop being such a whiny bitch, Steph. A photo isn't going to hurt you." Tate grabbed Steph's hand by the wrist.

"*You're* a whiny bitch," Steph said mulishly, yanking her hand away from Tate's grasp. "But fine. You keep it. I don't want your *sick photos* anywhere near me."

She held the photo out towards Tate. They glared at each other for a charged moment before he snatched the photo out of her hand.

17

"Hey, there's a sign here." Ollie was toeing something half-hidden in the long grass. With the flat side of his yellowing sneaker, he pried it free and flipped it over. It was a piece of sheet metal, painted white with red lettering on it. "It's all in Japanese."

Kenji came over. As he crouched down to read it, Eloise looked over his shoulder. It was painted in a shaky hand, but she could just about decipher it.

These are the ruins of the Royal Oceanview Resort, which completed construction in the summer of 1975 and was abandoned the same year. Access to this area is strictly prohibited. Takagusuku Park accepts no responsibility for any injury or loss of life to any individuals trespassing on this privately-owned property.
-Takagusuku District Governmental Office

"This might be a dumb question," Steph said after Kenji had finished translating the sign for them out loud, "But why the hell has it been, like, *forty years,* and they *still* haven't torn this junk-heap death trap down?"

"The answer's right there in the sign. Privately-owned property." Kenji pointed to the pertinent part. "It's local government jurisdiction. Sure, they can intervene, especially when the land has been obviously abandoned or if the owner got old and died—that happens a lot here, with our aging population, as long as they can wring the demolition costs out of the surviving family members. If not, it costs taxpayer money to demolish old buildings. It would probably cost a couple billion yen to raze this place to the ground, and for what? No one in their right mind would want to build anything new up on the cliffs around here. It'd be throwing away money. So, they just leave it right where it's rotting."

"It's sort of sad," Linh said. "This place was somebody's dream, and now nobody even cares that it's still up here."

Eloise glanced again at the instant photograph Tate was still clutching. It probably was a dud film. And Tate's stupid camera no doubt cost his rich East Coast Daddy a pretty penny, but that didn't mean it wasn't capable of taking a weird, blurred shot every now and again. What was the alternative explanation? Some kind of *curse*? The very notion was just...just *stupid*.

"Can I borrow that, mate? Cheers," Ollie said, and Miles handed the lighter over without a word. They watched in amazement as Ollie took a pack of Lucky Strikes out of his backpack's side pocket and lit up. He inhaled deeply, a look of bliss spreading across his face before twin plumes of greyish smoke curled up from the corners of his mouth like a handlebar mustache. "*Fuck*, mate, that's good."

"You smoke?" Eloise was mildly scandalized. Posers vaped, but no one their age smoked tobacco cigarettes anymore. It was gross, socially unsanctioned. Almost deviant.

"Hmm? Ah, yeah." Ollie chuckled. "I'm gonna quit. I *have* quit, but I caved at the convenience store. I can't get over how cheap they are here. It's mental. I figured I'd have just one last pack for the road, like. I haven't had a cig in *months*. Mishka doesn't like it. She wants me to cut down on my meat consumption as well. Not full-on veggie, but at least a few days a week. And less booze, of course. She's right. I know I'm not exactly in the best condition, like, but dad bods are due for a comeback, aren't they? I should take my health more seriously, though, of course I should. Don't tell her about this, will you?"

"Give me that," Steph snapped, snatching the lighter out of Ollie's grasp. "It's a disgusting habit." She let the lighter roll over on her palm. Eloise watched over her shoulder, mildly interested. The lighter was smeared with sweat, the gold surface glittering. It was beat up and old. There was a date engraved on it: *1971 AD*. And some sort of emblem, mostly worn smooth, hard to make out.

"I'm confiscating this," Steph announced, flashing Miles a challenging look. Miles shrugged, uninterested.

"Keep it. It's not mine. I found it on the road." With the toe of his sand-colored boot, he started knocking rusty flakes off an old hunk of metal that lay half-concealed in the long grass. It looked like it might once have been a car exhaust pipe.

"Nah, you're right, Steph, course you are. I dunno what I was thinking. This'll be my last one." Ollie smiled, no hint of annoyance visible on his pleasant features. He pocketed the Lucky Strikes, a squirrely look creeping into his eyes as he continued blissfully puffing away.

"It's a shame you forgot to pack your balls in that tattered old backpack," Tate said, a supercilious glint in his eyes. "Did you leave them behind for Mishka to use as a beach pillow?"

Ollie laughed, a throaty, infectious chuckle. Unbothered.

"I know, mate, trust me, I know, but, well...that's love, innit?"

"*Innit*," Tate repeated, giving Ollie a weak, open-mouthed grin.

They trooped through the broken doorway beneath the washed-out sign and entered a large, dim space dotted with rotting yellow chairs and overturned low tables. There were mounds of unidentifiable vegetative matter heaped against the walls and strewn across the bare concrete floor. Rusted-out drink cans and old coiled springs poked out here and there.

Even with all of the windows smashed out, the room was too wide to allow for much sunlight to penetrate and guide their way. Tate was the only one who'd thought to bring a flashlight. "I told you girls to come prepared!" he hissed under his breath.

Why he was whispering, Eloise couldn't guess. The dancing flashlight beam picked out the dust motes floating lazily in the hazy air as the others used their phones to navigate, eventually discovering a pair of swinging double doors in the back wall.

"Front desk must be this way," Tate said, shouldering his way to the front of the group and pushing open one of the doors. It took some effort, and he had to brace himself against it and shove hard to displace the drift of debris that had built itself up against the other side of the door.

They went through and entered a much brighter space, a long, meandering corridor that, with its large plate-glass windows smashed out on either side, seemed open to the elements, almost like it was an exterior walkway of some kind. A tattered, stained crimson runner ran down the center of the hallway. It might have looked rather grand back in its early days.

The walls were whitewashed concrete and would have been completely bare if it wasn't for the scrawled graffiti covering almost every available inch.

Tate got his camera and tripod out again and started shooting a mural depicting a man's cartoonish screaming face, with teeth sticking out of the gums at haphazard angles like untended graveyard stakes. As a piece of art, it wasn't too bad, technically speaking. But the demented look in the man's eyes and the smears of red paint, which meant to suggest blood dripping from the eyes, made Eloise look away quickly in disgust, an irrepressible shudder shaking her core.

"Maybe it's a portrait of the resort's developer, added as an homage to his tormented spirit," Tate said, grinning at Eloise. The glint in his eye told her he'd caught that shudder.

Don't. Don't give him any ammo. Don't give him the satisfaction.

The corridor was on a gentle incline, following the rise of the hill, little offshoot hallways on either side at staggered intervals. They investigated the first few but found that they led only to identical guest rooms. All had walls painted the same shade of queasy avocado green, the collapsed beds covered with moth-eaten, filthy comforters that might once have been candy pink. Seventies color scheme aside, the rooms were devoid of any particularly interesting features. Eloise looked around, taking in the piles of dead leaves strewn across the peeling vinyl geometric-print flooring and the upended rotting rattan furniture and—

"I can't believe *all* the ensuite bathrooms have got squatter toilets. Was that, like, a lot more normal in Japan in the seventies, Kenji, or was this just a really shitty cheap hotel?"

Apparently, Steph was really interested in the hotel's plumbing features. Eloise had been watching closely, but she couldn't pick up on any vibes between her and Kenji that would indicate they'd spent the previous evening hooking up.

They've both probably still got sand in unmentionable places, so how can she act like nothing happened? And why is he going along with it?

She scrutinized Kenji. He looked nonchalant enough. But there was a stiffness around his eyes— tension in the set of his jaw. He caught Eloise looking then, and she quickly averted her gaze, her cheeks burning.

The long hallway bent and twisted this way and that, maze-like. Eventually, it opened up into a wide space where a vast, glassless skylight allowed a thick shaft of daylight to rain down. There was a curved reception desk, the remains of a decaying yellow vinyl sofa, and a smashed glass table. Eloise stepped on something that crunched. Shards of a white porcelain coffee cup were scattered all over the ground. Vines snaked through the broken skylight and caressed the reception desk, their ropy tendrils like groping fingers.

They fanned out, exploring the area.

Why put the front desk all the way up here? Eloise wondered absently, gazing up at the open sky above. A cloudless square, impossibly blue. *It doesn't make any sense. You'd have to haul your suitcases and stuff all the way up that endless corridor and all the way back down, and then—*

"Ding, ding, ding!"

She jerked, whirling around with an alarm that quickly gave way to relief and then annoyance. Tate stood behind the front desk, still soundlessly tapping away at a broken reception bell that was stiff with rust. The others looked as annoyed with him as Eloise felt.

Pleased to have their attention all the same, he pointed above their heads. Eloise lifted her eyes, seeing a mezzanine floor with most of its balcony railings snapped off.

"Check that out," Tate said.

BEWERE!! KURENAI NO ONNA

The graffiti had been done with red spray paint in a shaky hand. The letters dripped like blood.

"Beware the Crimson Woman," Satoko translated, an excited grin playing on the corners of her mouth.

"This place is haunted, all right. I bet it gives the Overwatch Hotel a run for its money." Tate crooked his index finger. "Redrum, redrum."

"The Over*look* Hotel," Miles said disdainfully, walking past the reception desk, past Tate. He was following the long corridor that continued along the slope ahead. The others went after him, Tate more reluctantly, a shadow darkening his brow, his eyes trained intensely on the other man's back.

They passed a bank of rusted-out vending machines, and then the corridor ended abruptly at a T-section. They emerged through a set of glassless double doors into what really *was* a covered outdoor walkway this time. Several small, squat vehicles sat permanently parked and disintegrating into rust piles along both of the outdoor arms of the T.

"Are those...golf carts?" Linh wandered over to inspect one, curious.

"It's a big complex. They probably provided those for the guests' convenience." Tate kicked one of the rusted-out hubcaps, releasing a fine mist of corroded metal fragments.

"It didn't look that big to me. I only saw a few dozen rooms," Steph sniffed.

"Those were just the bougie suites for the rich guests. There's the bunkhouse cabins, too, tons of them dotted all over the hillside. And the guest cottages. *And* there's the waterpark as well. Don't forget about that." Tate's eyes had that manic, enthusiastic gleam in them again as he crouched down, shooting the most intact golf cart from all angles.

"I'm sure you'll make a point of reminding us," Steph said archly, swiping on her phone. "Shit, there's no signal up here. I can't get even a single bar. Guys?"

Linh swiped her own phone awake. "Nope. Totally cut off from civilization."

"There's nothing on this hillside. It's probably a dead zone. There are no cell phone towers around here. No need for cellphone coverage," Miles said.

"Great, that's just great." Steph sniffed again, shoving her phone into the back pocket of her shorts. "May as well cut off my freaking oxygen supply."

Steph was certainly attached to her phone for someone who never seemed to be able to respond to messages within a twenty-four-hour period. Eloise fumbled in her backpack for her own phone, a model at least five years older than Steph's. No bars. She'd forgotten to charge it, too, only 23% battery.

Mentally shrugging, she pressed the side button until the screen went black.

It wasn't like it was such a big deal. They could go tech-free for one afternoon. Steph was so dramatic.

"I was going to try to rent a satellite phone, but I ran out of time," Tate confessed. "Look, it'll be cool. Just as long as nobody goes diving head-first into a heap of rusted machinery, okay, 'cause we can't exactly rely on being able to call 911 up here."

"That might be because we're in *Japan*, genius," Steph hissed, scuffing the toe of one hiking boot hard against the gravelly ground.

"Can you chill out?" Tate groused, shooting her a disapproving look.

"That depends. Did you lure us all up here so you could murder us one by one for your little documentary? Or should I say *snuff film*?"

Tate grinned at her, entertained. Showing those straight white teeth.

"Don't go giving me any good ideas, Steph."

18

"What am I looking at?" Eloise asked, weighing up the risk of sounding stupid and deciding it was worth asking anyway.

They'd followed the covered walkway until it led them to a dirt-and-gravel path. At the end of the path, they'd found a decagonal-shaped building with an orange-tiled roof. Inside, there was an empty open space. However, its perimeter was ringed with a waist-height concrete wall, iron bars protruding vertically from it all the way to the ceiling. Tate took hold of the bars and stuck his neck between them, sniffing the air.

"Must have been the petting zoo. At one time, there must have been a regular menagerie here. Goats, pigs, kid-friendly stuff."

"Pangolins," Linh said dryly.

"Ostensibly," Tate agreed.

"What do you think happened to the animals when the resort closed? Do you think they were taken care of? They wouldn't have just abandoned them like they did everything else, would they?" Linh's big brown eyes were wide with concern behind her Coke bottle glasses.

"Oh, they were taken care of, all right." Tate pointed at Linh's head and made the sound of a gun cocking with his tongue, an explosion with his cheeks. Then he laughed.

Eloise and Linh shared a look of mutual disgust, united in their distaste for Tate. Not for the first time, Eloise wondered what she was doing here. She supposed that, in some odd way, making it to the resort had become a fixation. She didn't even know why she'd wanted to keep going so badly. She could have left at any point. She should have left, probably. Last night. That was the cue, and she'd missed it.

But, in a weird, inexplicable way, a part of her believed that if she could make it to the resort, she could prove that she wasn't afraid. Of other people, of what they might think of her. Not anymore. She'd prove she could be social, even without mass quantities of alcohol. Feel the fear and do it anyway, like the useless therapist she'd seen for five NHS-provided sessions kept repeating. It was a demented mantra. She'd had several. Push outside your comfort zone. Do the thing you think you can't do. But it wasn't helping. Eloise wasn't healing, wasn't moving on. She was limping through life, dragging herself along with all her wounds still festering.

And maybe you're really only here because this is exactly the kind of thing Chris was always encouraging you to do. But he's dead, El. Dead and gone. So why are you still trying to impress him? Doesn't that strike you as just a little bit insane?

"You okay?" Linh asked her, and Eloise's heart jumped in alarm. She gave herself a mental shake and smiled back at Linh, wanting to reassure her.

"I'm fine," she said in a voice that was so steady she could almost convince herself.

Almost.

They left the petting zoo enclosure via a flight of steps at its far end. The concrete staircase was wide enough for all of them to have walked abreast if it wasn't for the odd, jutting structure sticking out into the space above the stairs. In the end, they walked single file, although there was technically enough room to descend the stairs under the jutting part—if you crawled down them on your hands and knees, that is.

"Why is the architecture here all messed up?" Ollie asked. "It's like the geezers who built this place never saw an actual building before."

"Best guess?" Tate breathed air through his nose. "Cost-cutting measures. They must have hired the cheapest architects and contractors. But isn't it fascinating? It's giving Winchester Mystery House vibes."

"It's creepy," Linh said. "And the doorways are all different heights. Did you notice that? It's like a lunatic designed this place. Or someone on hard drugs. *Ugh,* I hate it."

The stairs led to the outside, to an open tiled plaza where the remains of sun umbrellas perched like vulture skeletons above mossy picnic benches. The ground fell away in a smooth slope on the right-hand side, offering a spectacular vista of the hillside below. Far beyond that, the waters of the Pacific glistened. Eloise spotted tiny boats bobbing far out on the horizon. She let her mind wander, idly lending half an ear to the conversations of the others as she scanned the overgrown mass of glossy greenery below. It seemed to quiver despite the scant breeze.

"Pripyat's too commercial," Tate was saying to Ollie. "I mean, I know it's basically the holy grail of Urbex, but you've got to pay someone to take you *in* and *out,* and you've got to sign waivers and get briefed and *duh-duh duh-duh-duh,* so much hassle. And really, the whole thing is just too edgy. Isn't it? I prefer discovering places that haven't already been picked over by tourists. I went to this abandoned hospital in Tochigi Prefecture last year. You wouldn't believe the stuff they left behind. Iron lungs, x-ray machines. There was even a brain in a jar."

"You're shitting me, mate," Ollie said.

"No, man, I've got photos of it. It was fucking gnarly. I'll send you the link. That was a killer location for Urbex. I mean, it was practically *untouched.* If I can squeeze it in, I definitely want to try to get to Gunkanjima before heading back stateside. Hey, you wanna come with? You're headed to mainland Japan next, right?"

"Ah, mate, I'd love to, but Mish...wait, Gunkanjima? Is that that abandoned island shaped like a battleship? The one with all those high-rise apartment buildings crammed on it?"

"Yeah, but again, we have to go on a tour, and since the buildings are so unstable, they won't let you actually go *inside* any of them. *My* plan has always been to sneak off from the group and—Fuck, fuck, fuck!"

The floor beneath Tate's feet was moving, and he threw himself backwards, Ollie rushing, grabbing him under the armpits, dragging him away. A slab of concrete slid forward from the spot where Tate had been standing, then plummeted down the hillside, gouging a deep furrow through the undergrowth as it fell. But the slab's wake revealed not bare earth but some sort of candy-bright fiberglass in faded red, yellow, and blue primary colors.

"Found the waterpark, guys!" Tate crowed, breathing hard as he scrambled to his feet. "Woo!"

Eloise put a hand over her thundering heart, willing herself to breathe normally.

"We almost fell right into the stupid thing," Steph grumbled as they all leaned over the bare drop, gazing down at the slanted hillside that wasn't a hillside at all but a complex of fiberglass channels.

Waterslides.

Now Eloise knew what she was looking at. It was easy enough to pick out the colossal swimming pool far down below, as overgrown with weeds and vines as it was. Its dark green tiled bottom had assisted with the initial camouflage effect.

There was a heavy scraping sound, and Eloise turned to see Miles dragging the remains of a plastic chair seat over to the lip of the slides.

"Er, what do you think you're doing?" Steph said, but Miles ignored her, placing the seat on the edge of the nearest slide and straddling it.

He looked up at the group. His eyes found Eloise's. He grinned. Then he let go.

The chair scraped its way down the slide, slowly at first and then picking up speed, clumps of moss piling up around the sides as the chair ate a channel through the slimy overgrowth that coated the slide like a fine skin. They all gasped, and Linh screamed a little as the chair finally shot off the end of the slide, sending Miles tumbling into the tiled bottom of the pool, the chair flipping through the air. He stumbled, arms windmilling for balance, boots skidding against the filthy bottom of the pool before he finally slid to a precarious stop. He turned around and grinned expectantly up at their group high above him.

Well, that was pretty dumb, Eloise thought, her heart in her throat. And was she *disappointed*? Maybe a little.

"What a lunatic." Linh finally broke the silence. "I am *not* doing that."

"Douchebag," Steph said disparagingly, her eyes flicking sharply to Eloise. Eloise took up the challenge and stared right back until Steph was the first to blink and look away.

After that, there was no dissuading the guys from following Miles's example. Tate, for one, seemed determined not to be outdone.

"If none of them break their fool necks, it'll be a miracle," Steph said to the other girls, who had all decamped to a safe spot away from the slope. "As our intrepid leader so sagely pointed out, calling *911* isn't exactly a possibility."

"Boys will be tools," Linh shrugged. "I'm surprised at Kenji, though. You'd think a legit educator would have a greater sense of responsibility."

"Hey!" Miles was yelling. "Look who I found at the bottom of the pool!"

"What's he got?" Linh inched closer to the edge again, squinting, the gold frames of her glasses glinting in the sun. "It looks like...like...oh, my *God*."

As Eloise watched Miles climb up the stadium-style steps they'd all somehow missed, her stomach lurched and bile filled her throat. Miles was cradling a child in his arms—a toddler, clearly dead and horribly pale, its eyes screwed shut, its mouth an open, gaping maw. The limbs flopped rhythmically as Miles loped nimbly up the steps. Reality seemed to be tilting on its axis, slipping to one side and leaving Eloise in a bizarre world in which nothing made sense. A world where Miles was grinning at her and brandishing the corpse of a dead child.

"It's a CPR dummy," he said, hopping up onto the tiled terrace, holding the floppy corpse aloft by its neck. Its bloated legs dangled and swung to and fro like a frog. "Little kid version." Miles held up one tiny dummy hand and shook it, speaking in a falsetto voice, a childlike lisp: "Hi, ladies."

"That's *disgusting*," Steph spat, glowering at him. "What the *fuck* is wrong with you?"

"What?" he smiled quizzically at Steph. "What's your problem?"

Eloise knew it couldn't have been a *real* child's corpse that Miles was shaking about. Of course, she *knew* that, but in trying to process what she was looking at, her brain had made the first possible connective leap. She remembered reading somewhere that when people discover a dead body, their first thought is usually always that it's a mannequin. Something about the brain not being able to process the reality of what it's seeing.

But then, why did my brain jump to the opposite conclusion? What's wrong with my brain that it would do that?

"That's the most *grossest* thing I've ever seen," Satoko said, scrutinizing the half-rotten dummy with fascination. Its lip and nose area seemed to have been eaten away by decay, and the back of its head was missing.

"Throw it away!" Steph's voice was high, sharp with anger and indignation.

"All right," Miles said lightly, tossing the dummy over his shoulder. It sailed high in the air, arms flapping. A long second later, there was a muted thud as it landed on the pool's tiled bottom far below.

"I didn't mean *like that*," Steph said through gritted teeth, her face a mask of disgust and contempt.

"Wow, there's just no pleasing you, is there, Stephanie?" Miles said in a soft, surprised tone, his eyes fixed on Steph, and there was a hot burst of jealousy in Eloise's chest, a sensation that shocked her with its suddenness, its violence.

"Everything okay, Steph?" Tate finished jogging up the steps to join them. He was breathing hard, blinking sweat out of his eyes.

"Fine." Steph turned and stalked off, heading for the far end of the terrace and another set of steps that led up into the hillside. Tate let his gaze slide over Miles before following her. Kenji, Ollie, Satoko, and Linh ambled along after them.

Cautiously, Eloise approached the edge of the slides and looked down. She could just about make out the gray, misshapen form of the dummy in the sea of moss and weeds below. Shuddering with disgust, she turned away, heading after the group, leaving the overgrown pool behind.

19

The sky overhead had grown muggy and white with thunderheads, and the scent of ozone hung heavy in the air as they stood gazing up at the towering structure before them. The Ocean-Viewing Platform was indeed unfinished, nothing more than a skeleton frame of gray concrete, fingers of rusted rebar poking out of the slabs like scarecrow hands. There were about six tiers to it, and while it looked sturdy enough, the lack of walls and the sheer drop on every side made Eloise half-sick with vertigo.

"I think I'll wait down here. Not a great lover of heights, me." Ollie shuffled, scratching his stubbled chin. "Anyway, I'm starving. I'm gonna dig into me lunch rations."

He ripped open his backpack, producing a small, wrapped package, a convenience-store rice ball. "Before you go, though, can anyone tell me what's in this? Because it looks like *Spam*."

Linh leaned in, eyes narrowing behind her glasses. "It *is* Spam."

"Ah, mate." Ollie's cheerful face fell.

"I thought you were cool with eating, like, literally anything."

Ollie grinned weakly. "I could murder a plate of me nan's Jamaican rice and peas." He started peeling the cellophane wrapping off his lunch. There was a certain gimmick to its design that was clearly lost on him, and he ended up tipping half of the rice into the dirt. "*Bollocks*," he groaned.

"Hey, someone lit a fire here," Kenji said, investigating the dusty barren area underneath the platform. "What's this?" He kicked something hard and metal.

"Looks like a canteen of some kind." Tate wandered over and picked it up. "It's busted. Looks military-issue. See the squadron stickers on it?"

"Fascinating." Steph crossed her arms below her chest. "Are we climbing this thing or not?"

Linh said that she would stay, too, to keep Ollie company, and Satoko didn't seem interested in climbing the structure either. In fact, she looked sick, dark swells of puffy flesh below her eyes.

Okay, Eloise told herself. *There's my out. I wouldn't be the only one. I can stay, or I can do the thing.*

Do the thing. That's what this was all about. Wasn't it?

So, she joined the others, trembling only a little inside, and started up the open staircase to the first tier. It held nothing remarkable. The first few levels, in fact, were completely barren except for some rotten foliage and a few dubious-looking rust stains. But as they reached the higher levels, a spectacular vista began to form all around them until they finally got the three hundred and sixty-degree panoramic view of Okinawa Island that was promised. Excitement hastened Eloise's footsteps as she ascended the final staircase and came out onto the top level, which had no roof and was completely exposed to the elements.

"Gorgeous," Tate said, camera held high on its tripod as he hurried over to one end of the structure. "The Pacific," he said aloud as if narrating a travel documentary, "And over here we have the East China Sea." He turned and shuffle-jogged over to the opposite side, his voice giddy with excitement.

The views were beautiful, yes, as long as you didn't look down, but Eloise was distracted by something else. For whatever inexplicable reason, there was a weather-beaten fairground carousel in the middle of the platform. It was built to a smaller scale than a true fairground carousel and actually looked more like some kind of coin-op kiddy ride. The paint had long since been washed away from the neighing faces of the horses, and the rotating base was rusted stiff, the metal opening up in gaping holes.

"The heck is this doing up here," she muttered, patting one of the sun-bleached noses.

"God knows. The guy who designed this place was totally non compos mentis if you ask me." Steph approached one of the horses and ran her fingers along its faded rump before rotating her hips and perching herself aboard the narrow back. She crossed her long legs, shorts riding up to reveal an expanse of honey-brown thigh. She swung her heavy boot back and forth, agitated.

"Non compost what? What's that mean?" Kenji lowered his phone after taking a shot of the Pacific and looked at Steph, his eyes glinting as they raked their way up her exposed thigh.

"It means crazy." Eloise swallowed past the hot lump in her throat. *Kinda like how I'm feeling. One good shove, and you could get her off the edge. From this height, her body might actually come apart on impact.*

Eloise's vision greyed as she pictured Steph lying in scattered, bloody chunks down below.

"Er, guys, the *view*?" Tate's voice was laced with sarcasm, his tone condescending. Steph's eyes flashed as she glared at him. Tate had never been Steph's favorite person. Eloise knew that, but she'd always humored him before. Been his bantering partner. Since they'd arrived in Okinawa, though, something seemed to have changed. Steph's jokey, exasperated tolerance of Tate seemed to have disappeared and been replaced by outright animosity.

"We've seen *the view*. In fact, I think we've seen everything this shithole has to offer. Can we leave now, Tate? Go to the beach? Maybe have some actual fucking fun for once on this trip? Oh, if you're done pursuing your Boy Scout badge in advanced 'urban exploration,' that is?" Steph's fingers hooked into quotation marks.

"Hey, nobody forced you to come."

"Go fuck yourself, Tate. This was a shit idea, you ask me. And we're all fucking stupid for agreeing to it in the first place."

Eloise's anger bubbled over, taking her by surprise. She was sick of Steph's bitching, the way she dominated every situation and forced the mood of the group to fit hers. She was sick of *Steph*. Her head felt like it was about to split open. Her raw toe was giving off full-body pulses of pain. She was hot, tired, and exhausted.

She opened her mouth to say something. She wasn't sure what. *Fuck you, Steph?* That would be a good start.

But before she could speak—

"Hey, Stephanie, why don't you do us all a big favor and, I dunno, shut your fucking mouth?"

It was Miles who had spoken. The others stiffened, tension rippling through them. Miles's tone had been disproportionately malicious, and it had set the air crackling. Eloise's temples throbbed. She always got a bad headache like this when the barometer dropped suddenly.

When a storm was brewing.

"Excuse me?" Steph turned her head very slowly and deliberately towards Miles.

"You heard me. I came up here to have some fun, like everyone else, but you've been acting like a psycho bitch and pissing on everybody's good time ever since we got here. I guess even getting porked on the beach last night didn't mellow you out."

Steph's mouth fell open.

Eloise's chest tightened like a vice. Her skin crawled with discomfort.

"Getting...I'm sorry, what?" Tate took a step forward. He snorted in disbelief. "When? Where? I mean, I mean, who the fuck *with*?"

"On the beach. Last night. Like I just said." Miles grinned at Tate. "As for *who with*...come on, champ, process of elimination. You're almost there. One last mental spurt, that's the boy."

Tate huffed air through his nose but didn't take Miles's bait. His eyes were still trained on Steph. "Wait, you and...and *Kenji*? For real?"

Steph grimaced and shrugged, looking down at her thumb. She brought it to her mouth and nibbled, working loose a jagged hangnail and peeling it away slowly, like the skin of a mandarin orange. A bead of blood quivered on her bottom lip.

Tate's jaw worked. He seemed to be cycling slowly through a kaleidoscope of disparate emotions, one after the other. In the end, his face settled into a huge, shit-eating grin, and he held one meaty palm aloft towards Kenji. "You hit that? My man!" he crowed, vocal cords straining. "Nice!"

Kenji shook his head, the corners of his mouth twitching. "Nuh-uh."

"Come on! Don't leave me hanging here, bro!" Tate's grin stretched to breaking point. Eloise hoped that Kenji *would* leave Tate hanging, that he wouldn't be piggish enough to indulge him in this display of disgusting machismo, this...this male-bonding ritual.

But Kenji was fully smiling now, a chuckle escaping him as he slapped his hand against Tate's.

"All right, all right, I did it." He brushed his hair back from his forehead with both hands. At that moment, Eloise felt utter disgust—with herself. For thinking that Kenji was sensitive, different somehow. He wasn't. He was a pig. And for some reason, she found herself thinking about that day on the bullet train back from Tokyo. Steph's chin trembling like a child's beneath the shadow of her baseball cap.

"You're sick, all of you." Eloise glared at them all in turn—Kenji, Tate, Miles.

"What did *I* do?" Miles had the indecency to look hurt, his tanned brow furrowed, his full lower lip caught boyishly between his teeth.

"The way you all *talk* about it. Us. Women. The *words* you use. Like we're just...just *meat*. Are all of you men really like this? I mean, is it really every single last one of you? Is that even *fucking* possible?"

"Listen, just chill out. You're being ridiculous. If Steph didn't want everyone knowing about her sex life, she should have gone for a little more discretion." Tate actually had the audacity to scoff.

Eloise's head was splitting. The rage was bubbling over again. She wanted to slap all of their smug faces, to kick all of them in the balls—starting with Kenji—when Steph mortified them all by bursting into noisy, gasping sobs.

Tate made a spasmodic, aborted gesture that indicated he'd thought of comforting her but then thought better of it. Steph turned her face away from them and pressed her cheek against the hard molded mane of the carousel horse. Her lower lip pulled free from her bottom teeth, and a ribbon of drool bungeed down from the corner, stretching almost to her shoulder before snapping back as she drew in a shuddering, slurping breath.

"*Fuck* all of you!" she gritted out, sliding weakly down from the horse's saddle. "Especially *you,* Tate."

"Me? What did I do? Don't blame me for the fact that you enjoy being a slut."

"I'm never going to fucking sleep with you, Tate. *Never.* Not after what you fucking did."

"What are you talking about?"

"I know, Tate. I know about the *fucking photos.*"

Tate's lips parted. "What?"

"The students told me what you did to them. They *showed* me. Your little photography project? You really thought you were going to get away with it, didn't you? You're *disgusting.*"

Tate swallowed—his Adam's apple bobbing. "Wow. That isn't cool, Steph. That is...that is extremely fucked up of you."

"Wait, what?" Kenji's eyes sharpened, his lower jaw coming forward in disbelief as he scrutinized first Steph's face, then Tate's. "What the hell is this?"

Tate laughed a sharp, mirthless bark. "I actually can't believe you'd accuse me of something like that. What's *wrong* with you, Steph? Jesus. You and I used to be tight. That is some sick shit to pull."

There was a protracted silence while Steph didn't say anything, and the others all held their breath. Only Miles wore a detached hint of a smile, standing a short distance away from the rest of them. His stance was comfortable, his legs spaced wide, and he was casually holding onto his belt with both hands.

Eloise might throw up. It was too hot, and there was too much happening all at once. She couldn't process it. Dimly, she thought about Tate's habit of making gross comments about some of his students, saying how they were all obsessed with him, totally *hot for teacher*, as he put it. Although, she'd brushed those remarks off as nothing but braggadocios, Tate-ish bullshit.

"You're a fucking predator," Steph spat, her features congealed with contempt.

Then Tate was rushing forward, closing the distance between himself and Steph in the space of a blink. And he was grabbing Steph around the neck, dragging her off the carousel horse, pressing his face up against hers.

Kenji yelled and grabbed Tate by the shoulder, but Tate clung on, his thumb sinking into the meat of Steph's cheek, distorting her lips and exposing the bone of her grimace.

"You take it the fuck back," Tate growled, spit whistling through his gritted teeth. "You take it back right now."

Steph breathed hard and slow through her nose, her wide, beautiful eyes fixed on Tate.

"Fine," Steph said. There was another interlude of agonizing silence, which the rustling of the trees and the relentless buzz of the cicadas suddenly swelled to fill. A gull cawed, wheeling high above. "Fine. I'm not serious. I made it up. Forget it. I don't know why I said it, okay?"

Kenji yanked on Tate's shoulder again, but Tate elbowed him away, his face contorted with anger, and he was still throttling

Steph. Eloise grabbed for Tate's arm, digging her nails into his sweat-slick flesh, panic tearing through her.

He's choking her. He's choking her.

But then, right before her eyes, Tate crumpled, breath bursting between his lips, and he went down to his knees, releasing Steph. Steph stumbled away, gasping and grabbing her throat, and Eloise reached for her, her fingers stiff and numb against Steph's chilled skin.

"Fuck," Tate gasped, knuckling his fist against his lower back. "You fucking…" he screwed up his face, retching. "Punched me…in the…kidney."

"You fucking deserved it," Miles said impassively, and if Eloise hadn't been so disabled with panic and shock, she supposed she might have been impressed.

"Are you all right?" Kenji's eyes found Steph's as he reached for her. She turned away, wiping her nose on her arm.

"I'm fine. Fuck off."

They all stood there, not speaking, for what seemed like minutes. Tate was still groaning and occasionally dry heaving, but it was starting to sound like he was putting it on. Steph was crying quietly. Miles was rubbing his knuckles. Kenji's face was stricken, his eyes blank. Nobody seemed willing to be the first one to speak.

Eloise chewed on her lower lip, massaging Steph's thin shoulders. Confusion clouded her thoughts. What the fuck was happening? How had things ended up like this?

A colossal crack of lightning split the heavens above their heads and turned the world photonegative for a beat. Eloise blinked, startled. She looked up. The billowing gunmetal-gray storm clouds above were finally opening up to release their bounty of rainwater. It started with a few spatters, but within seconds, fat drops of hail-like rain were crackling like pop rocks on the hot concrete all around them as the shower became a downpour.

Above the roaring of the sudden storm, there was something else. A high, sharp noise, ragged with urgency. Their faces stiffened. They all seemed to place it at the same moment.

It was the sound of Linh's voice ripping through the muggy air. She was screaming.

20

*D*on't slip. Don't fall. Steady. It's okay. You're okay. Linh. Oh God, what's happening? Why won't she stop *screaming?*

Eloise's mind was a jumble of panicked thoughts, all jangling loudly together like tangled coat hangers. It was a long way down from the top of the platform, and the sudden cloudburst had rendered the steps slimy and treacherous. A hot, wet hand grabbed Eloise's and she knew it was Steph's. It was comfort. An anchor. She couldn't fall. Not with Steph weighing her down.

She held on tight, and the two of them picked and hopped their way down together, evading the deepest of the puddles that had formed as if out of nowhere, the cracks in the concrete allowing the rainwater to seep down from the higher layers.

They reached terra firma again eventually, but it wasn't so much firm as it was soggy and mulchy underneath their skidding boots. The storm clouds had grown so dense that it was almost as dark as early evening already. Linh had stopped screaming somewhere around the fourth flight down.

The absence of the screaming was somehow infinitely worse.

Eloise couldn't process what was unfolding. Couldn't fathom what could possibly have *happened* to Linh during the ten minutes they'd been apart from her and Satoko and Ollie. She knew this wasn't a prank. That wasn't Linh, so then either she or Ollie or Satoko must really be in trouble, crushed by falling debris. Or maybe another explorer had stumbled across them, one with bad intentions, someone who wanted to hurt or rape one of them, maybe the person who'd left the fire pit and the canteen.

Satoko emerged from the dryness beneath the platform, the rain instantly soaking her. Her face was white, confused, with no hint of insight into the situation.

"What happened?" Steph yelled.

Satoko simply shook her head and pointed to the dirt track with a quivering finger. The dusty ground had turned into a soup of surging rainwater and treacle-thick mud.

They ran out into the open storm, emerging through the trees where the hiking trail let out onto a wider, dirt-and-gravel path. Bunching up together, they froze, gasping and blinking through the rain that streamed down their faces.

They'd found Linh crouched over Ollie, who was lying supine, and the only thing that seemed to be registering with Eloise was the fact that he had his jeans and boxer briefs around his ankles. Linh lifted her head slowly and looked over her shoulder at them, her eyes wide and staring and frantic.

"I can't get it off," she said, the storm's buffeting winds half-swallowing her voice. "I stamped on its tail, but it...it won't let go."

"Get back," Miles said, moving forward while the others remained dumb and stunned. He grabbed Linh by the shoulder and pulled her, and Linh stumbled back on her heels, still crouched, boots scraping against the ground. Inevitably, she fell backward onto her palms, wrists twisting, and now they could see all of Ollie.

He wasn't dead. His head was raised, eyes staring unblinkingly down the length of his torso to his groin where—Eloise's veins surged with terror and her throat constricted around a bubble of nausea as she realized what the long, rope-like thing lying across Ollie's quivering thigh was.

It was as long as she was tall, a mottled yellow-brown viper, its scales glistening with rainwater. It had a small, diamond-shaped head. The head was embedded in Ollie's scrotum, and his shriveled penis flopped passively over to the opposite side. There was no blood, but the entire area looked purple and swollen and livid.

"Get it off," Ollie gasped. "Please."

"He went to take a piss." Linh stared at the others, her eyes hopeless but pleading. "It was in the grass."

"Stay calm," Miles said. Then, quieter: "It should have struck once and let go. It shouldn't be hanging on like that." He picked up a stick and advanced upon Ollie. "Get off the path, Linh," he said, flexing his arm.

Linh scrambled to her feet and stumbled away, throwing herself at Eloise, who caught her and held her.

Another crack of lightning made the scene impossibly bright for a fraction of a second, and Miles seemed to advance several feet at once, like he was strobing.

Then there was a quieter crack and a muted hiss as Miles whacked the venomous *habu* snake's tail with the stick. It reared up, releasing Ollie's ravaged scrotum and striking at Miles, who leaped to the side.

Tail thrashing, the vile creature slithered in horrible undulating movements to the side of the path, disappearing into the grass.

As if a spell had been broken, the others all moved forward, falling to their knees on the ground around Ollie, who seemed to have lost consciousness.

"Oh shit, oh shit, oh shit," Tate was saying over and over. "Snake bit him on the fucking *balls*, man, oh shit."

"Calm the fuck down," Miles snarled. Tate stopped babbling and blinked, an affronted look in his wild eyes, muted anger distorting his features.

"Yeah, right, right, everyone just stay calm. So, first...first, we need to make a tourniquet, right?" Tate brushed water out of his eyes with a trembling hand.

Steph looked around desperately at everyone's faces, her hair clinging to her cheeks in sodden rattails.

"Don't we have to suck out the poison?" she asked.

Eloise clamped her hand over her mouth, fighting a sudden, terrible urge to burst into peals of hysterical laughter. Self-hatred surged. Was this funny? *Really?* Was this *fucking funny?*

"No." Miles came around behind Ollie, scooping his hands under his armpits and shoving him up into a sitting position. "No tourniquets, no sucking the venom out, none of that movie crap. It's bullshit. We need to keep his heart elevated above the bite, keep him still and comfortable, and get him some help as fast as possible." Miles patted Ollie's cheeks. "You still with us, buddy?"

Ollie stirred, blinked rain out of his eyes, and tried to focus on Miles's face.

"Listen, man. Eyes on me. We're going to get you some help. All right? You're gonna be fine."

"Is he going to die?" Linh's eyes were narrowed, her face scrunched up as if she couldn't bear to hear the answer, and yet, hadn't been able to stop herself asking the question. Miles looked at her sharply.

"He's not going to die. You're not going to die, man." Miles delivered this aside brightly to Ollie before addressing Linh again, his voice dropping into a conspiratorial register. "Not if we can get him some help soon. If he goes too long, he could end up in a bad way. There's a risk of organ failure, permanent disability...*Habu* venom's not as deadly toxic as a lot of viper venom, but they produce a lot of it, and it looks like that one was latched on for a while."

"I *knew* something like this was going to happen." Steph scrambled to her feet and started pacing up and down the sodden path, her dripping phone's screen glowing in the gloom as she tried to get service. Eloise fumbled for her own phone. No bars. In their place...

No Signal

The words swam before Eloise's eyes.

"Someone's going to have to hike down the mountain to where there's signal and then call for help." Miles sat back on his heels, lifting his chin.

"You can go," Steph said, glaring at Miles. "In fact, why don't all of you *men* go. We can stay here and take care of Ollie."

"No," Miles said evenly, *pleasantly*, even.

"What?"

"I'd rather shit in my hands and clap than take orders from you, Stephanie. No offence, though, sweetheart."

Steph blinked at Miles, rainwater spilling into her open mouth and pooling there. She pushed it out with her tongue, spluttering. "Are you *serious*?"

Miles ignored her. "Grab his legs," he instructed Kenji. "We need to get him out of this storm. Carry him back under that platform. At least there's some cover there."

Kenji and Tate helped Miles lift Ollie's limp form off the ground, Linh running over to pull up his jeans, to try to restore to him some small modicum of modesty. Then the guys carried him, slung between them, retracing their steps to the platform. The storm seemed to be growing worse, the trees and bushes whipping and shaking like angry, living things as the heavy winds buffeted the high clifftop. Under the platform, though, there was dryness and muffled quiet.

They lay Ollie down, and Miles told Linh to pull his jeans down again so he could splash bottled water on Ollie's crotch area, followed by whiskey from a silver hip flask he had tucked in his belt.

Everyone else looked away while he did this. They were all breathing heavily, eyes wild and frightened. Looking at Ollie, ravaged, poisoned Ollie, was bad. But the looks on the others' faces...the *fear* there...that was somehow worse. Eloise stared fixedly down at her boots instead, rainwater dripping from her chin in a long stream. The tan leather was black from the rain. She thought she could smell the whiskey. It disgusted her, how badly she wanted it.

"Listen. We have no idea how long this storm's gonna last. It could taper off in ten minutes, or it could go on all night. I'm volunteering to head down the hill." Tate grabbed his backpack and stuffed his camera inside it. "In fact, I think we should all go. This place is fucked. When we get somewhere with signal, we can call for help anonymously."

"Anonymously," Steph repeated. "What the hell are you talking about?"

"In case you'd forgotten, *Steph*, we're trespassing. You want to get arrested? In *Japan?* You know they can hold you in jail for twenty-three days here without charge? Does that sound like fun to you?"

"Are you…are you fucking kidding?"

"We can't leave Ollie here alone," Linh said. "I'll stay with him. The rest should go together, stay in a group. It'll be safer that way."

"I'll stay," Satoko said. "You go. All of you."

Linh shook her head, but Satoko insisted, raising her voice over the storm. "*Go*. I can't walk anymore. I don't want to be out there, in this. I still feel like shit. Hungover. My head is killing. I'll rest here, with Ollie. I don't mind."

Linh hesitated, then pulled something off her wrist and handed it to Satoko.

"Take it," she said. "The good-luck charm. Just in case."

Satoko stared at it for a moment, and Eloise was sure she'd refuse it, but instead Satoko just held out her hand and watched as Linh dropped the little stone into it.

"Thanks," she said quietly.

"Are you sure you're going to be all right?" Eloise handed Satoko her backpack to use as a pillow for Ollie.

"Yeah. I'm not scared," Satoko said, wringing out her dripping ponytail. "Just get help fast. Okay?"

21

They headed back into the resort, where the storm raged muffled outside, and sheets of water came cascading through the empty windowpanes. They followed the corridor again, and when they reached the front desk area, they found it flooded with brackish, thigh-high rainwater. There was no other option than to plunge right through it.

The water was ice cold, like a thousand stabbing knives, and it seeped into Eloise's jeans, dragging her down. Even after they'd passed through it, the sopping material clung implacably to her thighs, the tight, clammy sensation sending shivers of disgust through her.

"This storm is insane," Tate gasped as they slogged back down the dim, graffiti-riddled corridor. Another flash of sheet lightning outside turned day into night and back again. "There was nothing forecast, I checked. It doesn't make any sense."

The others were silent, save for the harsh noise of their ragged exhalations, as they passed back through the wide lobby and plunged outside into the storm once more. The rain soaked Eloise again instantly and she had to gasp to catch her breath as warm rivulets poured down her face.

Progress was slow, but the shimmering, puddle-strewn road was slippery and treacherous underfoot. They passed the shadowy guardhouse. The sky over the Pacific was so dark it was almost navy blue, but they could see beams of sunlight far off on the horizon, yellow glints shining like fool's gold out on the ocean.

When they rounded the bend, the deer carcass was still there on the road. But now the rainwater pelting down sent crimson droplets of rehydrated blood dancing in the air above it. They gave it a wide berth, Eloise's stomach contorting with nausea, and it wasn't until Kenji yelled in surprise that she lifted her head and saw what was in front of them.

They all shambled to a stop, no one speaking, disbelief heavy in the air as they stared down at the wreckage of the hillside below.

"It must have been a landslide," Kenji shouted. "The whole road's out."

It wasn't just out. It was gone.

Obliterated.

Eloise wiped water out of her eyes, trying to make sense of the yawning black crevasse where the road used to be.

"What do we do?" Steph asked, gasping.

"We'll have to go sideways. Cut through the trees. Try to make our own way down through the overgrowth, past the obstruction." Kenji started forward.

"Hold up." Miles held his arm up to block Kenji, rubbing his wet chin with the knuckles of his other hand. "We're not going through there. That's a dumb move. You want to fall into a ravine and break your neck? Get a snake hanging from *your* balls this time? Not to mention, this entire hillside is clearly unstable. We go tramping through the woods, and we could end up smothered to death in a mudslide. We need to regroup and consider our options. I think we should head back."

Head back? Up there? To the resort? The thought made Eloise's stomach grow leaden with dread.

Steph shook her head hard, narrowing her eyes angrily at Miles, blinking rain away. "We need to get help, you said it yourself. I mean, how much time does Ollie have?"

Miles shrugged.

"Maybe there's another road." Eloise knew she was grasping at straws, but she couldn't stand the thought of going back, even if it did seem like the only real option. Maybe they could wait until the storm passed, signal for help somehow, go up onto the Viewing Platform, see if they could spot another way down off the cliff. But Ollie might die while they did that. He might actually *die*.

"Please," she said, her voice cracking. "We have to at least try to find another way down. Let's just hike a little way through the woods. We have to *try*."

"It's not worth the risk," Miles said. "Right now, we've got one person seriously injured. You want to add to that number?"

"Fucking asshole," Tate hissed between his teeth, spit and rainwater spraying from his mouth.

"What did you just call me?" Miles moved forward quickly, closing the gap between himself and Tate. He was the taller of the two by about four inches, but Tate didn't seem to care about that just now. He shoved Miles hard in the chest.

"Stop it," Eloise croaked, her throat raw from shouting, her heartbeat pounding in her ears. Or was that the pounding of the rain? It was impossible to differentiate. The rain was violent, unstoppable. It felt malicious, almost. Malevolent. *Sentient*.

"You touch me again, and you're a dead man," Miles said, turning and walking away from them, heading back up the path. Eloise ran after him, grabbing his hand. Slick, it slid from her grasp. Hot tears burned her cheeks, joining the tributaries of tepid rainwater that slid ceaselessly down her face.

Another crack of lightning tore the sky apart above them, and one of the tall trees that fringed the road erupted with sparks.

Limb-locked with pure terror, Eloise gazed up at the toppling tree, at its encroaching dark shadow, with an almost detached sense of wonderment. Her thoughts were of Bonfire Night, the fireworks display that the council had every year back home, the night sky erupting with showers of pink and gold. She was still thinking about that when someone—she thought it might have been Miles—shoved her hard, and she went flying, losing purchase on the slick ground. She scraped the skin off her palms when she caught herself, but there was no pain.

In the gloom, Eloise heard Steph screaming. The tree began to hiss as the rain fell on its flaming, glowing trunk.

Moaning, animal-like, from the horror of what had nearly happened—the certainty of her almost death—Eloise scrambled to her feet. The fallen tree was between her and the resort. She would need to cut through the woods at an angle to make for the rough direction of the summit. Chest heaving and hitching, she plunged into the woods.

The others seemed to have had the same idea—she could hear Tate yelling intermittently, Steph calling her name, and the sound of tree branches breaking and cracking underfoot as they blundered separately through the wilderness.

With the thunderclouds still blocking the sun, the forest was almost as dark as night. In the low visibility, every noise seemed amplified. By Eloise's feet, there came a hissing sound, like compressed air leaking from a can. Another snake? She spotted a broken branch lying in the dirt and grabbed it, using it to thrash the foliage in front of her, checking for *habu*.

Gulping rain, she blundered through the dark beneath the oppressive canopy of the black trees. Time seemed to lose all relevance. The scenery all looked the same, like she was walking on an endless loop. It was just a constant sea of trees and draped vines and twisting roots, the darkness swelling to fill the spaces between them.

The trip, Tate, Steph, the others—they all seemed a little less *real* now that she was alone.

What am I doing here? Eloise wondered. *Am I really here? In Japan? That doesn't sound right. How did I get here?*

There were ghostly faces amidst the trees, shocked white faces spattered with blood. Their eyes were ragged black holes. When Eloise blinked, they were gone.

Something cracked behind her, low to the ground. She stiffened, hands tightening around her branch, the whorls and knots of the rough wood biting into her raw, abraded skin.

Then a low, moaning voice.

His voice.

Elllll...

She didn't want to turn. Her body did it all on its own, as if invisible fingers had taken hold of her chin and dragged her around.

He was standing there, indistinct in the half-dark, wearing the shirt she'd given him for his birthday.

The one he'd worn that night.

It was drenched black with blood.

"Chris?" she whispered.

He didn't move, didn't speak. But Eloise heard his voice in her head. Read the intent in his glittering black eyes.

You thought you could get away from me, El. But there's nowhere on this Earth you can go to run from me. I can get you wherever you are. And I'm never going to let you forget about me.

Terror spurted through her. He wasn't *here*, of course. No, that was impossible. She was imagining him—the panic and the disorientation combining to conjure a specter of Chris from the deepest recesses of her mind. But reason and rationality didn't seem to mean much when she was alone and lost in the desolation of an Okinawan forest, confronted by her mind's most visceral, most *intimate* fear.

"Leave me alone," she whispered, taking a step back, and something she stepped on gave way with a crack and an ooze. A dead animal? Distracted, she glanced down, and when her gaze flicked back up again, Chris was gone.

Completely disoriented now, blinking rapidly in the mid-day gloaming, she stumbled away, the branch held up in front of her, every chirp and rustle sending shockwaves of terror through her.

He's not here. He's not here. There's no one here, just the others. I need to find them. I need to find someone—

A tree root snagged her foot. She tripped and fell hard, her body weight pinching her fingers painfully between the branch and the hard ground. Sobbing, she used the branch for leverage and pulled herself to her feet, struggling on.

At some point, the rain started to taper off. The heavy storm clouds began to drift, permitting a few straggling shafts of real daylight to shine through. A glimmer of hope kept her moving forward as she picked her way through the undergrowth, feet squelching in her soggy boots.

But then she stumbled to a stop, numb fingers clenched tight around the branch, squinting, her eyes fixed on the *thing* in the mud just feet in front of her.

Steph called her name again, quite close by this time, but when Eloise opened her mouth to call back *Steph*, there was only a dry croak.

No.

She fought an urge to turn and run, her breath rasping in her ears.

Not real.

Squeezing her eyes shut, a moan burst against her clamped lips, but when she opened her eyes again, the inanimate *thing* was still there, a few feet in front of her.

No. Please. Not again.

But it wasn't Chris.

It was Kenji, lying face-down in the muck. He wasn't moving.

PART FOUR

BAD TRIP

"And Darkness and Decay and the Red Death held illimitable dominion over all."
—Edgar Allen Poe, *The Masque of the Red Death*

22

Takagusuku Park, Okinawa, Okinawa Prefecture

The afternoon of Sunday July 14, 2019
(The Day Before Marine Day)

Eloise stood freeze-frame still, clutching the branch. She was so numb with shock that there was no jolt of recognition when Steph came stumbling out from amongst the trees. She felt nothing.

Spotting Kenji immediately, Steph fell to her knees in the wet beside him and started tugging under his armpits. As she yanked on his rain-soaked shirt, he seemed to revive, coughing and spluttering and rolling onto his back. His face was black with mud.

"Eloise." Steph was saying her name. "*Eloise.* Put the fucking branch down."

Startled, Eloise looked down at her hands and, with some surprise, found them still clenched around the knobbed, dripping stick. She realized that Kenji was staring at her, his eyes wide and white in his mud-blackened face.

She flung the branch away from her as if it was a *habu* snake. Then she took a clumsy step towards Kenji, but he stiffened, his eyes narrowing.

"*Kun'na*," he growled, rough Japanese, a hard, defensive tone Eloise had never heard from him before. *Get back*. She shook her head, opened her mouth to speak, and that was when first Tate, then Miles, came crashing out of the trees and into the heavy tension that laced the muggy air.

"What happened?" Tate asked. "You girls all right?"

Kenji ran his tongue around his teeth and spat out a mouthful of black sludge. "Someone hit me," he said, his eyes fixed on Eloise. "With a branch or something."

"I..." Eloise swallowed. "I didn't..."

"It's okay, El," Steph said quickly. "No one thinks it was you."

Kenji coughed and seemed about to speak again but just shook his head. Steph unscrewed the cap from her water bottle and held it to Kenji's mud-smeared lips.

Miles wandered over to the clump of tangled vegetation where Eloise had flung the branch. Frowning, he picked it up and touched the ends, one by one.

"Is his head bleeding?" he asked Steph, who was helping Kenji into a sitting position. She glanced at Miles, then reached around the back of Kenji's head. Kenji hissed, and when Steph withdrew her hand, her fingers were wet with blood.

Miles moved over towards them, and Kenji stiffened again as Miles held the branch out in front of him.

"No blood on this," he said impassively.

"That doesn't prove anything," Tate said, for some reason smiling slightly and looking directly at Eloise. "I have to say I'm shocked, though. I never thought you actually *did it*, El."

There was a horrible moment of protracted silence while Tate's words seemed to hang in the air. From his phrasing, he clearly wasn't referring to Kenji's attack. No, his words implied something else. Something worse.

The air around Eloise seemed to swim, and a hot bubble of nausea filled her throat. For a moment, her vision blurred, a high, whining noise in her ears.

Please, please...no, I need to breathe, don't panic, don't panic.

She drew in a shuddering breath, her vision mercifully clearing. She needed to think. To process the situation. Something bad was happening. The worst. The worst was happening.

A branch cracked, its sharp report shattering the silence as Linh emerged through the trees, eyes wide and magnified behind her glasses. From the look on her face, it seemed she'd heard everything.

"What are you talking about, Tate?" Linh asked. The hard edge in her voice startled the smile off Tate's face as he glanced over his shoulder at her.

"I just…" Eloise started, although she wasn't sure what she was going to say. What the fuck *could* she say? She looked around the group, helpless, pleading. Tate smiled at her, with his shit-eating grin. Linh looked wary, confused. Steph's face had an odd, closed-off look to it. Miles's expression was clear and mild, like they were discussing the weather, or something equally mundane. And Kenji. Kenji was still glaring at her with accusation in his eyes.

Accusation—and fear.

"It's *fine*, El," Steph said. "Don't say anything. We need to get back…back to Satoko and Ollie. If there's someone dangerous on this cliff, then we need—"

"There's someone dangerous, all right," Tate said. His grin was back again.

Something tickled Eloise's cheek, a fly or something. She brushed it off and found the back of her hand glistening. Not a fly. She could taste the tears now, hot and salty in her throat. "I didn't…" she tried again. "Kenji, I…"

But Steph came around beside her and tucked her arm under hers. "Don't talk, El," she whispered, and all Eloise could do was watch helplessly as Miles grabbed Kenji's hand and hauled him out of the muck.

"Come on," Steph said in a voice with more life in it, false brightness. "Let's get back. *Now.* As fast as we can."

The storm was a distant memory. The late afternoon sun sparkled, and the world around them was green and refreshed by the time the group arrived back at the Viewing Platform. The air smelled heavily of petrichor—that after-rain scent Eloise always used to find so comforting.

They were all exhausted and sore, soaked to the skin and stiff with mud. But Kenji seemed to be doing relatively okay. He'd been able to walk back up the hill with them unaided, at least. He'd barely spoken to anyone, responding with noncommittal grunts, until they'd stopped trying, and the group had ended up hiking in silence.

Eloise's mind whirled with panicked, miserable thoughts. The walk back had been like a grim death march. Tate knew what she'd done. He knew about Chris. By the grin on his face, he'd relish the opportunity to tell the others. And Kenji thought she'd...what? Bludgeoned him in the back of the head? She hadn't. She *wouldn't*.

Ollie was lying where they'd left him, propped up on a pile of backpacks. His face was gray, and he was very still, but the gentle rise and fall of his shirt reassured Eloise that he was at least still breathing.

There was no sign of Satoko.

Kenji lay down on some dry leaves beneath the platform, groaning, while Steph washed some of the blood off the back of his head and assessed the damage. The others looked around for Satoko. Maybe she'd gone to pee, something like that.

"She wouldn't have just left, would she?" Linh asked, wiping her glasses against her shirt. "Maybe she got worried and came after us?"

"In the middle of a storm?" Tate scoffed. "She's not *that* dumb."

"She's not dumb at all, you jerk," Linh said darkly, and it was so unlike her to be outwardly hostile that Tate simply stared at her. His mouth was slightly open, and his bright blue eyes were surprised and affronted.

"Might want to see this," Miles called out, and they all moved over to where he stood, close to the path that led away from the platform to the maze of the resort's trails.

Eloise knew what it was instantly. The darkness soaked into the ground. Even though the rain seemed to have washed most of it away, there were still streaks of crimson remaining.

It was blood.

A lot of blood.

And in the middle of the dark patch, there was something like a pebble, or a small stone, looped through a black hair tie.

A ripple went through the group as they all recognized the object.

Eloise stooped and picked it up. It dangled from her fingers in the glistening sunshine.

It was Linh's good luck charm.

The one she'd given to Satoko.

Satoko was gone.

23

"I need that lighter, Steph. Got to make a fire if we're going to be stuck here overnight. It's going to get dark real soon." Tate had stripped to the waist and was hauling sticks and brush around. The others ignored him. Eloise, Steph, and Linh sat huddled together by Ollie, passing around bottles of spring water. Steph offered Eloise a granola bar, but the sight of food made her stomach roil, and she looked away wordlessly.

No one had spoken much. They'd compared phones to see if anyone had service, but they were all reading *No Signal*. Miles had gone up to the top of the platform to get a lay of the land and see if there were any other visible trails down. Kenji was sitting away from the others in silence, dabbing a wet, balled-up t-shirt to the back of his head. The heat had returned full force, causing coils of steam to rise from their damp clothes.

Eloise was waiting for someone to accuse her of attacking Satoko. For Tate to start in on her again about hurting Kenji. But that didn't happen. There was just a lot of silence. And she thought maybe that was worse.

Did she hurt Kenji? *Could* she have? She wasn't sure anymore.

Why, though? What for?

She wasn't angry with Kenji. Not really. And Satoko. She couldn't have done anything to Satoko, even if she'd wanted to, which she *didn't*. Anyway, none of them could have been responsible for Satoko's going missing. Not in the short amount of time they were all separated. It just didn't line up. Whatever happened to Satoko, it had to be unconnected. It couldn't be the same person who hurt Kenji.

Unless there was more than one attacker? Two or more, a coordinated group, working in tandem?

But why? *Why hurt any of us?*

It didn't make any sense.

Maybe something else happened to Satoko. An accident. A wild animal attack. Eloise tried to think what kind of animal attacked humans. All that blood—

She couldn't make any sense of what had happened to Satoko. Kenji, then? He was bludgeoned in the back of the head. A human being had to have done that. Blunt-force trauma, maybe a rock, a tree branch, yes, *okay*, or it could have been something like the butt of a gun.

A gun.

This isn't the movies, Eloise.

And guns weren't exactly a dime a dozen in Japan.

Wait. The old fire pit. The canteen. The military squadron stickers.

Eloise thought about what Tate had said back at the hostel. How so much of Okinawa was taken up by military bases. Could someone—

"Steph?" Tate's terse voice yanked Eloise out of her thoughts. "I said, give me the lighter."

Scowling, Steph tossed it at Tate, hitting him in his broad, shiny, bare chest. He grunted with irritation, a stupid, bovine sort of noise, and picked it up awkwardly out of the dirt.

They all watched, with a detached sort of interest, as Tate struggled to get a fire going. The kindling and stuff were dry enough, protected from the rains by the hulking platform. But it wasn't catching.

"Give me that," Miles said, descending the last few platform steps and snatching the lighter from Tate, whose face stiffened with anger. After rearranging Tate's kindling, Miles had the beginnings of a fire smoldering and flickering within a few seconds.

"Anything?" Linh asked Miles, who shrugged.

"Nothing I could see. It's all overgrown woodland on this cliff for miles around. Then sugar cane fields beyond that. No other roads, and if there's any hiking trails down, I couldn't make them out from up there."

Tate stared into the flames, mouth twisting.

"Here's what I'm thinking," Tate said, although nobody had asked. "I'm thinking our only option is to try signaling for help. There are military planes and helicopters flying all over this island. We only need one to spot us."

"What are you suggesting here?" Steph's voice was faint, tremulous, edged with fear. "We go up onto the viewing platform and spell out the letters SOS in dead branches? Then what? We just sit around waiting to be rescued and hope Ollie doesn't kick the bucket before the US military deigns to get off their asses and save us?"

"Yeah." Tate stared her down, mulish. "That's exactly what I'm suggesting."

"You mean just sit around and hope whoever attacked Kenji and Satoko doesn't come back to finish the job?" Linh's eyes were wide and frightened in her waxy, pale face, and Eloise found she couldn't look at her. Linh was her constant, her comfort person. Nothing ever rattled Linh. But now she looked like she was going to cry, and there was something so *wrong* about that that it filled Eloise with a dull, hopeless panic.

"We're making a leap here, assuming it was some random psycho stalker," Tate said, a hint of a grin playing about his lips, his gaze on Eloise.

Steph's eyes narrowed, her lips thinning. "El didn't hurt anyone," she said through gritted teeth, "so just fucking drop it."

Kenji inspected the balled-up t-shirt. It was blush pink now from his blood. He still hadn't looked at Eloise. Her heart wrenched, thinking about the books he'd given to her. That act of selfless kindness. How much those books had sustained her during that first lost year in Japan. And, as it turned out, he'd never wanted anything from her in return.

She wanted to say something to him now, but she didn't know what. Or how. And she was afraid that if she pushed it, misspoke, he'd turn the harsh accusations simmering in his brown eyes into words, giving form to them. Making them real.

"Relax," Tate said, wiping sweat off his brow, frowning at Steph. "I never said she did."

"Occam's Razor," Linh said, her voice low as she looked back and forth between Steph and Tate. "The simplest possibility *is* that someone from our group hit Kenji. As for Satoko, though, I can't—"

"Hold on," Miles said. "Let's think about this rationally. All right?"

There was silence while the fire spat and crackled, and nobody spoke.

"Say one of us hit Kenji, snuck up behind him, and cracked him on the head. The question you've got to ask yourselves is, who here would have the motive to do that?"

Eloise wished he hadn't said that. She could think of a few candidates. Tate, for one. His jealousy was palpable. He'd always had a hard-on for Steph. It was obvious that he'd been blindsided by the revelation of the sordid beach hookup. Clearly, he'd never seen Kenji as a threat.

And then, the second person likely to be harboring a grudge was Steph herself. They'd all caught the incandescent rage in her eyes. Witnessed her melting down after Kenji had bragged about...what was the verb Miles had used? *Porking* her. Could that have made Steph angry enough to attack Kenji?

The third candidate was the worst one of all. Because in terms of optics, who had more motive than Eloise herself? She hadn't been fooling anyone about her crush on him. But Kenji had rejected her and hooked up with Steph. And if you factored in what had happened with Chris—

Tate caught her eye just then, his lips curling in another grin.

Nausea surged, jets of saliva spurting over her tongue. The muscles in her alimentary canal went into spasm, and she turned away, gulping spring water from her bottle, trying not to puke.

I didn't hit Kenji. I didn't. I've never hurt anyone. Never. Never, never...

But as the sweet spring water washed the tide of acid back down her throat, something occurred to her.

Wait a minute.

Now, her mind seemed to be running on double time, her thoughts rushing past her, frenetic and blurred. There was something else, another reason why Tate would have wanted to hurt, possibly even *kill* Kenji. When Steph had insinuated, if not actually outright *claimed* earlier, that Tate was involved in something inappropriate with the underage students in his classes...something highly illegal...she'd said that in front of *Kenji*, who was a *teacher* at the junior high school. If Kenji decided to pursue this and investigate further, what would he find? What kind of repercussions could that have for Tate?

Everyone on that platform heard it, not sure about the others, waiting down below. Our voices could have carried. What if Tate's trying to silence all of us? Could he really be that desperate? That insane?

Eloise suppressed a violent shudder. She tried not to make it obvious that she was watching Tate from underneath her eyelashes. If she spoke up in defense of herself now, or in defense of Steph, that would only agitate the situation. Perhaps she should stay quiet and let Tate think he was merely one of a pool of possible suspects. Who knew what he might do if he felt exposed, how vicious he might become. A blow to the head like the one Kenji received could kill someone.

It was attempted *murder.*

And she was afraid for herself, too. A weaselly sense of self-preservation. Filling her with sickening guilt. Because if she took a shot at Tate, he'd tell the others what he so clearly knew about her. He'd lay it all bare.

She risked a glance at Tate, but he wasn't looking at her. He was scowling at Miles now.

"If you're implying I had anything to do with this, then you're wrong," Tate said coldly, his voice steady. "Listen. I was going to bring this up anyway. I saw someone. In the woods, during the storm. It was a guy. A tall guy. He was wearing dark camo gear. Must be one of the Marines stationed on this island. Remember that canteen we found earlier? The squadron stickers? What's a random US Marine doing skulking around up on these cliffs anyway? This site's supposed to be a no-go zone for anyone with SOFA status. So, what's he doing *here*?"

There was a moment of protracted silence. Tate laughed.

"Of course, you don't fucking believe me."

Eloise swallowed, her throat suddenly bone-dry, and brought the trembling bottle to her lips to gulp more spring water.

Maybe it was a gun, after all.

Assuming Tate was telling the truth, of course.

Which isn't fucking likely.

"Shit," Linh whispered. "Maybe he's right. Maybe there's someone else up on these cliffs with us. Someone dangerous. I mean, what happened to that deer? All that blood. Maybe a hunter, some lunatic survivalist, and he happened across Satoko while we were in the woods..."

Steph brought her fingers to her mouth. "It's not like it matters *who* it is. Whether it's a stranger or it's one of us, either way, we're trapped up here with *someone* who's got an actual screw loose. Like in some dumb fucking horror movie, and nobody knows where we are. Isn't that just fucking *great?*"

"Just relax, Steph, okay? Mishka. Remember her? Ollie's fiancée? She knows we're up here." Linh reached out and touched Steph's arm. Steph shook her off, gnawing at her nails, her eyes wild and unfixed.

Eloise really needed Steph to calm down. If Steph lost her shit, Eloise had a feeling she wouldn't be far behind her.

Ollie grunted something then, startling them. He must have woken up at some point, although he hadn't opened his eyes. His closed lids looked like two slivers of raw liver, purple and distended. Linh leaned over him, bringing her ear to his mouth.

"He says...Mishka's gone. She was so pissed at him for coming with us that she's taken the ferry to Ishigaki Island without him. They were supposed to go snorkeling. It's a three-day trip. She won't be back until late Tuesday."

"We don't need to rely on some *random girl* to raise the alarm," Tate snorted. "You people always underestimate me, don't you? Listen, in the top drawer of my desk in the faculty room is a letter explaining where we are and what we're doing. It's basic S.O.P for urbexers. You always make sure someone knows where you've gone in case you don't come back."

"Oh!" Steph threw up her hands. "A letter! Why didn't you say so? We're *saved*!"

Tate flipped Steph the bird, expressionless.

There was another silence while they all mulled over their situation.

"It sounds like we're stuck here until Tuesday at the earliest. When we fail to show up for work, and Ollie fails to meet up with Mishka." Linh uncapped her water bottle and took a long gulp. Her hand was shaking, the flimsy plastic bottle crinkling beneath her white knuckles. She was wearing the good-luck charm, the magatama, on her wrist again. There were still flecks of dried blood on it. "It's just an impromptu camping trip," she continued, her voice high, a faint note of near hysteria. "In an abandoned, snake-infested ruin with a crazed murderer running around. That's just the kind of relaxing Marine Day break I was hoping for."

"I think everyone needs to just take a breath and calm down," Tate said. "The situation is just being blown way out of proportion here. We'll signal a passing plane or a helicopter, they'll send someone to come rescue us, and we'll all be laughing about this later on tonight over double cheeseburgers and root beer. Trust me."

The silence hung heavy. None of them trusted Tate. And he was trying not to show it, but Eloise could see that he was getting antsy. That panic was setting in. That was it, the thing that had always annoyed her most about Tate. His need for approval, to be liked by everyone. But he'd blown that, attacking Steph up on the platform earlier. For a moment, Eloise was back up there, moments before the sky cracked open above them, convinced that Tate was going to strangle Steph to death. She could still see her friend's livid, purple face, distorted with terror.

Fuck Tate.

"We need to find Satoko," Steph said. "She must be hurt…injured. We can't just sit here. We have to do something."

"It's not worth the risk," Tate said, folding his arms across his bare chest. "For all we know, there's a dangerous psycho out there roaming around. And we're trapped up on this cliff with them. We need to stick together, safety in numbers."

"*God*, you're a piece of shit," Linh said, and Tate blinked, surprise and hurt in his eyes.

He really has no idea how he comes across, Eloise thought, with a kind of horrified awe. Maybe he was a sociopath, one of those people born without any empathy but able to observe it in others, to imitate. Masking their own pathology through pantomime.

"Weren't you sleeping together?" Linh asked him, and Tate stiffened, his blue eyes going cold. "Don't you *care* about what happens to her?"

"No," Tate said simply, after a long pause. "I don't care. All right, Linh? I don't fucking care. And you might think you do, but is it enough to risk your own safety? Your *life*? If so, then be my fucking guest. Go look for her. Go on."

Linh and Tate glared at one another. Linh's eyes narrowed with disgust and contempt. Tate's expression was almost nonchalant—as if he actually believed himself to have the moral high ground.

"I'll look for her," Miles said. "I was planning on heading out anyway. See if I can find a hiking trail down, maybe a stream we can follow."

"You're leaving us?" Eloise croaked, her voice faint and cracked from disuse. It felt like she hadn't spoken in a long time. A new clutch of fear, cold and implacable, seized her when she considered the prospect of Miles *leaving* them. He felt like the only impartial party, the only *capable* one among them. And with Ollie in such a bad way and Kenji injured, that would leave everything to Eloise, Steph, and Linh if Tate tried to...to hurt someone. The three of them could probably take him, but what if he had a weapon of some kind?

What if he's got a gun?

The thought was sudden, crazed, violating. Eloise pushed it out of her mind almost violently, scrambling to her feet, not sure what she was doing, but knowing that she had to do *something*. She couldn't stay here.

"I'll come with you," she said.

"El." Suddenly, Steph was beside her, her fingers gripping her elbow. "Don't, El. Please."

She looked back at Steph, blinking. Her friend's eyes were very wide and very beautiful in her mud-spattered face. Up close like this, she could see the individual pores on Steph's skin. For a moment, she wasn't sure she recognized her. Faces are weird, she thought distractedly. All the different moving parts. The glistening openings of the mouth and eyes. Skin covered in tiny hairs and tiny holes. How disgusting was that? *Humans* were disgusting, when you thought about it. Just bags of flesh. Animated bags of flesh.

"El?" There was concern in Steph's eyes now, along with fear. "Stay with us, okay? We'll...We'll keep each other safe."

"We'll be safer without *her* around," Tate sniffed. "Go on, Eloise. Fuck off. Guess you're a traitor on top of everything else. No wonder you had to run all the way to Japan. No one wanted you back home."

There was a charged pause, during which the air seemed to shimmer with the oppressive heat, and the creaks and the chirps and the thrumming of the cicadas intensified all around them as if someone had just turned up the volume.

Steph's fingers tightened painfully around Eloise's arm. Eloise squeezed her eyes shut and the dried snail trails of tears on her cheeks cracked. Then there was motion beside her, Miles charging forward.

Tate danced back, his eyes bright and frightened, grabbing something from behind him and brandishing it at Miles. It was a black tube, glass sparkling on one end. His flashlight. Silent, the two men faced off against one another, neither moving a muscle.

"I'll take that," Miles said, watching Tate carefully, as if Tate was some dangerous predatory animal.

"The fuck you will," Tate snarled.

"It's getting dark soon. You've got the fire. Give me the flashlight."

"Use your phone."

"I don't have a phone."

Tate laughed in disbelief, eyes flicking to Eloise. "Fuck, use hers."

"Give me...the flashlight."

Tate hesitated, chewing his lip. Then there was a momentary tussle, a painful-sounding thud, and it was all over. Tate on the ground, on his back in the black mud, Miles offering the flashlight to Eloise.

Numbly, she took it.

"Make yourself useful and light some signal fires up top," Miles said to Tate, who glowered up at him from the muck, all his dignity gone. "Light three fires, equal distance apart."

"I know how to make a fucking signal fire," Tate hissed.

"I'm sure you do," Miles said mildly.

Eloise looked down at the black flashlight in her hand. There were letters around the rim spelling out *Maglite*. It was heavy, solid. It could have been the thing that hit Kenji.

"Come on," Miles said, touching her arm very gently as he passed her. His touch seemed to crackle against her skin like static electricity.

Clutching the flashlight, she hesitated, eyes flicking back and forth between Linh and Steph.

If she left them with Tate...

"El," Steph said. "Don't be ridiculous. Seriously? You're abandoning me to go off with some guy?"

Then she laughed.

If only she hadn't laughed, El might have been mollified. She might have brushed aside the hypocrisy of her words. Steph was the one who'd abandoned her alone in Tokyo in the early morning hours. Wasn't she? *Steph* was the one who'd stabbed her in the back, hooking up with Kenji last night. For no reason. No real reason. Just to hurt her.

Wasn't she?

She could have brushed it all off if Steph hadn't laughed at her.

"I'll be back soon," she said, not looking at any of them. She kept her eyes trained straight ahead as she turned and followed Miles's broad, tall back. As she followed him into the golden haze of the oncoming evening.

24

It was dark inside the cave. *Dark as the grave*, a voice whispered inside Eloise's mind, the words repeating, echoing until she blocked them out.

She moved tentatively forward, almost blind, sliding the toes of her boots across the slick stone. The flashlight's skinny beam picked out one or two details at a time: slimy limestone stalactites dangling like precarious spears over their heads, the wet stone floor ahead, knobby and bumpy and treacherous, the glistening green walls. A scant subterranean river ran alongside the path, its slow-moving waters shimmering like dark treacle, or maybe even coagulating blood.

Miles held her wrist tight to prevent her from slipping, even though Eloise was the one leading the way. She had the blunt end of the black Maglite tucked tight against her shoulder, and she held it steady there in one tight fist, almost like it was a knife, and she was gearing up to stab someone.

They'd stumbled across the cave just a few hundred yards away from the old cemetery. The cemetery itself was small in scale, just a cluster of ancient, sun-bleached stone tablets, half-overgrown in a sun-dappled grove. It really wasn't far at all from the waterpark. The hotel developers had built their resort almost right on top of it. It felt wrong, somehow, to be there. Standing amidst the monuments of lives lost to time. *Trespassing*. On sacred ground.

The grave markers had all been old. Really old. The epitaphs smoothed away by time and wind. The stones furred with yellow-green moss. There were about a dozen of them and a large tomb with a curious humped roof that was built into the hillside. It reminded Eloise of a stone pizza oven, of all the ridiculous thoughts to have. The sight of it, such a grand monument to an unknown person, left untended out here in the wilderness and forgotten to time, made her feel sad and sorry and creeped her out at the same time.

But inside the cave, it was cold and almost silent, save for the occasional gloomy *plink* of dripping water and the dull whistle of moving air. In the dark, Eloise's remaining senses had already begun to heighten. Miles's grip on her wrist was tight and hot, his skin almost burning hers, and she could hear him breathing softly and regularly through his nose.

"If you rotate the head, you can widen the beam. Might help," Miles suggested. Eloise brought her hands together, twisting the bulbous head of the flashlight with one sharp, spasmodic movement, and a wide beam spilled out all over the floor.

Miles was still holding her wrist.

"Good," he said throatily. "Just like that."

She wanted to see his expression, but she couldn't shine the flashlight in his face, of course. He was indistinct, a conglomeration of smudgy shadows that undulated slightly in the dim light.

Eloise concentrated instead on the flashlight's beam as it fell on a cluster of stone tablets. They were nestled amid a nest of stalagmites that thrust up from the cave floor like obscene fingers. Eloise got her phone from her pocket and switched it on, the glow from its screen weak and insipid. Would turning up the brightness wear the charge out sooner? It was at 17%. Better not risk it.

She held the phone up in front of her and used its flash to take several shots of the stone tablets.

The shutter sound—obnoxiously loud but impossible to disable on Japanese models—was amplified in the cramped space. The phone's flash lit up the cave in brief slices of stark brightness, making visible the green-slime walls, dribbling wet and shiny, and what looked like a tiny shrine to some sort of deity. There were old green coins piled up in front of the tablets and a pewter censer filled with dark sand and studded with the burned nubs of incense sticks.

"What are those?" Miles asked. "Can you read them?"

Insecurity made her defensive, and she shrugged, although he wouldn't have been able to see that in the dark. "Not really. I mean, they're pretty eroded. And it looks like really old Japanese. See how it's a mix of katakana and kanji?"

Miles leaned into her personal space, checking out the photo on her screen.

"Oh yeah, absolutely. That's old Japanese, all right," he said, making her blow air out of her nose in amusement. "Yeah, I'd know it anywhere."

"I can read a few of the characters," she conceded, "but I don't really know what it's saying. I'm not sure if it's to commemorate someone who died, like an epitaph, or if it's something to do with worshipping *kami*—you know, gods."

"Mmm," Miles said, apparently not all that interested. Eloise studied the engraving on the markers again. Writing, scraped vertically into stone beneath some kind of crest—three magatama symbols, tails touching.

OCEAN, ETERNITY, WOMB, CRIMSON, FIRE, REBIRTH

Whatever that meant.

Shrugging, she switched her phone off and pocketed it once more.

"Oh, hey," Miles said, picking something black and flat up from the stone floor off to the side of the tablets. "This your friend's?"

It *looked* like Satoko's hiking flask, but Eloise couldn't be completely sure. And she was distracted by how odd it seemed for Miles to have just assumed that she and Satoko were friends.

"Maybe," she said. "Do you think she was here? In this cave?"

"I don't think it's just a cave," Miles said, taking hold of Eloise's wrist again and directing the flashlight beam. "I can feel air moving. I think it's a tunnel."

Eloise opened her mouth to suggest heading back, but Miles spoke over her thoughts.

"We should check it out. Your friend might be hurt down there."

Now, she'd sound callous and selfish if she said anything about leaving. The cave was horrible—dark, dank, and claustrophobic, but she didn't want Miles to think she was one of *those* girls. Weak, shrieking girls who freaked out over bugs and snakes and ghost stories.

So, when he started off down the tunnel, she went with him.

"I've been wanting to tell you," he said conversationally as they made their way through the dripping dark, "I'm sorry about the way I spoke earlier. You know, to Stephanie. On the platform. I got the sense you weren't too impressed."

"Uh…I wasn't. But don't you think *Steph*'s the one you should be apologizing to?"

He stopped smiling, his glittering teeth disappearing.

"Hard pass. I'm not sorry for what I said to Steph. She had it coming."

"Wow, seriously?" Annoyed, Eloise shone the flashlight right in his face, getting satisfaction from the way his pupils contracted to tiny pricks.

"Wait, you're misunderstanding me." He winced and held a hand up to protect his eyes. "Listen, Steph's perfectly within her rights to fuck as many guys as she likes. The issue is her attitude about it. Shame's a two-person game. Nobody can shame you without your permission. You have to be complicit in it. The sooner she stops feeling guilty about her life choices, the happier she'll be. I was trying to do her a favor."

"Your mental gymnastics are insane," Eloise said, still not mollified. *Shame's a two-person game.* Was that true? And if so, what did that say about her?

"I'm just sorry you had to hear it," Miles continued. "I never meant to use vulgar language like that in front of you."

She snorted. "You say fuck constantly."

"That's different."

"Is it?"

"Sure, it is. There are worse words than fuck. Hey, have you ever heard about *Kurombo Gama*? The Cave of the Negroes?"

Eloise blinked. It took a beat for her to realize he'd changed the subject.

"I don't...*what*?"

"It happened after the Battle of Okinawa. Sometime just before the end of the Pacific War. The US occupied the island then, and some of the Marines, a long way from home, you know, they started, well, acting out. Three of them, real young guys they were, they used to come by this tiny rural village every week. They were after the women, you see. And the girls. They were convinced the Okinawan villagers weren't a threat. They knew they weren't armed."

Eloise blinked, wondering what this was leading to.

"So, they kept coming back and helping themselves. Every week. But what they didn't know was that the villagers were setting up an ambush. There were these Japanese soldiers—holdouts—still hiding out in the woods, and *they* had guns. So, the next time the three marines rolled up to the village, the villagers had backup. All it took was five or six shots, and the problem was dealt with. The village was safe. But now the villagers are like...shit. Where do we hide the bodies? We've got three dead US Marines here. Well, there was a cave nearby. And, not far inside the entrance to the cave, there was this really deep drop. So that's where they tossed the Marines."

Eloise swallowed. It was audible in the dark, a thick, glottal sound.

"This was what? 1945? Anyway, the Marines are never seen again. They're written off as missing in action. In like 1997, I think, one of the villagers, he was a kid at the time, he's all grown up now, and he can't take it anymore. It's a different world, and the secret is eating him alive. So he goes to the authorities, and they search the cave. Eventually, the USMC gets wind of it. They identified each of the Marines by dental records. Pretty fucked up, huh?"

Eloise swallowed again, her throat hurting. "Is that true? Where was this?"

"Huh? Somewhere north of here, I think. Not sure. It's not important." Miles took a step forward, forcing Eloise to back up, her boots sliding across the slimy limestone. "Come on, let's keep going."

"Wait. Why did you just tell me that story?" Eloise widened her stance, bracing her feet as she pried Miles's fingers off her wrist. There was a little red warning light flashing busily on and off in the deepest recesses of her brain. Chris always said Eloise never knew when to leave well enough alone.

No. Don't think about him now. Not in here.

"Huh. You know, I'm not sure?" Miles chuckled. "I was thinking we should watch out for any sudden drops. I guess it just popped into my head, and I don't know why, I just said it."

"You could have just said, watch out for drops." She knew she sounded churlish, difficult, but she couldn't help it. "That—That *story*...it's horrible. And you didn't have to say that stuff about, you know, the *women and girls*."

"I don't get why it's such a big..." Miles trailed off, his fingers grasping for Eloise's wrist again, even as she yanked her hand away. "Oh, okay. I get it. I'm sorry. Shit. You must think I'm a total creep. I didn't mean to freak you out. I swear, I just wasn't thinking. I do this a lot. It was one of the things that really pissed Katie off. She used to say that I was—"

"Your fiancée?" Eloise interrupted.

Miles said nothing for a few moments, but she could hear him swallow.

"Yeah."

"You still haven't told me much—anything—about her."

"There's nothing to tell." He sounded sulky, all of a sudden, like a little boy. "Not anymore."

"Okay. I'm sorry." Apologizing came as naturally to Eloise as breathing. In confrontational situations, most people respond with one of the three fs: fight, flight, or freeze. But Eloise...Eloise fawned.

Miles was silent for a moment, the air between them heavy, as if her apology had annoyed him.

"You don't need to say sorry," he said eventually. "*I'm* sorry. I didn't mean to creep you out. This whole situation is fucked-up enough. Listen, let's just see what's through this tunnel. It looks like it slopes down."

Eloise led with the flashlight. They continued in silence for a while until she came to a stop, surprising Miles, who briefly placed his hands on her waist, making her gasp.

"Sorry," he murmured. "Why'd you stop?"

Eloise flashed the light in an arc in front of them. "It splits here."

One fork ended in a cave-in a few feet ahead. The other few forks shot off at haphazard angles, the tunnels narrowing where the floor and ceiling grew closer together, like slowly closing mouths.

"We should probably head back," Eloise said. "It's like a maze in here."

"No, it's all right," Miles said. "All we have to do is mirror ourselves. We take every right turn going in and every left turn going back. That way, we'll be fine."

That didn't make much sense to Eloise, but she stayed quiet, stuck close to Miles as they went right at fork after fork after fork.

The tunnel seemed to be sinking deeper and deeper into the rock of the cliff. Fear was starting to clamor at the back of Eloise's brain, claustrophobia setting in as the glistening walls seemed to shrink around them.

"I think that—"

Then Eloise stopped talking, the words dying in her throat.

There was something—a rasping sound—up ahead. It sounded like breathing—the gurgling whistle of someone struggling for their final breath.

A death rattle.

The panicked beam of her flashlight caught a swoop of red fabric in the gloom ahead. A hanging curtain of dark, dull hair, a filthy grey sock, and the ankle inside of it. Cocked at an impossible angle, as if badly broken, the foot dragged soundlessly across the wet stone floor.

Eloise's heart bashed against her ribcage. She couldn't swallow. Couldn't breathe.

She blundered backward into Miles's warmth but barely registered the feel of his hands cupping her upper arms, his voice in her ear saying: *What, what's wrong?*

Every animal instinct within her was shrieking at her to turn and run, *run now,* but she couldn't. How could she turn her back on it—the *thing* dragging itself along the cramped passage up ahead—

If I turn and run, it'll know. It'll be alerted. It'll come after me.

Eloise managed to make a sound, at last, a strangled mewl in her throat, like a choked kitten.

"Miles," she croaked. "Did you see..." but she couldn't finish.

Miles's fingers closed around her hand, the one that was gripping the flashlight, and he lifted it, Eloise's limp hand floating upwards as well. The beam spilled out ahead of them, down the tunnel. It was bare limestone, dripping, empty.

"I thought I saw..." Eloise's chattering teeth came down hard over her tongue, drawing blood. "I saw someone..."

"I didn't see anything. What's wrong? You're shaking."

"It was...I think it was a woman. Wearing red. There was something wrong with her, the way she was moving. She was *dragging* herself."

The red maiden...Tate's ghost stories...But that's im—

"There's nothing there, Eloise." Miles interrupted her thoughts, his voice firm, authoritative. "I was looking where you were looking, and there was nothing there. Okay?"

"No," she whimpered. "I saw it."

"All right. All right. Let's go back. Let's go back outside. Come on, now." He spoke softly, as if placating a fanciful child, his hand on her shoulder, turning her.

"No!" she groped for his hand, clawing it off her with fear-frozen fingers. "I don't want to turn my back on...on whatever that was. If I turn away, it'll come back. *Please*."

Miles paused. She could almost hear him thinking.

"All right," he said. "Here, take the flashlight. You got it? Okay. Now, put your hands on my shoulders and spread your legs."

"Spread my *what*?"

"Jump up and wrap your legs around my waist. You can keep watch over my shoulder with the flashlight while I get us both out. I'll feel my way along the wall. You okay? Still with me?"

Eloise mewled again, too terrified to care now about how she was coming across. Clumsily, she hauled herself up, clamping her legs tight around Miles, digging her chin into his shoulder. She trained the flashlight's jittering beam back down the passageway. It was empty, but she could somehow still *see* the tattered crimson fabric jerking and swaying, the fishbelly-white leg, the dragging foot.

Miles's chest was warm and solid against her as he carried her back along the dark tunnel. She felt his heart pounding away against hers, and she realized she could smell him. He smelled like soap, like sweat. Or was she smelling herself?

The metallic tang of fear still coated her tongue and the back of her throat as the light of the outside began to seep in, brightening the narrow walls around them.

But when they finally emerged, the fading light of the afternoon wasn't the comfort Eloise had hoped for. It would be getting dark soon. And it looked like they'd come out of the cave somewhere else. Not the same way they'd come in at all. The surroundings looked ominous, the shadowy trees unfamiliar. She clung to Miles even after he'd set her down, wanting the comfort of his contact. He obliged, holding her by the elbows, listening as she explained what she'd seen in the cave.

"You don't believe me," she said, the inflection at the end of her sentence going up slightly in a way that was almost a question, but not quite. "You think I'm crazy. Not right in the head."

Miles reached for his back pocket and pulled out his hip flask. Eloise grabbed it from him before he could offer it to her, spun the cap off with numb fingers, and took a greedy swig. The whiskey burned the back of her throat. The heat of it warmed her inside. A flood of relief. But not enough.

"I believe you. And I don't think you're crazy."

Eloise narrowed her eyes, not sure if he was just humoring her.

"I saw...fuck it. I saw something on the hike up here. Thought I was losing my damn mind if I'm being honest, but if you saw something, too..." He trailed off, rubbing his knuckles across his chin.

"What? What did you see?"

"I saw...a guy. You know, like Tate was talking about. I don't think he was lying about that. But it wasn't a Marine *I* saw. It was just some guy. He was wearing camo, yeah, but I'm pretty sure it was fake stuff. Like something you'd wear to play paintball. And he had...had the back of his head missing."

Eloise's trembling muscles locked up painfully. What were the chances of them both *imagining* dead people in the resort? Seeing Chris in the forest made sense. She saw Chris all the time. The stress of the situation could have, when combined with Tate's dumb ghost stories, pushed her miserable, broken mind into imagining some kind of horrific dead woman in the cave, too. But if Miles wasn't just lying to her—if he'd seen something as well...

"Did he...did *it* see you?"

"Yeah. But it was weird. He just kinda...stared at me. Then he turned around and walked away. The whole back half of his head was gone. You could see the rim of bone. Looked like half a coconut filled with blood."

"God." The skin on Eloise's arms shrank and tightened.

"There's something wrong with this place, I think. I don't think it's *ghosts,* or some kind of curse, anything that trite. Maybe it's more like we're seeing echoes of people who've been here before us. Imprints of souls. Old buildings, places like this resort that have a bad past...I feel like old energy gets trapped in the air. In the stones. Am I making any sense?"

"No," Eloise whispered. "Maybe. I don't know."

"Listen, that thing in the cave, whatever it was, if it wanted to hurt us, it had its chance, and it didn't take it. Like the paintball guy. Right?"

"Maybe it was waiting for the right opportunity." Eloise gnawed a flake of dry skin off her bottom lip, her gaze fixed on the empty mouth of the cave behind him.

What if it needs to get us alone...scattered, vulnerable, helpless.

Miles shrugged. "Yeah, maybe. But maybe not. This is my guess, though. I think these things, these visions...they can't actually *do* anything to us. Just think of them as projections. Old movie scenes, playing away eternally on a blank wall. It's just this old resort showing us its scars. But there's no one *physically* up on these cliffs except us. That's what I think, anyway."

"But there *is* someone here who wants to hurt us. Look at what happened to Kenji. If it wasn't the Marine—or the paintball guy—then who was it?"

Miles's eyes drifted away from Eloise, and her chest prickled.

"You think it was me."

"No, I don't. But the others do. You've picked up on that, haven't you? I saw it in your eyes. And you have to admit, Eloise, you've got motive."

"It *wasn't* me."

"I *know.*"

Eloise swallowed, the bittersweetness of the whiskey aftertaste on her tongue.

"If it was...was someone *human*, then I'd think Tate..."

Miles huffed air through his nose.

"Tate's the type of guy to shove a woman around, sure. We've seen that. But trying to take out someone his own size? No. He's a coward, if anything. I'm not buying it." Miles reached for her face and tucked a stray lock of hair behind her ear. The gesture of familiarity reminded her of when he'd touched her last night in the ocean, but it no longer felt like an imposition of her personal space.

Instead, it felt...comforting.

"You should stick close to me," Miles continued, his voice low, conspiratorial, although there was no one else around. "I don't think we can trust any of your friends. All right, El? I've got you. And even if the others are against you, I'll protect you."

She looked up into his steady eyes, wishing she was taller, wishing she could bury her face in his neck again and breathe in. She settled for butting her head weakly against his chest instead.

A part of her realized she was falling into a familiar old pattern. She'd gone through life always looking to the nearest man. For guidance, for protection. First, her dad. She'd run to him over scraped knees, closet monsters, and neighborhood bullies. Then he left. After that, it was Chris. Her lodestar, her true north. She'd relied on Chris for emotional support when she was up against an impossible essay deadline or warring with her flatmates. And now she was doing it again.

Turning to a man.

Taking the easy way out.

"Don't leave me alone," she mumbled, lips brushing against the soft fabric of Miles's shirt, not even sure whether he could hear her. But then his big hand cupped the back of her head, and the vice of fear around her heart began to winch itself loose, little by little.

25

Linh watched Ollie's chest rise and fall, monitoring for signs of life. As long as she had a job to do, as long as she kept busy, then the *what-ifs* wouldn't get a chance to take root in her mind.

That was the plan, anyway.

It was the silence that was getting to her. Tate and Steph refused to speak to one another, and Kenji sat by himself at the far end of the platform's cover. The only sounds audible were the sighing of the wind in the trees and the cawing of gulls circling the ocean cliff.

Eerily, even the cicadas had fallen silent.

And Ollie was looking really bad now. He kept drifting in and out, but there'd been some periods of lucidity, during which she'd dribbled water on his pale lips and asked him endless questions about his travels, anything she could think of to keep him with her. She'd *thought* he might still be doing sort of all right—that he was stable enough to hold out for rescue. At least, as long as it came soon.

But then there was a horrifying moment when he'd suddenly convulsed, vomit spilling down his front. A thin yellow-grey foam that seemed to be comprised of mostly stomach acid. Linh's heart broke a little when he apologized to her for the mess, and she had to swallow past a lump in her throat as she mopped him up and assured him that it was okay.

At least he still had his sense of humor. "You're a gem," he croaked, trying to grin at her. "If I die, I bequeath you my airline miles."

Steph had snorted air through her nose at the mention of the word *miles,* and Linh's chest had flamed with annoyance. Steph and Eloise, and Tate, for that matter, were acting like dumb teenagers, squabbling over who did what with whom, each one trying their best to cast blame and paint themselves as the wounded party. Linh thought she knew—had always known, really—what Steph's problem was, but this wasn't the time for it, and it certainly wasn't the *place* for it. It wasn't the place for *any* of this bullshit. And if Eloise wanted to throw her lot in with the big jerk with the creepy eyes and the stupid mustache, then as far as Linh was concerned, she could help herself. And Steph would just have to suck it up.

As for Eloise...well, clearly, she'd made her bed.

Linh *liked* Eloise well enough, but she could be infernally frustrating. For her part, Linh had already armchair-diagnosed Eloise back when they'd first met. The girl had a serious case of main character syndrome. She could be shockingly self-absorbed, confusing introspection for depth. That was it. The "I'm not like other girls" energy El radiated.

Linh worried for her, though. She worried that maybe those barriers she put up around herself wouldn't be enough to keep the world from crashing in and swallowing her up.

Maybe I should have given her the good-luck charm, Linh wondered, fingering the rough stone at her wrist. Shit. *Is that really the only thing I can do here?*

And why was it always up to her to fix everything, anyway?

She glanced at Steph. Her friend wore a look of abject frustration and impatience, but it didn't do enough to deflect from the fear and concern that darkened her eyes.

"Why don't you go look for them?" Linh suggested, hoping that Steph might feel better if she had something productive to do. And that she might take some of the negative energy away with her.

"If they're not back in five more minutes, I intend to." Steph sniffed, relacing her boots, wrapping the sodden strings around her hands and yanking them tight.

Tate tromped past them, his arms full of dead leaves. He'd been making pilgrimages up to the top layer of the structure for the past twenty minutes. Apparently, his plan was to light a big enough signal fire up there that they'd be visible even to the commercial passenger jets coming into Naha airport.

"Asshole," Steph muttered with acid in her voice, then stood up, brushing dead leaves from the seat of her shorts.

Ollie stirred, eyelids bulging as his eyes rolled back and forth beneath them.

"Ollie?"

He dragged his eyes open, blinking at Linh.

"Hey." His voice was croaky with pain. "Have they come for us yet?"

Linh's heart sank. He kept asking her that question. "Not yet. But they will, soon. They'll shoot you up with antivenom, or whatever it is, and you'll be fine. Good as new."

"Don't let them amputate my cock," Ollie said, trying to grin. "There'll be nothing left to live for."

Linh indulged him with a smile, but she was growing increasingly alarmed. She hadn't been able to bring herself to look at his injury, keeping her eyes trained on his face instead, but he'd lost so much color, and there were mottled, purplish bruises blooming under his eyes.

"Don't worry. We'll make sure we save the little guy. And, hey! You've got a wedding to start planning! Well, I'm sure Mishka will want to plan it. You can just show up in a tux and..."

"No." Ollie's eyes filled with sudden tears, tears which alarmed Linh more than anything she'd seen so far. "I don't want to marry her, Linh. I don't know if I ever really wanted to—*Fuck.*" Ollie screwed up his eyes, sucking his lower lip beneath his teeth, his face contorting.

"Hey, you don't mean that," she said, suspecting that he did, in fact, mean it.

"You don't know the whole story," Ollie said. His voice had grown weepy now, like he was a little boy wrestling with some unspeakable guilt. "She's the love of my life, but I can't *marry* her. She's already cheated on me once. She doesn't know that I know, but my mate Sy confessed. It was while we were traveling. We'd only been together a few weeks, me and her. And she's been texting my other mate, Ryan. I saw the texts. She's smart, she renamed all the contacts in her phone, but I compared the numbers. I don't want to marry a woman like that, but I *love* her, Linh. I don't know what to do. I thought getting married might help at first, if we had that commitment. But every time I look at her, there's a part of me that just wants to strangle her to death..."

Linh reached up to touch her nose ring, something she often found herself doing when she didn't know what else to do with her hands, but it was gone.

Just as well, maybe. Mom would murder me.

"You don't have to marry her," she told him softly. "Just tell her you changed your mind. People are allowed to change their minds, you know?"

"I'm scared of her." Ollie's mouth contorted again, a tear sliding down his cheek and getting caught in the stubble on his chin. "She's hit me a few times. I know it sounds stupid, a big bloke like me being afraid of a skinny little woman like her, but she gets these moods on, and I just...I don't know. I feel like if I can get things right, get myself together, be the kind of guy she deserves, she'd be happy, and then we could both be happy."

"You can't tie yourself in knots to keep someone else happy. You can't live your life in fear of what someone else thinks."

The irony of what she was saying hit her then, and she smiled wryly.

"I guess I'm one to talk. I'm twenty-three years old, and I'm terrified of my own mother. I told her I got into law school, but I never even...applied. She doesn't even know I'm in *Japan*. I can't believe it's almost over, and she hasn't busted me yet. Getting away with it has made me bold, I guess. Or maybe, just crazy. After EFA, I'm going to do an art internship in New York. I already got accepted. If she finds out about that, she really *will* kill me."

"What, your mum…doesn't…like art?"

"She doesn't like anything that's not directly related to either medicine or law."

"What is she, one of those dragon mums?"

"Dragon lady." Linh smiled again without mirth. "Tiger *mom*. But she's not, not really. She just wants me to have a better life than she did."

Ollie blinked, his eyes unfocused again. "I've got a tiger girl-friend. A real man-eater."

His eyes closed then, and he slept. Linh listened to the crackling of the fire and let her thoughts wander. Mom and Dad. Her mother was a force of nature, as ferocious and unstoppable as a tsunami or a cyclone. Her dad was the exact opposite. He had a sad face, like one of those dogs with droopy, weeping eyes. Whenever he looked at Linh, those eyes spoke silent apologies. Sure, he was sorry. But he never disagreed with Linh's mother.

He was actually her mother's second husband, even though they'd both left on the same boat. Neither of them talked about that time in their lives. Mom talked only of Hiep, the daughter she'd had with her first husband, the one who'd abandoned her once they reached North America. Hiep was the sister that Linh had never known, would never know outside of the grainy photographs. There were three of them in total, representing all her mother had left of Hiep. She'd only been about six when she died, but she'd been an uncommonly pretty child. Linh's features, in contrast, while pleasant enough, never seemed to satisfy her mother, who still mourned the beautiful child she'd lost. Linh felt like scant compensation for her mother's pain, her existence a pathetic consolation prize. Every time Linh hit a milestone or achieved something worth celebrating—like high school graduation or winning the regional figure skating competition—her mother would cry and talk about Hiep.

"All I've ever wanted was to have my own life," Linh mumbled, fooling herself that she was speaking to Ollie, though she knew he wasn't currently conscious. "I'm not afraid of dying up here. I'm afraid of...of a half-lived life. *My* life. At least I was trying to go my own way. At least..."

Linh trailed off, wiping her nose on her arm. The magatama stone scraped against her cheek. It was cold and very dry. The feeling was almost alien. Strange. When the world around her was so hot and wet.

"All right, I think we've waited long enough." Tate raised his voice as he came jogging down the steps. "It's time we headed out, found out what's keeping El and the dick with the 'stache." He approached Steph, who took several quick steps backward in alarm, leaves crunching beneath her boots.

"Chill out." Tate scowled, his eyes flashing. "Steph. Listen. This is ridiculous. I think we've got more immediate things to worry about than whatever nonsense a bunch of junior high kids made up. Haven't we? And for what it's worth, I'm sorry about earlier. Up on the platform. Okay? I hold my hands up. I'm not proud of what happened. You provoked me, but I shouldn't have lost my cool. Okay?"

Steph simply stared at him.

"Fine." Tate shrugged into his backpack. "Stay here then. I'll look for them *and* Satoko. Let's just hope the son of a bitch hasn't seized the chance to force himself on Eloise while you've been moping around down here."

"Excuse me? What about *you*?"

"I've been building the fucking *signal fire*," Tate hissed.

"Why don't you all go search?" Linh was sick to the back teeth with both of them. "I mean, I think you'd better. El and Miles, they've been gone a long time. Too long. Maybe something happened to them. Something bad."

Tate shifted his weight, his gaze flicking between Steph and Kenji.

Kenji. He's lucky he didn't get a concussion, Linh thought. There'd been a lot of blood but only a small cut to the back of Kenji's head, a nick, really. Still, this wasn't like the movies, where the hero gets punched out and springs back up later to save the day. Hitting your head hard enough to lose consciousness, now that was serious. Kenji needed medical attention. A CT scan, maybe. He should probably take it easy, at the absolute least. Although, Linh didn't really like the thought of Steph going off alone with Tate. And from the look on her face, neither did Steph.

What happened on that platform earlier? Linh wondered. *What did Tate do to Steph?*

Steph opened her mouth to speak, but Tate interrupted her.

"I think Kenji should stay. For protection. What if that Marine asshole comes along and finds you here, Linny?"

Steph laughed. Tate's face darkened. It was obvious what Steph was thinking. That there was no Marine. That it was *Tate* that they needed to be on their guard for.

Tate's a jerk, a creep, no newsflash there, Linh thought to herself. But it wasn't like he was actually dangerous...was it?

She needed to talk to Steph. Privately. *Whatever nonsense a bunch of kids made up...* What was Tate *talking* about?

She tried to catch Steph's eye, but Steph was too busy glowering at Tate.

"Fine." Tate heaved a sigh. "Linh, don't move from this spot. No matter what happens. And keep watch over the fires. We're all fucked if those fires go out."

"All right, all right, I'll watch the fires. Just come back before it's fully dark. I don't want to be up here alo—I don't want to have to leave Ollie and come looking for you, okay?"

"Fine." Tate looked back and forth between Steph and Kenji again. "Team of three?"

"I'm not teaming up with *you*. I don't think *anyone* should be teaming up with you. You go on your own." Steph jabbed an accusatory finger at Tate's face.

Snorting, Tate shook his head and walked off.

Without hesitating, Steph headed off in the opposite direction.

Kenji looked at Linh. There was resignation in his eyes. She shrugged slightly as if to say, what can *I* do?

After a prolonged moment, Kenji dropped his gaze, his head angled low as he trailed off after Steph.

26

Late amber sunlight filtered through the trees high above and cast dappled glints of golden light onto the forest floor and the backs of Eloise's hands. She held them up in front of her, the humidity making her skin sparkle where the flecks of sunlight hit.

Komorebi, it's called, Eloise thought. *Beautiful. One of those words English doesn't have a good equivalent for.*

The fallen log she was sitting on was knobbed and uncomfortable, digging into the meat of her behind through her thin jeans. But it was pleasant to sit there anyway, side by side with Miles, close enough for their arms to touch.

They'd paused to take a break, drink some water, rest up. They'd been walking through the forest for what felt like half an hour now, but the stark spire of the Viewing Platform, high above the tree canopy, never seemed to get any closer.

"What do you think happened to your friend?" Miles asked, breaking the silence, his tone conversational. "What's her name again?"

"Satoko," Eloise said, and there was a stab of guilt at the realization that she'd forgotten about Satoko. She'd forgotten about all of them, actually—Steph, Kenji, Linh, Ollie. *Tate.* And it had felt good to forget—to focus only on being with

Miles, on how easy it was. With him, there seemed to be no need to fill the silences. No need to mask.

"Maybe some kind of animal... attacked her." The thought wasn't pleasant, but it was the only plausible hypothesis she could come up with.

"No animal tracks," Miles said simply.

"But the blood..."

"Come on, Ellery," he said, and she noticed gold flecks in his blue eyes as he looked at her. "What if the blood's a red herring?"

"It's Eloise," she said, wounded. Had he actually forgotten her name? Her cheeks burned, and she felt herself shrinking inside, shriveling up like—

"Ellery *Queen*," he clarified. "Wait, you're British. Shoulda gone for Marple."

"I know who Ellery Queen is," Eloise said, embarrassed, trying to keep the indignation out of her voice. "But Ellery Queen was a man."

"No, she wasn't," Miles said. "She was the greatest super-sleuth the detective genre's ever seen."

She blinked at him, wondering if he was serious, or if he was just pulling her leg.

His eyes twinkled, and then his chin twitched. The next moment, he snorted with laughter, laughter so infectious Eloise couldn't help but join in.

She uncapped her bottle and took a swig of the lukewarm water. It felt good to laugh.

"What are you really doing in Japan, Ellery?" Miles asked her then, catching her off guard. She capped the bottle and tipped it from side to side, watching the way the sparkling golden water inside sloshed and bubbled.

"Teaching," she said, but she could sense him shaking his head.

"No, I mean, what are you doing *here*? Why Japan?"

She'd evaded this same question what seemed like a hundred times, but now she didn't have the energy to lie. And what did it matter, anyway?

What did it matter now?

"My best friend died," she said, and once she started talking, she found that the rest of the words came easy, like water spilling from a bust dam. "They...They died right before we both graduated from uni, and we had...we'd made all these plans. To go traveling the world together. It was...it was their dream to see all of Asia, to move from country to country, working in bars, teaching English. To live a borderless existence. Real freedom. It was just supposed to be a year, maybe two, then...then they were going to go to medical school, and I was going to train to be a nurse..."

"What happened?" Miles asked, and she could feel his eyes on her, but she couldn't meet them.

She shrugged and squeezed the bottle until the plastic began to crackle in protest.

"They died, and I was there when it happened and I...I didn't know how to cope with it. So, I just left and ran away like a coward. I did a *geographic*. That's what they call it, I guess, the impulse to start a whole new life somewhere else in the hopes it'll fix what's wrong inside you. Only, it doesn't work."

"I know it doesn't work," Miles said. "No matter where you go, there you are."

"Right," she said, swallowing, her throat dry despite the water she'd just drunk. She fought an urge to take another swig. Though she didn't want to think about it too hard, a nasty little voice inside her was whispering *you'd better ration that.*

"So, that's why Japan," she said. "I thought I could make things better by finding some new part of myself out here...t hought I could *kintsugi* my life back together. You know, like how they fix broken pottery with gold lacquer? It's a metaphor, kind of. You keep your flaws, your scars, but you make someth ing...something beautiful out of it anyway. Maybe that sounds dumb."

"No," Miles said, reaching for her wrist and rubbing his thumb along the inside of it. She realized with a flood of shame that her wrist was bare. She'd taken the wristband and her watch off earlier in an attempt to dry them, gotten distracted, and shoved them both in her backpack. Miles's thumb caressed the ropey scar she usually kept hidden, and she wondered if he could feel it, or if he'd already noticed it.

Why else would he be touching it?

But he didn't say anything, and neither did she, and they sat there in silence for what seemed like a long time, listening to the evening birds chattering back and forth in the trees above.

"No planes," Miles muttered eventually, almost as if he was talking to himself. "It's weird. So quiet up here."

They lapsed into another comfortable silence. When Eloise heard herself speak again, it was with some surprise. She hadn't intended to say anything. It was as if someone else had just spoken the words over her shoulder, borrowing her voice.

"Maybe I don't deserve to be saved."

And then she started to cry.

Miles let her cry for a while, his thumb rubbing reassuring circles into her skin. He didn't try to mop her up, or beg her to stop, or any of the usual things people do when confronted with a crying person. He just sat there, silent, as she let the tears slide down her cheeks.

"Come on, Ellery," he said when her chest finally stopped hitching. "Everyone deserves to be saved."

"I don't. I'm...I'm rotten inside. After what happened, I feel diseased—evil. *Angry.* I think terrible things about people all the time. About hurting people. People I love. I thought about hurting Steph...*killing* her. It's like I don't have any control of it. The thoughts just come, like movie scenes playing in my mind, and I'm always the villain."

"We aren't our thoughts," Miles said softly. "We aren't the people we convince ourselves we are whenever we get stuck in a self-loathing spiral. When we're drunk, or we come off wrong in an argument, or we face rejection. I think we all worry that we're bad inside, *wrong* inside, that if other people knew the things we really think, in the privacy of our own minds, they'd be repelled. But the thoughts aren't real. They aren't *us*." He brushed a hanging tear off her chin with his thumb. "You know, El...I have a theory about intrusive thoughts. I think they're some kind of ancient warning system, something left over from the earliest days of our existence. Something we've evolved not to need anymore, like tails or, I don't know, fucking earlobes. When someone represents a risk to you—a threat or an obstacle between you and what you think you need to survive—well, your brain makes you think about hurting them as a warning. To protect yourself. It's something primal. It's in the human blueprint. So, if you think about it rationally, blaming yourself for your dark thoughts is just really..." He trailed off, his blue eyes rising from her lips to meet her gaze.

"Stupid," she whispered, and Miles smiled. It felt like a reward, something special meant just for her, and in that moment, she felt so much better than she'd felt in...in longer than she could even remember.

"Your word choice, not mine," he said. "But you're not a bad person, Ellery. I promise you, you're not. And you're not a coward. The fact that you're here, that you're trying, despite what you went through...it's proof of that."

Was it true? This whole time, she'd focused only on the ways in which she was failing...failing Chris, his memory. Failing herself. But maybe Miles was right. Maybe trying was the thing that really counted. And she could try. She could always keep trying.

"If you feel like you need some extra courage, though..." Miles stopped talking, reached for the back of his neck, and paused a second while he fiddled with something there. "You can borrow mine."

He handed her the gold necklace he'd just unclasped, a fat embossed medallion lying on her palm with the chain curled around it like a snake.

"It's my Saint Christopher," he said. "My dad gave me this when...when I left to go traveling. It's for protection."

Christopher. The irony of it struck her. It made her shudder internally as she lifted the medallion by its chain and watched it twirl, the gold glinting in the early evening light.

"When we get out of this mess, you can give it back to me," Miles said, getting up from the fallen log with an abruptness that made Eloise think he was embarrassed about the gesture.

"Thank you," she whispered, hooking the necklace around her own neck and dropping the medallion down inside the opening in her shirt. It was cool, almost cold, but comforting against her feverish skin.

27

Steph was trying not to make her bristling anger too obvious as she and Kenji followed the dirt path in silence. They'd come across a creepy graveyard and a dank cave that seemed to lead deep into the cliff, but it didn't seem likely that El and the mustached jerk would have gone in there, so they'd taken a different path, one that snaked through the trees.

Steph had been regretting that decision ever since. She was haunted by the thought of El lying dead in the darkness of the cave, choked by natural gases or bad air, or crushed by a cave-in.

Or raped and murdered. Steph was trying not to think like that, but it was hard. Her mind kept going there, like a compulsion. Like a scab you just had to pick.

After all, she reasoned, they didn't know this Miles guy from Adam. He'd shown up, told them nothing about himself, latched on to their group like a blood-sucking leech. And then, he'd immediately started putting the moves on Eloise.

And it had worked, too.

"I'm sorry," Kenji said, apropos of nothing, and Steph was so taken aback—honestly, she'd almost forgotten he was with her—that she stopped dead, her boots crunching on the path.

"What?"

"I'm sorry. About what I said. How I acted. I guess I wanted to get a reaction out of you. I mean, I thought we had a connection last night, but you've been blanking me all day. I was out of line, though. I know that. All I can say is I'm sorry."

Kenji dropped his chin to his chest, staring down at the ground, arms flat against his sides. It was a gesture of remorse so completely Japanese, and on Kenji, with his laid-back Californian vibe, it was so...so out of place.

"You're not forgiven." Steph tried to keep her voice stern and steady, but she was wavering. "It wasn't cool, what you did. I mean, it doesn't matter what we did or didn't do together. The fact is that you...you shit on my honor. It was disrespectful. Do you get that?"

"Yes." Kenji was still looking at his feet. "I do get that."

"Well...listen, let's just move past it, all right? You're not forgiven, and I still think you're a dick, but I can put it behind me. Okay?"

Kenji finally lifted his head. "Okay."

They walked in a more companionable silence along the old dirt path, passing beneath an ancient-looking stone *torii* gate with knots of old rope hanging from it. The path was badly overgrown in places, and they had to navigate blackened, fallen trees and hack their way through bushes to stay with it.

"How's your head?" Steph asked.

"Better."

"You really think somebody whacked you?"

"I don't know. All I remember is a sharp pain, then waking up to see Eloise standing over me, holding a stick."

Steph smiled. "You can't seriously think Eloise whacked you."

"Could have been her. Could have been anyone. Could have been you."

Steph grinned. "Could have been. But it wasn't."

Either way, the thought of Eloise knocking Kenji out with a stick was laughable. Eloise was a weak kitten. And right now, she was lost God-knows-where in this forsaken, overgrown resort.

Steph was still thinking about Eloise, picturing her small, helpless form crushed underneath the weight of Miles's heavy body, his foul sweat anointing her skin, when Kenji made a small noise of surprise in his throat.

"What? Is it them?" Steph lifted her head. The path widened, and ahead, there was a collection of dilapidated cabins, a little complex of them studded here and there all along a downward slope. They seemed to be made of logs, some of them little more than rotted shells, lurching drunkenly on decaying stilts.

"I thought I saw something moving. Like smoke. Inside that cabin right there." Kenji pointed to one that was set back a little from the path. It seemed to be in better condition than most of its fellows. It had an intact roof and walls, at least.

Steph couldn't see any smoke, much less smell it.

"Are you sure?" she asked Kenji, who frowned, moving forward.

"It was weird." He moved past Steph, eyes still fixed on the cabin. "It was like red smoke...billowing inside."

"*Red* smoke," Steph repeated, her voice laced with irony. "Uh-huh. Like in Tate's dumb ghost story, I get it."

"I saw it earlier, too," Kenji muttered, his eyes unfocused, cloudy, as if he was dreaming. "I saw it in the forest...I was following it. That's when I got hit from behind."

"Oh, come on," Steph said. "Seriously, Kenji, this isn't the time for this. Okay? Cut it out."

Kenji's eyes widened suddenly, a look of alarm arresting his handsome features.

"*What?*" Steph asked, annoyed now, turning again to scrutinize the cabin. "What now?"

Kenji shook his head. He'd gone pale.

"I thought I just saw...it looked like a woman..."

Steph took a slow, steadying breath through her nose. "Right, of course. Of *course*, you saw a creepy woman in the window of the dilapidated old cabin in the woods."

"I don't know if that's what I saw or what," Kenji said. "I'm just saying it *looked* like a woman. I saw long hair. Black hair."

"Ghost shit! *Wonderful*!" Steph was pissed now. Beyond pissed. "Let's go say hi!" She shouldered hard past Kenji and started marching over to the cabin, her boots crunching on the grit-strewn path.

Kenji followed as she stomped up the steps to the porch. Circumnavigating several mushy spots and gaping holes in the wood floor, she stepped through the empty doorframe and entered.

The inside was trashed, although whether it had been entirely the work of the elements or if human hands had played a part, Steph couldn't tell. Nothing was on fire, obviously. The floor was a jumble of broken pieces of wood, old leaves, and the rusting remains of an old box mattress. She picked her way through the detritus, skimming the walls and entering the back room.

"Looks like they had their own toilet facilities. Swanky." Steph moved forward, the floorboards creaking under her weight. Remains of an old plastic unit bathtub. Rusted showerhead, lying on the bottom like a dead snake. She thought of Don, her mom's creepy-ass boyfriend. The trailer park. They'd had the same kind of cheap molded bathtub.

Nothing ever happened with Don. He'd never laid a finger on her. But he could have done it. Easily. Steph knew it. Don knew it. Even her mom knew it, Steph thought. And sometimes, late at night, when her run hadn't been strenuous enough, and the bed didn't feel soft enough and sleep eluded her, she thought about that glint in her mom's eye. That sly look that seemed to be saying: *I would have taken a side, Stephie. And guess what? Maybe you'd have been the only one on yours.*

Steph sensed Kenji shifting his weight behind her, and a mental scene began to play, like a projection on the back wall of her mind. It was grainy and crackly, fuzzy on the details, but in it, Kenji wrapped his strong arm around her throat from behind and dragged her down onto the filthy floor by her hair.

She whirled around, almost surprised to see that Kenji was just standing there, watching her with an open look in his calm brown eyes, his thick brows raised in question.

But he could do it. He could do it easily. After all, they'd already hooked up once, on the beach. He might feel he was entitled.

Steph wouldn't be able to stop him if so. And out here, no one would hear her scream.

"Did you find something?" he asked, and that was when the bathroom floor gave way beneath Steph's feet, and she plummeted through it, a jagged piece of wood scraping an angry red line up her back. It caught, for just a second, on the thin material of her untucked shirt. Then the shirt ripped, spilling her down onto the hillside below.

28

Eloise and Miles had found a sun-glazed meadow of knee-high grass and crossed it, emerging on the other side with their legs encrusted with sticky burrs. Passing through a brief thicket of dense trees, they'd come out right on the shore of a good-sized pond. Its surface was thickly laminated with shiny green lotus pads. Ringing the pond was a collection of seven stone cottages, each one with its own dock, in various stages of rot. Beyond the pond, high above the tree canopy, loomed the Viewing Platform. It looked close.

Miles nodded his head towards the closest cottage, the only one that still had all four walls and a roof. "Maybe Satoko's hiding out in there," he suggested. "Scared or injured. We should check."

Eloise didn't really want to get any closer to the pond, which stank. Nor did she want to poke around in a moldering stone hut on the off chance of finding Satoko cowering there. But Miles was right. They *should* at least check.

They walked over, thick pebbles sliding about beneath their boots. The door was gone, along with a good portion of the front wall, and the inside was strewn with bits of unidentifiable detritus. There was less graffiti here, just a few scrawls.

Climbing carefully over a heap of rubble and then a piece of crumbling wooden porch furniture, Miles pushed on the door, and it swung reluctantly inward on its hinge, revealing a room that was in much better condition.

Eloise followed him through. It was darker in here, a fallen tree outside blocking much of the light through the glassless window frame.

Miles was staring down at the bed. It took up much of the room. It was unmistakably heart-shaped, the rotten comforter a deep claret red.

"That's the most seventies thing I think I've seen yet," Eloise said as Miles nudged open the other door in the room.

"I think you spoke too soon." He grinned over his shoulder at her before disappearing inside, and when Eloise caught up with him, she had to agree.

The room held a sunken, heart-shaped acrylic bath the color of old chewed bubblegum. The curved wall above the bath was coated with almost full-length mirror panels, more than half of them shattered, burst rust bubbles mottling the edges. The floor was filthy, with black and white checkerboard tiling. A windowless anteroom to one side held a cracked toilet in the same dull bubblegum pink shade.

It was quite bright in the bathroom. There was a tall rectangular stained-glass window on the far wall, almost all of its glass littered across the tiles inside in glittering bright pieces.

Eloise caught sight of herself in the remnants of the mirror above the sink. Her face was streaked with grey dried mud, her hair limp and frizzy from the humidity. Quickly, she looked away, but she wasn't fast enough. Miles caught her checking herself out and gave her a grin that made her flush.

"No Satoko," she pointed out. "We should head out, and get back to the platform. The sun's going down, the others are probably worried sick about us."

"All right," Miles said, shrugging as if it didn't matter much to him what they did. He followed as she led the way back across the garish, love-hotel-style bedroom.

She spoke over her shoulder to him as they clumped across the wood floor in their heavy boots.

"Do you think it's true that this place was used as a—"

She meant to say *brothel*, but the word turned into a yelp of surprise in her throat, and the yelp evolved into a primal scream. Something large and dark had swung towards her, scratching a deep furrow into her cheek, gouging her skin. Her first thought was that a tower of old sticks—piled-up kindling—had toppled onto her. Branches poked and prodded at her face and arms. But as she stumbled aside, Miles yelled, and she realized it wasn't a pile of sticks.

They were *bones*.

Eloise fell back against the heart-shaped bed, its springs jangling, the heel of her hand shoved against her open mouth.

The skeleton on the floor still had remnants of skin, like a mummy. The face was shriveled like a walnut, brown papyrus stretched over puckered eye sockets, a black pinprick hole in the center of each wrinkled cavity. It wore a grinning smile of yellowed bone, each tooth appearing elongated by the lack of gum tissue, giving the corpse a vampiric look.

She could still feel the whispery, paper-soft touch of its desiccated skin against hers. The last caress of a man decades dead.

Eloise looked up at Miles, struck dumb with horror. There was alarm and concern on his face, and in a stride, he was with her, touching her cheek, his hand coming away bloody.

"You all right?" he asked her, and the question struck her as absurd. She could see the closet door now, hanging off its hinges. A shard of wood protruded through the back of it, and she supposed that was what had gouged her cheek.

But inside the closet slumped something else. Another mummified skeleton, this one dressed in a powder-blue skirt suit that had turned brown with age around the lapels. Strands of black hair trailed from the yellowed skull. A single white shoe with a boxy heel lay on the floor of the closet next to the remnants of a plastic bath stool.

The female mummy had a rope around its neck.

Eloise moaned and a slurry of vomit rose in her throat. She shoved past Miles, blundering blindly into the bathroom. Shards of colored glass skittered beneath her feet, and she bent over by the window, clawing at the wide sill and sucking in breath after breath.

The pond stench.

Her stomach hitched, and she heaved, but nothing came up.

Then Miles's hand was on her shoulder. "It's all right," he said. "You're all right."

She let out a dry sob, but her stomach settled itself.

Turning in his arms, she looked up at him. Looked for fear in his eyes, but they were steady, calm as an unrippled lake.

"Why didn't anyone find them," she asked him, her voice strained, cracking. "When the resort closed, why didn't they check the rooms? God...they really just left *everything*?"

"Maybe they got missed," Miles said. "Maybe they figured they left already, skipped on the room bill. It's all right, El. It was forty years ago. Fucking sad, but a long time ago. It's all right."

He stroked her hair like she was a nervous puppy he was attempting to soothe.

She blinked at him, trying to focus on him as her vision swam.

"All the rumors about the guests that committed suicide here," she said. "I thought it was probably bullshit, like half the stories about this place, but..."

Miles had taken his hip flask out and was shaking the contents onto a balled-up bandana he'd produced from his other pocket. Then, very gently, he started mopping up the wound on Eloise's face.

She hissed. It stung. "Sorry," Miles mouthed, but kept dabbing. "It's not that deep," he said. "Might leave a scar."

Eloise lifted her hand and touched his neck. "Like yours," she murmured. She traced the raised white lines with her fingertips. His stubble was like wire, the skin beneath like velvet. "What happened?"

"I fell through a plate-glass window at a college party. I don't really like to talk about it."

"Sorry."

"It's fine."

"I get it, though," she said after a pause, her voice faint, thoughtful. In her mind, she saw the couple in the closet. She saw them as they might have been forty years ago, filled with life, flesh on their bones, hot blood in their veins. Fixing the ropes around each other's necks. Closing the closet door on themselves, shutting out the light, the world outside, for the last time. One final kiss, perhaps, before kicking away the plastic bath stool.

Forty years together, dead in the dark.

"What?" Miles frowned.

"The kind of love it takes to do something like that," she said. "I get it."

She expected a shocked reaction, but there was no surprise in his eyes, no judgment. Just a kind of quiet understanding. As she stood there in the circle that his arms formed around her, she felt the urge to kiss him build to a fever pitch inside her. And she could see it, too, in his eyes.

It was some odd kind of reflex, perhaps, a primal urge to fight death with sex. Or maybe that was just a convenient excuse. Because this moment was inevitable, and had been inevitable since last night.

But Miles hesitated, kept her waiting. She half-closed her eyes, face angled up towards him, her throat tight, a pulse thrumming insistently somewhere deep down inside of her.

His breath was hot on her mouth.

There was a crunch outside the window, and he started to turn his head to say, "What was—" but Eloise grabbed his face in her hands and pulled him down towards her. Straining, she went up on the toes of her boots, her spine curving inward, and pressed her mouth hungrily against his.

It was an undignified sort of kiss at first, Eloise practically hanging around his neck, Miles almost overbalancing in his eagerness to indulge her lust. He curled his arms around her back, holding her up and tight against him as she attacked his mouth with hers.

A frenzied moment of pure bliss later, Eloise pulled her mouth away from his, turning her head to one side to avoid his eyes. He held on, reluctant to let go, but she pushed him firmly away from her by his chest.

As he stepped backward, boots crunching on glass, she ran her tongue over her bottom lip, tasting salt, the nerve endings all over her body still tingling.

She turned away from him, gazing at the smeared glass, out at the trees rippling in the breeze outside.

"El?" He murmured behind her, and before she could turn around, he wrapped his arms around her shoulders, nuzzling his hot, rough cheek against hers.

His warmth was against her back. Her ankle was itching badly. A mosquito bite was swelling and pulsating there, right on the bone.

She thought about the dead couple in the other room. She thought about Chris in the woods, his eyes filled with silent accusations. She thought about the dragging ankle of the woman in the cave. But none of it seemed quite so terrible now. It was like it had been filtered, diluted somehow.

Odd.

She tried to find fear, probing for it, like prodding a fresh bruise just to gauge how much it hurt. But for the first time in a long time, maybe since before Chris died, she couldn't find it. There was no fear anywhere inside of her.

"We should get back to the others." She twisted around in his arms and looked into his eyes, the pale blue, the dark limbal rings. She could see it there plainly now, whatever it was he felt for her. It had form. It was something she could trust, that she could rely upon. Something that could keep her safe.

He looked back at her for a long moment. Then he nodded, cupping his hands over her ears and pressing a kiss against her forehead. A chaste gesture of affection. A hint of mutual ownership.

"Come with me, Ellery Queen," he said softly, and she let him lead her out by the hand, averting her eyes from the closet and the heap of tattered bones on the floor as they went.

Outside, the evening sunlight hit her, and she emerged a little dizzy, a little thrilled, feeling lighter, somehow.

Feeling cleansed.

29

The stone cottages were only just visible through the thick growth of straw-like grass ringing the old pond. A hot afternoon wind blew, sending ripples across the black surface of the water and bringing with it the stench of dead fish and rotting weeds.

Standing next to Kenji, Steph wanted to cry, wanted to throw up. She settled for biting her tongue hard, knowing she'd never forgive herself if she let Kenji, of all people, see how rattled she was.

It wasn't as if she hadn't known it was going to happen. It had been inevitable. But she didn't want to have had to witness it in person. She didn't want to have seen *that*.

She'd been bruised and scraped, but she'd come out of her fall through the cabin's rotten bathroom floor largely unscathed. Kenji had run outside and galloped down the hillside like a gazelle, reaching her side in moments.

It was quite sweet, really. After making sure she hadn't broken anything, he'd carried her back up to the path before he set about examining her like she was one of his students who'd taken a tumble from the ropes during gym class. That had been indignity enough, but the scream that had escaped her when he'd pressed the skin on either side of the cut on her spine—to see how deep it was, he said—the thought of it still made her burn with embarrassment and shame.

Insisting that she was fine, she'd started off again, blundering along the path, moving in the opposite direction to the camp but not caring, and Kenji had come trailing after her. She'd rounded the corner, and there they were, a set of stone cottages ringing a desolate pond.

She'd been just in time to catch sight of Eloise's bright hair. She was entering one of the cabins, a step behind *him*, the hanger-on that had infiltrated their group.

"Should we go in after them?" Kenji had whispered to her, but she'd ignored him, going around the back instead, and that was where a busted window had afforded her an unobstructed view. A view of Eloise throwing herself on the guy, *Miles*, who'd seemed only too happy to receive her attention and respond in kind.

As she watched them paw at one another, practically eating each other's faces like starving dogs, Steph thought that she might faint. There was a whining sound in her ears that was growing louder and louder, and her hands and face were suddenly hot, cold, and numb all at the same time.

Kenji was by her side again, gently supporting her as she sank down to her knees. For a few seconds, everything in the nearby vicinity appeared dark, as if night had fallen. She could hear Kenji's voice in her ear, mumbling something that sounded like 'vasovagal reflex.' The snout of a water bottle nudged her lips, and she took a tentative, dribbly sip. It tasted salty. The whining noise slowly receded, and with it, the sense of gathering darkness, and she could see again.

Kenji's brown eyes were fixed on her, filled with concern.

"We should get you back to camp," he was saying. "Are you sure you didn't hit your head when you fell?"

Then there were footsteps, crunching against grit, Eloise and Miles moving away from the stone cottage, heading for the path. Miles's hand was pressed to the hollow of Eloise's back, a horribly intimate gesture, and vomit bubbled up in the back of Steph's throat again.

"Hey!" Kenji called out, and the two of them turned around. Eloise paused for only a second before she came running over, slipping a little on the loose ground, dropping to her knees in front of Steph, taking both of her hands in hers.

"What's wrong? What's wrong with her?"

Kenji explained about Steph's fall through the cabin floor, but Steph didn't bother listening. Instead, she looked over Eloise's shoulder at Miles. He met her gaze evenly, his expression neutral, but she'd caught the flare of anger in his eyes when Kenji had called out.

Anger. Not surprise. *Anger.*

Steph looked away from him, clinging tight to Eloise's hands, scrutinizing her friend's expression. There was a new cut on her face, and her cheeks were a deep red, as if stained with berry juice. Flushed from her exertions, no doubt. Steph could still *see* her attached to Miles's mouth, his hands roaming her back, stroking and kneading her flesh. Pushing Eloise's concerned hands away abruptly, Steph staggered to her feet.

"We've been looking everywhere for you." Her voice was firm, which was good, but she sounded too accusatory. She would need to tone that down. Pretend like she hadn't seen anything. El would only retreat into her shell, and she'd hate to give Miles the satisfaction of hearing her say what she'd witnessed out loud.

"We got lost somewhere between the caves and the path back." Eloise got to her feet again, too, swiping at Steph's kneecaps, brushing away the small stones and tiny twigs embedded there.

"Anything useful inside?" Kenji was asking Miles, nodding his head in the direction of the stone cottage.

Steph caught the brief look he and Eloise exchanged.

"No," Miles answered, impassively.

"We should all head back," Eloise said. "We've left Linh alone with Ollie for too long."

No one protested. They rejoined the path, returning in the direction of the Viewing Platform, the very top level of which could just be seen poking out above the tree canopy in the near distance. Steph hung back, eyes narrowed as she watched the shadows collect on the back of Miles's sweat-stained shirt. The sky was growing increasingly indigo in color. Within the hour, it would be full dark.

"I don't trust him, Els." Steph's voice was pitched low, her tone serious, intense. "He's a bad actor. Just listen. We don't *know* him. He could be dangerous. I really think he could be. We're alone up here, isolated, vulnerable...and the way he's been...*working* you...there's something calculated about it—"

"You're delusional," Eloise said, cutting Steph off, her voice closed and hard. "Look, we both know that Tate was the one who attacked Kenji. Miles didn't—*doesn't* have any motive to hurt Kenji. Or any one of us. And what do you mean, he's *working* me? You're coming off crazy right now. Paranoid."

Was she paranoid? Steph wasn't sure. And she was no longer as sure as she'd previously been about Tate being the mystery attacker, either.

"*Listen* to me." Steph made a sound in her throat, a frustrated gurgle, while Eloise sighed and briefly closed her eyes. "That sob story you told me, about Miles? The fiancée who jilted him weeks before the wedding? And you're the only one he told this to? Of course, you are. Wake *up*, Eloise. He's *lying*. To get you on his *side*. I can't believe you're not seeing it!"

"Just what exactly are you basing this on?" Eloise tipped her head to one side, a parody of genuine interest.

"It's...it's just a feeling I get from him. A bad feeling."

"A bad feeling." Eloise smiled. "I see."

They were still on the path that snaked through the forest, making the slow trudge back to the campsite. Miles and Kenji walked ahead, the backs of both of their shirts dark with sweat. Steph had pulled Eloise back, wanting to get some distance so they could talk things through. She'd started off sweet, cajoling Eloise into opening up and talking about Miles. But she hadn't been able to hold back her anger when she'd seen the smile in her friend's eyes.

Picking at her nail beds, Steph realized she was feeling sick again. It was probably the heat, the spill she'd taken through the rotten cabin floor. The back of her shirt kept sticking painfully to her wound. But none of that mattered. What mattered was that Eloise wasn't listening to her. She wasn't getting through. A rift had opened up between them, a rift that had started as a series of small, seemingly insignificant cracks in the foundation of their friendship. It had taken Kenji to break it wide open. And now that Miles had gotten his hooks into Eloise, she was long gone, and Steph couldn't reach her.

How was it possible that she couldn't see it?

The way Miles had spun the situation made it seem like it was him and Eloise against the rest of the group. Steph had heard the snide asides he'd made about Eloise's choice of friends. Even his body language and his physicality were calculated. Flipping Tate into the dirt. The way he'd taken charge of Ollie, of their situation. The hyper-confident, alpha male act. It was a performance he was putting on, all for Eloise.

He didn't even have to *do* anything. That was the really infuriating part. He'd known exactly how to play Eloise. No outright flirting. Keep her at arm's length. Let her come to him. Let it be her choice. That way, doubting him would mean doubting herself.

"You need to stop this, El. Pushing away the people who actually care about you. It makes you vulnerable, don't you see that?" Steph dropped her voice an octave, softening it. "I know you want someone that you think is somehow superior to you to validate you, to prove you're worth loving, but you're looking in the wrong places. You need to love yourself. I know you're still struggling with what happened back home. With what people think of you. If that guy in England hadn't been killed like that, if you hadn't been implicated, you wouldn't be looking for—"

There was a crunch of loose gravel as Eloise came to an abrupt stop. "Did Tate—"

"I found the articles online," Steph said, all in a rush. Then, more gently, "The guy was stabbed, wasn't he? You could have told me. I wouldn't have judged. I would have—"

"Stop talking now, Steph." Eloise stood trembling with anger, her eyes blazing, her face flushed in the dim twilight.

They stared at one another for a long moment, the noises of the forest loud around them. The sun was beginning to set, and the birds were restless in the trees. The rustling of their feathers sounded like harsh, angry whispering.

"I'm trying to help you." Steph's voice was dull now, hopeless. "You dumb bitch, why can't you see that I'm trying to help you?"

"Get fucked, Stephanie," Eloise spat, eyes glittering with crystallized rage. She paused for a beat, for effect. "*Again.*"

30

When she was thirteen, Satoko spent a night alone in the girls' toilet at school. It was her friend Mayumi's idea. Summer vacation, and they'd all gotten obsessed with this dumb reality TV show called *Test of Courage*. Groups of friends would dare each other to sneak into abandoned buildings and haunted places.

On the pretext of a sleepover, Satoko's group had snuck into the deserted junior high school. And it wasn't until Satoko heard Mayumi threading a mop handle through the door's latch that she realized she'd been tricked.

The other girls left her there overnight, and Satoko had passed the time trying not to have a complete freakout, while drawing up elaborate, cold-blooded plans for revenge. But when they came back for her a few hours after dawn broke, she was so relieved to be out of that dark, stinky, creepy toilet that she'd instantly forgiven them. Her well-stoked anger had evaporated like dew under the morning sun, and the terrors of the night past had diminished somehow, like a dangerous animal that's been de-fanged and de-clawed.

The memory returned to her now as the storm dried up, as the downpour gave way to a gentle, steady dripping from the trees.

Thank God the puking stopped, she thought, slowly sitting up on the stone bench inside the gazebo where she'd been dozing. The blood she'd vomited had frightened her, frightened her badly enough to make her dash out through the storm after the others, but it had only happened once, and after that, she'd felt...fine.

Good, even.

At least physically.

It didn't make any sense.

Must have been some weird hangover thing, she told herself. A burst blood vessel or something. Maybe a hallucination, even. The shock of Ollie being bitten, the heat, the humidity. It probably wasn't *blood* at all. A trick of the light, maybe.

Satoko took a sip of water from her flask and stretched, her back cracking. She hoped Ollie was all right by himself. She shouldn't have left him. She knew that, but she'd panicked.

How much time had passed? Maybe the others had already summoned help. It must have been around late afternoon, closer to evening. But the rain had been so intense, the sky so dark that it seemed like an entire night had already passed.

A night in which she'd seen things moving through the trees.

One of them was a man. A white man, tall with broad shoulders, so she'd thought it might have been someone from her own group. Tate, or maybe Miles. But it wasn't.

He'd moved slowly through the trees on the hillside below, unconcerned by the rain, which didn't seem to affect him—his hair and clothes were dry. This incongruent detail struck Satoko only later. Excited, she'd swung her legs down off the stone bench, lifting a hand, opening her mouth to call down to him, and that was when she'd felt something like an icy finger drawing a lazy path down her spine. That was when she'd sensed someone, or some*thing*, watching her from the entrance to the gazebo.

Two girls had stood there, silhouetted by the sheeting rain, their long braids like lengths of dripping rope. Their clothing was odd, old-fashioned, a sort of belted brown tunic spattered with dark raindrops. Satoko froze, heart-hammering, the hairs lifting on the nape of her sweaty neck as a tremor of fear seized her muscles. The girls observed her for a long moment that seemed somehow exempt from the ordinary flow of time, saying nothing, barely moving. But somehow, Satoko understood. They were *warning* her.

She'd cast her gaze back over the darkened hillside. She could still make out the man moving away from her.

She could see the open bowl of bone that was the back of his head.

Her breath caught in her throat, her hands forming panicked claws as she clutched at the stone lip of the bench beneath her. But when she looked over her shoulder to the gazebo entrance again, the girls had gone.

After that, she'd been too afraid to move. She'd convinced herself she was losing her mind, her brain conjuring up bizarre phantoms out of the storm. But now the storm had broken. The valley was full of amber sunlight, and it finally felt safe enough to emerge.

If she could find the Viewing Platform, she could check on Ollie. They could wait together to be rescued. It would feel better being with someone else.

There was something *in* this resort. Something bad. She *felt* it. Some ancient, dark malevolence that existed only in the gossamer-thin veil between this world and the other.

I'll find Ollie. We'll wait for rescue. It'll be okay.

Emerging from the gazebo, Satoko took a right, dripping the last few drops from her hiking flask onto her tongue. The spring water was oddly sweet, but it had apparently worked wonders. She was feeling steadier, the nausea of her hangover completely gone.

The ground ahead steamed as the heavy rainfall began to evaporate.

The long, low main hotel building stretched along the path to her left. Its concrete walls were almost entirely obscured behind a thick beard of shivering ivy. Fat raindrops suspended sparkling in a netting of spiderwebs captured a thousand tiny Satokos. Inhaling, she smelled the flat ozone funk of wet concrete. Before long, she passed the hotel's side entrance, which seemed to have been crudely bricked over. The right side of the path was dotted with annexes and small buildings of indeterminate function. Graffiti on their surfaces screamed swear words at her in English, but Satoko wasn't paying attention to her surroundings. She was much too lost in her own disjointed thoughts.

She was thinking about magnets. The door of their fridge at home was studded all over with brightly colored resin magnets. Their three-dimensional surfaces depicted famous city landmarks—The Eiffel Tower of Paris, the Golden Merlion of Singapore, Cambodia's Angkor Wat. All souvenirs Satoko had brought home from her solo travels. She pictured them as they would look years from now, thickly furred with dust.

I could leave him, she thought, the concept frightening her with its audacity. A blasphemy uttered in the face of long-held beliefs. Like the belief that her family's fortunes rested on her shoulders and hers alone. The belief that Shun, her fiancé, would be their best bet for the future.

How long can I spin it out, she wondered. Once they found out what was wrong with her, the ways in which she was lacking, it would all come crashing down. *Five years? Ten?*

It had been Shun's mother, the *mayor's wife*, who'd suggested the premarital medical checkup. *They're an accepted thing these days,* she'd said. *Standard procedure. After all, we want to ensure this union benefits all involved, don't we?*

A glint of sunlight on broken glass made Satoko think of the infertility specialist's spectacles. How they'd reflected her own pale, stunned face as the man had spoken, his lined face sad, his tone empathetic. *I'm very sorry to tell you this, Endo-san. But it will be very difficult—if not impossible—for you to ever conceive and carry a child.*

Maybe I can blame it on Shun, Satoko thought, feet scraping as she followed the path between the ruins of the old buildings.

Half of infertility cases these days are down to men, aren't they? Low sperm count. Low sperm motility.

But the idea of Shun taking responsibility for anything was laughable. He would always flip the script around on Satoko, accuse her of imagining things, things he'd claim had never even happened. He'd call her *crazy*. And by the end of the conversation, she'd be apologizing to *him* for being upset about what he'd done to *her*.

He is a prison, she thought, *a prison of my own making.*

Suddenly, there were running footsteps above her head.

Looking up, she noticed for the first time a covered walkway that stretched above the path from the roof of the main building to the roof of one of the sub-buildings. Curious, she ducked inside the sub-building, recognizing the waist-high partition that ran all around its interior. She was back at the remains of the old petting zoo.

Then, the platform can't be too far ahead.

Satoko caught a glimpse of bright red, a blur of color in the corner of her eye, and thought she heard the giggle of a child. She stood very still, not sure if this was her mind playing tricks on her, or if it was another of the resort's old spirits. But now she could hear something else on the hot breeze. A wall of ambient sound that was swelling and growing louder. It contained a mixture of voices, talking and murmuring. The joyful screams of children, the splashing of water. It made her think of the municipal pool in Yamaoku, the summer vacation days from her childhood that seemed to last forever. In her mind, she could see the rainbow oil slick of sunscreen on the surface of the warm, silty water and feel the rubbery tug of the yellow plastic floaties on her chubby child arms. She shook her head, trying to get the vision out, to get the noises out, but she wasn't imagining those. The din was deafening now, and close, just beyond the building.

Hurrying through and out, Satoko made her way down the haphazard flight of stairs and emerged into the daylight again, wet tiles beneath her feet. She blinked, trying to process the scene in front of her.

The noisy picnic tables on the pool terrace were packed with people, young women wearing white pedal pushers and chunky straw espadrilles, prominent collarbones peeking out of their ruffled gingham tops. Tanned men in tight shorts and white vests stood around smoking and holding plastic cups of beer. Chubby little boys in swim shorts and little girls in frilly one-piece swimsuits ran in every direction.

The tables were cluttered with plastic cups of beer, Styrofoam containers of fried noodles, and plastic dishes with tall peaks of lurid green, yellow, and pink shaved ice. Leggy waitresses in hot pants moved between the tables, delivering cucumbers on sticks in buckets of ice and clearing away garbage.

The candy-colored waterslides fell away in a precariously steep slope to the right-hand side, and the large pool far below shimmered with bright green water.

Somebody bumped Satoko, muttering, "Oh, excuse me!" She blinked as a teenage girl in a straw hat and a strawberry-print swimsuit nudged her way past her, flip-flops slapping against the hot paving. She led two errant toddlers along by their fat hands.

This is the resort from before, Satoko thought wildly.

Her eyes roamed the scene, wide and staring with disbelief, the hairs on the back of her neck prickling as pulses of disbelief and fear coursed through her veins.

Maybe Shun was right. Maybe she *was* crazy.

It took Satoko several confused seconds to realize there was a commotion going on down in the pool. Some of the people lounging on the terrace had abandoned their cups of beer and chilled cucumber sticks and had started milling around at the top of the slides. Looking down, they touched their faces in concern.

Down in the pool, a woman shrieked.

"Ambulance! Someone call an ambulance!"

A few of the men galloped down the flight of stadium steps to the pool. But one more enterprising one flung himself down one of the slide channels instead and was with the cluster of people in the water in seconds.

Satoko stood apart from the crowd, gazing at the scene and still wondering what the hell was happening to her, when a cold, wet hand slid inside hers.

The drowned child lifted his head to gaze at her. He had shiny hair in a bowl cut, the front part much too short, exposing thick eyebrows like two furry caterpillars. He might have been a beautiful child in life, but now his face was purple and livid, his lips black. Thick beads of water shone suspended on his head of thick hair.

"Where's Mama?" he asked Satoko, his voice sweet, childlike, but there was a cold, rasping after-echo to it.

She shook her head wordlessly, skin crawling at the feel of his damp, swollen hand around hers. She tried to yank her own hand away, but his grip was firm and terrible.

"Mama wasn't watching," the drowned boy said sadly. He must have been about six or seven. *Six or seven forever*, Satoko thought, and wished she could make her throat work so that she could find the release of a scream. Maybe she'd tripped and hit her head. None of this could be happening.

She reached down with her free hand and tried to pry the little dead hand from hers, but he clung on, his fat child fingers preternaturally strong. His thin chest was sunken in, his soaked red swim shorts plastered to his short, bandy little legs. Satoko tried again to scream, terror overwhelming her, but all that came out was a thin, reedy shriek, and the throng of people ignored her, too busy panicking over the drowning child in the water.

But there was no drowning child in the water. There was no water. The pool was empty, strewn with dead leaves and snaking vines, and glistening with rust-tinted puddles. The candy-colored waterslides were mossed over. The terrace was devoid of people, the picnic tables splintered from age and weather.

There was nobody else there now, just Satoko. Satoko and the ghost child clutching her hand.

"*Let go*," Satoko gasped, but the boy shook his head, the beads of water shivering on his glossy crown of black hair.

"Only one of you can leave," he said, his eyes solemn, like a child contemplating a tiny dead animal. There was sadness there, yes, but in a moment, it would be forgotten. The absence of empathy that comes with the innocence of childhood. "*Oneesan* said one of you can go. It isn't you, though. You're an *inferior vessel*. *Oneesan* said so."

The boy blinked up at her, his dark lips opening to reveal a black, bloated tongue. But it wasn't a tongue. It was a leech, glistening and shiny, squirming its way between the boy's yellow needle teeth.

"This place is ours," he said, words forming around the leech. It seemed to be growing bigger, fatter, with every passing moment.

Growing pregnant.

"You should never have come here."

Satoko screamed, yanking her arm again, and the boy's sharp teeth bit down on the body of the tongue-leech, making it explode like a burst black balloon. Blood sprayed Satoko's face and chest. He let go, and the unexpected freedom sent Satoko stumbling over the edge of the waterslides. She landed heavily on her side in the slick fiberglass channel. One arm bent painfully underneath her. The wet, mossy surface of the waterslide propelled her like a rocket down toward the hungry mouth of the empty pool below.

Seconds later, she shot off the end of the slide, landing hard on one shoulder and skidding through a puddle of brackish rainwater. Something crunched and snapped in her back.

Finally, her slide was over, and the world around her was still.

Then, wet, placid footsteps behind her. She couldn't turn her head, couldn't move at all. Her body was broken, useless. She knew the child was behind her. She lay there immobile, the brackish rainwater seeping into her clothes, her cheek raw from scraping against the concrete bottom.

"Please," she begged, coughing blood. "*Please...*"

A tiny body fell with a thump against the hard ground a few feet in front of her as if it had been tossed. Satoko screamed again, her throat raw, her ears ringing.

The child's corpse rolled over, one arm flopping against the floor of the pool, and she could see its scrunched-up face, its bald, half-rotten head. It was a dummy, not a real child at all.

The O-shaped mouth of the plastic dummy opened wide, and the smooth yellow-brown body of a snake came oozing its way out of the face, slithering towards Satoko in undulating movements.

Then redness seeped in, obscuring Satoko's vision. The red mist was within and without. A swirling cloud of crimson particles. Hungry, it swarmed over her broken body. *This is what dying is like*, Satoko thought, her mind detached from her corporeal body, from the feasting that was being visited upon it.

Then there was no pain, no more fear. There was simply nothing.

Nothing at all.

PART FIVE

GHOSTS OF 1975

"The world was the Overlook Hotel, where the party never ended. Where the dead were alive forever."
—Stephen King, *The Shining*

U.S. SERVICEMAN'S DEATH OFFICIALLY RULED AN ACCIDENT, MARINE CORPS FORBIDS ENTRY TO ABANDONED RESORT SITE

Okinawa English News, September 8th, 2017
By Ted "Woody" Hudson

The dilapidated Royal Oceanview Resort in the Takagusuku Park region has been added to a list of sites decreed off-limits to US Marine Corps personnel, said Lt. Gen. Arnold Bradbury in a statement on Monday last week.

The remains of the now graffiti-scrawled resort, a partially burned-out husk that has long been a favored destination for off-duty thrill-seekers and amateur paintball/airsoft aficionados, have been added to the veto list as a result of safety concerns that arose following the untimely death of Seaman James Scrivener, who tragically lost his life at the site.

Seaman Scrivener, who entered the resort's grounds while off-duty to play paintball and camp out with a number of his Marine Corps buddies, was killed when a section of the concrete structure he was standing on collapsed. The decedent sustained devastating head injuries and died at the scene before medical assistance could arrive. An investigation was conducted into the incident, but no evidence of foul play was discovered, and it has now been officially designated a tragic accident, one that could have been entirely prevented.

Under the SOFA (State of Forces Agreement) between the US and Japan, the decree forbids all active-duty Marine Corps sailors, their families, and civilian personnel affiliated with the Marine Corps from accessing the site. Any individuals caught illegally entering the area may be subject to punitive action by the US military.

The sprawling complex of concrete buildings is said to pose a significant risk of injury and loss of life due to the instability of the decaying structure and the hazards posed by the large amount of rusting metalwork and broken glass that litter the site.

The Royal Oceanview Resort was an ambitious leisure complex that faltered and closed its doors soon after opening in the summer of 1975. A series of bizarre deaths reported to have occurred at the resort lend credence to the rumor that the complex is cursed, a direct result of its being built too close to the site of an *Utaki*, the name for a sacred place in the ancient Ryukyuan religion.

Indeed, a long-abandoned gravesite complete with ornate tombs located close to the resort complex itself has long held a kind of magnetic pull that appeals to ghost hunters and fans of the macabre alike...

31

Takagusuku Park, Okinawa, Okinawa Prefecture

*The evening of Sunday July 14, 2019
(The Day Before Marine Day)*

They arrived at the campsite to find the fire burning low. Linh was curled up beside Ollie, her cheek resting on her backpack, apparently asleep.

They were all silent as Miles set about adding more kindling to the fire. Kenji offered to do something for the raw scrape on Steph's spine. Still, she brushed him off, sitting down beside Ollie's motionless form and watching Eloise intently as her friend rummaged in her backpack for bug spray. Steph caught a glint of something gold around her neck. She knew that Eloise didn't wear jewelry except for her watch. And she couldn't even stand that touching her skin. She had to wear a sweatband underneath it. It was one of her weird sensory things, like food items touching each other on her plate or labels in clothing.

So, where did that gold chain come from?

Once Miles was done, he and Eloise sat down by the fire together, away from Steph. They had their heads together, talking in low voices, the orange flames licking their faces.

Steph sighed, reaching into her own backpack for her phone, as Linh abruptly sat up beside Ollie, coughed once, and then vomited blood into her own cupped hands.

There was a moment of complete stunned shock during which nobody moved or spoke. Linh gazed down at her bloody hands in astonishment, her eyes wide and glassy in her pale, waxy face. Then they were all moving and talking at once, and even though Steph had been standing the closest, Eloise was the first one to reach her.

"It's okay, you're okay, Linny, come here, just let me...Okay..." Eloise was babbling soothing words with no meaning, holding Linh's wrists as the blood seeped through her fingers and began to fall onto the dirt ground in thick, dark globs.

"What have you eaten?" Miles stood over them both, his jaw tense. "What have you been drinking? Water?" Linh nodded wordlessly. "Water from where?"

"Convenience store," Linh choked out, more blood dribbling down her chin. "Refilled it. From the spring."

"We all refilled our bottles from that spring," Steph whispered.

The salty-sweet taste. She swallowed hard. The trace memory of it coated her tongue like a film.

Miles shrugged and rubbed his chin with the back of his knuckles again. The gesture was becoming familiar. And irritating. He didn't seem to be aware that he was doing it. "Eloise?"

"Yeah, I mean, I did. I refilled my bottle as well. Do you think there was...something wrong with the water?"

"Linh?" Miles crouched down, touching Linh's forehead and lifting her upper eyelid. "How do you feel?"

"Okay," she said. And the odd thing was, she *looked* okay. Her full cheeks were flushed now, her eyes bright. "I mean, I don't feel sick. I just felt like I needed to cough all of a sudden, and then..."

"Doesn't make any sense," Miles muttered under his breath. "Cyanobacteria poisoning would present with other symptoms...convulsions, tremors..."

"Poisoning?" Eloise's voice was panicked, shaky.

"What if it wasn't the spring?" Steph tasted blood and dirt on her fingers and realized she was gnawing on her nails again.

Stop *doing* that, Stephie.

She forced her hand away. "What if it was Tate again?"

"But why would he poison Linh?" Eloise frowned up at her. "She wasn't there, on the Platform. She doesn't know what the rest of us know."

"What? Can someone please fill me in?" Linh looked back and forth between Steph and Eloise, her eyes wide with fear. "*Steph?*"

"Show me your water bottle," Steph demanded, and Linh dug it out of her backpack. She held it up. It was smeared with blood from her hands.

"That's *mine*. I always tear the label off like that." Steph ran her hands through her hair. Her raw fingers stung. "Jesus."

"Calm down and give her a minute," Miles said. *Dick.* "Linh? Can you stand up and try walking a few steps for me?"

Linh lowered her bloody, trembling hands and pushed herself off from the ground, scrambling to her feet.

"I feel fine?" she said again, walking over to the campfire. "I mean, I can walk and all."

The line between Miles's eyebrows grew deeper, filling with shadow.

"What is it?" Eloise asked him, but he shook his head, crouching down to touch the half-coagulated puddle of Linh's blood vomit. He rubbed his thumb and fingers together.

"I don't know. I don't know what it is he's given her. But I want you all to stay here." He straightened up. "Kenji, man, you feel like coming with? I think we need to find Tate and...*secure* him."

Wow, what a fucking hero.

But Miles was still talking.

"I should've never just let him roam around. Not with your other friend still unaccounted for in the resort somewhere. What was her name again?"

"Satoko." Steph paced back and forth in front of the fire. She felt like an animal in a trap. She bent down, picked up a random stick, and threw it into the flames to have something to do with her hands. Something *else*. "God, he really tried to poison my water? Just because he knows I found out about his dirty little photography project...?"

Then she trailed off, the realization hitting her like a bucket of ice water to the face. "This is my fault," she breathed. "I brought it up. I said it out loud, *here,* and now...now he's going to take this chance to silence *all* of us. Everyone who knows what he's done."

"These are high school kids he took photos of?" Miles asked her, his mouth twisting.

"Junior high," Steph muttered. "One of my students wrote to me about what he was doing. She left me a note in her English homework. When I asked her about it, she said she was too scared to tell the school. She didn't want her parents to find out, but she thought I might be able to get Tate to stop. Then, some of her friends came to see me, too. He's been putting the photos on the internet. I think he...I think he makes money on them."

Why didn't you say *something?* The guilt was like a knife twisting inside her gut. *It's all your fault. Linh didn't know. Whatever is in that water, it was meant for* you.

Linh coughed, spitting blood between her feet.

"This is the kind of person you choose to associate with?" Miles asked, his voice thick with disgust, not addressing any one of them in particular, but Steph knew he was speaking to Eloise.

And is he talking about just Tate, or me, too?

"Let's go." Kenji moved forward, grimly patting Miles on the shoulder. His face was dark with anger. "Let's go, now, and deal with that asshole."

"Yeah, all right," Miles said, taking Eloise's hand and pressing the heavy flashlight against her palm. "Stay here. We'll be back."

32

Tate had sixteen mosquito bites at last count, including the new one, the biggest and juiciest one, somehow located on the globe of his right buttcheek. It throbbed as he shifted his weight on the low stone wall.

He had his chin resting on his hand, like that statue of the thinking guy. And Tate *was* thinking. Thinking about what a colossal, steaming pile of shit his life had somehow become, all in the span of one afternoon.

He had no idea how Steph knew about the photos. He'd been careful, but the girls must have squealed to her. He hadn't been expecting that. He knew they would never go to the faculty or their parents, but Steph was young, female, technically an outsider, and the students all liked her. An oversight. *Stupid.* The word of a gaggle of junior high girls wouldn't usually count for much, but if Steph backed them up, he was screwed. He could have handled the girls, placated them somehow, just enough to keep them quiet until he made it out of Japan. But Steph was the issue. There would be no placating Steph.

Fucking bitch. This whole trip had been set up for her. He'd even invited Satoko, that clinging gaijin hunter, to help him put the screws on Steph. All he'd needed was the right setting, the right opportunity, a chance to show Steph what she was missing. But he'd fucked everything up. And now *he* was fucked.

Tate straightened up and began cracking his knuckles

Actually, it wasn't even about Steph anymore. Now that Kenji knew, Tate was doubly fucked. Irrevocably fucked. He'd need to get out of Japan as soon as possible. If there were any repercussions after that, Dad could take care of it, and they could lawyer up. Tate reminded himself that it was just a few pictures, nothing even explicit, just suggestive. It was *art*. And he'd *paid* them. The girls sure hadn't been distraught when they were out shopping for luxury brand bags or whatever dumb shit they'd spent their cut on.

Not that it mattered. They'd be baying for his blood, the good residents of Yamaoku City. The fact that he'd never laid a finger on any of the girls wouldn't count for jack shit, of course. Best case scenario, he was facing deportation and public shame, if not actual time in a Japanese prison. He'd heard that Japanese prisons were the worst.

Okay. So, he'd just get the fuck out of dodge. Before Kenji got the chance to make his move.

All Tate needed to do was get off this god-damned cliff and make it to the airport. Fuck going back to Yamaoku. He'd get on the first flight he could find, to Taiwan, Hong Kong, or whatever. Slip away while the others were distracted.

And avoid that creepy fuck, Tate reminded himself. Miles was *off* in some way. Tate knew that of all of them, Miles was the only one that could have possibly brained Kenji like that. The girls didn't have enough arm strength to knock out a grown man.

What Tate didn't know was why. The other American had told them nothing about himself, and yet he'd let little things slip, things that set off Tate's bullshit radar. If that guy was a backpacker, Tate would eat his fucking camera.

What *was* his motive for whacking Kenji, though?

Maybe just the fact that he was a homicidal fucking lunatic, one who saw a chance and decided to capitalize on it?

The girls hated Tate now. To them, he was scum. Still, he didn't want them getting hurt or worse. Miles may have started with Kenji, but where would it end?

Maybe what Miles wanted was to get the girls alone. To render them defenseless and vulnerable. He'd already been putting the moves on Eloise, after all. If it was the girls that Miles ultimately wanted, then his next target would probably be Tate himself.

Tate drained his canteen, grimacing over the odd, sweet taste of the spring water. He'd be needing a refill soon. Sighing, he heaved himself off the stone wall and started walking, without any real purpose. He was so distracted, and the shadows had now grown so thick that it took him a few seconds to notice the woman on the path a little way up ahead.

She was medium-height and fashion-model thin, with bobbed black hair, and she was leaning against the smooth wall of the main hotel building smoking a cigarette.

As Tate froze, she pitched the cigarette, pushing herself off the wall and smiling at him. She wore a canary-yellow shirt dress, belted at the waist, with white tights and clunky, old-fashioned platform shoes. Tate stiffened as the woman came striding towards him on the path, her hips rolling, her lips spreading in a glossy red smile.

"You're late," she said, amused impatience in her tone. She said something else after that, but Tate's Japanese was—though he hated to admit it—little more than a glorified smattering of traveler's survivalist vocab, and he couldn't make sense of her. It was clear, though, that she wanted him to follow her. She beckoned with slim, white fingers, the long nails painted cherry red.

His feet moving without his input, he followed her to the broad, horseshoe-shaped doorway of the hotel's side entrance.

That was odd. It was bricked over a few moments ago.

Once inside, he rotated slowly on the spot, looking around him in confusion, gazing up at the dim orange sunset glow that streamed in through the intact glass ceiling. The floors were polished tiling. The yellow leather chairs, the low glass table...they were all clean and shiny and whole. People were sitting in the chairs, chattering, laughing, smoking, and sipping coffee from fat white cups. The air was hazy with wisps of grey cigarette smoke, but underneath the fug, it smelled clean, like disinfectant and fresh flowers.

A man and a woman stood by the check-in desk with brown leather suitcases piled up beside them. The man wore a beige flannel suit, with a trilby hat perched on his head. The much younger woman wore a powder-blue skirt suit and white boxy high heels.

A small boy in a patterned robe ran laughing past Tate, sleeves flapping, his bowl-cut hair lifted by a breeze of his own making. His face was a gappy grin of delight. He was pursued by a slightly older boy wearing the same sort of robe, his slippers slapping against the smooth flooring. The scent of shampoo wafted past.

The little gold bell on the counter sounded—*Ding! Ding!*—as the man in the trilby hammered on it.

No one paid any attention to Tate except the woman, who glanced over her shoulder at him, still smiling her glossy red smile. He followed her down the corridor. Warm, mellow light spilled through the plate-glass windows on the western side in sheets, dust motes dancing like glitter in the air.

A preteen girl with a glossy ponytail walked ahead of them. She wore sandals, bell-bottom blue jeans, and a sleeveless white blouse. As Tate watched, she plucked the seat of her jeans out of the crack of her ass with a total lack of self-consciousness, never once looking behind her.

His companion ducked down an offshoot. She paused in front of one of the guest room doors, produced a key with a diamond-shaped plastic key fob dangling from it, and unlocked the door. Flashing him an inscrutable look from beneath her heavy dark lashes, she gestured with the flat of her hand, indicating that he should step inside.

What's happening, Tate wondered, his mind thick and heavy and slow. Everything seemed slightly blurry, and he found that if he didn't intentionally slow down his movements—if he didn't keep his head as still as possible—the blurring effect got worse. It was like being drunk.

The next few moments passed in a series of disjointed vignettes with no discernible flow to the passage of time. He entered the room. The woman latched the door. He sat down on the bedspread. The floor was hard somehow, beneath his stockinged feet, but it hadn't even occurred to him to remove his shoes. Where had they gone? The woman crushed out a cigarette in the glass ashtray on the desk, a cigarette he didn't remember seeing her light. She exhaled a plume of gray smoke between glistening white teeth.

"I wasn't expecting a foreigner," she said, and Tate found that he could understand her, though he was sure she wasn't speaking English. "It's an extra charge for foreigners. Please understand."

Tate nodded, although he didn't understand. Not even a little.

"You have to bathe first. I can bathe you, but that will also incur an extra charge. What would you prefer?"

Tate shook his head, wanting to ask the woman who she was, what was going on, what all of this was *about*. But the act of shaking his head caused a bright bolt of pain to slice through his brain, right between his eyes, and he hissed, pinching the bridge of his nose.

The woman went over to the curtains and twitched them shut, cutting off the amber glow and shrouding the room in darkness. She moved over to the dresser, picked up a neatly folded white cotton towel and a similarly folded blue and white robe, and offered them to Tate.

Now, he stood alone in front of a fluttering half-curtain in an empty hallway, with no idea of how he'd gotten there. There was no more amber glow but only purplish moonlight streaking through the corridor's bare windows, and all was quiet.

The curtain fluttered invitingly, as if blown on by teasing lips, and Tate stared at the character printed on it in a curly white font. He knew that the character meant *Hot Water*. He ducked under the curtain and entered a white, pristine space. The walls were lined with wooden benches and cubbyholes, and somewhere, there was an audible drip, drip, drip. It was hot and steamy inside, and as Tate shuffled over to one of the benches, he realized he was completely nude.

"Don't worry. It's reserved," the woman said behind him, and Tate turned, registering with some surprise the fact that she was also naked.

She had narrow shoulders and prominent collarbones and was very pale, but her skin was soft when she brushed past him, reaching for one of the empty wicker baskets. Her small breasts barely swung as she bent over, clutching the towel and robe he didn't remember handing back to her. Her dark, shiny hair hung over her face. He couldn't make out her expression, but Tate could see the individual hairs of her scalp against her stark white part-line as if they were suddenly in sharp focus.

Everything else remained hazy and indistinct, like the dreamlike effect you saw in old glamour photography.

Vaseline on the lens, that's how they did that, Tate thought, randomly, dimly aware that something very odd was happening. He was sure he was supposed to be somewhere else. It was a long way away from here. He knew that much. Not in the dimension of space but in the dimension of *time*. A place where a snake with a false name was, even now, slithering through the rubble and the undergrowth, tracking its prey under the moonlight.

"I have to get back and protect them," Tate said, his tongue fat and numb inside his mouth.

The young woman straightened up and, as if he hadn't spoken, slotted the basket into the empty cubbyhole by Tate's elbow. Then she turned and walked away from him, sliding her white feet out of her plastic sandals and stepping barefoot onto the raised main floor of the room. It was an area that contained a double row of silver mirrors and sparkling white sinks.

She stood there for a moment, not moving, before coyly looking over her shoulder at Tate. A deep dimple formed in one round buttock as she shifted her weight to the other foot, smiling her cherry smile.

"Come," she said, and Tate shuffled forward, his slippers falling away from his feet as he stepped up out of the changing area to join her.

"So much hair," the woman said, wrinkling her nose as she raked Tate's body with her eyes. "Dirty."

She turned to face the sink, picking up a shining silver straight razor that rested on the edge of the basin. Tate reached for her wrist in alarm as she turned to him, holding the razor aloft, and she smiled.

"Just relax," she said. "Let's clean you up."

She moved behind Tate, pushing him down by his shoulders until he could see himself framed in the shining square of the mirror. His face was flecked with mud, and he'd caught the sun on the planes of his cheeks. The skin there looked angry and red.

The woman brought the razor up slowly, holding the flat of it against Tate's neck.

She smiled at him in the mirror. Her reflection had black gums and black teeth. There were camera lenses in the sockets where her eyes should be, the lids black plastic shutters jittering and ratcheting. Tate cried out in disgust and horror, knocking the woman's hand away as he whirled around to face her.

"*Hai, cheese,*" she rasped, holding up Tate's camera. The one he'd left in the cubbyhole. But no, this wasn't Tate's camera. It was an old Seventies Polaroid. The camera flashed, the bulb popping, blinding him. Tate lunged for her, the camera falling to the floor and shattering into multiple pieces.

His hands closed on nothing but empty air. His breathing came ragged, his heart hammering in his chest. Tate looked wildly around the room. It was broken down and filthy now, the mirrors bubbled over with rust, the sinks cracked and stained, the floor strewn with dead leaves and rotten hanks of wood. Beyond the sliding doors that led to the bathing area came the sound of splashing water.

Tate's bare toes bumped against the fallen pieces of the Polaroid camera, sending them spinning and clattering aside. Picking his way through the debris in his bare feet, Tate inched across the room, pausing by the sliding doors to the bath area.

A greenish glow filtered through the opaque plastic. The woman was singing softly inside, her voice sweet and melodic above the sound of sloshing water. Tate's nerves screamed at him not to do it, but he slid the door open on its tracks.

The woman wallowed in the filthy, brackish water of the sunken tiled bath. It was almost large enough to qualify as a small swimming pool, and as Tate watched with disgusted disbelief, she began to swim lazy laps back and forth, mulchy leaves and foamy brown scum adhering to her neck and back.

The wall adjoining the bath was one large empty windowpane that led directly to a small, enclosed area, open to the outside air above. Rotten vegetation and unidentifiable debris filled the small space. Moonlight streaked in, giving the woman's pale swimming form an anemic blue hue.

"What's happening?" Tate demanded, his voice cracking. She smiled, gums pink and healthy once more, teeth white and glittering. The water she floated in was now crystal clear and lightly steaming. The air filled with the scent of shampoo and floral body wash.

The woman rolled over onto her back, seal-like. Her small breasts bobbed lightly, white peaks protruding just a little from the surface of the water like tiny twin icebergs.

"Why don't you join me?" she suggested, and Tate shook his head, the scene blurring before his eyes, pain streaking through his brain once more.

"Imamura-san said to do anything you wanted," she said, reaching the side of the bath, clutching it with her slim, white fingers, the lacquered red nails clacking against the tiles with a chitinous sound.

"I don't know who that is," Tate muttered, backing up, the wet tiles slippery, treacherous beneath his feet.

"He's the manager, of course." The woman smiled, her cheeks pink from the heat, her skin jeweled all over with glistening water droplets. "He's still here, you know. We're all still here. All of us who died at the resort..."

"Stop," Tate whispered, taking another step backward. "This isn't real, this is some kind of—"

"*Ara*. Checkout time so soon?" the woman asked, speaking over him, an element of sadness in her voice. "It's a shame he couldn't stay for the party."

Realizing, after a few seconds' delay, that she was talking to someone behind him, Tate whirled around.

A middle-aged woman stood there. She wore a Japanese hotel maid's dark pajama-like uniform, and she was brandishing another silver razor. Or perhaps it was the same one from before. Only now, the blade was dark and dull with rust. It still sliced easily through Tate's jugular vein, so smooth, he barely felt it. Blood sprayed in a freshet, sprinkling the woman's stiff, unmoving face.

Tate went down to his knees, clutching his neck, eyes wide in disbelief as blood started to pool beneath him on the shining tiles.

The sliding door trundled on its hinges as the maid stepped out. She was followed in due course by the naked woman, who heaved herself out of the bath and paused for just a moment beside Tate's crumpled form. His watery blood swirled and eddied around her slim white feet, bubbling up between her toes.

Then the sliding door clattered shut behind her, and Tate was alone, the room filling with swirling steam, the scent of floral shampoo, the metallic stench of blood.

His eyes grew glassy, his body sliding forward until he lay prone on the wet floor. His lifeblood pumped out over the tiles in dark, rhythmic spurts.

Where it met and mingled with the water, it spun and whirled and spread out, forming little crimson tendrils like curling smoke.

Sometime later, the sliding door opened again with a juddering sound. A pair of battered brown leather boots came sloshing over the sodden tiles, stopping just in front of Tate. He blinked and jerked, snorting and coughing at the same time, expelling a double lungful of blood. He tried to speak, to form the word *Help*, but his vocal cords didn't seem to be connected anymore.

With a dripping red hand, he reached out, a dying man grasping for salvation.

Then his fingers closed, curling weakly as hope drained from him faster than the blood he was so rapidly losing.

He knew those boots.

33

The burnt umber of dusk seeped between the trees like an insidious gas, rendering everything around in stark black silhouettes. Below the concrete canopy of the platform, Steph lay on one side, head against her backpack, resting her tired, aching body. Linh and Eloise were close by. Slumped, reclining shadows, the three of them formed a lazy ring around the campfire.

Steph found the crackles and pops emanating from its red glowing core to be oddly comforting. It was almost like this was just a camping trip, friends having fun out in the woods. Maybe later, they'd roast marshmallows, drink beer, and play *Never Have I Ever*.

Or maybe later, they'd all be dead.

Steph cast her mind back over the events of the afternoon. The dead deer carcass. The weird photo glitch. That disgusting CPR dummy. Tate...Tate's steel fingers closing around her throat. The *habu,* the storm, the landslide. Kenji, face down in the muck. Bloody vomit pouring from Linh's mouth.

It's too fucking much. Anger bubbled in the pit of Steph's stomach. *Too fucking much to process.*

Her feet felt like hamburger meat. The scrape on her spine stung like acid. Why hadn't there been any planes? Any helicopters? Why hadn't someone seen their signal fires? Why hadn't anyone come to help them?

She shifted, the hard ground lumpy and uncomfortable beneath her. She wondered, again, what could have happened to Satoko. If she was still alive, then she was alone in the resort. At least Steph had that.

At least she wasn't alone up here.

Something buzzed beneath her head, like an angry, insistent wasp. She frowned, irritated, rocking her head back and forth. *Cut that out.*

Then it happened again.

Steph sat bolt upright, grabbing at the zipper on her backpack. *My phone?* She located it with fumbling fingers and unlocked it with a snap.

That's weird. I thought I switched it off. Preserve battery life. I wouldn't...

She groaned, her eyes going right to the battery percentage. 3%

Shit!

But wait a minute. Was that a bar? Was that a *fucking* bar?

It was. Just the one. But one was all she needed. Right?

The phone buzzed again in her hand, the screen filling up with message notifications and push alerts. They almost completely obscured the background, a shot of herself and Eloise in colorful *yukata* robes at Yamaoku's summer festival last year.

Breathing fast, Steph thumbed the notifications away with irritation, tapped the big green call icon, and punched in 119.

She set it to speaker, but there was nothing. No dial tone. Just silence. She brought it to her ear to check. She couldn't hear anything.

She tried 110. Same deal. She remembered hearing somewhere that there was some sort of international emergency number, but she didn't know it. In desperation, she tried 911.

Nothing.

The single, solitary bar popped out of existence, replaced a nanosecond later with the words *No Signal*.

She closed her eyes briefly, mouthing obscenities. But there'd been a *bar*, and right now, that seemed huge. Maybe if the others still had charge, they could try again, they could...

Steph opened her message app, thinking she could at least skim her texts before her battery gave up the ghost.

2%

There was somehow only one new text message from an actual person in amongst the usual mess of app notifications. She thumbed it open, brows knitting over the name of the sender. She had them saved as *Jenna (Annoying Girl from EFA Orient. Tokyo.)*

What the fuck is this random girl texting me for? Steph wondered, skimming down, and as she read, the skin on her arms prickled and shrank, and her guts turned to lead.

It was some sort of link to an article with a preview bubble loaded beneath it.

www.lifeonokinawa.co.jp/news/2019/07/14/awol-marine-wanted/

AWOL Marine wanted for questioning in connection with suspected death of Iowa girl in 2012...

A manhunt is underway today for a U.S. Marine stationed out of Air Station Futenma. 25-year-old Adam Preston Davis absconded fr...

The preview bubble had a photo showing a pretty, laughing girl of about high school age with multicolored brackets on her teeth. The photo bore a legend inset:

Presumed deceased: Cadence Marie Walker

Life on Okinawa...a US Marine...

Steph scrolled down, blinking beads of panicked sweat out of her eyes, her throat knotted up into a hot little ball.

Jenna—(Annoying Girl from EFA Orient. Tokyo.)

Hey saw your post! Beachy keen! You in Okinawa rn yea??? Maybe watch out for THIS fuckin guy! Sounds like a real gent! Never trust a man with a mustache am I right? BE SAFE babes xo

"*Shit*," Steph hissed between her teeth, and there was a rustling and a crackling of leaves as Eloise and Linh slowly sat up on their elbows to look at her.

"What?" Linh said blearily, then again, more harshly as she took in the look on Steph's face—"*What?*"

Steph's eyes shot down to the screen again, sweaty thumb scudding over the smooth surface as she looked frantically at the tiny number in the corner.

1%

She clamped down with her finger and thumb, pressing the side buttons for a screenshot. Although what the fuck good that was going to do them, she didn't know, and as she opened her mouth to say something like, *you need to see this*, the screen went black.

In disbelief, Steph hammered the power button with her thumb.

It was no good.

The phone was dead.

34

Splitting up was Kenji's idea.

That suited Miles just fine, though it really highlighted Kenji's ineptness. You never split up in unfamiliar terrain, especially not when pursuing an enemy that could be armed. Clearly, the guy had never heard of the buddy system.

Miles toyed with the idea of looping back for Kenji but decided he'd rather prioritize dealing with Tate. He didn't like to think of himself as the kind of person who enjoyed violence for the sake of it, but he was quite looking forward to this. He'd keep it quick and clean, although maybe he should let the rich prep school boy get a hit or two in on him. That might make for better optics. Perhaps he'd let Eloise mop him up afterward. He got the feeling she'd enjoy that.

Miles crunched down the covered walkway, taking a path they hadn't explored yet. He was trying to put himself in the mind of the enemy. If Tate was hiding out, his first instinct would be to find an enclosed space to hole up in. He'd be inside somewhere, seeking the false shelter of the building.

Ahead, the path petered out, but there was a long, low building along there. It was some kind of facility, although Miles had no idea what it might be for.

He ducked through the half-collapsed doorway, entering a corridor. A wispy scrap of curtain hung from an alcove. No, it wasn't an alcove. It was another corridor, one that ended in a filth-encrusted plastic sliding door a few short feet in.

Miles slid the door open as slowly as possible, trying not to make a sound, but it was hard going. The track was stiff with rust.

The space inside resembled something like a gym locker room. Half-rotten cubbyholes, a line of cracked, stained sinks. It seemed he'd found the resort's communal bathing facilities.

Something crunched beneath his feet. An old Polaroid camera lay on the filthy floor in bits and pieces. There was even an old Polaroid photo sticking out of the slot as well. It was just a black square, a dud shot.

There was another sliding door, a dim bluish light seeping through its moldy plastic. Miles paused in front of it for a few moments before slowly inching it open.

He saw the body right away, his brain registering the fact that it was naked, his eyes focusing fast on the shard of blood-streaked glass lying on the wet pink tile. It appeared to have fallen from the man's white, dead-crab hand.

Stepping inside, Miles finally recognized Tate. The man's face was gray and bloodless, his handsome features slack, the eyes vacant and staring.

Miles crouched down, touching the body's damp, clammy back. It was still warm.

"All this over a couple of dirty pictures? Fuck, man." Miles shook his head. "I'm sure Daddy would have cracked his wallet and gotten you out of it. Still...thanks for taking the trash out for me. That was real nice of you."

He patted Tate's clammy shoulder.

That was when Tate gasped.

One moment, he was lying dead in a puddle of his own blood. The next, he was jerking and coughing, his eyes suddenly alive, bright and panicked.

"Jesus, fuck," Miles growled, almost angrily. He reached for the shard of ruby glass, but then there was a touch on his shoulder, an insistent tapping.

He looked up to see the Marine standing there, offering him a knife. Wordlessly, he took it. Then, grabbing Tate by his sodden blond hair, he pulled his head back and slit his throat. Ear to ear, a neat cut just above the original jagged wound. Easy, like slaughtering a pig.

Tate gurgled, wild eyes fixed accusingly on Miles as the last bit of life seeped out of his body.

When it was over, Miles got to his feet, wiping the knife against his leg, his upper lip curling back from his teeth with mild disgust. When the knife was mostly clean, he held it up, recognizing it immediately.

"Thanks, man. Thought I lost this."

The Marine chuckled. "Found it lodged in a tree trunk. After it bounced off the back of that Japanese guy's head."

Miles turned to face the man, who was standing behind him, dressed in red-splattered camo. "Lucky fuck, huh?"

The man in the camo smiled.

Miles reached for the small of his back and pulled a brown leather knife sheath from his belt. Almost lovingly, he slid the knife inside it before snapping it back onto the belt, fastening and untucking his T-shirt over it, concealing it from view.

"Wanna hazard a guess why he's naked?" Miles asked the Marine, who said nothing.

Not that it really mattered. Tate was obviously sick in the head. It was just a weird detail, that was all. And where did he leave his clothes? Maybe he'd stripped off, piece by piece, on his way here. People did that sometimes, when they were losing their minds.

"Give me a hand, would you?"

Miles hummed to himself as he grabbed Tate's ankles. The two men dragged the body over the filth-smeared green tiles to the sunken bath. Positioning the body parallel to the edge of the tiled hole in the floor, Miles braced his foot against Tate's hip and then, with a grunt, rolled him over.

Tate's body rotated, arms flapping like a broken marionette as it fell several feet to the hard-tiled bottom. The impact knocked Tate's final breath out of his body, a belch of air bursting between his pallid lips.

"I know, I know," Miles said. "Got to cover you up, though, man. Don't want the others stumbling on you all naked and gross and dead, now, do we?"

Miles looked down at Tate for a moment, rubbing his knuckles against his lips.

Pink. And marble-white.

Like a freshly butchered hog.

Miles shook his head and resumed humming to himself. Then he grabbed an armful of dead leaves—there were plenty strewn about the bathhouse—and dumped them on Tate's corpse.

Once Tate was mostly covered, Miles dusted off his hands and crunched back outdoors into the fading twilight.

Outside, the man in the splattered camo was waiting for him.

"AJ," Miles said.

"Jimmy," the man responded, taking Miles up on his offer of a handshake. Jimmy's hand was ice-cold, but that was because he was dead. "Miles" already knew that. The socking great hole in the back of the guy's head was a dead giveaway.

"What happened to you, man?"

"Paintballing accident."

"That's paint?" Miles indicated Jimmy's red-splattered fatigues.

"The floor collapsed. They couldn't get the chopper up here in time."

Miles licked his lips. "Yeah, I think I remember hearing about that on base. Sucks, man."

Jimmy smiled, inclining his head. "They're looking for you, you know. Got a BOLO out."

"Yeah, I figured. I thought about running, trying to get off Oki, but..." Miles sniffed, knuckling away sweat from beneath his nose. "I've got a different plan now."

Right. Ellery Queen. One last chance.

Focus.

Reaching behind him, he unsnapped the knife again.

"That's the plan?" Jimmy's glittering black eyes fixed on the dark blade.

"Huh?"

Jimmy inclined his head again. He was smiling. "Weren't you going to take them all out?"

Miles stared at Jimmy.

"Hey, the guy in the bath was a mercy kill. You saw it. He was on his way out already. I just...helped him along."

"And the Japanese guy?"

Miles rubbed his knuckles against his lips.

"All right, fine. I'll level with you, Jimmy. First, I was just gonna take the Japanese guy out. On principle, you know? Fucked that up. Then the naked freak in there started causing me all kinds of headaches. The British guy was never going to be a threat—too weak, too out of shape—but either way, it doesn't matter now. That pit viper already did my work for me there."

"We aim to please," Jimmy said, still smiling.

Miles smiled back, his brow slightly furrowed. "What's that?"

"All of us. All of us here at The Oceanview. Our goals...align with yours."

"Yeah?" Miles thought about that for a second. "All right. In that case, there's something else you can help me with."

"What's that?"

"With Tate checked out early, I have to do all the staging by myself. I've still gotta really finger him for what happened in the woods earlier, see. Get that bitch Stephanie off my back. Get all the girls on Team Miles, once and for good. You get me?"

"I get you, AJ."

Miles held out the knife. "Be a pal and stab me."

Jimmy raised an eyebrow.

"Come on. Stab me. And if you can, make it look a lot worse than it is."

Jimmy shook his head.

"We facilitate. You do the real work yourself."

Miles paused for a moment, considering this. "All right," he said.

It didn't take long for Miles to locate a suitable stretch of wall, one with a crevice about the right height. He readied the knife. The blade was sharp. Ka-Bar, standard Marine Corps issue. He pulled out his old lighter, the one he'd taken back from the geeky girl with the glasses, and quickly sanitized the blade. Then, as an afterthought, he pulled out his hip flask of whiskey and splashed the knife with the amber liquid. Knocking his head back, he drained the last few drops of the whiskey. Then he wedged the handle of the knife into the crack in the concrete until it was stuck in there nice and tight and deep, the blade horizontal, poking out about four or five inches.

He was still humming. It was a good song, an old one by one of those new-wave eighties British bands his mom used to listen to for hours on end. He'd be sent home early from school for some infraction, to find the walls pulsing softly with the bass line. For some reason, it had been stuck in his head all afternoon, like an earworm that had crawled inside him, burrowed deep inside his brain. What the fuck was it called, again? It was something about a snake. It was driving him insane.

"You know that song, Jimmy?"

Jimmy said nothing.

Miles turned and positioned the tip of the knife against his shoulder, wriggling around until he found the right spot.

"Got to make sure not to hit the brachial artery," he told Jimmy. "Otherwise, I'm just gonna bleed out like a damn fool."

Jimmy said nothing.

"I know what you're thinking. I could slash myself in the arm. A flesh wound would look impressive enough, sure. But it wouldn't have the convincing *verisimilitude* of a stab wound to the back. Only a lunatic would accuse me of doing something like *this* to myself, right?"

Jimmy said nothing.

"Besides, if this doesn't work, it doesn't work. It's a gamble, sure. But what the fuck do I have left to lose?"

Jimmy said nothing.

"Die trying. That's my motto. Hold tight, Jimmy."

Hissing as the sharp blade's tip began to needle against his skin, Miles took a deep breath. Mentally, he was preparing himself, waiting for the right moment to rear back, to slam himself against the wall, to let the knife eat its way through his shoulder. He was confident that he had the tip in the correct spot between his collarbone and scapula. It should slide right through.

He stopped humming, fumbling the knife's leather sheath out of his pocket and slotting it in between his teeth. Then he began to hyperventilate, spit whistling around the well-worn leather, soaking into it. He would need to be quiet.

He took five deep, rapid, panting breaths and then rammed himself back against the wall. The tip of the blade popped through the front of his shoulder, piercing the fabric of his shirt, blood blooming across the material. At the same time, he released a long, muffled mewl of agony, his teeth chomping down into the leather sheath, marking it.

"*Fuck,*" he gasped, spitting out the sheath. "*Fucking hell.*"

Taking a few more short, panicky breaths, he waited for his blurred vision to clear before slowly leaning forward, the knife sliding back through him with a sucking sound.

Finally, it was free, and he could stumble forward, falling to his knees, clutching his shoulder. Blood dripped through his knuckles. He remained there, crouched in the dim early evening light for several minutes, eyes screwed shut, breath whistling harshly through his gritted teeth.

Finally, he got to his feet, snatching up the discarded knife sheath.

He was alone again.

Jimmy was gone.

Bracing himself against the wall with his good shoulder, Miles tugged the bloodied knife out of the crevice with a grunt and wiped it perfunctorily against his shirt, making sure it didn't look too clean. Then he slotted it back into its bulky leather sheath before tucking it into the back of his belt again. This last part, the re-sheathing of the knife, he did from pure muscle memory. It was deeply ingrained, basic knife safety, nothing more. He didn't give it a second thought.

His shoulder ached like a gunshot wound. He looked down at it, chin tucked tight against his chest, holding his shirt taut so he could see the hole. The blood was oozing but not pumping. He hadn't nicked the artery after all. He huffed out a triumphant lungful of air, lost for a moment in delighted disbelief.

Finally, something was going his way.

And somehow, the act of self-mutilation, the revelatory sight of his own rich red running blood, had unlocked something inside him. It had brought everything back into sharp focus.

Ellery.

He smiled and set off slowly, his shoulder throbbing, making his way through the darkening woods in the direction of their camp.

He was humming again.

35

Steph had lost it. That was the only explanation. Eloise stared into her friend's wild, frantic eyes, trying to nod understandingly. Something about a text message, someone called *Cadence*, Miles being some guy called Adam, an *escaped killer* from a nearby base. There was a warbling trill of insanity to Steph's voice, her words running into one another as she gripped Eloise's arms with fingers of hard bone.

"And we need to get away from here, from *him*, before he comes back, before he kills the rest of us..."

Did she really believe this? Oh, God, she *did*. Eloise would need to humor her, talk her down gently. The stress, the situation. She watched as Steph's cheeks colored, livid with sudden anger. Then she flinched as Steph brandished her dead, black smartphone in Eloise's face.

"Are you fucking *listening* to me, Eloise?"

Miles. An escaped marine. A crazed lunatic. All he was missing was a hook for a hand. Eloise tried to keep her mouth and brows in a straight line, tried to look like she was taking Steph seriously. But you couldn't reason with someone in a delusion. Could you?

"Steph," she began, making an attempt. "Everything Miles has done has been to help us. Who pulled Tate off you when he had his hands around your neck? Who helped Ollie? Who was the only person willing to look for Satoko?"

Steph stared at her, her entire being seeming to radiate fury and impatience. Eloise swallowed hard and opened her mouth to speak again, but there was a crunch of old leaves behind her, and they all lifted their gazes to see...

To see a man stumbling down the path towards them. He was clutching his shoulder, his shirt dark with blood.

Chris?

The man staggered towards Eloise, his blue eyes clouded with pain. He winced as she reached out, trancelike, to touch his blood-streaked arm.

"Tate," he rasped, going down to his knees.

"You...found Tate?" Steph demanded, stepping back, her voice flat, her face black thunder.

"Stabbed me," Miles coughed. "In the back. Shoulder, I think. He ambushed me and ran off like a coward. Left the knife in me. I pulled it out. I think..." He coughed again. "Think I maybe shouldn't have done that."

A knife...

"A knife?" Steph was a blur, her finger-bitten hand drifting slowly to her mouth. "*Tate* had a knife?"

"Yeah. Just a sec." Miles brought his legs out in front of him, reaching around to the back of his waistband. He fumbled there, beneath his shirt, for a few seconds, gasping with effort before slowly pulling out a long knife with a dark, shining blade. He held it out to Eloise.

She stared at it. Made no move to take it. Her hands flexed by her sides, her chest heaving with rapid breaths. For once, her inner monologue had nothing to say. She was completely blank. Hollow. Her mind was an open void.

"El?" Steph took a step closer. Reached for her.

Eloise wheeled around, taking one stride away and stumbling, falling to her hands and knees in the dirt.

"*El?*" Steph's hands were on her shoulders, and Eloise heard a high-pitched whistling sound. It was coming from her own throat. "What's happening?"

"She's having a panic attack," Eloise heard Miles say, his voice sounding distant.

"Shit. Fuck. What do I *do*?"

"Talk to her. Get her to name..." Miles grunted, then gasped. "...three things in the vicinity."

"*What?*" Steph spat.

But Eloise had heard him. She grabbed onto his words like they were flotsam, floating past her. She was drowning, drowning in the sea of her own lungs.

"Knife," Eloise gasped. "Backpack. Linh."

"Good. Now...do sounds."

"Fire...fire crackling. Leaves...rustling. Steph breathing."

"All right. Good. Touch your nose."

Eloise did so, holding her breath, then gasping and coughing. Her lungs opened. She found that she could breathe.

"Touch your shoulder...knee...how's that?"

"Better," Eloise gasped. They waited. She coughed again, swallowed, and rubbed her shaking hands over her face. She was suddenly freezing. Her body was drenched in rapidly cooling sweat. "I'm...all right. Can you put that...away somewhere?"

"All right." Miles reached behind him and tucked the knife into the back of his belt. He showed his palms. "See? It's gone." Then, groaning softly, he leaned back, eyes closing with pain.

Not Chris. Not Chris. Chris is dead. Breathe. Please breathe.

Forcing herself to inhale slowly, Eloise shrugged Steph's hand off her shoulder and crawled over to Miles. Kneeling behind him, she cupped the back of his head and gave him her lap to lean against. His face was pale, a smear of dark, dried blood beneath his chin.

Steph stood over them. Eloise ignored her.

"So, Tate had that? The knife, I mean?"

"Yeah. He's gone...fucking crazy. Must have had the knife on him the whole time. It might have been what he used to attack

Kenji. He threw it at his head. I'm guessing Kenji was lucky and got the handle end. Tate tried..." Miles coughed. "Tried to kill him."

"God..." Eloise muttered. *Fucking Tate.*

"What about Kenji? And Satoko?" Steph demanded.

"I don't know. I didn't see the girl. Kenji went off alone. They're out there somewhere in the resort. And Tate's still roaming around out there, out of his fucking mind."

"What are we going to do?" Eloise asked, her voice faint.

"Nothing," Miles said, shifting and wincing painfully. "We do nothing. We stay here. Wait for rescue. No one goes off alone. We stick together."

"What if Tate comes back here?" Linh spoke up then, from by the fire. "What if he comes and attacks us here?"

"Well..." Miles plucked the stiffening material of his shirt away from his wound, blood smearing across his fingers. "We've got his knife, at least. But I'm not sure I can protect you girls like this. I mean, I'll try. But if he comes here, I think one of you is maybe going to have to use it on him."

"You mean, like...scare him off with it?" Eloise stroked a fleck of mud out of the golden hairs of Miles's eyebrow.

"He's beyond that now. You're going to have to take him out."

"Take him *out*? With a *knife*? Are you *insane*?" Steph got to her feet, looking terrified. "You're saying we're going to have to *kill* him?"

"I guess that's your choice," Miles said, looking up at her. "Kill or be killed."

"Fuck sake," Steph said, turning and walking off towards the fire, her expression inscrutable.

"Are you...going to be okay?" Eloise asked, gazing down at Miles's face. His blue eyes gazed back at her, gray in the dim light.

"Honestly? I don't know. I think the bleeding's slowing down. If he got an artery, I'd have bled out already. I think I can hold on. As long as someone comes for us soon."

"But we don't even know if anyone *is* going to come for us," Linh said. "I haven't heard one plane or helicopter since we've been here. I haven't even seen any commercial jets. Don't you think that's odd?"

Miles didn't answer her. He was looking at Eloise. Gauging the fear in her eyes.

"I'm sorry," he said. "I wanted to protect you."

"I know," she said. "It's okay. Just lay still."

Eloise asked Linh to find her something she could use to staunch Miles's wound, and Linh gave her a wadded-up T-shirt from her pack. Coaxing Miles's trembling hand away from his shoulder, Eloise hissed air between her teeth as she saw the place where the knife had come out. It was a raw, angry black slit in his tanned skin, oozing slippery red blood. She pressed the shirt against it and held it there tight, murmuring sympathetically as Miles gasped.

When she lifted her head, Steph caught her eye and held it.

Sure, Miles *is the crazed killer. Whatever you say, Steph.*

Eloise looked away in disgust.

After that, there didn't seem to be anything left to do but wait. Wait for the night. Wait for a rescue that might never come.

Wait for Tate to appear, looming out of the darkness, grinning with insanity. To finish us all off.

36

Kenji was following the girls.

There were two of them, as alike as twins. At first, he'd thought they were real. Real girls, lost up on the cliffs somehow. But he knew, almost straight away, that it couldn't be. They weren't acting like lost girls. They walked with purpose, hand in hand, feet scuffing along the moonlit path. And when they paused to whisper together, the light illuminating their pale faces, he could see that they were both dead.

He knew who they were. He'd seen photographs of the schoolgirls who had belonged to the Lily Corps, the ones who'd been forced to act as field nurses in the war. Both girls wore their black hair in long braids on either side of their face, their pale foreheads bare. Tags hung from the breast pockets of their belted tunic uniforms. They appeared to be in their mid-teens. Maybe fifteen or sixteen years old.

He hadn't spoken to them, not yet, but he thought they were aware of him. Aware, but unafraid. He'd been following them for a while now, so engrossed in what he was doing that he'd barely noticed the sun disappearing in the west, the night rolling in. He'd forgotten all about Tate. And the others.

Should he call out to them? He had no idea what he would say.

They were leading him somewhere.

The girls paused under a walkway that stretched between the main hotel building and the petting zoo. For a moment, they were shrouded in darkness. One of the girls looked over her shoulder at him. Then she leaned in and whispered to her friend, cupping her hand around her ear. Giggling, the two girls ran off into the darkness. Alarmed, Kenji set off after them. He passed under the walkway and caught another glimpse of the girls ducking into the side entrance of the hotel.

When Kenji reached the doorway, he found it half-blocked by debris. An old, rusted oven. He kicked it aside and scrambled over it, entering the room, eyes scanning the cluttered space. He was distracted for a long moment by a familiar face smiling charismatically up at him from the filthy floor. The campaign poster was yellowed and brittle with age. However, Kenji recognized him right away—a greasy politician who'd been disgraced in the mid-seventies for corrupt land purchases.

Another giggle spilled in from the hallway, and Kenji crunched over to the door, poster forgotten. He quickly scanned the corridor, wincing against the throbbing headache he'd been silently suffering with ever since he'd gotten whacked.

The girls were standing there in a patch of square moonlight that filtered through the empty windowpane. Kenji froze, and the girls turned their heads slowly, looking at one another.

"Are you all right?" Kenji called out pointlessly because, of course, they weren't all right. They were *dead*—and one of the girls shook her head as the other held a finger to her lips.

Kenji swallowed, moving slowly toward them. The girls turned and began walking away. He followed them down the corridor, realizing that it had turned cold. A whistling, desolate wind with a sharp bite came gusting through the yawning black windows that flanked the corridor. Kenji suppressed a shiver, noticing the sudden absence of the muggy summer night heat.

Ahead, the girls stopped. Facing a closed door. Slowly, they lifted their hands in unison, index fingers pointing towards it.

Kenji inched closer, scrutinizing the faces of the girls. Their cheeks were still full of baby fat, their brows thick and youthful. One had a smattering of teenage acne on her temples. They didn't look at him. Their eyes were focused on the door.

Kenji lifted his gaze. There was a plaque on the door, green with corrosion. The plaque read *Manager*.

"In there?" Kenji murmured, but the girls ignored him. They weren't even blinking. Kenji reached out and turned the door handle. It shrieked in his hand, grating metal. The door slowly swung open. Kenji stepped inside, looking over his shoulder at the girls. But the girls had gone.

He shivered, even though the air was now hot and close once more.

He'd been guided to some sort of office. There was a large oak desk in front of a cracked and smeared window through which a shaft of desolate moonlight fell. The floor was strewn with damp, rotting books, their pages yellow and curling.

Kenji moved over to the desk. It was covered with leaves and broken pieces of glass. He brushed some of the mess aside and picked up a framed photo. A few shards of glass still clung to the frame. The photograph was a posed studio shot. A man in a dark suit stood next to a teenage boy, his hand on the shoulder of a woman seated on a chair in the forefront. Her feet were together in *tabi* socks and lacquered sandals, and she wore a pale-colored kimono with a tight smile. Kenji narrowed his eyes, focusing on the man. He wore his black hair neatly parted, and he had kind eyes behind thick, yellow-tinted glasses. The frames were so large they covered his eyebrows. Was this the manager, Imamura?

Kenji placed the photograph back down on the desk, glass kernels crunching. The desk had several heavy drawers, and Kenji rattled the knobs, but they seemed to be locked.

He stood there in the dim blue light of the room for a few moments, wondering why the girls had brought him here, what it was they wanted to show him.

He moved over to the window and looked out. Through the streaked, milky glass, he could see nothing but overgrown vegetation and the dark night sky above.

As Kenji shifted his weight, there was a small, barely audible click from the floor beneath his feet. He looked down. There was a line running across the floor in between the leaves and pieces of books. He swept the debris aside. There was a slight square depression in the floor. A silver handle and a round combination lock protruded slightly from it.

Excitement pumping through him, Kenji crouched down, hands roaming over the floor safe, testing the handle, tugging on it. It gave only a little. He spun the combination lock's dial one way and then the other.

It had to be important, relevant somehow. But it was locked, just like the desk drawers. Guessing the combination was impossible. He didn't even know how many numbers were involved in the unlock sequence.

Frustrated, Kenji got to his feet, casting his gaze around the room again.

His eye fell on the desk. Crunching back over to it, he picked up the framed photo. Flipping it over, he pulled the prop tab on the back and untucked the photograph from the frame. And there it was, written right there on the back.

L2 R9 L7 R1

"Are you freaking kidding me," Kenji muttered, hurrying back over to the floor safe. He crouched down again and spun the lock. Nothing happened. He paused for a second, hearing his own harsh, excited breathing. He turned the handle and pulled it. The hatch lifted.

Swallowing, Kenji leaned forward, peering inside. There was a briefcase in there. He pulled it out, eyes closing for a pained moment as he saw that it, too, had a combination lock. But when he pulled on the gold latches, they popped open. It was already set to the right combination.

He lifted the lid. There were papers inside, some handwritten documents, a bundle of yellow newspaper clippings, a sheaf of old photographs—some Polaroids, all held down by spring traps.

Kenji peeled the top photograph off the sheaf and held it up to the light. A beautiful young woman smiled over her shoulder at him, her hair long and black and shining, a backdrop of rose bushes behind her. There were more photographs, most of them showing the same girl. Kneeling in a pale cream kimono, plucking a long-necked *sanshin*. Emerging from the surf in a crochet bikini. Lolling on a bed in a hotel robe, cheeks flushed. In a handful of them, she was naked, wearing nothing but a leather thong necklace, a pendant nestled between her white breasts. Those ones were warped somehow. The eyes were black, glittering blobs, the mouth a smear of red.

Others showed her and Imamura laughing with the ocean behind them, his arm stretched out towards the edge of the frame, her arms around his neck.

The last one was a posed studio shot. The girl was younger, seated on a chair, wearing a navy high school sailor-type uniform, her eyes sparkling, her lips in a tight, shy smile. She held a framed diploma of some sort. Behind her stood a woman in a salmon-pink kimono with streaks of gray in her black hair. Her white hand was on the girl's shoulder, and she was beaming with what looked like pride.

Kenji frowned, picking up the yellow newspapers. They all had to do with Satoshi Imamura in some way—articles about his achievements in business, the properties he'd developed. Many of them were about the Oceanview.

Finally, Kenji picked up the handwritten document. The writing was spidery and shaky, the characters wobbling across the page. Two characters were written at the top of the paper, fat and blotchy with smeared ink. The characters read: CONFESSION.

As Kenji crouched there in the moonlight, deciphering the first page, his ears faintly registered the sound of a helicopter flying somewhere overhead.

37

The indigo hue of night crept through the trees, but the fading of the evening sun did not affect the temperature. If anything, it seemed to be getting hotter. The din of the cicadas had swelled to a lasting crescendo, and the scurrying sounds of crepuscular creatures of all kinds seemed to intensify as the evening settled in around them.

Steph had given up poking the fire, which was giving off a thick, acrid smoke that made her eyes stream. Now, she sat on her own, gnawing strips of skin off her fingers. She'd nibbled the thumbs down as far as she could get them and had started work on the pinkies. She was arguing silently back and forth with herself, trying to put things together in a way that made sense.

He couldn't have stabbed himself.
Could he?
Was that text even real?
What text? Her phone was dead. Useless.
Did I imagine the whole thing?
Maybe.
Am I fucking losing it?

She was trying not to look at Miles and Eloise, trying not to listen as they talked. Miles still had his head in her lap, and Eloise was bent over him, hanging on his every word.

"You know," he was saying now, "It's sweet how you were so concerned about me earlier."

Eloise smiled. She was visibly embarrassed, her cheeks tinged pink. Pretty.

"It's not just that. I mean, I was, but...I have this...this thing. With knives."

"I figured." Miles was staring up at Eloise with those creepy eyes of his. "This related to...our talk earlier?"

"Yeah." Eloise chewed her lip, scratching her wrist.

Steph bristled, goosebumps travelling along her sweat-laced arms. The conspiratorial way they were speaking. Eloise had never opened up to her like that. *Why not?*

They were silent for a while. Miles had his eyes closed. From this short distance, Steph could make out the sweat glistening on his forehead. He wasn't handsome. Wasn't charming. Psycho-killer or not, he was *weird*. So why was Eloise smiling at him like that, like he was the best person she'd ever met in her life?

"Eloise?" He opened one eye, checking on her. "Still with me?"

"Yeah."

"Tell me something."

"What?"

"Anything." He smiled.

She returned it.

Gag me.

"I mean, a prompt would be nice."

"I don't know. Movies. Books. What's your favorite book?"

"My favorite book?"

"Yeah, you don't have a favorite book?"

"I've got hundreds. It's not that simple. You can't just ask someone what their favorite book is."

"Sure, I can. Look, I'll do it again: What's your favorite book? Just name one."

"Okay..." Eloise drew air between her teeth, apparently thinking hard. "Maybe *Wuthering Heights*."

"Seriously? Ugh. I hated that book. It's just terrible people doing terrible things to each other and then wandering off to the moors to die of spite. And why do half of the characters have the same name? How's anyone supposed to keep the story straight?"

"It's a classic. It's one of the most romantic books of all time," Eloise said, looking affronted.

Steph's hopes rose a little.

"Sorry. Okay. *Wuthering Heights*. Yeah, it's a classic, right?" Miles sang a few bars of the Kate Bush song, mimicking the singer's distinctive high-pitched voice, and Eloise disappointed Steph—deeply—by snorting with delight.

"So, you read books like that? Classics, I mean?" She tried, but Eloise hadn't been able to hide the surprise in her tone. Now Miles's eyes were narrowing. He'd picked up on it.

"Just because I don't have some fancy four-year college degree like the rest of you doesn't mean I don't know how to read."

"I know, I..." Eloise trailed off, looking dismayed by the hard edge that had crept into his voice. "I didn't mean that."

Steph tried not to breathe in case she missed something.

Miles closed his eyes again, his lips set in a slight pout.

"So, what do you do?"

"Hmm?" he said.

"Like, for a job. Or whatever."

"Or whatever," he repeated. "If you want to get to know someone, the last thing you should ask them about is their job."

"Maybe, but it's just what people say."

"Is it?" He frowned, shifting his head against Eloise's knee.

But Steph was no longer listening to their conversation. There was something else in the night air now, something out of place.

"Hey, do you hear that?" Steph asked, her voice startling Eloise, who'd apparently forgotten she and Miles weren't alone.

"What?" El said.

Steph walked over, looking up at the sky, which was now a dark navy, sprinkled with early-evening stars.

"I think it's a helicopter," Steph said. "It's getting closer."

Miles sat up abruptly, startling Eloise again. "Helicopter?" He started to get to his feet. Eloise made a grab for him but missed, and he stepped away from her. For some reason, he looked slightly frantic.

"Where? Do you see it?" Miles looked up at the night sky, which was clear except for a few light streaks of dark blue clouds. They all spotted it at the same time, the dark shadow of the chopper moving slowly across the sky above, lights flashing, the steady *whup-whup-whup* noise of its rotor blades. It was getting lower and lower in the sky as if coming in to land.

"El, you should take the knife," Miles said, pulling it out of the back of his shirt and holding it out to her, and when Eloise shook her head, panicked, he pushed it into her hands. "*Take* it, just in case. It's fine. Listen, they're just thoughts, right? But I think that helicopter's landing. I'm going to follow it."

"Don't be stupid," Steph said. "You've been stabbed. You'd better lie down again before you pass out."

"I'm fine," Miles said irritably. "I think it clotted over. I need to get to that helicopter. Give me the flashlight, El." Eloise grabbed the Maglite from her pack and handed it to him, holding the knife loosely in her free hand. Even secured safely in its thick leather sheath, she was clearly terrified of it.

"You can't leave us here," Steph said as Miles activated the flashlight and started down the path that led away from the platform, the white, round beam jittering where he trained it ahead. "What about Tate?"

"Fuck off, Stephanie," Miles said, brushing past her, and then he was gone, swallowed by the dark.

Steph stood staring after him for a few moments, catching glimpses of the flashlight strobing through the thick overgrowth. He was moving fast, way too fast for someone who was that badly injured.

Steph gnawed on her thumbnail, working a hank of flesh loose. Blood oozed over her tongue, hot and metallic. There was a horrible feeling in the pit of her belly. It was like the feeling you get when you've forgotten something deathly important.

"Something's wrong," she whispered to herself. "I *know* it is." She turned and headed back to the camp where Eloise stood staring at her with wide eyes, the knife dangling from her limp fingers.

The knife. The fucking *knife*.

Steph ran the last few steps, almost crashing into Eloise as she snatched the knife out of her hand. Holding it up to the firelight, she tried to breathe around a sudden knot in her lungs, blinking stinging sweat out of her eyes.

The knife was inside a brown, heavy-duty leather sheath, a thick strap with a snap button securing the handle. The words KA-BAR were embossed in the stained leather. There was a round symbol below, and underneath that, an acronym.

"USMC," Steph muttered, her stomach dropping with dread. *I fucking knew it.*

She lifted her gaze to meet Eloise's wide, uncomprehending eyes. "USMC, Eloise. Do you see that?" She held it up in front of her friend's eyes, and she recoiled. "Where did this fucking United States Marine Corps *knife holder* come from, Eloise?"

"I don't...what...?"

"Where did it *come* from?"

"I don't *know*. It was already on it when Miles handed it to me..."

Steph brought her hand to her mouth, fingers pressing against her lips as her heart hammered away inside of her. *Fuck.*

"You can buy those kinds of knives on *Amazon*, Steph, it doesn't *mean* anything—"

Steph laughed, a furious bark of disbelief. "Where did he *get* the holder, Eloise? If Tate supposedly stabbed him in the shoulder with the knife and ran off, leaving said knife in his fucking shoulder, then *where did Miles get the holder*?"

Eloise was shaking her head, muttering something that sounded like *No, no, no*. Steph grabbed Eloise by the back of the neck, and Eloise shrieked, shying away from Steph's right hand, the one that was still gripping the knife.

"Oh my god. It was him. It was him all along. It's his fucking knife! Why else would he *lie* about it?" Steph thought she might pass out. She gasped, taking in a shuddery breath of air as the trees seemed to close in. "El. Eloise. Listen to me."

"No," Eloise said more clearly. "Maybe Tate dropped it, and Miles picked it up. That would explain it. Right? You can't just..."

"Tate's dead! He *killed* him!" Steph screamed at her, and Eloise flinched away again, her face scrunching as if she expected Steph to hit her. They stood there, locked together, as the light of the fire flickered on their faces.

Linh lifted her head from over by where Ollie lay and said, "Eloise...I think she might be right."

There was a long silence. Steph let go of El, tucked the knife into the side of her belt, and started to turn away. Eloise grabbed her wrist. "What are you *doing*?"

"I'm going after him," Steph said. "He doesn't want us getting off this cliff. If there's someone in that helicopter who can help us, I need to reach them before he does."

Eloise swallowed, hesitating, before holding out her palm. "Give me the knife back, Steph. *Please*."

Steph stared into her friend's eyes. The hope and pain and confusion there.

"No, El," she said softly. "I can't."

Then she turned and ran, kicking up clods of wet earth, skidding a little in her heavy boots, disappearing around the bend in the path, the darkness swallowing her.

PART SIX

THE OTHER AMERICAN

"Murder is murder. Everything else is just details."
—Keigo Higashino, *The Devotion of Suspect X*
(Translation: Alexander O. Smith)

38

Takagusuku Park Nature Preserve, Okinawa, Okinawa Prefecture,
Just past midnight, Monday July 15, 2019
(Marine Day)

Smudged pink and purple nebulae swirled high in the sky above the clifftop field, strewn through with billions of stars.

Steph was making her way silently across to where Miles stood, alone in the open field, the evening breeze rippling his clothing. The crash and roar of the ocean, off to the side and far below, didn't seem to even register with him. He was staring, transfixed, at the metal husk of the helicopter.

It had to be the same one. Steph had seen it catch fire and come down *right here*, burning sparks erupting from its tail, shooting through the night sky like summer fireworks.

But it couldn't be the same one. This copter had to have crashed years, *decades* ago. Thick blades of green, unburned grass danced and swayed throughout the skeletal mass of half-disintegrated brown metal.

"Stephanie," Miles said, his back still turned as she approached. "Thought I told you to stay back."

"Tell it to the fucking Marines," Steph spat. "*Adam*."

He turned. There was no surprise in his eyes as he took in the bristling, determined sight of Steph, moonlight shining down on her hair and face. His Ka-Bar glittered as Steph held it up in front of her face, her stance untrained, hands trembling.

"I was hoping we could skip this, Stephanie," he said. "All I wanted was Eloise. I was going to let the rest of you go. You and Linh. The other girl. Ollie, too, why the fuck not. I'm not a monster. But now, you..."

He took a step forward, and Steph stiffened, the blade wavering.

"You could have been a good girl, stayed out of my way, been more like Linh. But now I'm going to have to deal with you, Stephanie. Aren't I?"

There was a sadness in his voice that almost sounded genuine. He took another step forward, and Steph danced back, swiping the air between them with the knife.

"Who the fuck are you, really?" Her voice was tremulous and panicky, but there was a steely edge underneath it that she was glad to hear. She had the knife. She had the upper hand.

"It doesn't matter who I am," Miles said. "Not anymore. I'm not getting off this island alive. I always knew that. I was going to end it all the first day, find a cliff, throw myself off it. I don't want to face it, you see, what I've done. Maybe I *am* a coward. But this place...I feel like it's embraced me. I feel like it wants to help me out. All I want is to do things on my own terms. Go out with a smile on my face. That's what we all want, right, deep down?"

"You're crazy," Steph spat. "You're a fucking lunatic. You tried to kill Kenji. You probably killed Tate and Satoko."

"I never touched the girl." Miles scowled, his brow darkening, deep shadows forming in his eye sockets. "I haven't even fucking *seen* her. But you're right, Tate's dead. Only, he killed himself."

Steph shook her head. "No. I don't believe you. You're fucking pathological."

Miles moved toward her, and Steph slashed at him with the knife again, narrowly missing his ribs. He stopped short, brows rising.

"I'm impressed, Stephanie. But you're not going to stop me from being with Eloise. I knew I had to be with her the moment I saw her on the beach. You all were splashing about in the water, playing Marco fucking Polo like children, and I saw *her*. But you get what I mean. You're in love with her yourself."

"What?" Steph blinked, and that was when Miles sprang, grabbing her raised knife arm and twisting it painfully to one side. He kept twisting it beyond the axis of her elbow joint, beyond the breaking point. Steph screamed, going with it instead of fighting, trying to mitigate the pain, letting him slam her onto the ground. The knife fell from her limp fingers, and he pressed the weight of his knee into the nape of her neck, scrambling for it with his free hand and grabbing it up off the grass.

"You're fucked now, Stephanie," he said, breathing hard with exertion, tossing the knife away, grabbing Steph and turning her over. She reared up, trying to headbutt him in the face, but he pulled back, lifting her by her shoulders and then slamming her head back down against the ground. It was soft, still soggy from the rain, but the shock of the impact was enough to stun her as he pinned her wrists down on either side of her head.

Steph tried to lift her hips, to shove against him with just enough force to pitch him forward, over his center of gravity. In her mind's eye, she saw him release her wrists to catch himself against the ground. Then, she would twist and spin and get out from underneath him.

In reality, though, none of that happened. Steph bucked her hips against him, once, twice, and he smiled down at her, a confused, amused sort of smile.

"I've got seventy pounds on you," he reminded her. "That's not going to work."

Steph grunted, bucking her hips against him again, but she barely even managed to jostle him. The weight of him was pressing her down, impossibly heavy, as immovable as solid rock.

"Please," she whispered, and he grinned.

"Yeah?" His eyes glittered, empty and black, as he gazed down at her, scrutinizing her face, drinking in her fear. Steph let out an angry sob, yanking her wrists against his iron fists, feeling the wet grass soak into her sore back.

This couldn't be happening. Not to her.

She squirmed beneath him, hating the feel of his heavy body lying on top of hers, hating the absolute power he had over her. *I can do anything I want to you*, that power said. But Steph knew that if he really wanted to render her incapable of fighting back, he could have just punched her in the face, knocked her senseless already. He wasn't doing that. Wasn't doing anything. He was just lying on top of her, holding her down, enjoying her helplessness and her fear.

She closed her eyes, and for a crazed moment, she thought that it was Don on top of her—Don, her revolting stepfather, finally making good on the implicit threat in his ever-watchful eyes. *Don's* sour nicotine breath on her face, *Don's* damp, meaty hands holding her down, *Don's* paunchy beer belly crushing out her air.

Waves of terror washed over her, and she thought of the dark water crashing against the shore far below.

"Please," she said again, and then she was babbling, half-incoherent with fear, thinking about how Miles would leave her dead body here on this desolate clifftop underneath the stars, leave her to get picked apart by gulls. "Please, I'll do anything you want. I'll do anything, I don't want to die."

Miles reared back, putting the full weight of his extended arms on her pinned wrists. His expression showed disgust.

"I don't want *you*, Stephanie." Slowly, deliberately, he shook his head. "You've got nothing I want. The only thing I want from you is for you to die."

Steph sobbed, looking past him at the stars, twinkling in the sky, light years away. *The stars can't help me*, she thought, and then something black and solid cracked Miles across the back of the head. He pitched forward with a groan, releasing Steph's wrists and catching himself against the wet ground.

Finding her hands suddenly returned to her, she didn't hesitate. Her fingers scrabbled across the stiff material of his shirt, nails seeking the wound in his shoulder. Then she dug her index finger into the raw, wet hole, right up to the last knuckle. Miles roared with pain and threw himself away from her. She scrambled free, gasping in deep lungfuls of the muggy night air, looking up wildly to see Kenji standing there, silhouetted against the moonlight, a black briefcase dangling from his hand.

"Steph, are you—" he started to say, and then Steph remembered the knife.

"Kenji!" she screamed, and Miles reared up like a snake, plunging the knife into Kenji's belly. Kenji looked down, eyes cloudy with confusion as Miles dragged the knife out sideways, and a cascade of blood and visceral matter came sloshing out of Kenji as if his guts had been unzipped.

Steph scuttled backward on her hands and her heels, and she wanted to scream, but her throat was closed up, her vocal cords paralyzed.

Kenji fell heavily to his knees, and Miles turned his head, very slowly, towards Steph. As he got to his feet, grinning, he lifted the knife, Kenji's blood gleaming crimson on the blade, and advanced.

Stopping just in front of her, he lifted the knife, still grinning. His eyes were dark, empty holes. As he brought the knife down on her, Steph grabbed the Maglite from his belt and hit out at him with it, deflecting the knife with a screech of metal.

Miles blinked in confusion, but before he could ready his arm for another strike, Steph smashed the chunk of concrete she was holding in her other hand against his temple, closing one of his eyes and sending him crashing to the ground.

Gasping and sobbing, Steph scrambled to her feet and ran to Kenji. He lay face-up, his brown eyes open wide, reflecting the night sky above, his lower body awash with blood.

"Steph," he said, a blister of blood bursting between his lips, "case."

She blinked, confused, and her fingers bumped against the black leather briefcase he was still clutching in one hand.

"Hold on, Kenji, please, just hold on..."

Kenji took a breath and opened his mouth as if to tell her something, but the words never came. The breath remained in his lungs as his eyes went blank, and his hand fell away from the handle of the briefcase.

Gasping, Steph fumbled her fingers over his neck, trying to find a pulse.

There was a groan behind her, and she stiffened, eyes darting over her shoulder. Miles was stirring, half of his face stained red with blood.

Steph stuffed the flashlight down the back of her shorts and gathered the briefcase up into her arms. She scrambled to her feet, backing away from Miles. He was still holding the knife, dragging it through the mud as he struggled to get up onto his hands and knees. Steph backed up two, three, four paces before turning and running. She streaked across the clifftop field beneath the stars, making for the resort, which loomed high on the hillside ahead.

The resort was blazing bright. It was as if every light in the place was on. But that couldn't be. It was impossible. As Steph reached the tree line and plunged into the woods, she realized she could hear distant music. Lungs burning painfully, she crushed the briefcase tight against her chest as she crashed through the undergrowth, emerging eventually in a clearing. The clearing housed a towering, A-shaped building made of logs, large plate-glass windows blazing with bright light, the air vibrating with music. Dark shapes moved around inside, silhouetted against the windows, and as Steph approached the front steps, her legs failed, and she sank.

The last thing she saw before the blackness rose up to swallow her was Kenji's briefcase, flying loose from her fingers and skittering away from her across the glistening wet ground.

39

It was dark in the boat. Cold bodies pressed together. The night sky above was black, starless. Close enough to touch. Not sky. A coffin lid. Linh opened her mouth to cry out for help, but she had no voice. Her cracked lips tasted of salt. Someone was sitting on her legs, they had fallen asleep. Wriggling her toes triggered a violent cramp that twisted her calf muscles. Sitting up, she reached for her leg, crying out, trying to crush the pain away with her fingers.

There was no boat. She was in the resort with Ollie, under the Viewing Platform. Night had fallen, and she'd fallen asleep.

The night air around her was thick and dark and filled with steaming sheets of rain, host to all manner of unimaginable, faceless terrors, and some that had faces…handsome faces, the familiar faces of Tate and Miles, although that didn't make the prospect of them looming out of the darkness any less chilling.

It wasn't the isolation or the dark that frightened her. Nor was it the fact that she'd vomited blood again, twice, since Eloise and Steph ran off and left her in their pursuit of Miles. The blood was alarming, of course, but she felt physically completely fine. *Good*, in fact. Except for a gnawing hunger, which she'd only half satisfied by eating the two boxes of hiker's nutrition bars she'd helped herself to out of Tate's backpack.

It was for Ollie that she was really afraid. He'd been having seizures, small ones, since late afternoon, but they'd been coming at increasingly frequent intervals, and his pulse had dropped so low that it was barely detectable. Hot waves of panic washed over Linh each time she prodded his neck with her stiff, shaking fingers, waiting for the beat, waiting to see if he was still with her. He'd stopped responding to her a few hours ago, but he'd continued talking for a while. Having conversations with people who weren't there. *Ask Dad to check the footy scores*, he'd said. *Tell Mum I'll be stopping at Lee's. Tell her I won't need anything for tea.* But he'd been quiet for a long time now.

Ollie was going to die. That was clear by this point. It was also clear that she would have to sit there and watch him do it. The prospect of that was the scariest thing of all. She could leave him—she toyed with the idea, but where would she go? The resort was a dark labyrinth of crumbling concrete and twisted, rusting metal, overgrown with jungle-thick vegetation. And filled with snakes.

At least here, the light of the flickering fire was some small comfort.

Another, albeit smaller, comfort was the stone amulet she wore on the hair tie around her wrist. For the past few hours, she'd been taking it off and turning it over and over in her palm, the hard weight of it grounding her. It seemed to her now like the one link she had to normalcy, to the last point when things had been right. There'd been a very clear break in reality, this she was sure of, and it had happened when Ollie fell out of the undergrowth with his jeans around his ankles, that horrible, hideous viper hanging from him. When the storm came and washed away the path back down, that was the turning point. Linh was sure of it. Everything looked different now, even the way the raindrops rolled off the smooth surface of the leaves like tiny drops of dark sky filled with stars.

She couldn't bring herself to believe she might die up here. Surely, when dawn broke and brought with it the relief of daylight, they would be able to regroup, to find some other way down from the cliff. But the absolute silence that lay heavy on the hills and the emptiness of the vast sky above, the lack of airplanes, flashing lights, and signs of human civilization, it all combined to fill her with a sense of cold dread, like a stone fist crushing her insides.

The rain stopped then, with an abruptness that startled her. Everything was suddenly still, but for just a moment, Linh could have sworn there was music playing somewhere far off. Probably someone's phone running out its battery at the bottom of a backpack, she told herself, easing away from Ollie's side and getting to her feet to stretch her legs, to feed a few more dry branches to the fire.

There was nothing else to do. She couldn't help Ollie. She touched the magatama talisman again, gazing through the hole in it at the wet ground below.

It *was* music. She could still hear it. Linh lifted her head, straining her ears. It was coming from somewhere in the resort.

But there was something else. Something closer. Singing. A sweet voice, soft on the night breeze. It was coming from the top of the Viewing Platform.

Kariyushi nu ashibi
hari uchi hari iiti kara yaa
yunu akiti tiida nu
hari agaru madi madin...

When Linh reached the top level and stepped out under the moonlight, she found that Tate's signal fires had long fizzled out, extinguished by the downpour. The painted, grinning faces of the carousel horses met her with grotesque mockery. Averting her eyes, she edged past their immobile, prancing forms. The roof was otherwise empty.

The singing had stopped.

Planting her feet as close to the blind edge as she could bear, she looked down and out over the resort.

The Oceanview was coming to life beneath her. Lights popped on one by one, blazing, spilling from the empty rounded windowpanes, the red-orange glow lighting up the hillside.

Shadows moved about inside the resort. The lights flickered as the shadows shifted in the rooms and drifted along the corridors.

The music, which was louder now, was obviously not coming from an errant electronic in one of her friends' backpacks at all.

It came from a long, blazing A-frame building at the end of a snaking path far back in the resort's hills. There were other sounds now, too, from the direction of the petting zoo Scuffling and snuffling sounds, reptilian roars, the frenzied jangling of chains. The ammonia stench of animal excrement laced the muggy air.

The spectacle of the blazing resort, unspeakably and inexplicably alive, was terrible. But beyond it, as Linh lifted her gaze, there was something worse, something that terrified her to her core.

The landscape beyond the resort boundary was an expanse of black nothingness that stretched across the breadth of the island to the glittering ocean on either side. It was a void, an abyss, a stark, uninhabited expanse of empty land between the seas where not a single human light shone.

We really are all alone up here, Linh thought, and she stepped back quickly from the edge, convulsions jerking her to her knees as she vomited thick black blood onto the steaming concrete.

Why won't it stop?

As she coughed and gasped for breath, she could hear the singing again. She lifted her head.

Red smoke billowed before her. Crimson particles swirled, suspended in the night air like ocean mist. The particles formed the shape of a woman.

As Linh fought for enough breath to scream, the carousel horses watched. They watched, and they waited, and they grinned.

40

Eloise hugged her knees to her chest, trying not to shiver. The stone cave floor burned like dry ice through her jeans, but it was still better to be in here, out of the deluge roaring outside.

The rain came down in diagonal sheets of water, obscuring the surroundings, and a long, low rumble of thunder voiced its menacing threat somewhere over the ocean.

She'd lost sight of Steph while chasing her, gotten turned around somehow, and found herself wandering the resort grounds, disoriented. That was when the downpour started. There were only a few fat drops at first as she tried to head back to the Viewing Platform, its concrete slabs looming indistinct in the evening gloom. But then the sky darkened fast, and the rain began bucketing down, soaking her to the skin in seconds. With no other recourse, she dashed for the cave, which was closer, and huddled up just inside the entrance, afraid to go in any further, afraid of what—

the woman with the long hair and the broken, dragging ankle
—of what dangers might be lurking in its depths.

She'd been sitting there hugging herself for a long time now, hating the feeling of her sodden bra and underwear clinging to her skin, when there was a rustle in the bushes outside.

Her head came up, and she froze, trying to bend her hearing towards whatever might be out there, making the sound, but it was difficult to hear anything over the din of the storm. Visibility was poor, too, with the sheeting rain, but then a jagged fork of lightning hit somewhere to the west, and for a moment, the figure was clear, a big hulk shambling its way towards her.

Get up. Get up and run. Now!

Scrambling to her feet, Eloise panicked, caught between fleeing into the nebulous black depths of the cave tunnel behind her or taking her chances and breaking past the hulking creature outside.

Then the creature spoke.

"Eloise," it said, and there was a flick and a pop, a bright light blazing in an aloft hand. White hot fear ripped through her, followed by a rush of relief when she recognized the face. Half of it was as white as the belly of a dead fish, while the other half was filthy, smeared with what looked like chunky blackberry jam.

Miles fell into her arms in the mouth of the cave, and they both went down on the hard stone floor, Eloise gasping as her breath got knocked out. The lighter skittered across the rock, but the flame kept burning.

There was a horizontal slit in Miles's forehead, just above his right eyebrow, and that seemed to be where most of the blood was coming from. There was also a horrible sunken depression in his skull just above that.

He's dying. He's not going to survive that, not going to last until we can get help.

She tried to think. Pressure. Something to stop the bleeding. Was that right? There was nothing around she could use. Her socks? They were soaked through.

"What...Miles, what *happened*?"

He looked up at her, blinking blood and rainwater out of his left eye—the right one was swollen shut.

"Kenji," he said, after a pause of a few seconds—it was as if he was having trouble speaking. The sunken part of his skull terrified Eloise.

Don't look at it, El. Don't. Stop.

But she *had* to look. Couldn't stop herself. What was Miles saying? Something about Kenji?

"Kenji? Kenji, *what?*"

"He's lost his mind. Hit me with a...a rock. Had to...kill him."

Kill him?

Kenji was dead?

No, that wasn't possible. Kenji was too strong. He'd lost his *mind?* No. That didn't make any sense.

None of this makes any sense!

"What did he—Why? Miles, that can't be what happened, there must be—"

"You think I did this to myself?" Miles's voice was cold and angry, blood bubbles bursting between his lips as he spoke. Eloise was silent for a moment, trying to make sense of what was happening. She couldn't. It was impossible. This whole thing was impossible.

Maybe I'm the one who's lost my mind. Maybe I'm hallucinating all of this. Maybe I went crazy after Chris died, and I'm locked in a rubber room back in England right now, completely out of my fucking gourd.

She tried to focus.

Kenji? Kenji was the one? The one who...but why? And the wound on the back of his head, he couldn't have done that to himself.

The pieces weren't fitting together. None of them were.

I can't give up. Think. I still need to help Miles. I need to find Steph. Find a way off...

Steph.

"Miles, what about...what about the helicopter? What about Steph? She didn't catch up to you?"

"No." Miles grimaced, trying to sit up. "I didn't see her. And the helicopter...it came down, and I followed it, found it, but Ellery...the thing had to be decades old. I mean, it crashed decades ago. It was just rust."

"*What?*"

Miles coughed, blood burbling up in his throat. He swallowed. "I don't think we're getting off this cliff, El. I think...I think we're out of time."

"Don't say that. There's still time. We can still get help, we—"

"El. Listen to me. We're *out of time*. I don't think we're in the right time *period*. I think...I think something happened to us, and we've gotten trapped in some kind of...some kind of limbo state. Some dimension that doesn't really exist anywhere. I think the things we've both been seeing are real, after all. They're real, and they're here with us *now*. Do you understand what I'm saying?"

Eloise shook her head, her lips moving with disbelief. "What does that *mean*?"

"It means..." he coughed again, turned his head to the side, and spat blood. "It means...no one's going to see our SOS message. It means the US Marine Corps ain't coming to save us." He smiled again, but there was no humor there. His teeth were a darker red now, and in the dim moonlight that filtered into the cave entrance, it looked like he'd been drinking too much wine.

"You should lie down," she said, wishing she had her backpack to use as a pillow.

"Lend me your lap," he said, coughing again, and Eloise sat back, letting him put his head on her knees. Her fingers hovered in the air over the crushed section of his skull, the deep black slit in his forehead.

"Don't die. Don't leave me," she whispered. She reached for the fallen lighter, propping it upright. The flame danced, sending black shadows sliding across the cave walls.

"I'm sorry, El." His good eye closed. "I don't think it's...up to me."

Wiping her nose with the back of her hand, Eloise tried to think of some other way out of this, some way to get Miles down from the cliff in time, to get them all some help. But if Miles's theory was true...

Why can't I think? I just want everything to stop. Just until I can figure out what to do. Just please stop.

"My boyfriend died. In our last year at university. He was... stabbed."

What the heck are you doing, El?

She was going to stop there, was going to *make* herself stop, but Miles opened his eye again. There was an expectant light shining there, an understanding light, one that gently urged her to continue.

"I was there when it happened. It was...it was at the Red Lion...at the *pub*, on a Saturday night. I'd asked him to meet me, and he thought it was a date, but I wanted to talk about...about how I'd just found out he was cheating on me. With my flatmate. And the girl on his course. There were multiple girls."

She shook her head, eyes closing again. Still, all these years later, she couldn't believe it, even after what happened.

If only I could be angry. If only I could have that release. But what's the point of being angry with a dead person?

"He admitted to everything. It was almost like he expected...like he expected *points* for finally being honest. I thought I was going crazy. It was like nothing made sense. And I couldn't accept it. That wasn't Chris. He wasn't *like* that. He used to read me to sleep at night. I thought we had one soul."

Eloise stopped, wiping her nose on the back of her arm, swallowing the tears that were pooling in the back of her throat. "Well, I was wrong. The pub was packed. Chris went to get more drinks. There was a scrum at the bar, and I went to try to find him, to tell him I was leaving. I was done. But then people started screaming. Chris was there, and there was blood all over my dress, all up my arms. It was so crowded. The surge of bodies. I couldn't *see* anything."

She was dimly aware of Miles's cold, slippery fingers closing around her hand, squeezing it tight.

"Go on, El," he said.

"They never found the knife. The police thought it was me, of course. I tried to tell them about the...the rough blokes Chris and I bumped into on the way into the pub. There were two or three of them. Not students. Older. I tried to tell them about the altercation, but there were no witnesses to that. Just me. And half the pub had seen me crying, shouting at Chris..."

"A knife...that's why you freaked out on me earlier. My shoulder."

"When I saw you bleeding, for a moment, I thought... I thought you were him. Chris. His ghost."

Eloise exhaled, rubbing her stiff, frozen cheeks. "God, I never talk about Chris. I don't even let myself *think* about Chris. Even Steph doesn't know. Or didn't know..." She trailed off, looking down at Miles's handsome face, the dark crust of blood beneath his nose, the hairs of his ridiculous moustache clumping together, and felt a rush of affection for him. He wasn't looking at her with disgust or revulsion. The sickening glint of hatred and suspicion she'd grown used to seeing in people's eyes once they realized it was her—Eloise Tiller, murder suspect—there was none of it in Miles, just quiet understanding.

"So they...didn't charge you?" he asked, his voice soft.

"If they could have, they would've. I think they knew they couldn't make it stick. After that, I had to get away. Everyone back in England thinks I'm...a murderer. The press camped out on my mum's doorstep. Digging through our rubbish bins. My *life* was over. Even after things died down. Every time I meet someone new, I have to wonder if they know who I am. I lost my old friends. I think some of them believed me, but I pushed them away. I felt like...like I was tainted. Like...like my soul had been stained, somehow, with Chris's blood. So, I left England and came to Japan. But it didn't help. It's too late."

"It's never too late, El," Miles muttered, squeezing her hand tighter, and hot tears streamed down her face.

It's like someone finally understands. The rush of relief was like a hit of feel-good chemicals straight to the brain. *God, I've been so desperate for someone to understand.*

Miles was truly on her side. An ally. Steph had been wrong about him, of course. She'd been jealous and selfish and wrong about everything. Miles was her friend. He'd come here to be with her. He'd been her friend all along.

Eloise brushed her fingers against the back of Miles's cold, sticky hand, wondering how much longer they had together.

If he leaves me, I don't think I can go on. I think, maybe—

The cliffs. It would be easy, wouldn't it? Better than dying like rats trapped in the resort. Maybe Steph and Linh would see it that way, too.

"Miles, why did you have that knife holder?"

"I—What?" Confusion in his voice.

"The holder. When you handed me the knife earlier, it was in a leather sheath. Where did it come from? I mean, Steph thought it was...thought it was odd."

"Picked it...up. After Tate ran off. Dropped it."

Eloise exhaled. "See, I knew that's what it was."

"Your crazy friend Stephanie...thinks I'm some kind of...homicidal maniac."

"I know. But don't be too hard on Steph. She's not coping. She's confused. She said she got a *text* saying you were an AWOL Marine. A murderer. Some guy called Adam."

Miles's good eye was fixed on her. He wasn't saying anything.

That was when Eloise glanced down the length of his body and noticed something odd.

It was the outline of something hard. The wet, clinging fabric of Miles's shirt tented around it, where it protruded just above his belt.

The knife?

He couldn't have the knife, though. *Steph* had it. And Miles had just told Eloise he hadn't seen her.

Why would he lie to me?

Eloise's fingers hovered above the object, too afraid to touch the indeterminate mound and make sure, too afraid not to.

No. No, Eloise. There's an explanation. He can't be lying. It can't be him. An escaped Marine? A man wanted for murder? Steph...Oh, my God...

She was shaking hard now, a full-body tremor. She tugged her hand out of his cold, tacky grip. Her knuckles found her lips and mashed them hard against her teeth.

Don't. Don't whimper.

She tasted his blood. Her lungs screamed for air.

I know it's the knife, the same knife, she thought, heart hammering in her chest, her muscles knotting with terror.

And it would be the same lie again, wouldn't it? One just plausible enough to be true. I found it. I picked it up.

No. Because it's his knife. It was his knife all along.

Carefully, with shaking fingers, she peeled back the short sleeve of his sodden t-shirt, revealing the blood-smeared tattoo on his upper bicep, the one that looked oddly familiar.

In the hostel bath, Steph thought it was a rooster. But it's not. It's an eagle.

An eagle, perched atop a globe, skewered by an anchor.

USMC. United States Marine Corps.

"No, Miles," she whispered, her fingers retracting, and she shrank away from him, an animal reflex. Oh, she wanted to believe him. She wanted him to explain it, to say something, anything that would make it so she could keep on believing he was her friend. So that she didn't have to be alone. But it was too late. She already knew, could never again un-know.

Steph was right. Steph was right about Miles, about how stupid I am, about everything.

But before she could even think about whether to run or go for the knife, Miles grabbed hold of her hand again.

"I was going to tell you everything, El. You know what it's like to go through something that traumatic, something that splits you into two separate people. Who you were before and who people force you to be for the rest of your life. You understand. I know that now for sure. I'm really glad you told me."

His fingers tightened around her hand, pinning her down, anchoring her to him.

"I'll tell you the truth, El. About what I'm doing here. About who I am. I think I always wanted to tell someone before...before the end. Maybe my dad knows. He always had this look about him after she died. This dismayed kind of look. I think he thought I wouldn't pick up on it, but I saw it. I couldn't *not* see it. It was a look that said…that said…*Adam, this is a disappointment.* That was the worst part, I think. The worst part of it all. That look in my dad's eyes."

Adam.

The AWOL Marine.

He's killed Steph, Eloise realized, black spots dancing before her eyes. *And now he's going to kill me.*

41

Steph was in a bathroom. The walls were overlapping wood planks, rough-hewn and rustic. But the sinks were ornate. Marble, perhaps, and sparkling like they'd been installed recently.

Her reflection stared out at her from the mirror over the sink. The reflection wore a blood-red satin dress, formal and figure-hugging. Jewels sparkled at her ears and her throat, catching the light from the crystal fixture overhead. Her hair was swept up in an elaborate style. She was heavily made up, with glossy red lipstick. Someone had powdered in her brows. They looked much too dark. And her eyes were wide and staring, filled with fear and panic.

She was aware that something terrible had just happened, but she couldn't remember what it was. It was difficult to think, as if someone had packed her brains with cotton wool.

Shuffling painfully in the red stiletto-heeled shoes she was somehow wearing, she inched toward the door. She could hear voices outside, an indistinct hum. Before she could grasp the knob, the door swung open, away from her. She fell into the arms of a man in a black dinner jacket with a thunderous expression on his face, who shoved her away as if disgusted.

"It's *stage time*," he admonished her, muttering something about stupid foreigners under his breath. He grabbed her by the wrist and dragged her through the glass entry hall and a set of double doors into the party.

The venue was dimly lit, the night lurking outside the plate-glass windows that took up both walls. She stumbled, her ankle twisting in her high heels as the man dragged her through a crowd of people. They all wore fancy attire, the women in cocktail dresses, dripping with jewels, the men in tuxedos. The air was thick with cigarette smoke.

The eyes of the guests raked her as the man yanked her through their midst, and they reluctantly parted to let her through.

He dragged her past a line of white-clothed trestle tables, groaning under golden platters of food. Fat children, boys and girls, in tiny tuxedos and sparkly party dresses, sat gorging themselves.

Finally, they reached the stage at the far end of the party hall, where a band stood behind their instruments, waiting expectantly, all of them watching her.

The man in the dinner jacket dug his fingers cruelly into the small of Steph's back. "Get on with it," he growled.

Steph staggered up onto the stage, teetering in her heels. Thick, crimson curtains hung down at the back of the stage, fluttering slightly in an impossible breeze. She didn't want to turn her back on them, but she had no choice. Looking out at the audience, she blinked as a microphone was thrust into her hands.

The band began to play, something with a lugubrious beat, a haunting melody. Steph knew it by ear right away, although it took a moment to find the lyrics inside her memory. *Marimba rhythms. The lazy ocean.* Opening her mouth, she began to sing along to the band as if in a deep dream, half-mumbling into the microphone.

As she struggled her way through the song, her eyes roamed around the hall. The guests stood watching her, none of them moving to the music or even nodding their heads.

The women glittered, tiny shards of light bouncing off their pearls, their brooches, their diamond earrings. Their faces were dull and matte with powder, brows inked over, cheeks livid with spots of berry-colored blush.

The young men had blue-black hair that shone like raven's wings under the spotlights. The old men had bald, shiny white pates like freshly peeled boiled eggs. The sickly-sweet scent of their myriad colognes and perfumes hung over the crowd in an intermingled floral fug.

They were here for a celebration of some sort—there were black balloons and gold streamers strung from the high rafters and a banner strung above the entry doors. Steph couldn't read the kanji characters, but she understood the numbers and the words written in simple *katakana* script.

1975 ROYAL OCEANVIEW RESORT GALA OPENING

The sign had been written with crude brushstrokes in black paint. The paint had run in several places.

As the song was drawing to its close, Steph noticed the man slumped over in the corner by the trestle tables. He wore a tuxedo and shiny patent shoes, but his hair was disheveled, sticking up in clumps. His head was down, between his knees.

The other guests had given him a wide berth, and Steph could see him clearly—his shoulders were heaving. As if he was laughing...or sobbing.

Her eyes slid to the trestle tables, where guests stood holding matte gold plates. Distracted, they ate one-handed as they stared at Steph. But it wasn't canapes they were eating. Their plates were piled high with some sort of greyish, rubbery meat. As she watched, a man dug his fingers into the pile and crammed a fistful into his mouth, gulping greedily without chewing, like a snake. Still unsatisfied, his black tongue darted out to lap at the grease and juice that glistened on his chin.

Throat constricting with nausea and disgust, Steph looked away, scanning the crowd again. Nearly everyone clutched a glass in their hand, but they weren't flutes of champagne, as Steph had somehow thought earlier when she'd passed through their silent midst. Now, they held glasses of red wine.

One of the women knocked her head back, draining her glass and spilling its contents on the bosom of her pale dress. The wine stains sat atop the fabric, not soaking in like normal wine would. The spill looked more like congealed blood, glistening under the bright spotlights. The woman smiled, catching Steph's eye, letting her mouthful of—

blood

—wine spill out of the corners of her mouth, letting it drip and dribble down her chin and neck as she held Steph's gaze.

Steph's heart was a panicked bird, flapping its wings in desperation against the cage of her ribs. The song was about to end, she realized, her voice cracking and failing on a high note. She would have to play along. She couldn't let them know she'd noticed something was wrong.

If I just play along, I can get away and keep looking for...
Who?

Who was she looking for?

She couldn't remember.

The band played a final flourish. Steph gasped into the microphone, her mind racing, adrenaline spurting through her veins as the crowd broke into scattered applause, turning to whisper to one another.

The man in the dinner jacket took the stage and grabbed the microphone from Steph's hand, scratching her with his nails as he did so. She gazed at the back of her hand, three deep red furrows beginning to well up with blood.

"Ladies and Gentlemen," he began in English before switching to Japanese. "Welcome to the grand opening of the Royal Oceanview Resort!" the crowd whooped and clapped their approval.

"Unfortunately," the man continued, signaling for silence, "Unfortunately, the man of the hour, Manager Imamura, is not feeling in *quite* the party mood."

The crowd all turned their heads in the direction of the man slumped on the floor by the tables. His wretched sobbing was now clearly audible.

"Should have stayed out of the caves, Imamura," the man in the dinner jacket said. "You were warned. Was he not warned, my friends?"

The crowd clapped again, hooting their assent.

The man in the dinner jacket turned to Steph. His mouth fell open. His tongue was black and shiny, lying in his mouth like a gelatinous slug. His teeth were nicotine-stained nubs, the back molars crammed with gunmetal gray dental amalgam. His hair was slicked back, glistening with pomade, shot through with ragged streaks of gray. White specks of dandruff clung to the comb tracks in his hair and peppered the shoulders of his jacket. The crowd was utterly silent, hanging on his next word, and Steph forced herself to smile.

She couldn't let them know. Once they realized the jig was up, they'd kill her. Somehow, she knew it.

"Allow me to introduce our special musical guest! All the way from America, this is—" he thrust the microphone under Steph's nose. Swallowing, Steph muttered her name into it, her own voice booming back at her from the speakers hanging in the rafters.

"Stephanie Elliot-san!" the man repeated, tucking the microphone under his armpit with a whine of feedback, clapping with all the eagerness of a dolphin performing tricks. Taking their cue, the audience followed suit.

"Well then," the man said, then remembered the microphone and untucked it. "Well then, Miss Elliot-san, what do you think of our splendid Oceanview?"

The microphone grazed her chin when he thrust it towards her face again.

"It's very...very good," Steph said, her Japanese pronunciation awkward, the words cumbersome in her mouth, but none of the crowd seemed to mind. They applauded again.

By the tables, a fat little girl in a sparkly tutu put down her plate and belched loudly.

"*Wonderful!*" the dinner jacket man said in thickly accented English. "Splendid. Because you're never going to leave, Miss Elliot-san. You and your friends have won a permanent stay at our lovely resort! Yes, a round of applause!" he half-screamed, and the audience clapped madly, whooping and cheering.

Steph smiled weakly out at them, struggling to breathe, the tight bodice of the satin dress pinching under her armpits, constricting her chest like a snake wrapped around her, denying her the ability to take a full breath.

Behind her, the crimson curtains billowed and flapped.

Then, the doors at the back began to bang and shake in their frames, the hinges rattling. The dinner jacket man's face darkened as the crowd all turned to look behind them.

"She is not of us," he said to the assembly. "Pay her no heed." His hand reached out and grabbed Steph's wrist, his eyes sliding to her face. "*Sing*," he hissed, and the band struck up again, but Steph ignored them, eyes fixed on the banging doors. The crowd began to move as one in alarm, edging away from them.

The banging continued, audible even over the clashing noise of the band. A woman screamed as the doors flew open, and a figure came shambling through them. The music died in the speakers, a whine of feedback fizzling out as silence fell.

Steph strained to see as the figure came into the light. It was a young woman in her twenties, perhaps. She had very long black hair and wore a white blouse and a red skirt, but no shoes. Her legs were thin sticks. The crowd parted in alarm, surging away from her as she staggered up the hall towards the stage.

As she grew closer, Steph realized one of her ankles was clearly broken, dragging uselessly behind her, and the side of her head was caved in. Her pretty face was splattered with blood and gore, the ragged waterfall of her hair matted with clumps of jellied brain.

The woman dragged herself over to the stage, and Steph stepped back, terrified, as she heaved herself up the steps. Determination blazed in her eyes, which remained fixed on Steph.

Soon, the woman stood before her, swaying slightly. Her breathing was audible, harsh, and rasping. The crowd muttered. The man in the tuxedo was still sobbing loudly on the floor. The woman blinked at Steph, and Steph gazed back, looking right into the woman's eyes. She had kind eyes, sad eyes that seemed almost to be soliciting Steph's help.

She looked a bit like Linh.

The woman reached for Steph's arm. The motion juddered as if the scene was being rendered in stop motion. Her fingers were warm. When Steph looked up again, the woman was no longer bloody and horrible. She was beautiful, transcendentally so. Her skin was impossibly white. Her hair was like shimmering black silk, and she had a dewy freshness to her skin that made Steph realize she was younger than she'd thought—little more than a teenager.

The girl reached for Steph's hand and pressed something hard and cool into her palm.

"*Unigeh*," the woman said, but Steph couldn't understand her. It didn't even sound like she was speaking Japanese. "*Unigeh sabirah*," she said again, closing Steph's fingers over the object in her palm.

The lights in the hall grew dim as curls of some red mist, thick as smoke, began to unfurl from the rafters and descend upon them all. A flutter of alarm went through the crowd, dark mutterings and low groans.

Steph clutched the object the girl had given her in her fist as the girl's hands fell away from hers. The lights in the hall grew dimmer and dimmer until the only light left seemed to be coming from the girl's eyes. Steph saw something glimmering down in the depths of them, like a vast black pool shimmering somewhere deep beneath the earth.

Then the eyes closed, and there was only blackness.

Something hard was pressing into her ribs, and Steph shifted, debris crunching beneath her. When she opened her eyes, she found she was lying on a dirty floor, gazing into a filthy toilet stall, its walls peeling, the bowl cracked. Raising herself on one arm, she realized she was back in the bathroom, but now it was strewn with dead leaves. The mirrors above the sink were cracked radially like spiderwebs as if a fist had punched each one. The marble sinks were brown with filth.

Sitting up, the skin on the back of her hand tightened, and she hissed with pain. There were three red scrape marks there, the edges of the wounds white and raw. She turned her hand over and opened her fist.

It was empty.

No, there was something. A smudge in the center of her palm, rust particles stuck inside the minute grooves of her skin. The smudge was shaped like a weird six. Or a nine. But she'd seen that shape before, somewhere. She just couldn't remember where.

She remembered the others, though. Linh and Tate and Kenji and Satoko and Eloise and Miles...

Miles.

Scrambling to her feet, Steph threw her weight against the bathroom door, falling through it and crunching through the glass entry hall. She smelled the rain even before she plunged out into the downpour. Descending the steps, she kicked something hard, sending it skittering away from her. The briefcase. She ran for it and snatched it up, trying to orient herself.

Miles was still alive. He was still alive, and she had to get to Eloise before he did.

42

Miles...*Adam* rotated his head to look up at Eloise, his skull slowly grinding against her cold thigh. Her jeans were already soaked and sticky with his blood. It was on her hands, too, streaks and smears of it all over her pallid skin, horribly black under the pale moonlight, like tar.

She was pulsing, the adrenaline coursing through her veins. Her fight or flight reflex had hijacked her nervous system, setting off clamoring alarms throughout her body. She was hungry for air and had to suppress an urge to yawn, to expand her aching lungs, which had gone cold and tight.

The blunt end of the knife poked through the back of his shirt again, like a broken dock piling, revealed only briefly by the withdrawing of the tide. Eloise was filled with a wild compulsion to snatch it from his belt and—

And what, El?

Miles started to speak and started coughing. It went on for a long time, but he had her hand in his vice grip. She couldn't escape.

Eventually, he stopped coughing, spat one final time, then rolled onto his back again, his blue eye gazing glassily at the dark roof of the cave.

"I'll tell you everything," he said. "Everything that led to this point."

"1971 AD," she murmured. "Adam Davis. You didn't find that lighter. It was yours."

"My *dad*'s lighter. A gift from my grandfather. The year Dad joined the Marines."

I missed it, another clue. I wasn't listening to Steph. I didn't want to listen.

"El. Ellery. I need you to know...I came here for *you*. To be with you. It was a risk. I knew that. I was going to talk my way onto a fishing boat...use my knife for leverage, get some distance, and think about what to do next. I'll admit my great escape plan wasn't exactly sophisticated. I was just thinking as far as buying time until they caught up with me. I was going to take the clean way out, maybe use the knife once I was certain it was all over, that there was no hope left. But then I saw you on the beach. I *saw* you, Eloise."

"The beach?" Eloise struggled to focus on what he was saying. It didn't seem to matter very much either way, the specifics. Miles was a killer. A murderer. He'd been a murderer already, right from the moment she'd met him. She'd thought real murderers were *different* from normal people. That once you'd killed someone, it showed in your eyes somehow. It *had* to.

How did I not see this? God, Eloise, you're so fucking stupid...

"You were swimming in a white dress. You looked half-crazy, like some kind of demented, I don't know...sea witch? You called me to you like a siren. There was something so beautiful about you, all lit up under the golden sunset like that. You reminded me of her, I think. You have the same color hair. And your eyes. So, I watched you horsing around in the water with your dumb friends. It was clear that you were different from them. That you were *special*. I knew I had to get away, but I ended up following you back to your hostel. I watched you go into that bar. I attached myself to some randoms hanging around outside your hostel, looking lost, and suggested we head to that same bar for drinks. Tourists with guidebooks and backpacks.

They thought I was like them, just another hostel guest. It was easy after that. Your group was very welcoming, I have to say. It made sense later when it turned out that you were all *English teachers*, fresh out of college, naïve as fuck. But you were the most welcoming of the whole bunch, Eloise. You were so sweet. That's why I decided to stick around for you. I slept on the beach that night. Fucking crazy, I know. But you had me. You *had* me, Eloise."

"Did you kill Steph?" she whispered.

"In a minute," Miles said. "I'll explain. I need to tell you about Katie."

"What?" Eloise shook her head, confusion clouding her mind. "Katie?"

"No, no," the corner of his lip quirked up. "Not Ka*tie*. Ca*dy*. Cadence."

Cadence...the girl Marine...the girl he'd murdered. She'd misheard him all along, been thrown off by his accent, by the way Americans sometimes turned a t into a d. *Wadder, ledder, Harry Podder*. When he'd talked about his fiancée, the one who'd abandoned him while they were traveling...she'd thought he was saying *Katie*.

You could have figured all this out earlier, she realized with a sick jolt, *like when Steph told you about the text. You could have put it together. The lighter. The initials. The tattoo. Cady. For fuck's sake, El, you could have* listened *to Steph. But you didn't.*

And now, Steph was dead.

"I don't want to know about that," she said, her throat raw, a sob trapped in her chest. "You killed Steph. You killed Satoko and Tate...Kenji..."

"No," he said. "Only Kenji. In self-defense. Not the others."

"Why?" she sobbed, yanking her wrist against his grip. "Why are you *still lying*? Where's Steph? What did you do to her?"

"I *told* you, I don't know what happened to Steph. I didn't see her. She doesn't fucking matter. Listen. I was going to get you away from here, Ellery. You and me. It was the deal. I had to *facilitate*. You and I were going to start over, somewhere new. But something happened. Something... I can't remember."

Miles...*Adam*'s good eye clouded over with confusion. He trailed off, lips moving without sound. He seemed to have dropped the thread of his thoughts. It was like he wasn't able to make the right neural connections in his swollen, bleeding brain.

"Miles, what are you talking about? Please. I don't know what you're *talking* about."

"Cadence was my high school girlfriend," Miles spoke conspiratorially, as if he and Eloise were tucked in bed sharing post-coital secrets. Not huddled in a dark cave, both of them soaked in his blood while he confessed to having murdered someone.

How did I end up here? Eloise wondered. *How did I get so far from home, so far from everything that was ever safe and familiar?*

"I really loved her, Ellery. Cady, I mean. I still love her, I guess. She was my anchor. The missing piece of my soul. She was the only person I could talk to about...I don't know. Anything. My dad's a great guy, but he was...a stickler. He used to whup my mom, sometimes, when she did something that really pissed him off. Until she ran out on us. I blamed *her*, I know that's fucked-up. But after that, he'd give me and my brothers our lumps when we let the side down, when we brought home a bad grade, or he thought we hadn't given something our all. When we were being *slackers*."

"Miles, *please*."

"In high school, I was so damn angry all the time. It took a while, later on, to realize I was angry at my dad. He was my *dad*, you know? When you hate someone you respect more than anyone else, you've got to find somewhere else to put all that hate. I guess I internalized it. Then Cady came along. Things were better, great, even, for a while. We had all these plans for after school. Applied for the same colleges...but then..." Miles trailed off, and there was a long silence filled only by the dripping of the leaves outside, the scuffling of hidden creatures going about their own tiny-minded business somewhere deep in the vegetation, and Eloise's harsh, panicky breathing.

She knew she should indulge him. Keep him talking. Buy some time.

Time for what, Eloise?

"Then, she took everything that we had, all the plans we made, our whole future...and just dumped it in the trash. She dumped *me*. She got talking to this other guy...some fucking loser she met volunteering at the hospital, and all of a sudden we were done. Fuck college. Fuck prom. Fuck *you*, AJ." He scowled, his lips drawing back from his blood-stained teeth.

Eloise's skin crawled. *Get off. Get him off me.* She picked at his fingers and tried to prise them off her hand. It was no good. He had her.

"I got her to leave with me after prom. She was drunk out of her mind, pissed my date was voted prom queen, not her. Her popularity took a real nose-dive after she started dating that loser. I think she was jealous, then, finally. You know, that I'd taken her friend to prom. She hated that bitch. Like how you hate your friend Stephanie."

"I don't," Eloise said, by reflex, but he snorted, her denial apparently deeply amusing to him.

"You hate her, but she worships you. It was the same kind of deal. I took Cady to my family's cabin. To talk. I knew that if we could talk it out and reconnect, we could get back what we had. The cabin was sort of a special place for us. So we drove there, hooked up. But when it was over, it was like a fucking...flip had switched. She started getting all delinquent, getting up in my face, shoving me, cursing at me. She said she was going to tell everyone I forced myself on her, was going to ruin my reputation, contact the Dean of Admissions, and make them revo...resci...*take back* my early acceptance. I don't know where it all came from, El. She was never like that. She changed. People change on you when you least accept it. Don't you fire that?"

He was rambling, the words spilling into one another. The part of his brain that controlled language was pulling the wrong ones, jumbling up phrases. He was deteriorating rapidly, that much was evident. He was disgusting and evil, but now he seemed sad, too, pathetic and broken, a victim of an abusive upbringing and toxic masculinity.

It's not an excuse. None of this is an excuse. I don't want to hear anymore.

But Eloise had to keep Miles talking. She had to get away from him. She had to get...

The knife.

"So, you...you killed her."

"I didn't *mean* to. It's not murder if you don't *mean* to. We were fighting, and she got hit somehow...she went down. I tried to help her up, but she started...*biting* me. She bit my upper lip damn near clean off. I had to get twenty-six stitches. I had to tell the cops I got jumped at the gas station on the way home from prom. That didn't help my fucking case, let me tell you. Anyway, she bit me, and she scratched me, and she went for my eyes. I think she *thought* I was trying to kill her, but I wasn't. I swear to God I wasn't. I had to hold her down by her neck to keep her teeth away from me...I mean, it was self-fucking-defense, don't you see? But then she was just...limp. She was *gone*. Nobody tells you, do they El, how fucking easy it is to kill someone. Even with your bare hands. Even when it's completely by accident. And more so when it's a woman. You're so...soft. Fragile. Like baby birds. Hollow neck bones. It was done before I even realized I was doing it. And then I was all alone. It was just me. And I had to clean up the evidence. She was gone, and I couldn't help her. She was beyond helping. It wasn't my fault." His eyes found Eloise's, seeking her understanding.

Eloise shook her head wordlessly.

"What?" he asked, his voice cold, hard.

"I don't...I don't know."

"You *do* know. You know *exactly* what that's like."

"I didn't kill Chris."

"You don't need to do that, Eloise. Not with me. I *understand*, don't you see? I *get* it. Anyway, I got away with it. Just like you did. Until now. My dad called from the States yesterday morning. He said I needed to get away, that the police were digging out by the cabins. I guess part of the body must have shown up. That's all I can think of. I buried her as deep as I could, but the sun was coming up, and I didn't have all that much time. I thought about going back after that. But that would have been stupid. You never return to the scene of the crime. Dad sold the cabin soon after Cady went missing. I guess he knew...I guess he figured out that's where it happened. Fuck, I think he probably figured out everything. All of it. But he still covered for me. That's love, El. When you know the worst thing someone's done, and it doesn't change how you feel about them. That's fucking love."

"You're sick," Eloise muttered.

Oh, fuck. I said that out loud. Oh, God. Oh, shit. Oh, shit.

"I could have really loved *you*, Eloise," he said, his voice suddenly heavy with sadness. "It was going to be you and me at the end of everything. If only we had more time. It would have been...It would have been...nice."

His head nodded forward. He was silent now, chin resting on his chest. Either sleeping or unconscious.

You need to go now, El. You need to get out. You need to get away—

Trying not to breathe, Eloise cupped his head in her hands, his short hair scratchy against her numb fingers, the back of his head matted stiff into a crust of blood. Gently, she lowered it to the stone floor, tugging her legs out from beneath his shoulder. Then she tried to get to her knees, to get to her feet and escape, but her legs had gone dead, numb. Agonizingly painful needles were shooting up from her toes, the muscles cramped up, useless...

His hand shot out and clamped around her wrist, his good eye snapping open. He started to sit up, his mouth moving. He was saying something.

No! No! No!

Her free hand snaked around his back to his belt, grabbing the knife and yanking it free. He snatched for it, missed. Falling on him, pushing him down with her weight, her elbow in his cheek, Eloise somehow managed to wrest her other hand from his grasp. Grunting, she locked both hands around the handle and brought the blade down on him as he rolled beneath her.

There was a muted thud, like the sound of somebody getting a dull punch on the arm, and all of a sudden, Eloise's hands were empty.

Gasping, moaning, Eloise flicked her frenzied gaze back and forth over him. It took several seconds until she finally located it. The handle of the knife was embedded in his neck.

"Oh, fuck," Eloise moaned, and Miles rolled onto his back, his eye burning into hers with a look of disbelief, of deep hurt.

Please, I'm sorry, Chris, I didn't mean to...Please, God.

"El," he gurgled, blood streaming from the corners of his mouth.

"I'm sorry, I'm sorry," Eloise babbled stupidly, her slick fingers slipping on the bloody handle of the knife.

"Don't," he said, pushing her hands away. "I would never...never have hurt you, El."

"I don't believe you," she said, and she was sobbing hard, salty snot coating her top lip, dripping down the back of her throat. "You're a fucking liar."

He blinked, blood oozing between his clenched teeth.

"I didn't mean for any of it." There was a bubbling sound, air escaping the opening in his neck. "I swear I didn't mean it."

His hand groped for hers, and she tried to shake him off, but he held on tenaciously, still surprisingly strong, even seconds from death.

"Hold my hand," he begged, and there were faint scratches on the back of it, little raised wounds like rusty strings, already scabbing over. Eloise remembered the tiny kitten Miles had saved from being eaten by crows just that morning, out in front of the hostel.

But in her mind, she saw him, plucking the kitten from its hissing mother cat's side. The tiny life a mere prop, something to use on her, to manipulate her emotions.

"Watch...your six...Ellery," Miles rasped. "Please...tell my dad...tell him..."

But there was nothing more. Miles's cold fingers slackened, and his hand slid from hers, the arm flopping to the stone floor. Then his chest ceased shuddering, and he lay very still, his one clouded-over eye staring, fixed and unblinking, at the dark cave roof that hung low above their heads.

43

Eloise stumbled and went down for the third time. Mud oozed between her splayed fingers, her knees raw and stinging against the spongy forest floor.

The knife had been lost to her, wedged intractably in the cartilage of Miles's neck. She had nothing with which to defend herself, and she could hear voices in the trees. Some sounded human. Some didn't.

The air, too, was pulsating slightly. Eloise felt, rather than heard, music coming from the glowing lodge. She avoided the building by instinct. She didn't know how she knew. But something bad resided there, some kind of dark sentience beyond her capacity to comprehend.

The night was dripping, steaming, and moving all around her. The shadows capered on the path ahead, the moonlight filtering through the trees. Silver slices of this light, like tiny daggers, bounced off the raised bumps in the wet mud. She thought about the dappled sunlight she'd enjoyed that afternoon when Kenji wasn't dead, and she could still so easily discredit Steph as jealous and irrational. When Miles was just an exciting, handsome man she'd met. In the levity of the afternoon, when escape had seemed not only possible but inevitable.

A cold, rasping voice laughed close to her ear, and she jerked, forcing herself to her feet. The mud sucked at her boots as she struggled on through the dark. She had a vague goal in mind, of course. The Platform. If any of her friends were still alive, still capable of movement and thought, they'd know to go there.

Miles is dead. Kenji is dead. Steph is almost certainly...

But she was trying not to think about Steph and what Miles must have done to her. Miles. That wasn't his name, of course. It was Adam. *Was* Adam. Past tense. Because he was dead now. Eloise had...killed him.

I had to do it. He would have killed me.

Would he, Eloise? He told you himself that was never his intention. And even if it was...he was mortally wounded, wasn't he? Not only stabbed but bludgeoned in the head. His brain leaking out of his nose and his ears. And you say he was a threat to your life?

Shut up. It was self-defense. Miles killed Kenji. He killed Steph. He was going to kill me.

We both know the truth. You wanted to kill him. You enjoyed putting that knife through his throat. It brought you release. Didn't it? But if that helps you, then sure, go on believing you were defending yourself. Although, you were only delaying the inevitable, weren't you? It's this place that really wants you dead, Eloise.

"Shut up," Eloise said out loud. "Leave me alone."

The platform reared above the treeline high ahead, like the dark skeleton of some gigantic prehistoric creature, the moon hazy and indistinct behind it.

Eloise looked for the fire to guide her, but it was cold and black and dead, and the silvery light was weak down here in the shadows. The white concrete of the platform seemed to emit its own meager glow, and Eloise used it to orient herself.

There was a dark, still mass on the ground not far from the fire. When Eloise stood over it, she realized that she could see its open eyes, colorless in the dark, shimmering with trapped moonlight.

Ollie.

A scuffling sound from high above caught her attention, and she craned her neck, backing up enough to make out someone standing on the top layer of the structure, a dark shape silhouetted against the moon.

"El?" the shape called down to her.

"Steph?" Eloise's voice came out in a cracked whisper. Something crashed through the undergrowth beyond the platform, some wild beast or specter of the old resort, and Eloise's nerves clamored with alarm.

It's so dark.

She couldn't remember what had happened to the flashlight. She needed to make her way to the top of the structure, but in the dark, she thought she might fall.

"Steph?" She called out again, her voice a dry feather, tickling her throat, making her choke.

What if it's not really her up there? Eloise thought, her mind moving heavy and sluggish as if her head was filled with coagulating mud. *What if it's the resort?*

Eloise wasn't sure when she'd started thinking of the resort as an entity, a sentient thing that thought and hungered and hated. But it made sense that there was something here, after all, a malevolent, ancient force. It had been here long before the resort, before Okinawa was Japan, before history had even begun to be written down and recorded.

It's down in the cave, its true form, Eloise thought. Baseless conjecture, surely, but at the same time, she knew it to be true. *But how? How do I know?*

"Eloise?"

The voice, plaintive and afraid, so high above, and Eloise knew that it was Steph's voice, but was it really Steph up there? She imagined climbing the structure, finding nothing but pale moonlight, those horrible carousel horses grinning with flaking, yellowed teeth. The night curling like smoke around her feet, propelling her helplessly to the ledge, where the ground yawned dark and cold and hard below.

Then, a beam of light wavered across the ground in front of her. *Flashlight?*

"I'm coming up," Eloise called, entering the dark shadows of the open staircase, climbing as quickly as she dared.

The blazing lights of the main resort building blurred and shifted around her as she climbed beyond the canopy of the trees. Above, she found Steph, an indistinct shape, the flashlight's beam puddled at her feet. She was cowering by the dark mass of the broken-down carousel.

The realization flooded Eloise.

She's alive! Steph's alive!

As she drew near, still stunned by the discovery, Steph reached for her and pulled her close. Steph's hair tickled her nose. She smelled of sweat, dirt, and fear. Eloise grabbed her and held on to her as hard as she could, the hug almost painful, blinking away hot tears of relief.

"You're alive," Steph said, inhaling deeply near Eloise's ear before abruptly releasing her. "El. Listen. I think Linh's been taken."

Taken? Miles?

But Steph pushed something into Eloise's hands, something smooth and hard, plastic.

"It's Linh's camera. This was sticking out of the slot." Steph trained the flashlight's beam on something—a photograph. The light bounced off the smooth surface, and Eloise had to squint, to take hold of it and angle it in order to make it out.

Most of the photograph was obscured by an orange blur, probably a finger that had gotten in the way of the lens. Beyond the blur was a white oval amidst blackness, a face without features save for two black glittering holes. From the angle of the shot, it appeared to have been taken from the ground, pointing upwards.

The black background had some texture to it. Eloise realized it was hair, hanging down on either side of the face. And there was a white, gnarled hand, like a dug-up tree root, reaching towards the lens.

"Linh wouldn't have left Ollie alone." Steph pulled another object from her pocket, training the beam on it. It was Linh's phone, the screen dark and cracked. "I found this below as well. It was smashed and stamped into the dirt. And there was something else."

Eloise saw it, then. Linh's hollow stone bead, the protective talisman, dangling from a black hair tie around Steph's wrist.

"Ollie was holding it," Steph said solemnly, meeting Eloise's gaze. "He was holding it in his hand."

PART SEVEN

THE MAGATAMA

"The world breaks everyone, and afterward, some are strong at the broken places."
Ernest Hemingway–*A Farewell to Arms*

44

Takagusuku Park Nature Preserve, Okinawa, Okinawa Prefecture,
Early Morning, Monday July 15
(Marine Day)

Steph descended the last concrete step of the Viewing Platform, boots sinking into the mulch, El close behind her. The moonlight had completely disappeared, as if it had been snuffed out. There was only darkness, dense and cloying, pressing in on them from all sides. The realization that El was alive, that Miles hadn't hurt her, had filled Steph with an almost painful relief.

I need to tell her about Kenji. We need to come up with a plan, a way to save Linh.

The night was filled with noise. The music from the forest lodge had faded away, but voices had taken its place. Most audible among them were the screams of children, screams that could have been innocent joy but sounded more like screams of terror. There was laughter, too, the roaring of men, the high shrieks of women. The noises came from the illuminated guest rooms, faint shadows roaming the corridors.

There were other noises, too. Doors slamming. Feet pounding up and down the threadbare carpet runners. Water splashing busily somewhere in the vicinity of the bath house.

With the fire and the moon gone out, Steph's flashlight was their only source of light. They huddled together close to Ollie, who was somehow still breathing but cold. Steph kept the beam of the flashlight trained away from his face. She didn't want Eloise to see what she'd already seen.

She'd left the briefcase beside him. Fingering the black leather, she licked her lips and tried to find the words to tell El about Kenji, about how Miles had killed him.

"Steph," Eloise said, her voice cracking.

"What is it?" Steph reached out and brushed a fleck of mud off Eloise's cheek, right under her eye.

"I killed Miles," Eloise said, her eyes finding Steph's, apparently searching them for signs of disgust.

He's dead?
El killed him?

"God." Steph blew out a breath, her chest empty and cold. "He attacked me, the bastard. He said he was going to...kill me. And he killed Kenji. Right...right in front of me."

Eloise's cold fingers found Steph's, closed around them.

"He said Kenji went crazy and attacked him."

"Another one of his damn lies. He attacked me, and while he was...while he was toying with me, Kenji hit him over the head. With this."

Steph fingered the gold catches on the leather case, its shiny black surface a pale blue where it caught the light.

"His head was all bashed in," Eloise said. "When he found me in the cave."

"I did that. Hit him with a chunk of concrete. But I couldn't finish him off. I just ran. I grabbed the case first. Kenji seemed to...he seemed to think it was important."

"I put Miles's knife through his neck. That's how I did it. I stabbed him. Like...like what happened to Chris."

Eloise drew her knees up to her chest and pressed the hollows of her eye sockets against them. Her shoulders shook. Steph waited with her arm tight around Eloise's shoulder.

You're in love with her yourself.

Was she?

No, her mind insisted. *No, it's not like that.* It was *purer* than that. She'd kissed plenty of girls. If she felt that way about Eloise, she would have just gone for it.

It means so much more than that to me. Eloise *means more than that to me.*

Eventually, Eloise's spasming sobs stopped. She lifted her head, wiping her nose on the back of her hand, leaving a smeared snail trail. She was gross, but Steph smiled at her anyway, feeling an infinite tenderness that was almost too intense to bear. Even with her face streaked with mud and snot, her eyes dull and exhausted from fear, her friend was beautiful, and alive, and still with her.

"It's okay. El. It's over. And...and he deserved it."

After a long pause, Eloise put her hand softly on Steph's knee. "I'm sorry, Steph," she said in a small voice, and Steph got the feeling she was apologizing for more than just the stuff about Miles.

They sat in silence for a while, Eloise's shoulders still hitching every now and then.

"Did you see any sign of Tate or Satoko?" Steph asked, at last, removing her arm and shuffling her seat against the uncomfortable hardness of the ground. "If Tate wasn't the one trying to hurt us after all, then...then maybe Miles got to him, too? Maybe he and Satoko are both dead. Miles told me Tate killed himself, but...I can't believe that."

"It's not just him. It's not just Miles. This *place* is out to get us. I can feel it. And Linh's been taken. What the fuck are we supposed to do?"

There was another long silence, then Steph held out her hand. Eloise passed her the flashlight.

Taking a deep breath, Steph trained the wavering beam on Ollie's face. It looked like all of the flesh had been wasted away, leaving only skin stretched over a bare skull. The rise and fall of his chest was now barely perceptible.

"We should never have come here," Steph murmured.

"That old woman. She was right about this place," Eloise said. "Have you opened that briefcase yet?"

The briefcase.

Kenji died for this.

It had to be important.

Steph picked up the case and placed it on her lap, fingering the gold catches. They popped open with a sharp snap, making them both jump.

"It's…just papers." Steph lifted the spring traps and began leafing through the mess of photographs and documents. She lifted the top photo, a Polaroid shot, then dropped it in alarm as though it was hot enough to sear her fingers.

"What is it?"

Steph picked the photograph up again and held it up, hand trembling.

"It's the same girl," she said in disbelief. "I've seen her. Here, in the resort. In the lodge. Her face was all messed up. I think I was dreaming, but…she spoke to me. She handed me something. One of those magatama stones. And she said something."

"What?" Eloise leaned forward, looking at the sweet smile of the beautiful young girl in the photo.

"I don't know. It didn't sound like Japanese. Okinawan, I guess? But I know that she wanted something from me. It was in her eyes. Like she was…pleading for something."

Eloise picked up the stack of photos and flipped through them. Most were faded yellow-brown Polaroids, amateur snaps. Some were glossy prints, studio shots taken against a backdrop screen. The girl smiled innocently in a school uniform, posing beside an elegant-looking woman with salt-and-pepper hair. But most were candid shots of the girl alone, the framing and composition presenting her through a lascivious gaze.

"Oh, God." Her mouth twisted as she picked up a Polaroid of the girl and an older man, a rumpled hotel room visible in the frame behind them. "Look at this guy. He looks old enough to be her dad."

"It must be the guy whose briefcase this is," Steph mumbled. "Jesus. Look at this one. What's wrong with her face?"

They both stared at the photo. The girl was naked in the shot, but it was her face that was more disturbing than anything else. She wore cherry-red lipstick, smeared all over her chin. And her eyes. There were no whites to them. They were completely black, glittering, like the night sky.

"Remember? The same thing happened to those photos Tate and Linh took of us. In front of the resort. Linh's eyes." Steph turned the Polaroid over, the black plastic backing reflecting the moonlight. She remembered taking that group shot. Laughing, arguing, enjoying the adventure. Creeping each other out with talk of curses and ghosts. It felt like it had happened days ago. "Do you think she's dead?" Steph fought the urge to gnaw her fingernails. "The girl in the photo. In my dream, she was really badly injured, dragging her leg behind her..."

"Dragging her...Steph, I think..." Eloise's breath hitched. "I think I saw her, too. Down in the cave. *Shit.* There has to be something here." Eloise seized the briefcase and upended it, spilling its contents on the ground. "Kenji found *something*. You said he gave you this case, right? Like it was important? Maybe there's something that can help us."

"Right, but what?" Steph reached for the scattered papers and started automatically sorting them into piles. "How can some old photos and business documents help?"

"I don't know." Eloise chewed her lip. "Maybe there's some blueprints? Or, like land surveys? Maybe there's another way down? A tunnel in the caves or something?"

"I don't see any blueprints. It's just text. Can you read this?" Steph held up what looked like a contract of some sort. The page was dense with kanji characters.

Eloise took it, the paper trembling under the light of the flashlight. "Steph," she said, her voice faint, strained. "My Japanese is maybe good enough for everyday...I mean, I can just about make it through a newspaper article if I have to, but legalese, technical stuff...it's beyond my capacity. Way beyond."

Steph took a short breath. "El. I need you to try. I can't. You're the only one of us who actually studied this stuff. Just try to get the gist of it. Anything we can find out could help us. Could help Linh."

Eloise exhaled, and Steph heard her swallowing.

"It's some sort of...I don't know. Let's see...Intent to purchase property...Party A agrees to the terms and conditions laid out in...I can't...I can't *read* this, Steph. I've never even *seen* half of these characters before."

"Wait, there's something here that's handwritten." Steph grabbed a sheet of yellowed paper, covered all over with spidery black handwriting. "What could this be?"

"Steph, I can't make anything out of this," Eloise said, frustration in her voice, defensiveness. "This writing is chicken scratch."

"Well, what about the title? That looks pretty legible. Just try, El."

"You don't know what you're *asking*—"

"*Kenji died giving this to me!*" Steph realized she was shouting, paused to rub her hands over her face, and took several deep breaths. Then, softer: "I'm asking you to *try*. I know you can read this. All those hours locked up in your apartment, studying. Please try, El."

Eloise exhaled again, and Steph waited, holding her breath as El ran her shaking finger over the faded ink, the spiky writing.

"It says...Huh?"

"What?" Steph leaned closer.

"It says...I think it says, *confession*."

Eloise lifted her eyes from the page, and the two stared at one another for a long moment.

Somewhere in the resort, a woman screamed with laughter. The foliage whipped as something came crashing through the undergrowth towards them. Terror-stricken, Eloise trained the flashlight beam in the direction of the disturbance, but the noise stopped abruptly. There was nothing there.

"Can you *read* it, El?" Heart still hammering, Steph returned her gaze to Eloise, expectation filling her with hope. It was an expectation born from her belief in her friend. But whatever faith Eloise had in her own abilities seemed to have abandoned her.

"I can't." Her voice cracked on the words. "Steph, please. I can't do this. Don't make me do this. I'm not capable. I just want..." fresh tears rolled down her cheeks, seeping into the corners of her mouth. She whispered the rest of her sentence, "I just want to go home."

"Home." Steph shifted, taking a deep breath, holding Eloise's gaze firm. "Right. We're *going* home. We're going to get out of here. We'll get some help for Linh, Ollie, and the others. Then we'll go home. We'll *all* go home. And one day, I'll come visit you. And you'll come visit me. And this will all just be a very bad, traumatic memory. Just a memory. But I need you to help me now. You can read this. I know you can. The answer has to be here. I saw it in Kenji's eyes. This girl...she's connected to this place, to the man this briefcase belongs to. She's the root of all of this. I *know* it. So tell me," Steph picked up the handwritten pages and shook them slightly under Eloise's nose, "*Tell me what this says.*"

Taking the pages, the fight gone from her, Eloise blinked the tears out of her eyes and stared at them.

"Just read the first line," Steph encouraged her softly. "Just the first line."

"Confession," Eloise began, her voice catching. "I, Imamura...Imamura somebody...I can't read that character. I, Imamura, have a story I must tell, if not for my own sake, then for my beloved South, South flower...that's a name. Nanoha? For the sake of my beloved Nanoha, whose real...whose truth I could not believe."

Eloise stopped, the heavy weight of Steph's expectation hanging in the air over both of their heads.

Licking her cracked lips, Eloise held the shaking flashlight closer to the page and kept going.

45

I, Satoshi Imamura, have a story I must tell, if not for my own sake, then for my beloved Nanoha, whose truth I could not bring myself to believe.

When I bought the land for my proposed leisure resort, I was besieged by a barrage of angry phone calls and lengthy missives from a local temple. The monks' warnings were tenebrous, rambling, and seemed grounded in nothing more tangible than spiritual hokum and resentment towards me, an outsider.

The bulk of their ire seemed centered around an ancient gravesite located within the bounds of the property I had already purchased. But the graves were very old indeed, and seemed untended, and though I tried to make inquiries, to track down the descendants of those whose bones were interred there, my efforts were fruitless. If any still lived, perhaps they had moved away or felt nothing but indifference towards their ancestors, towards those ancient monuments and tombs.

Perusing the gravesite, I found nothing of note, but close by yawned the mouth of a cave. Nothing so unusual on this island, which is something of a massive rabbit's warren of caves, some mere pocks in the limestone, others vast networks, deep and complex. This cave was of the latter variety.

I resolved to return before construction began, to explore the cave complex more thoroughly. Perhaps this was a resource I might exploit, a bonus feature of the cliffside location I had purchased that could be spun into an additional money-making venture, incorporated, as it were, into the resort complex itself. I thought about wiring it for electricity, conducting tours, perhaps, or even constructing some sort of subterranean gift shop or café.

But when I mentioned my plans in an offhand manner to my young companion, (a local girl I'd been mentoring, in a fashion, and who made my frequent trips to the island much more enjoyable) her reaction was visceral. It is hardly my usual policy to discuss business with my companions, much less a girl of her unseasoned years. Heretofore, I had found her local quirks amusing. Colorful even. She had become critical of the resort venture over time, poisoned, no doubt, by the whisperings of her hag of a mother. The old bitch was some sort of spiritual medium or witch doctor, I'd never cared to inquire further, and so her superstitious ramblings should have been easy enough to ignore, even for her devoted daughter, who was a bright girl with an analytical mind. She would have had a promising future had she not been dragged up by a deranged woman who scratched out a meagre living providing spiritual "services" to other island folk as delusional as she.

But Nanoha insisted that her mother was some kind of priestess, still practicing the ancient Ryukyuan religion. One of the *kaminchu*, or godly people. Following the Battle of Okinawa, these priestesses were scattered and their numbers dwindled. Some remained in small villages, and often in close proximity to *Utaki,* or holy sites.

Nanoha's mother claimed that the fascinating cave complex I'd uncovered was one such *Utaki*, that it housed the spirit of a prehistoric, female deity who had, for many centuries, been worshipped by the local people.

As the legend goes, when time began, a young shrine maiden was burned alive in sacrificial crimson fire to appease a malevolent sea god who had wracked the island with terrible storms. Storms that had lasted for a year and a day. The virgin girl was burned alive, and with the offering of her agonizing death, the violent storms at long last abated. Grateful, the islanders entombed the sacrificed girl in the deep caves and enshrined her there to be worshipped ever after, as a *kami*, a sacred spirit.

To trespass upon the land, to develop it for commercial use, therefore, would be to invoke the ire of the ancient sacrifice's *kami*, the spirit slumbering deep in the caverns beneath the rock of the high cliff.

But I have no use for fanciful folklore. I am a pragmatic man, a thoroughly modern man. Japan is entering a period of great prosperity, and the potential for the accumulation of wealth and success beyond any man's dreams is now entirely within the grasp of those who would only reach for it. The Takagusuku cliff site was a perfect score. A prime location, ripe for development. Was it not Henry Avery, that intrepid foreign explorer, who said: *I am a man of fortune, and I must seek my fortune*?

I, too, am destined for greatness. For great fortune.

Or so I believed.

To appease the nervous heart of my dear Nanoha, I coaxed and cajoled and finally convinced her to join me on a sojourn into the caves. Once she saw the potential of the area, I felt sure she would finally be able to break from the crazed mother and align herself fully with me. I saw that to win her over, I could offer her not marriage and respectability, of course, but *enterprise*. Not content to be a mere companion, Nanoha, with her sharp mind and keen acumen, wanted in on the Imamura business, to participate and innovate, to share in my success.

I have many regrets. I regret the resort venture in its entirety. I wish I had never embarked upon any of it. If only I had developed elsewhere, and thus spared us all of this. But my most grievous mistake was bringing Nanoha into the caves that night. Because her presence there served as some sort of ritualistic catalyst, I believe—perhaps it was the influence of her mother's *kaminchu* blood, or some spiritual gift of her own.

Had I, an ordinary man, been the one to liberate the magatama from the ancient corpse's neck alone, perhaps nothing would have happened at all.

But I am getting ahead of myself. The magatama, of course, takes its proper place later in the telling. First, I must describe the chamber that lies deep in the rock. In the lowest recesses of the cave complex, there is a long, narrow tunnel, bored by ancient means, perhaps, or else a complete coincidence, some natural formation. The tunnel opens out, at length, into a vast subterranean chamber—a cavern with a roof of rock so high that it is invisible in the blackness, and where a deep, glittering lake shimmers. In the very center of the lake, there is a flat slab of rock upon which rests a vast stone sarcophagus. I regret, very much, that I opened the sarcophagus. But how could I not? Curiosity clutched me tight in its claws and compelled me to slide aside that heavy slab and peer within.

Never have I seen such beauty. She seemed perfectly preserved, as if she were crafted from pure marble by the greatest artisans who ever walked the Earth. She was but a young girl, barely out of her teens—of an age, in fact, with my Nanoha, who, rather than shrinking from the embalmed vision, leaned over her in her coffin, spellbound. I can still recall how her long, black, silken hair fell upon the beautiful corpse, how it shone like starlight in the faint beam of my helmet-mounted light. With infinite care, her fingers brushed the beaded string the young sacrifice wore about her slender neck.

Let us take it as a token, I suggested, and though she balked at this and claimed she would not accept it, she did not attempt to prevent me as I removed one ancient stone bead from the string. The young sacrifice never stirred, of course, for she was centuries dead. But when I was sliding the stone slab back into place, I thought for one fanciful, irrational moment that I saw her eyes open, so bright, so *sentient*, glowing with a strange, starlike light.

I made Nanoha wear the bead on a string around her neck. Part of me hoped the old bitch might see it, might know its symbolism—the devoted daughter was no longer hers. Her precious child had renounced her and all her spiritualistic mumbo-jumbo. In my perverse heart, I wanted her to know that I had claimed the girl as my own, that together we had desecrated an ancient tomb.

But the mother, it transpired, said nothing. I cannot believe that she didn't notice. I saw her once, after that. She seemed diminished, somehow, her eyes grown dull. As she stared blankly at her daughter, her worn features registered defeat.

Not long after that, the vomiting began.

Nanoha said she felt fine. *Never better* were the words she used. I suspected pregnancy at first, which would have been most inconvenient. But a doctor's examination ruled out that possibility. Nanoha was infertile and had no womb. I considered specialists. A doctor of the gut, perhaps, as what spewed from Nanoha's insides on an almost daily basis was not bile nor vomit but a dark red liquid resembling blood. But there were no answers. Nanoha was in perfect health.

How could someone vomit blood in such quantities and yet have such a bright complexion, such vitality, such a hearty appetite?

Not long after the bloody vomiting began, Nanoha started to talk about crimson shadows, like swirling smoke, that came whenever she was alone. She grew fearful, clingy, her mind filled with insane notions and baseless fears. She became deathly afraid of snakes and would not come near the resort for fear of the forest. The cliffs were crawling with deadly vipers, she insisted, my guests would be poisoned by the waters, by the very air, and perish en masse.

As if her words had spoken into existence a curse against me, things began to go wrong with the resort. There was a collapse during construction. A man was crushed to death. A costly payout to the worker's family closed that matter, but things began to unravel further. A child drowned in the pool. I couldn't explain it. I'd employed lifeguards. The pool was overcrowded with so many day guests. Someone should have seen the child in distress. I paid more condolence money, but it wasn't enough. The newspapers caught wind of the tragedies. Then the whispers of protest began.

And all the while, Nanoha grew more and more monstrous. She had been exceptionally beautiful to begin with. I assure you, I would not have risked my marriage and reputation otherwise. But since that night in the cave, her beauty took on a lascivious, demonic quality. The luster of her skin and the sheen of her hair bordered on obscene. Her skin grew impossibly milk-white, her eyes blackening until the pupils merged with the iris, until she barely looked human. I could no longer lie with her. I could no longer deal with her. She grew wild, uncontrollable, insane. I feared for my reputation if she were to be allowed to carry on unchecked. She seemed determined to ruin me.

But perhaps I was ruined already. The resort was faltering before it had even begun to find its feet, the venture an obvious failure. And I owed unfathomable sums of money, much of it to unscrupulous individuals. Men who would just as soon take what was owed them in blood, if no money was available.

And so, I made my plans to flee. But first, the Gala Opening party. It was a farce, of course, a mere pantomime. It was obvious the resort venture was dead in the water. In hindsight, I should have made my exit long before. But the investors would be in attendance. I suppose I wanted to live my dream for just one more night. One last, magical night, where I could be a glittering success, where I could pretend that everything I'd worked so hard for had come to fruition, instead of rotting, untasted, on the vine.

But Nanoha betrayed me. She denied me that one perfect moment of golden triumph. And she flung herself from my beautiful Viewing Platform, in full view of the guests, the investors, my wife, my son. One last shocking death, the most dramatic of them all. The crowning event, as it were. That incident was the final death knell for my resort, my marriage, and my career.

It occurred to me later that I could make amends, of a sort, by returning the magatama to the corpse's sarcophagus. Could this appease the spirit of the young girl who had been sacrificed, the virgin maiden whose soul had been put to sleep beneath these island cliffs, oceans of time ago? Perhaps. But I could not get the magatama. It had been given directly to Nanoha's mother. And the old bitch would not receive me.

A broken man, no hope left, I stumbled through the halls of my empty resort alone, pulling on a bottle of whiskey. We had no paying guests. The staff had all left. The creditors were closing in upon me. I had lost Nanoha, and my wife had taken my son. My reputation was dirt.

As night fell, I lit a fire and huddled by its comforting glow, beneath the unfinished Viewing Platform. At some point, I must have slept, for I had a strange dream. A procession came by, a dozen wizened crones in white robes, with long folding fans and dangling beaded necklaces, clutching burning lanterns. Between them, they carried an ornate palanquin of black lacquer and gold filigree. A young girl rode stiff and solemn inside. I knew at once that it was my Nanoha. Compelled, I followed the procession as it led me to the ancient gravesite. The big tomb, the turtleback one, was open, its doors leading into blackness. I hid behind a grave marker and watched as Nanoha alighted from the palanquin. She was dressed all in white robes, and her hair fell down her back like a waterfall of night. She paused, for just a moment, looking over her shoulder, and I thought I saw an odd, shining light in her dark eyes. Then the entire procession disappeared into the tomb.

When I awoke, the dawn was a grey mist about me. Filled with a sudden certainty, I ran through the woods to the old graveyard. The tomb was sealed, of course, as it had been for centuries, but something compelled me to dash to the mouth of the nearby cave. I had only a lighter with which to make my way, but I relied on my memory to guide me down through the endless dark, to the long, deep tunnel, to the glittering water-filled cavern.

It was empty, silent, save for the gentle sloshing of the deep water. I made my way along the raised stone platform to the great sarcophagus. When I slid aside the slab and looked down upon her face, my breath turned to solid ice inside my lungs.

It was Nanoha asleep in the coffin.

My confession ends here. I have nothing more to say for myself. I am aware, painfully aware of my hubris and conceit. I will hide this confession away, lock it tight in the safe in my office. I admit that the writing of it was more for my own psychological unburdening than to serve as any form of penance. There can be no redemption, of course, for my soul. I hope that no one will ever read these words, for the truth brings me deep shame. At the same time, however, I suppose I don't particularly care if anyone ever does, for I will not be around to know of it. I thought of flight, somewhere remote and overseas. But when I attempted to leave the resort, I found that the road down had been obliterated by some arcane means. A gaping chasm cuts me off from the rest of the world.

The resort is a prison of my own making, and now, I am its prisoner.

As I write, crimson smoke curls around the crevices in the door, and I hear strange laughter echoing through the empty rooms.

Once I finish, I intend to wander deep into the woods and end my own life.

I wonder what will become of my resort. My sincere hope is that it is left to rot.

Please forgive me, Nanoha.

Satoshi Imamura

General Manager, The Royal Oceanview Hotel and Leisure Resort

September 24, 1975

Eloise let the pages fall to her lap. It had taken her a long time to get through them, and there were several characters she'd claimed she couldn't make out, let alone attempt to read. But she'd made it to the end.

The confession was fantastical, filled with long, rambling sentences, and the writing was obviously deeply subjective. But after everything that had happened, Steph thought they had reason enough to believe every word.

"If what this confession says is true...then Linh is..." Steph trailed off, allowing her fingers to drift towards her mouth. Eloise reached out and caught her wrist, surprising Steph, distracting her from the bloody stumps of her fingernails.

"Don't you *see* it?" El asked, her eyes wide, glimmering. Steph frowned, shaking her head almost imperceptibly.

See what?

Dropping Steph's wrist, Eloise used the flat of her hand to fan the photographs out on the bare ground between them. Spotting the one she wanted, she plucked it up, turning it around so that Steph could see it.

"Steph...look. Look at this woman."

Steph leaned forward, perplexed. "What? What about her?"

"Look at her hands."

They both studied the photograph in silence. It looked like a high school graduation photo. The girl, Nanoha, was wearing a sailor suit and a shy smile. She was seated in front of a smiling woman, who looked elegant in a crisp kimono. Nanoha was holding a framed diploma on her lap. The woman's hand was on her shoulder, the fingers thick and white.

White gloves.

"The old woman, the one from the hostel? She wore white gloves. Linh said she had tattoos on her hands. What was it Kenji said? Some Okinawan women got the tattoos when they came of age. But over time they became taboo and the practice died out until they became *incredibly* rare."

Steph blinked at Eloise. "You can't seriously think it's the same woman?"

"If it *is*...If it is the same woman, if the old lady at the hostel was Nanoha's *mother,* then that means that this..." Eloise trailed off, holding the stone bead up to the light.

Steph reached up to touch it with a forefinger, setting it spinning as it dangled. "Shit," she whispered, her face hot, her chest cold. "It's the same one. That's why Nanoha took Linh. *That's what she wants.*"

It was at that moment that the battery in the flashlight gave out, the light sputtering, then fading away to nothingness.

46

If she'd been alone, Eloise wasn't sure she'd have been able to force herself to leave the safety of the camp, either real or imagined, and venture out again into the depravity of the resort. But Steph's hand was warm inside hers, and in her other hand she held Linh's magatama, gripped so tightly it hurt.

Fumbling in the darkness, they'd tended to Ollie as best they could, soaking Steph's camisole in bottled spring water and draping it over his corpse-like forehead. Then they left him where he lay, stealing away into the shadows of the night.

The cave was beyond the graveyard, which the half-overgrown path close to the platform ought to lead to. But the path branched and forked, and it was now so dark they could barely see their own hands in front of their faces. On either side of the path, the trees and bushes rustled as though restless creatures huddled within, watching as Steph and Eloise inched their way past. It was as if the resort knew what they were up to, as if it was biding its time, safe in the knowledge that its helpless prey was already trapped.

We just need to get to the cave, Eloise told herself again.
And then what?
Bargain for Linh's life with this—this magatama.

You're dreaming, you stupid bitch. You really think that's going to work? Based on what? Conjecture? Horror movie logic?
Stop talking to me.
"What?" Steph whispered.
"Nothing," Eloise murmured, and then something skittered across the path in front of them. Something that moved low to the ground, hissing like an angry snake.
"What was that?" Steph froze.
"Linh's camera." Eloise reached for Steph, fingers fumbling along her arm. "Does it still work?"
"You want to take a *picture*?"
"The flash. We can use the flash to see ahead."
The bushes on one side shook again. Steph lifted the camera and depressed the shutter button, but nothing happened.
"Wind the film," Eloise whispered, and there was a sharp ratcheting sound, impossibly loud, as Steph thumbed the wheel.
Something broke from the bushes again, right in front of them, and Steph shrieked as the camera flash went off, lighting up the environment and the path ahead.
A dark shape with long, pale fingers, low to the ground on its hands and knees. Eloise got a glimpse of matted, reddish-brown hair hanging from a head that wobbled erratically on a clearly broken neck. A black rubbery shoe dragged a deep furrow through the mud behind it. The next moment, the absolute darkness flooded out the light again, and the apparition could only be heard, crashing into the tree cover on the opposite side.
Then there was silence.
"Was that real?" Steph whispered, her breath hot and panicky in Eloise's ear.
Eloise couldn't speak.
That red-brown hair. Those expensive hiking shoes. Satoko.
Steph's hand slid under Eloise's armpit, and she pulled her close. "Don't let go of me, El."
"Steph!" a male voice boomed from the undergrowth where the scuttling woman-creature had vanished. It was Tate's voice.

Sickening familiarity. A bubbling undercurrent of malice, something horribly inhuman. "Steph...you should stick with me. I'll keep you safe. There's a murderer running around, you know." The voice was followed by a childish giggle.

"Go away, Tate," Steph responded, her voice cracking.

"Go fuck yourself, Stephanie." The thing with Tate's voice giggled again.

"Let's hurry," Steph said, but Eloise shook her head.

"No. It wants us to panic, wants us to lose our heads. If we run, I feel like...I feel like it'll get worse. We have to pretend to be calm. It's our fear this place wants. We can't let it feed on us, Steph."

"Shit, El. Okay."

Eloise gripped the magatama harder, the jagged surface biting painfully into the soft meat of her palm. "We have to get to the cave. I think that's the fork up ahead. Take another picture."

Eloise steeled herself as Steph raised the camera again, tugging the last photograph out of the slot and tossing it to the ground. The flash startled both of them once again, but in the slice of light it provided, Eloise recognized the path ahead, the fork. The decaying rope that slung between two trees indicated the way to the graveyard.

"Go right," she whispered.

When they emerged in the graveyard, the moon appeared from behind a black cloud, lighting up the grave markers and the old turtleback tomb. Steph's hair was shining, too, the strands glinting like white gold. Eloise thought about the beach, the glowing plankton, Miles touching her bare shoulder. The excitement of being young and free in a far-flung land, and the adventure of it all. Now Miles was dead, curled up in the mouth of the cave like a dead spider, the knife still buried in his neck.

"The cave's up ahead," Eloise said, her voice almost gone. The thought of stepping inside the dark mouth of the cave again terrified her, but not as much as the thought of having to step over Miles's corpse. She hesitated, feeling Steph's eyes on her. "How many shots left?"

"I don't know. It's too dark to read the dial."

Eloise thought back. "Linh said it's got...what, ten shots? She took one photo outside the resort. And at least one more, of Nanoha. We just took two. That leaves six."

"Linh could have taken more."

"Oh, yeah."

Something stirred in the darkness by the turtleback tomb. Eloise grabbed Steph's arm. Dark tendrils curled through the crevices of the doorway like groping fingers. It was the red smoke. The tomb was billowing with it.

"How are we going to do this?" Steph whispered. "How are we going to make it into the deepest part of that cave and back again with six light flashes? And that's the best-case scenario."

"It's afraid of us," Eloise heard herself murmuring. "The bad thing at the heart of this place."

"You mean Nanoha?"

"I don't know. What if...what if Nanoha's afraid, too? What if she's a victim of this place as much as we are? If we help her...maybe she'll help us get out. We need to find her tomb. The sarcophagus Imamura wrote about. The cave's pretty narrow inside. We'll have to feel our way, save the flash for when the path forks."

"If we go in that cave, what are our chances of coming out again?" Steph's question hung in the air, unanswered.

Eloise took her hand instead.

The moonlight held up long enough to illuminate the cave mouth. But as they stepped inside, it was swallowed by clouds again. They found themselves in complete blackness, the cave walls dripping all around them.

He's in here. His body. His dead body. Right in here.

The camera dial began to make that ratcheting sound again.

"What are you *doing*?" Eloise gritted out, half-crazed with fear.

"I need to see the body." Steph shifted, lifting the camera. "I need to know he's dead. I need to see it for myself."

"Don't," Eloise whispered. She wasn't going to look. She closed her eyes, her mind projecting images of Miles sprawled on the cave floor in a pool of his own blood. But she couldn't help herself. She opened her eyes as the flash lit up the cave, breath catching in her throat.

Glistening walls, bare rock floor shining with red, wet blood—

Miles's body wasn't there.

They stood there in the cave mouth, stunned. Steph turned the dial again. Eloise was too numb to stop her as she ripped aside the ejected photo and set the flash off a second time. Nothing. Only the nest of dripping stalagmites, the stone markers. And the blood.

"Is this where..."

"I left him right here," Eloise said, speaking over Steph. "He was dead. How can he be gone?"

"I thought I saw..." Steph cranked the dial again, ignoring Eloise when she gasped *stop*, lighting the cave up again. But there was something wrong. There was something hanging out of the photo slot of the camera Steph was clutching. It was like old, black rope, some sort of frayed, dark hemp.

Black hair.

Steph screamed, dropping the camera. It crashed to the stone floor, shattering, little plastic shards bouncing off into the darkness.

"Jesus! Jesus, fuck," Steph moaned, and Eloise heard her brushing her hands hard against her shorts, as if she could wipe away the feeling of it.

"Shh," Eloise soothed, as Steph gasped and sobbed beside her. "Shh, it wasn't real. It's just this place. None of this is real."

Once Steph was calmer, Eloise crouched down and felt around.

"I saw it, too. There's something here."

Metal against her fingers. A scraping sound, a pop. Orange light lit up Eloise's face, and she straightened up, holding the lighter. The flame flickering against her breath, she rubbed her thumb over the engraving: 1971 AD.

"There's something else." Steph grabbed Eloise's wrist and angled the lighter down towards the cave floor. Stooping, she picked up something flat and dark and shiny from where it lay in the drying pool of tacky blood.

"That's his knife." Eloise swallowed, feeling the blood rushing in her ears. "I buried it in his neck. He can't still be alive. I killed him."

"Are you *sure*?"

Eloise swallowed.

"El...what if, on top of everything else...*he's* down there?"

Eloise thought about it for a moment. Then she held out her hand, palm-up.

"Give me the knife."

"You don't have to, El. I can..."

"Give it to me." Eloise's fingers closed around the thick handle. "I stabbed him once. If I have to, I think...I think I can do it again."

47

Eloise and Steph pressed forward, Steph holding the lighter up in front, trying not to breathe on the flame and make it judder. Eloise followed, gripping the knife.

They passed the fork with the dead end, where Eloise had first seen Nanoha, hours before. Beyond that point, the tunnel began to grow shallower and narrower, and they had to crouch down and then crawl. Eloise started to worry that the tunnel would grow so narrow they'd have to pull themselves through it on their bellies, like snakes. It was a relief when the tunnel began to widen out again, but a further series of sharp bends disoriented her.

Then they emerged into something like an antechamber. The ceiling was still so low they had to stoop, and the walls were cluttered all around with giant earthenware pots.

"Bones," Steph whispered, and something cracked beneath Eloise's boot. Sickness washed over her.

"There are so many of them…Why…"

Steph lifted the lighter, illuminating a section of the cave wall covered with scratches and gouges.

"It's a petroglyph," she said. "An engraving in the rock…"

They moved forward, their breathing very loud in the hush of the cramped antechamber, both trying to figure out what they were looking at.

Crude lines were scratched in the limestone, depicting a female figure burned on a pyre. A magatama symbol. A woman, clutching a baby in her arms.

"What does it mean?" Eloise whispered. She sensed Steph shaking her head beside her.

"I can feel air...moving air." Steph lowered the lighter, and the engraving became a blank black wall again. "There's a passage," she murmured, and Eloise took the hand she held out low behind her. Steph's fingers were cold and sweaty in her grasp.

They followed the passage. Eloise felt cool air on her cheeks.

When Steph came to a stop, Eloise walked into her back with a grunt of surprise.

"What is it?" her voice echoed, reverberating around what sounded like an immense space as her eyes adjusted.

The cavern *was* immense, the roof so high above that it wasn't visible. But there must have been an opening somewhere. A shaft of silvery light illuminated the cavern, reflecting off the black ripples of the dark subterranean lake that filled it, highlighting the stone slab that rested on a dais in the very center.

"It's the sarcophagus," Eloise muttered over her shoulder to Steph. "I think we have to open it."

A stone walkway stretched across the pool. It was worn smooth and partially submerged in places. Eloise and Steph inched their way along it. The waters undulated slightly on both sides, as if teased by underwater currents. When they reached the platform, they both moved instinctively to stand on the right side of the stone sarcophagus.

"Help me lift it," Eloise said, taking hold of the stone lip of the sarcophagus's lid. It was cold, rough, and incredibly solid. Gummy cobwebs covered it like a sheer film, sticking to Eloise's fingers.

Together, they heaved the slab aside just enough to allow the silvery light to illuminate what was inside.

Steph's shriek repeated, over and over, bouncing off the cavern walls. Eloise's heart clamored, and she clutched for Steph, gasping in lungfuls of the cavern's fetid air as the echo-shrieks finally faded away to silence.

Linh lay face up inside the stone coffin.

"Is she..." Steph began, reaching to touch Linh's face. Eloise grabbed her wrist.

"Don't touch her," she warned.

Together, they looked down at their friend. Linh was pale, her eyes closed. The body was dressed in a white kimono, folded with the right side over the left in the funeral style. One pale hand clutched a rusty sword. A cracked black mirror lay near her other hand. Draped around her neck and chest was a necklace, crudely hewn stone beads strung along it, interspersed by smooth yellowish cylinders of what looked like bone.

"There," Eloise said, pointing. "The missing magatama."

Someone had cut the necklace, then loosely tied a knot where the pilfered magatama had once been. Picking the knot apart with her fingernails, Eloise looped the thin, brittle rope of the necklace through the hole in Linh's magatama and re-tied the knot.

"What now?" Steph whispered.

"Help me close it up."

Eloise sensed Steph looking at her with incredulity, but she said nothing. Together, they reached across Linh's supine form and grabbed the lid again.

Behind them, something emerged from the water, gasping and choking, emitting a colossal splash before sinking back below the surface. Steph shrieked again, grabbing hold of Eloise and almost pulling them both into the dark lake. Eloise managed to grab the side of the coffin at the last moment. Craning to look over her shoulder, she squinted at the churning water.

"Linh?"

The figure bobbled up again, choking and spluttering.

"*Linh!*"

Together, they dragged Linh out of the water. She fell against the side of the coffin, coughing as a dark spurt of liquid burst from her lips and splashed down against her neck. Then she gasped for breath.

"Where am I, what's happening?" Her eyes sought out Eloise's. But Eloise shook her head, letting go of Linh, dragging herself to her feet. Holding onto the lip of the sarcophagus, she peered inside once more.

"It's empty."

Steph peered over the lip as well, looking down into the coffin. Only the sword and broken mirror remained. And the necklace of magatama beads, coiled at the bottom like a limp snake.

"Do you think it worked?" Steph murmured. Her eyes found Eloise's. "Is that right? I mean...is it over?"

"I don't know. But we did our part. And we've got Linh. We need to leave now, I think. Help me with the lid."

As they slid the heavy slab back over, Eloise thought she saw Nanoha in the coffin for a moment. Thought she caught a glimpse of the glittering black pools of her eyes. But it was only for a moment. The coffin was empty. The lid of the sarcophagus settled back into its grooves, closing with a dull thud that echoed around the vast, desolate cavern.

48

When they emerged from the cave, it was broad daylight. The brightness hurt badly at first, the light overwhelming after being down in the deep darkness of the cave complex for so long. Linh blinked and shielded her eyes, pain needling at her brain. She was foggy, confused. And dimly aware that she'd lost time. The last thing she remembered was climbing the Platform, gazing out at the nothingness that had engulfed the island.

Then darkness.

The other two let Linh rest at the graveyard. She leaned against a crumbling grave marker, holding her head in her hands, waiting for the nausea to dissipate.

Once they'd all re-acclimated to the bright sunlight, they discussed what to do next. Linh suggested returning to the Viewing Platform camp to see if anyone else had made it back there. She caught a glance exchanged between Steph and Eloise, but they said nothing.

The sun was hot and high in the trees above them as they walked. It warmed Linh and helped to lift some of the shakiness she still felt inside. It felt like early afternoon. Last night's mud had solidified, and the ground beneath her boots was baked hard. The path ahead was dappled with golden sunlight that filtered through the tree canopy above. The horrors of the night now seemed remote, and the resort was silent and peaceful, the only noise the chirping of the cicadas and the twittering of birds. Somewhere far off, Linh made out the roar and rush of the ocean.

"It's like nothing happened," Steph said, as they rounded a bend in the path and the Viewing Platform came into view through the trees ahead.

But when they approached their makeshift camp, they realized that something was different.

Ollie was gone.

They wandered aimlessly around the camp, searching for signs of him. Their backpacks were all there in a pile, the remnants of their fire a blackened circle on the ground. A mellow, warm breeze blew through the trees all around, shaking their branches.

Linh stared down at the depression in the mud where Ollie had lain, her vision blurring behind her glasses.

"He was dying. He couldn't have just gotten up and walked away."

Eloise went to her, but Linh fended her off with her elbow as she wiped her nose on the back of her hand.

"Maybe someone came to help in the night. Maybe they took him to a hospital." Steph picked up one of their half-full water bottles, then thought better of it and drained it onto the ground.

Linh looked at Steph with disbelief. "Yeah, right."

"Do you hear that?" Eloise was distracted, head tilted back, looking up at the concrete structure above them.

"Hear what?" Steph frowned.

"I think it's a plane..."

They could all hear it now, the drone of the engine. They bolted for the platform's stairway, dashing for the top layer.

Linh emerged onto the roof first just as the plane flew over her head, low in the sky, seeming almost close enough to jump and touch. It was fast, with a sharp nose and a glass bubble cockpit, a fighter plane.

The noise of it was immense, and they all went down onto their knees on the concrete platform as it zoomed over them and out over the cliffs to sea, seemingly without having spotted them.

"We should try to signal, there might be more..." Eloise gasped, and Steph was nodding, agreeing with her, but Linh ignored them both, drawn to the edge of the platform.

As she looked down at the vista of the hillside below, shivers danced up and down her spine. Beyond the resort boundary, there lay the rest of the island...its towns and villages, the snaking roadways with their moving cars. And out on the oceans, hundreds of tiny fishing boats, bobbing merrily on the waves.

Everything was as it should be. Everything was intact. *Everything*.

Linh turned to the others. They stared back at her.

"The road," she said simply. "It's back."

PART EIGHT

LEAVE

"Even if she be not harmed, her heart may fail her in so much and so many horrors; and hereafter she may suffer...both in waking, from her nerves, and in sleep, from her dreams."
Bram Stoker—*Dracula*

SEARCH FOR MISSING HIKERS ON OKINAWA OFFICIALLY ABANDONED, OCEANVIEW SITE DEMOLITION TO COMMENCE NEXT MONTH
The Tokyo Reporter, August 15th, 2019
By Jason Berger

The rescue effort to locate a group of international hikers still missing on Okinawa Island comes to an end today after just under a month of fruitless searching.

During a press conference, local police announced their decision, saying that at this point they consider any further efforts to attempt to locate the missing hikers or their remains to be 'an exercise in futility.'

The announcement comes following weeks of hard storms that have battered the Takagusuku region of the island, where the hikers disappeared on Marine Day.

Presumed dead are James Tatum Caldwell, 23, from Boston, Massachusetts, Satoko Endo, 25, and Kenji Ohkawa, 24, both from Yamaoku City in Shiga Prefecture, Oliver O'Connell, 22, from Bristol, UK, and an individual known to the group only as Miles (age unknown) of whom there are no available records. Police have mooted the possibility that this individual could, in fact, be AWOL United States Marine Corps Private and wanted murder suspect Adam Preston Davis Jr, 25, of Cedar Rapids, Iowa, USA, who absconded from a US Marine Corps base the day before the group went missing.

The alarm was raised for the missing hikers by three surviving members of the group, who alerted officers on duty at the Ginowan Police Station in the early afternoon of July 15th. The Takagusuku Three, as the media has dubbed them, are English teachers Eloise Tiller, 23, from Hertford, United Kingdom, Stephanie Jo Elliot, 22, from Ten Sleep, Wyoming, and Linh Nguyen, 23, from Markham, Ontario, Canada.

The three young women were questioned extensively, first by Naha police and then again by experts from the Tokyo Metropolitan Police in the weeks immediately following the disappearances. The story they told was a fantastic one, described as "stretching the limits of credulity." Their initial individual reports were noted to be consistent, differing in only certain inconsequential details. As a result, experts believe that many elements of their testimony are consistent with a group hallucination or an instance of shared psychosis.

This has been attributed to several possible causes: asbestos poisoning from exposure to the internal structure of the abandoned Royal Oceanview Resort, heavy metal poisoning caused by drinking tainted spring water, or methane poisoning stemming from exposure to coal seam gases in a complex of caves located near where the hikers made their camp. Experts say that substances such as these can also cause HPPD—Hallucinogen Persisting Perception Disorder—delusions and flashbacks that may continue to occur for many months or even years after the initial effects of the exposure wear off.

With the incident being officially designated a tragic accident, most likely resulting from a combination of ill-preparedness and disorientation brought on by the as-yet unidentified substance, none of the surviving three female hikers are being considered legally culpable for the tragic losses that occurred on this ill-fated excursion.

The Royal Oceanview Resort, a sprawling concrete eyesore blighting the cliffs of the Takagusuku Nature Reserve, has long been a point of contention for locals. The resort has a seedy past, which includes allegations of money laundering and harboring an illicit prostitution ring.

The owner, disgraced leisure tourism and recreation magnate Satoshi Imamura, went missing in 1975 and was declared legally dead in absentia a decade later.

Following nearly thirty years of intermittent protests and lobbying by local residents, the prefecture finally seized control of the privately-owned property this month, citing safety concerns. The razing of the site was officially announced on August 10th, with demolition work due to commence in September.

The project is expected to cost the taxpayer approximately 200 million yen.

49

Yamaoku City, Shiga Prefecture, Japan

August 2019

Kemuri had been a mistake. Eloise knew it the moment they walked in. For the first time, there was no bellowed greeting from the staff. When the bell over the sliding door tinkled to announce their arrival, they were met instead with a loaded silence and averted eyes.

"Let's sit outside," Steph whispered in Eloise's ear, and so she led the way through the smoky space, fighting disgust as the opaque plastic curtain wiped its grease against her cheek. Outside, they found the tables half-empty, the naked crimson bulb lights casting the space in a familiar red glow that now seemed unfriendly, even menacing. They took seats at the same bench where Tate had held court, only around a month earlier, laying out his plans for the ill-fated urbex trip.

The waitress, a young woman with shaking hands, took their order for draft beers, fried chicken, and soybeans. They picked at the food and ordered more beer, aware of the eyes that were on them.

After it was all over, they'd taken the inexplicably restored path back down to civilization, happened upon a police box, and found an officer on duty inside. They'd caught him on lunch break, reading a magazine at his desk. He'd been so disturbed when they'd trooped in, three foreign girls with filthy faces and thousand-yard stares, that he'd tipped his steaming polystyrene cup of noodles onto his lap. It had taken a frustrating amount of time for him to finish tending to his potential second-degree burns, recover his composure, and begin listening to what they were trying to tell him.

Adopting honesty as their policy had been the first of a series of stupid mistakes they'd made. Mistakes that led to interrogations, accusations, and ostracization upon their eventual return to Yamaoku City.

They'd told the truth, halfway, at least. About the storm and the landslide, about the *habu* snake that bit Ollie, about the stranger calling himself Miles who'd murdered Kenji. By mutual instinct, they neglected to mention Nanoha Shimabukuro, Imamura's confession, the underground cavern. The other *things* they'd seen at the resort. Not that it mattered. The police hadn't believed a word of their accounts regarding what happened on those cliffs. There had been no tropical storm on Okinawa Island that weekend. There was, evidently, no landslide. And there had been no bodies recovered. As far as the police were concerned, Kenji, Satoko, Tate, and Ollie had simply vanished.

As for Miles, a man from one of the US bases had come to see them at the Naha police station that first day. He'd shown them a photograph and asked if this was the man they'd been with on the cliffs. Eloise had studied the photograph for a long time. The young man in it wore a uniform and looked much younger, his vivid eyes bright. He was smiling in the photo, an enthusiastic, hopeful sort of smile.

They'd been excused from teaching duties for the remainder of their tenure, effectively dismissed with pay. It was presented as an act of compassion, after the trauma they'd experienced. But that wasn't it, at all. Eloise, Steph, and Linh had been tainted by scandal, by the stigma of death. They'd brought a shadow home with them that now hung over Yamaoku.

"They can't wait for us to get out of this town, can they?" Steph muttered darkly, popping the soybeans out of their fuzzy pods and fiddling with the depleted skins.

"We should have come up with a story, something simple, made sure our accounts matched. Some kind of accident, maybe." Linh sighed, shadows pooling in the ridge between her eyebrows.

Steph and Eloise said nothing. Linh was right, of course. They should have taken a moment to collect themselves, to come up with a sensible explanation for why only three of them had returned from their "hiking excursion" to the Royal Oceanview.

The police had been incredulous, immediately suspicious. They'd found themselves swiftly separated, quizzed about alcohol and marijuana. Eloise was just glad she'd had the foresight to fling Miles's Marine Corps knife off the side of the Viewing Platform, along with his lighter, before they'd left. It was illegal to carry a knife in Japan, and they were body-searched at the police station. It was only later that Eloise realized the police were looking for drugs.

It all really kicked off once the investigators from Tokyo arrived and the press got their teeth into the story. Tate's father and older brother flew in and began threatening legal action against the EFA Program. A wrongful death lawsuit was apparently already being drafted.

Ollie's fiancée, Mishka, also went public with her story. She was convinced the rest of the group had murdered Ollie, that they'd lured him out to the Oceanview for some kind of satanic, orgy-based ritual. The British press lapped that one up.

The Japanese public reacted to the story with subdued bemusement. It was the overseas news media who'd gone into a frenzy, and the online discussion was dominated by rabid true crime fans, spinning wild conspiracy theories on enthusiast forums. The truth was too out-there, and so it was easily dismissed. The pervading theory was that the entire group had succumbed to madness on the cliff, experienced some form of elaborate group hallucination.

Delusional psychosis. That was what Eloise overheard the man in the wire-framed glasses and white coat whispering in the corridor after he'd examined her.

It didn't help that Linh kept changing her story. At first, the timeline of events she'd given matched Steph's and Eloise's, but after her first interrogation, she'd backpedaled, started claiming amnesia. She was growing increasingly worried about her parents, about their reputation within the local community back in Canada. Eloise tried to be sympathetic, tried to remember what it was like to have a reputation to ruin. But Linh seemed to be in denial more than anything else. Casting about for something that might explain what had happened, Linh's mind had returned to the spring. The odd, sweet-tasting water they'd used to refill their bottles. Some of the talking heads who were being interviewed on TV were saying certain kinds of minerals could cause poisoning, inducing vomiting and psychosis. Eloise couldn't believe that. But Linh seemed to be clinging to it as an explanation for everything.

"Linh." Eloise touched her hand, and Linh blinked, as if suddenly remembering where they were. Nearby, a table of salarymen laughed raucously, but there was something deliberate, almost nervous, about the way they averted their eyes from the girls' table.

"Linh," Eloise spoke again. "Steph and I were talking earlier about the others. Satoko and Ollie, Tate...we think...we think there's almost zero chance that any of them are still alive up there. And even if they are, I don't think we can get to them. I think that the resort that we were in belonged to another...a nother sphere of existence. The magatama we brought up there was the key that opened the gate, do you see? And now the gate is closed."

"I wasn't going to suggest going back." Linh pulled her hand out from underneath Eloise's. "I'm sorry for the others, I truly am. But I never want to go anywhere near that place again."

Steph and Eloise nodded, their faces crimson beneath the bulb lights.

"I think we should adopt a policy of total silence from this point forward," Steph said. "Okay, Linh? We make a pact. We never talk about this again. We say it was all some kind of hallucination, a sort of sickness. A tragically unfortunate accident."

Linh nodded, her eyes suddenly brighter. "Listen. I know I keep saying this, but what if it *was* a hallucination? Some kind of group delusion, an elaborate narrative we built for ourselves using the ghost stories Tate talked about as some kind of...I don't know...framework?"

Steph shifted uncomfortably in her seat. "Linh. *It wasn't.* We were there. We saw those things happen."

"But they *didn't* happen, Steph, did they? Remember what the police said? There *was* no typhoon that night. It was completely clear weather. Everything started to happen after we drank the water from the spring, right? First the deer carcass, then those photographs, then I started getting sick..."

"Linh..."

"If it wasn't the spring water, then maybe it was the asbestos in the resort, or the natural gases..."

"Linh." Eloise put down her glass of beer. The frost coating it was burning her hand. "It was *real*. An untenable reality, maybe, but it happened. We were all there. We all saw it. All three of us did."

Linh blew out a slow breath of air. "I know what I *saw* at that resort. I'm just not sure that what I saw was *real*. I don't *want* it to have been real." She looked back and forth between Eloise and Steph, her eyes quietly pleading. "I just want to forget about it. I want to get on with my life."

Get on with my life, Eloise thought.

How?

They fell silent, watching as a feral cat's head emerged underneath the clear plastic curtains that kept the outside out. Spotting a filth-encrusted squid ring lying under one of the tables, it darted forward, snatching the morsel up in its jaws before bounding back to the safety of the curtain. As it flattened itself and squeezed underneath, the curtain bunched up, revealing a litter of bedraggled kittens on the other side, anxiously awaiting sustenance.

"Excuse me," a terse voice said, above their heads. Bewildered, Eloise looked up, recognizing the owner of the bar. A middle-aged man with a tanned face, pale lines of crow's feet. Before, he was always friendly, had often fussed over the girls, sneaking them appetizers and shots of shochu on the house, but now his face was closed and dark.

"Is something wrong?" Eloise asked in polite Japanese, but he wouldn't make eye contact.

"There is a ninety-minute limit for tables," he said, staring at a wooden support post. "Please leave."

"No, there isn't," Eloise said, a cold sort of sensation spreading out in her chest. "We've been coming here every weekend for ages."

The bar owner cleared his throat, one eyelid twitching. "You are inconveniencing other patrons. Please leave."

"Let's just go," Steph said, thumbing some bills out of her wallet and dropping them onto the table.

The relieved laughter of the salarymen followed them as they slunk back through the bar into the night outside.

50

Eloise awoke with a start. She'd been dreaming of the resort. Of Miles. The two of them were standing in the dried-out swimming pool, vines coiled around their feet. Miles was holding a snake, trying to make her touch it.

"Bite it," he said. "It's not venomous."

As the dream drained from her, she became aware of the guy sitting opposite, a stocky white guy. His well-built body was wedged uncomfortably between the hard arms of the airport seat. He'd dropped something heavy—a water bottle. Its muted thud must have been what had awoken her.

She watched him as he went through his backpack, wedging the water bottle inside. That done, he folded his arms across his broad chest, tipped his head back, and closed his eyes. His forearms were thick, roped with veins, his upper lip almost obscured beneath his thick mustache.

Am I going to keep seeing him wherever I go? Just like Chris?

She watched the man sleep, letting her thoughts wander. Things had been a lot quieter inside her mind since the resort. A lot of things seemed clearer now, ever since they'd emerged, blinking, from that black cave.

Maybe that was why she was here, sitting in an airport waiting lounge, clutching a boarding ticket that had grown damp and begun to disintegrate around the edges.

It's not too late. You could call that school in Seoul back. Tell them you can start next week. You don't have to do this.

But Eloise was homesick. So homesick it physically hurt. Not just for England. For her old life. An ordinary life. Before Chris, before running away to Japan, before everything changed.

You can't go home. You read the articles.

She'd read the articles. It wasn't as bad as it had been right after Chris's death. This time, there was no body, no evidence of bloody violence. And it wasn't just her. This time, she had Steph and Linh to share the load of suspicion. But the UK press had eaten Eloise up, just like they did last time.

WOMAN IMPLICATED IN UNI BOYFRIEND STABBING INVOLVED IN DEADLY HIKING ACCIDENT IN JAPAN

The articles were bad, painting Eloise as a drug-addled, thrill-seeking, potential murderess, but it was the comment section that stuck in her mind, repeating over and over.

—*I went to school with Chris. He was a sweetheart. Everyone knows she stuck a knife in him in a jealous rage. Bitch.*

—*I was at uni with Eloise Tiller. She was quiet but nice. And she seemed really into that bloke. Just goes to show, you can't trust anyone.*

—*A mate of mine said she was a massive cokehead when he knew her! She probably stabbed them hikers while she was off her tits on something.*

—*I think u meant Eloise* Killer.

"Ladies and Gentlemen, we will soon begin boarding for Flight 44 to London Heathrow…"

Eloise was on her feet. Dragging her backpack, pushing past bodies, stumbling away from the gate.

I can't do this. I can't go back there, I—

Someone grabbed her shoulder and turned her. She looked up into the face of the man who'd been sleeping. His eyes were very dark brown, so dark you couldn't see the pupils.

"You dropped this."

He walked off without waiting for her response. Eloise looked down at the hard object he'd placed in her hand.

A flat gold disc, a chain snaked around it. Eloise rubbed her thumb over the embossed surface, over the words engraved there.

PROTECT ME

I should throw it away, Eloise told herself. *I will, when I get home. When I...*

"Miss?" A soft voice, a familiar accent. She looked up at the gate attendant, her vision blurring, then clearing. "Is this your flight?"

Eloise slid the medallion, Miles's medallion, into her back pocket.

"Yes," she said, testing her voice, finding it strong. "Yes, it's my flight. I'm going home."

Eloise approached the gate. Watched as her boarding pass was scanned. The gate opened, and she walked through.

EPILOGUE

Somewhere Over the Pacific

Late August 2019

It was around six hours into the flight. The sun was an orange streak on the horizon 35,000 feet below. Linh lowered the window shade, trying not to wake Steph, who was asleep, her head resting against the window shade, the travel pillow around her neck dark with drool.

The flight was full, and Linh had a terrible headache. She always got a splitting headache on planes. Her guts hurt, too, a dull, crushing ache.

Maybe I ate something with dairy in it again, she thought absently, grimacing against the pain, which seemed to radiate to her lower back. Unbuckling her seatbelt and stuffing her flimsy in-flight headphones into the seat pocket, Linh struggled to her feet, trying not to yank on the headrest of the person in front of her.

Steph had spent most of the flight asleep, leaving Linh feeling utterly alone. There was something so inhuman about flying. Hurtling through the sky, hundreds of miles removed from the world, packed in a compressed metal tube for hours on end with total strangers.

Linh knew she should sleep, too. She had a six-hour layover at LAX to enjoy before boarding a flight to Ontario. But she couldn't relax. She felt shaky inside, feverish, as if she was getting sick. Just nerves, no doubt.

She was going home. Maybe for the last time.

If it gets bad with Mom, I can just leave. She can't keep Dad from me. She can't disown me for everyone else. I won't let her. I'm strong. I know I am. I'm stronger now.

Another cramp. *Jesus, that hurts.*

In the dark, she made her way down the aisle to the toilets in the back. Both were occupied. Peering out of the window embedded in the aircraft's bulky door, she could see the black ocean, a long way below. A feeling of vertigo washed over her, and she closed her eyes, swallowing, her lips gummy.

"Are you all right, miss?"

Linh opened her eyes. The attendant gave her a reassuring smile.

"I'm okay," Linh said. "Just thirsty."

"We'll be bringing water and juice around in just a few minutes," the attendant said, flashing Linh another smile as she squeezed past.

When the bathroom was finally free, Linh locked herself inside and studied her reflection in the mirror. She looked worse than she'd expected, her skin waxy with a bluish tint, her lips rimmed with white lines of dried spit. Disgusted, she scrubbed at them with a handful of toilet paper.

The suck and roar of the toilet flush made her jump. As she turned to wash her hands, she caught a flash of herself in the mirror again. But something was odd.

Blinking, she leaned in, focusing on her reflection. The reflection smiled at her.

Milk-white skin. Long, shining black hair. Dark, glittering eyes. Dressed in a white kimono, a string of stone comma-shaped beads around her neck, interspersed with cylinders of yellow bone.

Linh's mouth opened, her fist rising. Mashing her lips against her teeth with her knuckles, she began to moan, a desperate, keening sound. But the reflection remained tight-lipped, still wearing its satisfied smile. As Linh's heart thundered in her ears, the apparition held a finger to her lips, a silent pantomime. *Shh.* Then she opened her mouth, revealing blackened teeth.

In a blink, the apparition was gone. Linh was left panting and retching, clutching the half-bowl of the sink, staring at her own sweaty, panicked face. Her eyes were wide and wild, no whites to them, no brown irises, just glittering blackness.

Her guts cramped, twisted again. No, not her guts. Something was moving in her womb. Little flutters, like a tiny eel. Flopping and squirming around inside her.

A memory came. A hot morning, the beachside road. Gnarled old fingers stroking her palm, folding the magatama inside it.

Linh reached for the door handle, rattled it, all her senses screaming, the stuffy air of the cramped bathroom like a coffin tight around her.

She wasn't trying to warn *us*—

And she heard the old woman's rasping voice in her mind.

She sleeps...The maiden...

Linh clawed for the emergency call button.

Beneath the dull drone of the engines, nobody on the plane heard her scream.

CHECK OUT THESE OTHER THRILLING READS FROM ROWAN PROSE:

E.M. Lund holds a BA in English & Creative Writing, and a BA in Japanese Studies. She is a freelance translator of Japanese fiction for the global market. She's an avid reader of horror and dark fiction, and loves to creep herself out by looking at photos of abandoned places. She is originally from the UK, but resides in Japan.

www.ingramcontent.com/pod-product-compliance
Lightning Source LLC
LaVergne TN
LVHW041654060526
838201LV00043B/434